MW01489813

THE DAWN

THE DAWN

KAITLYN AND THE HIGHLANDER

DIANA KNIGHTLEY

Copyright © 2024 by Diana Knightley

All rights reserved.

No part of this book may be reproduced in any form or by any electronic or mechanical means, including information storage and retrieval systems, without written permission from the author, except for the use of brief quotations in a book review.

 Created with Vellum

For my Mom, thinking of you a lot these days, wishing we could talk all of this through... I miss you.

PROLOGUE

$\mathcal{T}$his is where we left off in *Long Live the King*...

Magnus and his family have discovered that they have a new enemy, Asgall. Unfortunately, by the time they noticed him, he had already gained a great deal of power, amassing wealth and land, and becoming a King of Scotland in 1296.

This is especially irritating because in the book *Magnus the First*, Magnus had gained the Scottish throne *before* Asgall. Magnus (called Mag Mòr) had been crowned at Scone in 1290 and while he hadn't been back to that time, and though he had used the Bridge to clean up the timeline, it might still technically be his throne... *maybe?* Probably.

Asgall had also kidnapped Lochinvar's new love, Ash, a modern woman from Florida. She was held captive in a compound in the year 1296. (She had no idea about time travel, yikes!)

Because of all of this danger, the household fled Florida for the relative safety of Balloch castle.

Then, Magnus, Fraoch, and Lochinvar rescued Ash. (Thankfully!)

During the rescue Magnus decides that the best way to stop Asgall before he gains the Scottish throne in 1296 is for Magnus to return to 1291 and sit on the throne and hold it.

Through all this, Archie is having nightmares about becoming the king, terrified that Magnus will die. This is another good reason for Magnus to retake his throne — to set his son's mind at ease.

Magnus and Fraoch go to Stirling in 1291, walk up to the castle and, lo and behold, Mag Mòr is still king. Perfect!

He decides to rule for a bit, and guess what? It works — Asgall is knocked off the list of kings, the wheel turns, and Asgall loses, for this round at least.

Magnus and Fraoch send a message through time to their family asking them to please come to Stirling castle.

Kaitlyn, Archie (about 8), Isla (4), Jack (1), Hayley, Chef Zach, Emma, Ben (7), and Zoe (3), all go to Stirling castle. Magnus's brother Sean, who has never time traveled before goes with them.

While Beaty and Noah (1) and Sophie and Junior (a few days old) remain at Balloch, Quentin and James go on a supply run for weapons and diapers. Once they return from this errand,

Quentin will deliver weapons to Magnus at Stirling in 1291; and then they all plan to move there to be with the rest of the family, eventually.

Lochinvar and Ash are also at Balloch resting while she recovers from a dislocated shoulder. Ash needs to travel to Florida to tell her friend Don that she has survived the kidnapping, but after that she and Lochie plan to meet Magnus at Stirling.

Phew, this is a large family, in a bunch of different places and times.

For Magnus and his family in 1291 Stirling, this story begins the following day.

 For everyone at Balloch, it's the same day as when we last heard from them, May 27, 1710.

*And in case you were wondering, Lady Mairead is running Riaghalbane (Magnus's future kingdom) all alone.

The Dawn begins.

—DK

PART I

CHAPTER 1 - KAITLYN

MIDDLE OF THE NIGHT, THE KING AND QUEEN'S CHAMBER, STIRLING CASTLE - JUNE 16, 1291

I woke up with a start.

My head was on Magnus's warm chest. He said, "Wha—?"

"Sorry... didn't mean to wake you."

He tightened his arm around me, sleepily, but then fell right back to sleep.

I breathed in the scent of my medieval husband. I had grown used to him like this, his look over the next few weeks and months would grow wilder, his hair would knot, his beard would lengthen. I would wonder, was it the air that caused this wilding? Or was it the weight of the past, everything was more dire here, heavy and significant, it coarsened the men's skin, lengthened their hair, roughened their manners. Even their laughs would grow deep, their meetings solemn with responsibility, their movements measured. Living in the medieval world, there was always something on a modern man's mind: the curses of the age, the bitter chill of the rooms, the shadowy gloom of the corners, the drab taste of the food — everything carried more consequence.

A humorous story told around a fire in a castle in the dark ages always felt just so... medieval. I breathed in again.

The dark heaviness would be terrifying, if not for Magnus's warm, comfortable, familiar presence.

Then, as I was thinking about how comfortable he was, he grunted and rolled like a big bear, grasping my waist, pulling me close, his head nudging against my breast, getting comfortable as if I were his pillow

I wrapped my arms around his head and kissed the top of his head. He was fast asleep again.

I wasn't, I was peering out around our room, dimly lit by the fire in the hearth. The room was unfamiliar as I was newly arrived. I wasn't used to servants who lurked around at all hours, a wee bit oppressive in their helpfulness. I had asked that the canopy not be closed around our bed, but I had changed my mind now. Beyond the bed were shadows that made me uneasy.

A darkness lay behind the wardrobes containing the bottom layer of our costumes: my dresses and cloaks and Magnus's outer layers were kept in another room and would be brought in when we needed to dress.

I vaguely remembered where this magical room holding the Queen's Wardrobe was, and somehow it contained dresses, jewelry, and a crown for my use. I had been here at one point, long ago, even though the shifting of time had changed my memories.

Cailean had welcomed me warmly but without much recognition, but I *knew* him. I had met him once long ago... I had stayed with Magnus at the abbey and palace in Scone just after he had been crowned king, and then I remembered following Cailean as we had ridden our horses on a journey to Stirling. Magnus's standard had been flying above us against the blue sky, the rumble of an army of men on horseback around us, the scent of horse and Scottish forest. But after that my memory grew hazy.

I couldn't remember what happened next.

I looked up at the canopy, my fingers circling around one of Magnus's locks, wondering about the men and women who had lived in this room before us, and who would live here after us. Kings and queens who were named in the history books, who were remembered by school children, and here we were — Mags and Katie.

If I thought about it, in the darkness of this medieval room, we were usurpers.

We had taken a throne.

Whose throne?

I didn't know. My Scottish history knowledge was patchy at best.

Who were we replacing, and would everything be okay?

We didn't know, had no way to know, we were holding the throne, that was all... holding... Magnus tightened his hold on me and smacked his lips, sleepily.

Then he mumbled, "Ye havin' trouble sleepin', mo reul-iuil?"

"A little, new bed, new room—"

"Auld familiar worries."

I said, "Aye, I know *why* we are here, and I understand you're going to solve this, but it's got that feel..."

I smoothed my hand down the skin of his shoulder. "We've had this feeling before — have we been removed? Are we out of the way, distracted? And in the meantime, is something big happening? It seems like a storm is brewing, and we are unable to see it coming."

"Och nae, ye canna sleep with those kinds of thoughts in yer head."

His hand went up under the hem of my chemise, drew it up, and clasped my breast, playing and fondling there.

I breathed, slowly in and out, then he drew his fingers ever so slightly away and I arched ever so slightly to meet his touch. My exhale sounded like — *please more.*

He chuckled, very low, and said, "Ye distract easily, mo reul-iuil," as his mouth settled on my other breast. His hand pulled tenderly down along my skin, and found its way between my legs and played there, driving his fingers between the folds — oh god oh god oh god. His mouth drew along my skin, his lips and his tongue, tasting and suckling. His fingers probed — I was drawn to the heights of climax, but a moment before going over the edge alone, he climbed onto me and entered me in a rush. He pressed his mouth to my lips, kissing me deeply, his hips pounding against me... oh, oh, ohhhh, I climaxed within a second, so fast, so big, a gigantic rush roaring through me. My muscles contracted and released, pulling him in and in and...

He growled a long drawn out, low rumbling occhhh, then raised above me and drove into me, over and over, his breaths bullish, heat rising. I pressed against the headboard and raised my hips to meet him, more and again, until he climaxed, and with a long exhale collapsed on me, his fingers clutching my buttocks, holding my hips tightly against him. We stilled in place, as our insides relaxed and softened, until, as the feeling ebbed, we grew weighted, my hips lowered to the bed. He followed me down, above me at first, then on me, then heavy on me. He kissed my lips, long and lingering, an elbow on each side of my head, his fingers entwined in my hair, his thumbs against my temples. Then he rolled off onto his side. "Twas verra fine, I for one want for nothin' now."

"Me neither." I peered around in the darkness, "Except... can we close the curtains? I mean, that's the royal 'we'."

"Ye want *me*, the king, tae close m'own curtains? Dost ye ken who I am?" He cleared his throat.

A voice said, "Aye, Yer Majesty?"

My eyes wide I whispered, "Oh my god, he's in the room, watching?"

Magnus chuckled. "The next room, but he hears everythin'."

I burrowed under the covers and hid there like a child while Magnus's manservant pulled the curtains closed around our bed.

Then I whispered, "The coast is clear?"

"Aye, ye can come out now, he's left."

I flung down the covers. "That is hard to get used to, I will be much quieter in the future."

He said, "Och nae, ye canna promise it, mo reul-iuil, or I will grow saddened by the quietude. I need yer sweet howlin' in m'ear tae ken ye are properly bedded."

"My 'sweet howling'?"

He chuckled. Then he shifted and rocked trying to get comfortable. "This is a lumpy mattress."

I patted my arm so he could put his head on it. I put my thigh up on his hip. It was lovely with the curtains pulled, dark, quiet, and warm.

He asked, "Did ye hear Sean say that he has heard of Mag Mòr in the list of Scottish Kings?"

I stroked my fingers down his cheek, "Yes, he told us at Balloch."

"Men will ken of me."

"You've been a king for a long time."

"Aye, in the future, mo reul-iuil, but m'name wasna in the history books. How often has it happened, dost ye think, Kaitlyn, that a man lives long enough tae ken he has gone down in history?"

I pressed my lips to the bridge of his nose. "I never... I didn't really think about it that way."

"Aye, and ye are likely in the books as well."

I exhaled, long. "I hope they get my story right — none of that YouTube nonsense."

"Och, twas just an inconsequential part of yer life. Think of all ye hae accomplished since then, ye are a queen, the mother of a future king, ye hae vanquished yer enemies—"

"I don't know if any of the vanquishing is in the permanent record."

"Aye, likely not."

"None of the bloodline and history of Riaghalbane exists in the historical record either."

"Tis true, and there is the rub. If time travel daena exist... and it daena according tae most, we are simply a medieval king and queen."

"People will say, 'Kaitlyn and Magnus, huh? You have the same names as that old king and queen.' And we'll say, 'Yes, it's uncanny how that happened.'"

"Twill be our secret."

"No one will ever know that you, the medieval King of Scotland, had the high score on Fortnite."

He chuckled. "Och, it only lasted for an hour and only because Chef Zach was cookin' dinner at the time. Even Archie beats me now. Alas, nae one will ever remember me for m'gamin'."

I laughed. "So we will have to be content with how history remembers us, a medieval king and queen, not much else, because written records are rare. We hold this kingdom for how long?"

"Long enough. Tis still being written."

I nodded against his head.

"...there is an English King who wants the power, Scottish lords who daena like tae be ruled, an arse-wipe named Asgall causing trouble, and a kingdom in the future that I must trust m'mother is guardin' well. This is an empire."

"That makes you an emperor."

"Aye."

His hand clutched my buttock and pulled it closer, his face burrowing against my throat.

"Sleepy?"

He nodded there. "If ye wake, mo reul-iuil, and I am nae here, I hae gone tae the walls."

"I thought you were the emperor — do kings and emperors have to guard the walls? I don't think that's how it works."

"Aye, I will likely surprise the castle guard once I do, but Sean will go tae the walls. I will need tae be there tae keep him company, or he will think me too unconcerned."

"You're a king and you're still worried about what your older brother thinks?"

"Och aye, tae twist something he says often, older brothers are born tae force younger brothers tae prove themselves."

"I can't believe he came — I think he's trying to prove himself to you."

His forehead quietly nodded against my neck. Then he said, "But if I am nae here, tis where I hae gone."

"I understand."

CHAPTER 2 - ASGALL

A BROTHEL IN STAUNTON, VIRGINIA - 1775

I tossed my tricorn onto the rack by the front door. My favorite harlot leaned over the rail of the stairwell and called down, "Fancy a roust, sire?"

"Nae." I took off my coat and hung it upon a hook.

"You look weary, sire, a little—"

"I said, Nae, bring a whisky."

She left tae get m'drink.

I ran a hand through my hair and loosened the cravat at my neck as I walked down the creaking wooden floor of the hall into the low-ceilinged sitting room. I sat down on the cushioned chair in front of the fireplace, opened the cigarette box on the table, and lit one with m'lighter.

I leaned back in the chair and drew a long inhale of the cigarette, exhalin' smoke rings toward the ceiling.

The harlot entered, barefoot, her breasts uncovered, a corset and nae skirts, just cunt and arse, carrying a glass with whisky in it. She moved sultrily taeward me, passed me the glass, and sat down, unbidden upon my knee.

"Ye requested me, sire?" Her fingers went tae the back of my hair and twirled through it. Upstairs a bed was banging against the wall, a man was groaning with pleasure.

I scoffed. "Why would I request ye?"

She pressed against me, her mouth moved tae m'neck. "Ye enjoyed yerself last week, sire, I believe."

"Who is upstairs?"

"Yer man, Master Greyson, sire, he arrived early for yer meetin'."

"Up — ye are sweaty and soilin' m'breeches." I pushed her off as I leaned forward, tae put the butt of m'cigarette out in the ashtray.

She said, "My apologies, sire."

I brushed off m'knee. "Open the windows wider, tis hot as Hades in here."

"Of course, sire." As she turned tae leave I smacked her arse, settin' a pink mark in the shape of m'hand, marrin' her pale skin. Twas satisfyin' tae hear her squeal.

I opened the box, pulled out a second cigarette, and lit it while watchin' the lass open the windows.

Then I looked around at the furnishings, the upholstered chairs, the long, heavy draperies, and the woven rugs. This was a well-appointed room for the time, a fine brothel. And close tae Richmond. I scheduled many of m'meetings here, because I rather liked the lawlessness of the age.

Yet the heat was unbearable, I needed tae remember tae check the weather before I arrived.

I drew in a long drag... There were drawbacks tae the time of course, lack of air conditionin' being one of them, but the men were on the cusp of greatness and the colonies had just begun their revolution. I felt invigorated by the impending war and relished the novelty.

I flicked ashes ontae the rug as Jim sheepishly came down the stairs, tucking his shirt intae his breeches, running a hand through his hair. He looked damp from exertion, and ashamed of havin' kept me waiting.

Good.

I said, "I will give ye a moment tae get yer coat on."

"Oh, of course, I took it off because of the heat."

I nodded and settled my gaze on his face through the smoke that I had exhaled around my head.

He pulled his coat on, verra nervously, sweat blooming on his upper lip. He dinna use tae be so nervous, but he had likely heard what I had done tae his predecessor.

Jim settled in the settee, placed a leather portfolio on the table, unzipped it, and began spreading out papers.

The oil lamp on the table dinna do much tae beat back the darkness, yet I could see a drip of sweat roll down his temple.

I said, "I will need more light."

"Of course, my apologies, sire." He jumped up, went tae the hall, and returned with a battery-powered lantern. He put it on the table and turned it on, emitting a bright light around the room.

He sat back down and returned tae goin' through his papers.

The brothel-keep entered with a bottle of whisky. "Welcome back, sire, your room is prepared upstairs."

"Good, good."

"Would you want a top-off of your glass, sire?"

I nodded. He refilled my glass, and left.

I sipped the whisky. "Ye dinna even take one minute, Jim, tae mention the locale — are ye enjoyin' yer visit? Ye time-traveled, are ye havin' a fine experience?"

He looked startled. "Oh, um, yes, sire." He leaned back against the pillows of the settee, his knee jigglin' nervously. "Thank you for giving me the opportunity, and this is a fine land... though I must say it is... very hot."

"Ye are visitin' the American colonies, surrounded by the enlightened men of the Revolution, and ye're complainin' about the heat?"

"My apologies, sire."

I called down the hall, "Brothel-keep!"

He entered. "Yes, sire?"

"Send in the last lass tae fan me."

He rushed away and a moment later a harlot with a wicker fan stood beside m'chair, fannin' my face. The exertion caused her breasts tae quiver delightfully.

I inhaled more cigarette. "I daena ken, Jim, I find the temperature tae be verra fine."

Another bead of sweat rolled down his temple as he watched the lass fan me.

I said, "What are ye lookin' at?"

He said, "Oh, um, the... nothing."

"What dost ye think of m'lass?"

"She's um, lovely..."

"Why did ye think ye could partake of the lassies? Did ye ask my permission tae go upstairs?"

"No, sire, the brothel-keep told me it would—"

"Do ye think I pay ye tae fornicate with the harlots, and dost I want ye sweatin' upon m'papers?"

"No, sire."

He used his sleeve tae wipe his forehead. I huffed and gestured for the lass tae hand him a handkerchief.

He dabbed at his forehead.

"Better."

"My apologies, sire." He flipped through the papers, once more, and passed me a small stack.

I looked them over. More leases, a patent, and a title to a new ranch.

"Good, good." I tossed them tae the table and picked up my cigarette from the ashtray, took a drag, then picked up my whisky glass and drank.

We sat in silence for a few moments, while he dabbed at his damp face. Meanwhile I tapped the side of the glass, slowly, countin' the days since Magnus and his brothers had stolen the woman, Ash, from m'compound.

I dinna like tae hae lost that round. Twas not in my nature tae lose. "Did ye bring me the information I asked for?"

Jim said, "Yes, sire."

He placed a small stack of papers on the table.

I nodded, jabbed my cigarette out in the ashtray, and pulled the papers closer tae read.

He interrupted, "That is all you need to win back your throne."

I flipped the page tae read the next. "I daena want m'throne back, I want Magnus's throne *ended*."

I picked up my glass, drained it, placed it on the table, and snapped my fingers at it. The harlot put down the fan, poured whisky in the glass, handed it tae me, and began fanning me again.

Jim asked, "Do you hear that?"

"What?"

"Sounds like wolves. Are there wolves?"

"Of course there are wolves, we are in the middle of nowhere, Virginia, the wilderness is right outside."

He nodded.

I picked up the papers again and read. The fan wafted back and forth beside my face. From the corner of my eyes I watched the quiver of her flesh as she moved.

Jim glanced at m'whisky, but dinna ask for one, though he looked tae be desperate for a sip. Streams of sweat rolled down his cheek.

The sound of a long, low wolf howl again. He looked at the open window nervously, "It sounds closer, does it sound closer?" He pulled his shirt collar from his throat, then realized I was watching and quickly dropped his hand.

I punched that cigarette out in the tray. "Nae, I am not interested in gainin' a thirteenth century crown."

"Perhaps the Kingdom of Riaghalbane, sire, we discussed challenging them for their throne—"

"I meant tae," I waved my hand, "but I daena hae the bloodline, and I hae grown disinterested in all of that anyway—"

"I thought you looked forward to training for the arena—"

"It has lost its luster. Think of it, Jim, really think —

Magnus built an arena, ye expect me tae enter it and play by his rules?"

"No, sire, that does not—"

"It would be a lark, of course, tae train and challenge him, let it all play out."

I leaned forward for yet another cigarette, saying while I did, "I would rather *enjoy* beating his arse, possibly in a long duel, with blood and gore and a great deal of brutal pain, even havin' my own arse beat — I'm not much interested in failure, but I do enjoy *someone* havin' their arse kicked, even if tis m'own... and ye ken, I wouldna die. *He* would die, I would like tae *see* him die, but it needs tae be a game — this is... see, Jim, this is the problem — I like a game. I want revenge — I'll remind ye, he walked intae my compound and stole the woman who I had contracted tae be m'wife and the unborn son who was legally mine. Magnus would deserve the cruelty, daena ye think?"

"Yes, definitely, sire, revenge is the best idea." Then the color left his face as a wolf howled again.

I listened. "Sounds like wolves are comin' closer, would ye like tae hae the window closed?"

He gulped and tugged at his collar. "No, we need the air, I think, sire, but... how big are wolves, would they fit through the window?"

I shrugged. "I imagine they would... We are in a brothel on the edge of the New World. The Old World belongs tae the wolves and beasts of the past, they howl in the night. They might want tae come see what we are up tae."

There was a long faraway howl.

I said, "Speaking of the Old World, I asked ye if Magnus would deserve the cruelty."

He nodded. "He would, yes, this is his problem, he is a traditionalist. He believes in thrones and bloodlines."

"And he keeps his family close."

I stared at the burning ember on the end of my cigarette. "I daena want his throne, but I would like him tae suffer. And I would like tae get the woman back. Tis why I hae had ye gather all ye could about them."

I drained the whisky in my glass.

"My plan will be tae menace and dismay King Magnus, not for the throne, but tae ruin him — twill be fun. I will watch him twist in the wind, tryin' tae save his family and his throne, only tae realize I wanted naething more than tae bring him tae a miserable end."

"I have arranged another meeting with King Edward of England. He looks forward to beginning the campaign."

"I suppose I will hae tae return tae the thirteenth century — see, Jim, this is Magnus's problem, he has honor, he does what he says he will do — it sounds particularly unpleasant, daena it, Jim? Tae be ruled by duty? Tae feel bound tae live in the thirteenth century?" I shivered. "I tried livin' back then, I lasted a week."

"Yes, sire, it sounds bleak."

"Especially once the English King begins lobbing cannonballs at his castle. Och aye, I look forward tae it. I imagine Magnus will be verra discomposed by the attack. Wallace is joinin' us?"

"Yes, page six, you convinced him."

I flipped tae that page and chuckled. "Och, tis verra entertainin' — William Wallace! I canna wait tae see the look on Magnus's face."

I shuffled through the stack, finding one that mentioned the layout of Stirling castle. "The walls are built of timber and stone — if I give Edward a catapult, specially made — better yet, a tank." I flicked ashes on the rug again.

Jim said, "His whole family is there... Both sons and his daughter. His wife, his brother Fraoch, and others."

"Where is Lochinvar and m'wife? They arna there?"

He looked at the front and back of a paper. "I am not certain, I believe they are at Balloch Castle in the year 1710 or—"

I narrowed m'eyes, "They never left?"

"I sent spies as you requested, but I am not certain. They are either in 1710 or 1683."

"Send Maxwell, tell him he can use the drones, I would like tae ken where they are — I want her back. She inna worth anything, but I daena like tae be tricked."

I stamped out that cigarette in the ashtray and lit another, getting more excited about my plans. "Lady Mairead is of course at Riaghalbane? I do appreciate how well that device I bought from Johnne Cambell works, I never used it before, I stop vessels, direct them off course. Tis wonderful for creatin' mayhem."

"Divide and conquer."

"More like draw and quarter. If Lady Mairead canna find her son and her grandchildren... twill be verra entertainin' tae watch her suffer."

I watched him nodding, sweating on the furniture. I scowled. "Ye ken, Jim, ye ought tae go now, this has been enough."

He faltered for a moment, then started tae gather his papers—

"Leave them."

He stood. "You will leave in the morning?"

I leaned back in my chair. "Aye, but ye canna stay, besides ye hae work tae do."

He said, "Um... with the wolves howling and..." His eyes searched the darkness. "Hear it? There are more now."

"I hear it, they likely want a weasel for their meal, ye ought tae leave before they smell yer fear."

He bowed awkwardly, and rushed from the room.

CHAPTER 3 - KAITLYN

THE KING AND QUEEN'S CHAMBER - STIRLING CASTLE - JUNE 16, 1291

I woke up and patted beside me, the bed was empty. I raised my head to see one of my lady's maids, uncomfortably near, waiting for me to rise so she could wash and dress me. *How long had she been in the room?*

This whole process would be complicated without Magnus here to translate when necessary.

I shoved the heavy bedding aside, and climbed from the bed.

The maid bobbed her head and set about pulling my chemise off and washing me with a rag from a basin of water. She kept her eyes averted and submissive and was too shy to try to communicate with me.

Another two maids entered and helped the first to dress me in a clean chemise in a pale linen color that went down to my ankles. Then they covered it with a tunic-style dress in a deep royal blue. The dress had long sleeves with an interior fur lining. It was warm and toasty in the drafty castle.

My hair was brushed back and twisted in a piece of ribbon. Then a pale white cloth was placed over it, held down with a gold crown with a red garnet stone in the center.

A rust red cloak, with a fine embroidered edge was placed on my shoulders, and fastened at my neck with a golden brooch.

The garnets in the crown and my brooch both matched the one in my wedding band.

It was all heavy. The look was beautiful. I felt dignified, and incredibly royal.

It was a lot to wake up to. My days of going down to breakfast in my yoga pants were apparently over.

Jack woke up fussing in the other room. He had perfect timing, I was basically dressed.

I rushed in, trying to soothe. "Hey little guy." I picked him up and grimaced. Ugh, he was ripe. We had brought diapers, but not many and there would need to be more, and yes, potty training needed to happen — stat.

I looked around, finding the box of my stuff in the corner. I ripped open the top and was interrupted by a lady's maid who wanted to do it for me, but of course had never seen a diaper before. She watched me change him on his bed. I showed her how.

Then, holding him in my arms, I sat in an armchair and the lady's maid pulled on my socks and leather ankle boots. These boots didn't match the time period, but they were unobtrusive enough. She tied the laces.

I stood up and said to Jack, "There, we look perfect."

Jack, who had fussed through most of it, grinned.

I said, "I am glad, Mr Jackie-poo, that you have a happy personality, because when we run out of diapers, things are going to get dire around here. You will need to be extra charming."

Jack said, "Baba."

I said, "Exactly. Now where are your sister and brother?"

We left the room and I looked up and down the hall. Where was Zach and Emma's room? Guards fell in behind me. I actually wasn't entirely sure where I was going, I had been given a tour yesterday, but had been tired and overwhelmed by the gloomy surroundings and hadn't paid much attention. Dumb. I had been trapped in castles before, it seemed like I would have learned to look for escape routes and weapon-rooms first thing.

And I should definitely know where my kids were staying — just down the passage a door burst open: Isla, Zoe, Ben, and Archie rushed out. "Hey babes! Where you going?"

Archie yelled, "We're going to the Great Hall for breakfast!"

Isla's eyes went really wide. "Mammy, you look like a beautiful princess."

"Thank you, sweetie, you made my morning. It took a long time to get dressed."

Jack reached out with his pudgy hands. Isla gave him a kiss. "Bye! Going to—"

She made to rush off, but I pulled her back and made her focus, to take a moment to calm and center before she ran wildly through the halls."Hey, Love, Good morning." I kissed her forehead.

She said, "Good morning, Mammy."

I said, "You know your way around the castle already?"

Ben said, "We've already been *everywhere*!"

Archie said, "Just like Balloch, I bet we've been places you've never been, Mammy."

I laughed. "That does seem likely. Well, Master Ben and Prince Archibald, don't leave Isla and Zoe *anywhere*, they might not know the layout quite as well as you do."

Emma came from the same room. "They have been up for *so* long. Wow, look at you, you look like a medieval painting, how long did it take to get dressed?"

"So long, I feel like it's been hours. The style is much simpler than the eighteenth century clothes, but I have to wear it at royal-level."

"Now I feel lucky, mine's comfy and I don't have to wear a crown." Her dress was much like mine, but the colors were muted. Her cloak was pinned with a plain brooch. And of course, she didn't have a gold band on her head.

"Why don't we get to wear long flowing dresses like this in Florida?" She waved an arm. "It's got the kind of sleeves that will knock over the drinks on the table if you want to cause drama."

I laughed.

She asked, "Want me to take Jack down?"

Jack put out his arms.

I said, "I'll meet you down there, I'm headed to go see Magnus on the walls."

CHAPTER 4 - KAITLYN

THE ROOF OF THE KING'S TOWER - JUNE 16, 1291

I came to a stairwell at the end of the passage and the two guardsmen who were following me, paused as if waiting for me to decide which way to go. I didn't know if this was the right stairwell, but it also felt awkward, so I just acted like I knew where I was going.

I didn't want to look like an idiot, so I just started climbing a staircase going who knows where, like an idiot.

I came out on the roof, blinking in the morning sun, relieved to see Magnus standing at the end. He was with Sean and Fraoch, all nodding stoically, listening to Zach tell a story.

Zach had a modern physicality, his head bobbed and his shoulders weaved, his arms waved, with an energetic vibe. As I strode toward them I guessed at the story, it must have involved a... concert?

He started playing air guitar — yep, a concert. The men all laughed.

Magnus was wearing a crown much like mine. He was wearing a pale blue tunic, belted around his waist, with his good boots. His cloak was a woodsy green. It was a good color, dyed from local flora, and matched the hills — he looked like a mountain.

The other men were also wearing tunics, their colors muted, their fabrics less fine.

I had grown used to seeing Zach's tall lanky body in kilts, but seeing him in a long saffron colored tunic was wild. He was so thin it made him look a little like a pencil, except for the bit of tattoo sticking out of his shirt collar and down his wrists.

Magnus met my eyes and smiled. He put out an arm and kissed me on the head. "Och, ye look beautiful."

"Thank you."

"Ye found us."

"I did, wow, this is quite a view."

Magnus said, "Aye, tis a good view, twould be perfect if I couldna see that the walls are built of timber. We hae been discussin' finishin' them in stone, makin' the castle more formidable."

"That would be good, is that what you were talking about right now?"

Zach said, "Nope, I was telling them about the last Metallica show I went to — man, it was fucking wild." He looked around at the horizon, "Not as wild as this, but a good show."

It was a gorgeous day, the sun rising in the sky, a bit of a breeze, but warm on my face, and my layers cut the chill.

Zach asked, "Where's Em and the kids?"

"They went to the Great Hall,"

He said, "Cool, good..." As we all looked out at the gorgeous view, he said, "Wait, it's their first day at the castle — she went down to the Great Hall on her own with all the kids?"

My eyes went wide. "Uh oh, she's going to be in way over her head."

He said, "Alright, I'm headed down."

Magnus said, "Aye, this is a verra different time than she is used tae. Tis time for breakfast, ye ready for food, Sean?"

"Aye."

Fraoch said, "I am famished, I will grab Hayley and meet ye there."

He went to the stairwell on the other end. We turned to go down the stairs I had climbed, while Sean talked about building the walls. "I also think ye need a bulwark on the south curtain wall, I spoke tae Ian—"

"Already?"

"Aye, while ye were sleepin' like a bairn, without a worry in the world, someone needed tae get tae work. He said we could get stone from the quarry south of here."

Magnus held my hand. Guards surrounded us as we crossed the courtyard to go eat a meal.

This is the scene that greeted us — a medieval hall crowded with people, a cacophony of laughing, talking, and yelling, as people served from platters and baskets down the middle of a wooden table, and shoveled food into their mouths before rushing off to their pressing duties of the day. It was a little like a buffet in a train station — loud, busy, crowded.

Emma rushed up with Jack. "Thank heavens! I just followed the kids down here and wasn't paying much attention. I walked in and stopped in my tracks — I don't know anyone! I couldn't remember where you guys were. I wasn't sure what to do. This is intense."

Zach said, "I'm sorry, babe, I didn't know you were down here."

She whispered, grimacing, "It's Campbell men, but ten times worse."

I scanned the room. "These are dark-ages Campbell men."

Magnus said, "And I am their king."

As the crowd realized Magnus had entered, the busy hall grew quiet and everyone bowed. Then at Magnus's nod the clamor resumed.

Emma said, "From now on, I will only go everywhere with you, I think."

CHAPTER 4 - KAITLYN 29

I said, "Good idea, we got 'No traveling alone in the passages,' added to, 'Don't go anywhere without a man with a sword.'"

Hayley and Fraoch walked in. She said, "Holy cannoli, this is a lot of Campbell men."

"Yep, that's what we're saying. And you should have seen it five minutes ago. They're on their best behavior because Magnus entered, but five minutes ago it was wild, and Emma was in the middle of it with all the babies."

She said, "I bravely go where no modern woman has ever gone before."

Zach said, "I fucking love your Star Trek references, babe."

Magnus spoke to someone and we took our seats at the high end of the table, with plates of food in front of us.

Emma said, "I see that we need Magnus if we want anyone to pay attention to us."

Magnus said, "Madame Emma ye hae bravely entered a medieval Great Hall on day one without an introduction. Tis tae be admired, but I will give ye a bit of advice, ye daena want three quarters of these people tae pay any attention tae ye."

Zach asked, "Who runs the place?"

"Cailean runs the kingdom for me. He's my... what dost ye call it — the large painting?"

Zach said, "Your big picture guy?"

"Aye, he does the big picture of it all. Cailean's castle, Innis Chonnel—"

I said, "The ruin on Loch Awe?"

He nodded. "Aye, in this time tis kept in good order, the castle is strong, Cailean and his sons are verra good at management. Sean, when ye are talking about the stone with Ian, bring Cailean in on the conversation. He will oversee the work when ye arna here."

Sean said, "Good, I will meet with Cailean today."

"And I will ask Cailean if his son Niall and his wife can come and take over the runnin' of the household." He squeezed my hand. "His wife, Mary, speaks English, so there would be nae language barrier, but she must always be acknowledged as the most important person in the castle."

I laughed. "Great."

He chuckled. "'Tis why I haena invited her tae come yet, she can be a trial. I imagine twill complicate yer relationship, Kaitlyn, as ye are the queen, but as she will be able tae communicate with ye, ye might not mind her pride, and if ye tell her she has done a great deal of good she might be easy enough tae manage."

I laughed. "I've learned to manage a few women like that in my life."

Hayley said, "Lady Mairead falls under that description, but on steroids."

The Great Hall had grown quiet as the crowd dwindled. I sighed, "This is going to be a lot to get used to."

Fraoch said, "Aye, but we are in it taegether."

Zach shrugged. "Are we? We seem kind of spread out across time: we got a kingdom in the twenty-fourth century, we got James's newborn baby in the eighteenth century, we got one of our best fighters, besides me of course, in the eighteenth century." He looked at his watch. "I think right about now we have James and your Colonel in the twenty-first century..."

Magnus nodded. "When ye put it like that, in the light of the day, we appear tae be on our back foot."

Sean said, "With mostly timber walls."

Magnus exhaled. "'Tis not all timber, some are stone, the corners are stone, there is some wood but—"

"Och, ye are tryin' tae justify it, the stone is too short, the south west is timber, the east is too thin. Ye must build properly, Young Magnus, a thick, strong, stone wall first thing. If Lizbeth were here she would never stop laughin' on it."

"Och nae, fine, aye, I agree. I daena want any wood on the walls, and the timber side must be done first. And I *definitely* daena want Lizbeth tae mock me."

Sean raised his glass and said, "Tae Lizbeth, may she always think kindly upon us."

Magnus raised his glass and the two brothers drank.

We were eating a meal of warm grains with some pears and cream, there was honey and some eggs, thick bread with a soft cheese to spread on it, and white fish. Fraoch stacked it all on his bread, making a very tall sandwich.

Zach said, "You can't do that Fraoch, you have cheese on honey on oats, on bread, with fish!" He pretended to gag.

Fraoch tapped the side of his head. "But if I pile it up it looks like more food."

Zach said, "But it doesn't *taste* good."

Fraoch pressed the top of the sandwich and prepared his hand to grasp the sides to lift it. "I daena care about taste. I only want tae fool m'self intae believin' m'self well fed."

Zach said, "If I had known that you didn't care about taste it would have saved me a *lot* of trouble."

Magnus groaned. "Daena listen tae a word he says, Chef Zach, the taste is the point of it all."

Fraoch opened his mouth very widely, had to go even wider, and struggled to take a bite. He chewed, grimaced, and swallowed. "Och nae, I am talkin' from m'arse, I hae made a great deal of mistakes in puttin' this all together — ye might like fish, ye might like honey, and oatmeal is delicious, but ye canna put them all taegether without regret."

CHAPTER 5 - MAGNUS

RIDING WITH ARCHIBALD IN KING'S PARK - JUNE 16, 1291

*A*fter breakfast, I asked Archibald tae go for a ride.

He followed me out tae the stables, where I asked for Dràgon and Mario tae be brought tae us. While we waited, people bowed and curtseyed as they passed. One man startled when he saw me, then bowed and groveled.

I nodded and sent him on his way. Then chuckled and raised my brow. "What dost ye think, Archibald?"

"This is wild."

I said, "I think so as well, and we are becomin' wilder tae match our surroundings."

Our horses were brought. We climbed in the saddles and I turned Dràgon and led us from the castle courtyard toward the King's Park, with Haggis bounding along beside our horses' legs.

We had four guardsmen followin' us.

While riding, Archie looked thoughtful, then asked, "Do you like it when they bow to you, Da? I don't know if I would."

I smiled. "Ye are thinking of what it will be like tae be king?"

He nodded.

"Are ye worried about it still?"

"No, not much..." His voice trailed off. "Yeah. The worry went away, a little bit."

"I think yer concerns will probably sit here on yer back." I leaned over and patted him high on his back between his shoulder blades, just under his neck. "Twill be much like a yoke, always present, perhaps yer whole life, Archibald. Tis yer fate."

He nodded.

"Yer job will be tae straighten yer spine and strengthen yer back, so the yoke winna wear ye down so much. And ye ken the best way tae do that?"

"Bench pressing?"

I said, "Aye, but also, ye do it by lookin' out on the horizon. See me in my saddle? If I am lookin' down..." I slouched forward. "...the yoke, here..." I attempted tae pat that place on my own back.

He giggled. "You can't reach it, Da."

I laughed and tried again. "Nae, m'muscles are too big, I am stuck with the yoke, even if I wanted tae throw it off. But if I sit up straight in m'saddle and look out, see how m'back straightens?"

He straightened his back in the saddle.

"Good, ye feel it. The other place ye will feel it is when ye are up on the walls lookin' out over the lands, ye look out and yer back will be straight and strong, nae matter the weight. And whatever comes ye will be ready."

"That sounds good, Da, on the walls and on Mario I'll practice."

"But that is not all... another way tae strengthen yer resolve is tae enjoy yerself, tae hae fun with yer friends, tae love a fine lass, tae eat a good meal — when ye lean back in a chair and laugh as ye look around at yer family and friends, ye will also strengthen yer—"

"Because your family and friends are kind of like your horizon."

"Och aye! That was well said!"

We rode for a moment, in quiet, looking out over the land-scape, watching Haggis run off after something that moved in the brush and loping back without anything at all as if he had forgotten why he left.

Archibald broke the silence. "... isn't it strange that I have to have a straight, strong back, but everyone else bows?"

I said, "Archibald, as Chef Zach would say, 'Ye hae exploded m'brain.'"

Archibald laughed. "I don't think you said that right."

"Probably nae, but tis part of m'charm."

We rode through the wide green fields and then turned tae go on the easy path around the perimeter of it. "And, about the bowin', I am 'not a fan' as yer Aunt Hayley would say. I would make a rule that they canna bow, but I tell ye, Archibald, sometimes, ye want them tae bow so they will quiet or they all will be talkin' at once. Tis necessary tae follow tradition and keep order — tis crucial. Our subjects are many, they might decide someday tae remove a tyrant king from the throne — in America, the story goes that they fought a bloody revolution tae free themselves from a king and his taxes... so a king ought not be a tyrant, but a king also canna allow his subjects tae get a high idea in their head, or the king might be overthrown."

"Emma read to us about the revolution, I guess... I never thought that you're like the king in the story."

I laughed, "Och nae, Archibald, I am not like that *English* king! I think, after bein' a Scottish King and livin' in Florida for so many years that I would side with the rebels."

"Good, me too."

I teased, "Unless the rebels are tryin' tae overthrow *my* throne, then I will side with m'self. I promised my descendants a throne, I mean tae deliver it."

He nodded and from the corner of my eye I saw him straighten his back.

I said, "Tis not all terrible though, Archibald, ye will hae fine breakfasts and ye will sleep in a lavish bedroom, ye will hae heavy responsibilities but ye will also be surrounded by friends and family. Ye will live in Grace from God, and will be wise and just, and laugh from yer belly when ye are havin' fun, and ye winna hae tae worry about rebels overthrowin' ye, because ye will be fair, and yer subjects will join yer army when ye make the call. That is the best measure of a king, ye ken. The downside, alas, is I daena sleep much. Ye will see, one day ye will be as weary as I, with the same wrinkles." I smiled tae crinkle the wrinkles around m'eyes.

He laughed. "You make it sound fun."

I laughed too. "It seems like hard work most days, but has become vastly more fun now that ye and yer mother and sister and wee Jack are here."

We watched Haggis scamper off and return.

I asked, "Did ye notice the carvin' of the wolf on the wall of the castle?"

He shook his head, then said, "You mean the one on the Great Hall?"

"That's the one."

"Ben and I thought it was a carving of Haggis."

Haggis looked up at Archie and barked.

Archie said, "I'm talking about you, did you hear me talking about you, good boy?"

Haggis frolicked, his tail wagging.

I said, "He is a funny dog, tis hard tae see him as a descendent of wolves."

Archie laughed. "So it's a carving of a wolf?"

"Aye, the story goes that wolves once lived in caves on the cliffs of Castle Hill and on one fateful night, the men who lived here long ago were fast asleep when Vikings attacked—"

His eyes went wide. He whispered, "They attacked *here*?"

"Aye, but as they crept up on the castle, one of the Vikings stepped on the paw of a sleeping wolf, and the wolf woke, and the wolf howled a mighty howl until all the wolves woke, and they all howled. The mighty men of Alba woke up and began tae fight, and they won, Archibald, they beat the Vikings and brought peace tae our lands. Those men are our ancestors and that is why the wolf is a symbol of Stirling."

"I like that story — I think you should call yourself the Wolf King."

"Tis a good idea, except maybe Fraoch would tell me I am an arse for thinkin' too highly of m'self."

He said, "That sounds like Uncle Fraoch."

I watched him ride for a moment on the long wide field. "Ye hae become a verra good rider."

"Thanks Da, want to race?"

I said, "I daena ken..." Then I commanded Dràgon, "Ruith!" and set him chargin' across the field.

Behind me Archie yelled, "Hie!" and set Mario tae chase.

We galloped across the plain. I let Archie pass me and he began tae howl like a wolf as he rode, a fine sight, full of bravado and confidence. My pride in him swelled in my chest, I howled, too, as I passed him. I pulled Dràgon tae a stop at the edge of the far field after winnin' the race.

He pulled up a few moments behind. "Aren't you supposed to let me win?"

I narrowed my eyes. "Let ye win? Why would I let ye win?"

"Because I'm a boy."

"Ye are a prince, why would a king let ye win?"

He shrugged.

I laughed. "I was just tellin' ye that whole story about how ye canna let yer subjects get high ideas in their heads, or ye might be overthrown — tis the same for princes."

Archie said, "Oh, yeah, right."

"Someday ye will beat me."

"How do you know?"

"Because I am a time-traveler, I met ye in yer future. Ye will grow tae be a big man, a worthy king, and most importantly a good horseman."

"Most importantly?"

"Aye, tis the way tae my heart, ye ken."

He said, "Aye...." Then he asked, "So what happens when someday I beat you?"

I shivered. "Och, I daena like the sound of it, Archibald, I would prefer not tae dwell on it, but I will say this, ye will be a man and I will be proud of ye, and I will say, 'Well done, son,' and then I will go about my duties as king — just because ye can ride fast daena mean ye get tae replace me."

"I don't want to replace you."

"Then we daena need tae worry about it, tis verra far in the long away future. But ye are well, ye arna worried on it?"

"No, I am well, but Ma said something that I've been thinking about, 'Do what makes the best story.'"

"Aye, her Grandma Barb used tae say that. It makes ye feel better?"

"Yeah, I have a cool story coming, and there's not much I can do about it. You're a king, I get no say in it."

"Aye, ye will be a king, tis a bloodline, tis harsh but tis true, ye canna do much but accept that this is yer story."

"Yeah, and *if* this is my story, that I *have* to be a part of... I could fight it, I could be a brat and not play along nicely, *or* I can be the hero of it, you know?"

"Aye, I ken, with power comes a great deal of responsibility."

He laughed. "Da, you just quoted Spider-man."

"Did I? I dinna notice, I am a man from the past, I daena ken what a 'spider man' is."

"You do too, it's one of your favorite movies."

"Aye, I love that movie. Tis true. My favorite though is Thor, he is verra heroic even if he is a Norseman."

We turned and headed tae the castle.

I added, "So, what ye are saying, Archibald, is ye hae become accustomed tae the idea of becoming a king?"

"I don't know, how did you get used to it?"

I chuckled. "I daena think it came easily. I fought against it, tried tae hide from it, I dinna want tae do it — ye ken why I finally decided tae become the king?"

"Why?"

"Tae keep ye and yer brother and sister safe, that is the whole reason. Ye hae a royal bloodline coursing through yer veins, ye hae tae sit on a throne or ye winna ken peace."

He nodded. "That's what I mean, we are in a story and we can't get out of it, so we ought to make it good — like you might as well call yourself the Wolf King. That sounds like a good story." He howled, "Aarh-oooooooooooh!" Then said, "And if you are worried about an English attack, you can think like a Wolf King."

"Where did ye hear about an English attack?"

He shrugged. "I hear things. If an English attack is like a Viking attack, we need to wake the wolves."

"'Tis true. And the men." I smiled.

He howled again, bent back, aloud to the sky, "Arwhoooooohhooo!" Then said, "You just have to Wolf King it. That will make the best story."

"I agree. So ye will remind yerself, Archibald, when ye hear things that frighten ye, that ye are just the prince — ye hae long years afore ye must be king, more long years afore ye are a Wolf King." I teased, "And ye canna even ride a horse fast at all. Ye will be strong and wise long afore ye must be king. And in the meantime ye can think tae yerself, 'I daena want tae be king,' while telling yerself, 'but I must, and so I will make it the best story.'"

"And you will keep riding fast, Da, but occasionally you will let me win, sometimes… I promise if you do, I won't try to overthrow you."

I laughed. "'Tis a deal."

Then he asked, "The King of England is starting a war?"

"There are rumblings that he is wantin' war, how frightenin' do ye find it?"

"Terribly."

"Tis nothing we canna handle, Archibald, and think of the story we will tell of it after we kick his arse."

He laughed as we rode through the castle gates.

CHAPTER 6 - LOCHINVAR

THE HIGH WALLS - BALLOCH CASTLE - MAY 27, 1710

*A*sh asked, "So, what do we do in a castle in the... what century is it?"

"Tis the dawn of the eighteenth century."

She counted on her fingers, "Okay, so it's the early 1700s, that is crazy. I wouldn't believe a word of it if I wasn't wearing a too-tight bodice and looking down on a cart rolling through a gate from up on a castle wall." Her eyes scanned the horizon, "I can't believe this horizon, it's gorgeous."

I said, "Ye want tae see somethin' that will give ye pause? Look down from the other side of the wall."

She went over to the other side and looked down on the courtyard. Twas teeming with crowds: rolling carts laden with bundles and baskets and piles of sacks, many horses — an odor rose tae our noses, it smelled like heavy work with not enough bathin', and there was a great clamor.

She gulped. "I feel like such a numbskull, you would say crazy things and I believed you were talking about modern day Scotland, like it's some kind of archaic place. Let me guess, Scotland, in my time, is just normal?"

"Tis likely, I haena seen it. I hae seen past Scotland, the future kingdom, a lake house in Maine, and New York City."

She laughed. "That is an odd assortment, I imagine that inside your head you have a really weird view of how the world works."

"Aye, tis why, when faced with a beautiful lass who I want tae win, I canna think of anythin' tae say."

"You, Lochinvar the Lord of Time, do just fine."

He joked, "Tis because I won ye a'ready."

"Ha! That is true, but I suppose that might mean I'm too easy. Should I have made you fight for me first, led you on a bit?"

He scoffed. "What was I doin' at the walls of that compound? I think I was riskin' m'life, I fought for ye plenty hard."

"I guess that is true. I just meant, made you fight for my love."

"I daena think ye understand anythin' about m'love for ye, Ash, if ye think I dinna struggle tae win yer love. I stared out at the rain, soppin' wet for a whole night."

She smiled. "One night! I ought to have strung you along for at least a month, caused you a bit of worry."

I clutched my heart. "Nae, it might hae killed me! One night was all I could stand, where in the story of the world hae ye heard that ye ought tae cause turmoil in yer man's heart afore ye profess yer love tae him?"

"Everyone *kens* it, Lochie, all the stories, every love story comes from turmoil."

I waved my hand at her. "Och nae, this is similar tae something m'brother, Magnus, said about the turmoil and intrigue and danger caused by brothers strivin' for the throne — I told him that because *some* brothers were duplicitous, daena mean that is the way of all brothers. I think the history of the world is more likely tae be written by brothers who collaborated with each other tae win power for their family."

She leaned against the wall on the other side, looking out over the Scottish landscape once more, green fields, a deep dark forest, a ring of majestic mountains beyond. She said, "That might be true."

I continued, "And then ye hae a lord and his lady — ye think tis better tae cause turmoil in the beginning? Tae start with pain and agony and distress? Och nae, the way of it is much better for me tae say, 'Hello, m'lady, m'name is Lochinvar, and I do believe ye are verra bonny, might I hae a slice of yer pie?' and for her tae say, 'I do so like the sight of yer knee, m'laird Lochie, I made ye a pie, I will serve ye a slice of pizza, and then I will take ye tae m'bed and press m'thumb tae yers, and we will live happily from then on.'"

"When you put it that way, it does seem better."

I took her hand and held it. "There was plenty of turmoil with yer kidnappin', I daena think we need anymore."

She said, "I like that you're the orphan of the family and you're the one telling everyone they ought to trust each other's loyalty more."

I said, "I hae been alone m'whole life, I think that if I hae decided tae take on a family that they ought tae believe me when I say I am loyal tae them. If I am holdin' yer hand, Ash, I want ye tae ken, I mean it, ye daena need tae cause me anguish. I am yers, ye are mine. We daena need tae fret over it, we get tae be each other's family."

She smiled, "I really like that, I mean it too."

I smiled, "This is amazin', Ash picked me even with all the extra excitement that I bring." I put my arms out. "The scent of the garderobe, the terrible food, the uncomfortable bed, the lack of air conditioning."

She chuckled. "I haven't been in the garderobe yet… just used the pisspot, it's disgusting."

"Och, ye daena even ken how bad it can get."

"M'laird, are you trying to talk me out of staying here and being your family?"

"Nae, never, I just want ye tae be clear, there inna a PlayStation here, not for centuries."

"I do love playing GTA. I used to play a *lot* when I was on base."

"We canna here, tis just a fact. One year the family lived at Kilchurn, and they ran electricity tae the castle—"

"How?"

"I think twas a magical wheel in the water."

She nodded. "Hydropower, good idea. Who did that, Quentin?"

"He and James, likely. But it dinna work well for a gamin' system, it dinna hae a lot of power, it cut out all the time, tis almost worse than not havin' it at all. They used it for light mostly."

"It's interesting — it's a little like living on the frontier, but with access to everything in history to get comfortable. You could outfit this place with electricity, put up a satellite, fire rockets from here, drill for oil in the sixteenth century, bring a car—"

"They have brought what they call ATVs here before, ye ever driven one of them?"

"Yeah, I have — so what stops them from bringing everything they could ever want?"

"Magnus told me he daena want tae ruin the history of the world. If ye bring one lamp, and it lights the night, that pool of light might cause someone tae become complacent, tae not invent the light. Then where will light come from?"

"That is a really good point."

"Aye. Men must experience hardship tae want tae build a world, so we canna get too comfortable." I pulled her hand closer so that she was standing right in front of me. She was shorter, smaller. I put m'arms around her, bent down, and kissed her shoulder. "How is yer arm?"

"Much better."

"Good."

"So what do we do here in the eighteenth century?"

"I am thinking that Laird Lochie and Lady Ash ought tae go tae their room and see if they can get more comfortable."

She smiled. "I thought you would never ask."

CHAPTER 7 - ASH

BALLOCH CASTLE - MAY 27, 1710

*L*ochie led me by the hand to the stairwell, and then down the spiraling stair and along a passageway. I was able to pay more attention, my head growing clearer as the painkillers wore off, but that clarity was making my head swim with the reality — I was in the past.

I had been in the past for days. I had been kidnapped, now I was in another place, each different from the last, and nothing like the normal, ordinary, modern world.

I looked down at Lochie's hand, entwined in mine.

I had known him for hours. It could barely be called a full day, not really. *What had I done?*

He slowed in the stairwell and turned with one leg up, one down on the steps. He pulled me to his chest in a big embrace and kissed the top of my head. I kissed him back, but just then above us were footsteps as two big guards descended.

He whispered, "Press tae the wall. Turn tae me."

We pressed and the two men passed. I took a furtive glance to see one looking me over, the other asked, "Lochie, what ye doin' with the lass?"

"She is mine."

They laughed and continued down the stairs.

The exchange was short, but tense, common enough, but also my heart was pounding — it had seemed dangerous. "Who was that?"

"Guards, ye canna walk alone in the castle, Ash, the men arna trustworthy. Ye are used tae walking on yer own on the island but this is different, these are Campbell men."

I grimaced. "That sounds dire. But wait... aren't *you* a Campbell man? What about your brothers, wait... aren't they *all* Campbell men?"

"Aye, ye ought not trust a one of them unless ye ken them tae be trustworthy, ye ought tae trust three tae five men, tops."

"Okay."

He took my hand and began leading us down the steps again.

I asked, " Why did you stop and kiss me on the stairs?"

"Because I hae been tae yer home and as we came down the stairs I was thinkin' twas verra different here, ye are far away, and I thought ye needed a kiss, I could tell."

"I did, you guessed correctly."

He drew me down the passageway, darkened for lack of windows, but enough ambient light that we could make out our way to the door. He opened and we went in.

He asked, "Would ye like tae go tae bed?"

"In the middle of the afternoon, good sir? But it took so long to get dressed! And won't there be a meal soon, I am famished, must be all this fresh air, and... no, I don't think we can go to bed."

"Och nae," his face fell.

I smiled. "But we could do something else fun."

His eyes went wide. His arms went around me and pulled me close. "Like what?"

"We could just—" We were interrupted by a knock on the door.

Lochie dropped his arms and we stepped apart as a maid entered. "Dost m'lady need anything?"

"No, I don't need anything, thank you."

"Would ye like me tae wait for ye?"

Lochie said, "Nae, we need some privacy."

"Aye, sire." She backed from the room.

Lochie's arms went around me again. "What were ye sayin', Ash?"

"I thought we might just access our fun, private parts under our skirts."

"Tis a verra good idea..." He kissed my neck. "It has been centuries since I..." But then he straightened. "But och nae, Ash, it means I winna get tae see yer form. I hae only gotten the one look at ye, on the one night and briefly in the mornin', it daena seem fair."

"Life isn't fair, Lochie, but we will do our best, next time I am undressed I will let you really look." I put my good arm up around his neck and we kissed long and luxuriously.

While kissing me, he began drawing my skirts up. There were two layers of fabric, it took a few moments to bunch them up on the sides, and then — we heard many men running down the hall.

He froze.

Men shouted to each other as they passed the door.

Still holding my skirts up he faced the door listening.

I whispered, "What is happening?"

"Somethin' has caused them tae go on alert." He let my skirts drop down. He looked down on me. "I must go and check what is happenin'. Quentin and James hae gone on a supply run, and with Sean gone, Lizbeth's husband, Liam, will need me. He has been left in charge."

I shook my head. "But... what will I do?"

He kind of looked right and left in dismay as more commotion sounded outside. "I daena ken where tae take ye, ye need tae stay here. I am sorry, Ash, I need tae go see what the commotion is."

My heart pounded. "I can't come with you?"

"Ye hae an injury — we daena ken what is happenin'. I canna risk it, I daena ken what tae—"

There was a loud knock on the door and Lizbeth's voice called in, "Lochinvar, is Lady Ash with ye?"

"Aye, come in!"

She pushed in and closed the door behind her. "A group of men hae arrived, all the women and children are tae go tae the nursery. I came for Lady Ash."

"I will escort ye there." We all rushed from the room, Lizbeth in front, Lochie running behind me, looking in all directions — we made it down the steps to the doors of the nursery, now being heavily guarded. Lochinvar kissed my forehead before rushing away.

I called to his retreating back, "Stay safe!" and went into the nursery to sit among a whole bunch of medieval women I had only just met. I felt alone and really alarmed, made worse by more than one baby wailing in despair.

I said to myself, "Och nae," and slid down the wall to sit on the floor.

Lizbeth sat properly in a chair. "Daena be frightened, Lady Ash, we are safe here. This is only until they can ascertain the meaning of the visitor."

"Does this happen every time someone visits?"

She shook her head. "Nae, if we hae been sent tae the nursery tis because the visitor seems suspicious."

I dropped my head back against the wall.

She said, "Usually tis because of some trouble that Magnus has brought, but he inna here."

Beaty sat down beside me, leaning against the wall, holding her son in her arms.

Sophie sat in a chair beside Lizbeth holding her small infant.

Lizbeth said, "I hae sat here many a day with Kaitlyn, waitin' with trepidation tae see what trouble has arrived at the gate."

I asked, "Do you think this involves me?"

Beaty said, "'Tis likely, Ash, but it inna truly about ye, tis always about Magnus and his throne. This is part of the excitement of marryin' one of his men."

I gulped.

CHAPTER 8 - KAITLYN

RIDE IN KING'S PARK - JUNE 16, 1291

*M*agnus asked, "Where are the bairns?"

I said, "The kids are in their lessons and Jack is napping."

He said, "Perfect, would ye like tae go for a ride in the King's Park?"

"I would love that. Do you need our horses readied?"

He smiled. "I already did it."

"You have been planning this?"

"From the moment I called for ye tae come tae this century, I hae been thinking on our rides. I took Archibald out this morn, now I want tae ride with m'wife." He put his finger to his lips. "But Isla stamped her foot at me and told me I was only allowed tae take ye if we dinna hae any fun, so we will hae tae tell her twas terrible, even if tis wonderful."

I laughed, "Perfect. It will be just us?"

"Just us and four guardsmen. We must pretend as if they arna with us tae hae the whole effect of our private romantic ride."

"In your mind you're a great deal more unencumbered."

We walked together across the courtyard tae the stables with Haggis happily following along behind. "Aye, in my mind I am not a king, I am just a Scottish man who wants tae shew his wife a verra fine trail tae take in the glorious view of the landscape. Alas, I am the king of all of it, so it inna quite as romantic as it ought tae be."

"I don't know, seems to me like plenty of women would swoon at the idea of a king showing them a view of his kingdom. This sounds very romantic."

He laughed. "It could be, but in this scenario ye are thinking of yerself as a 'woman' instead of a queen."

I joked, "Och nae, that is not how I want to be seen. I wish I was a lot more unencumbered too."

"Exactly."

We came to our horses, stable men bowed, and Magnus held the reins so I could pull myself up, making it, after all these years, almost effortlessly.

He passed me the reins with a look of appreciation in his eyes.

I asked, "Did you like that?"

"Och aye, I liked it verra much, it has been a while since I hae seen ye on a horse."

He climbed on the back of his horse, and pulled alongside mine. Haggis, ever the sentry, walked alongside. The four guards drew their horses behind us, and we left through the gate to the grounds.

As we passed along the grassy hill sweeping away alongside the path, I said, "It's odd how this is all familiar. We were here in the thirteenth century, but time was shifting, we were in two different places, it was all so confusing. And then we were also here with Mary of Guise, in 1551. It looked very different then."

"Aye, in a little over two hundred and fifty years we will be here. There will be games held right over there. They will cut down a great many trees." He pointed.

"*That's* where I kicked all the ladies' arses at archery."

He chuckled. "Twas another fine sight."

He drew his horse around behind mine.

I said, "Wait, aren't you supposed to be in the lead?"

"Am I? We are only goin' there." He pointed toward the place where the path cut into the woods at the edge of the King's Park. "And I do greatly prefer the view from back here."

I said, "You, Master Magnus, are incorrigible."

He said, "Did ye say something, Madame Campbell? Tis hard tae hear ye over the sight of yer..." He pulled his horse alongside mine, leaned in, and I kissed him on the lips.

I glanced at the guards, they were pretending to look elsewhere.

We came to the woods and entered his park.

He pulled in front of me, looking around at the trees surrounding and arching above us.

I said, "I only see 'trees', what trees are these?" Because I knew it was one of his favorite things to talk about.

"Dost ye see there, Kaitlyn, tis an ancient oak, think on it, ancient, *already*."

I looked up at it. "Wow, that's amazing, imagine what that tree has seen."

"Much of what it has seen has been lost tae history, men who are nameless." He pointed, "And there is a birch, and a grouping of pines."

The ground was carpeted with mosses and ferns, I pointed, "Look! Bluebells!"

"Aye, the fae planted them. They hae been at work all around here." He breathed in. "Och, I love the scent of a Scottish forest."

I inhaled. It was the aroma of pine carried on a breeze mixed with the odor of musty, loamy soil. It was hard to describe except it smelled thick and old and deep. Heavy.

We drew to the field, where we had jumped, then rode across it and our path began to climb.

He said, "Ye can continue on?"

I said, "Aye. Did you bring Archie up here?"

"Nae, we kept tae the fields on the edge of King's Park, but I wanted tae speak tae him alone for a time."

"Is he doing okay? I haven't had the time to check in."

"Aye, he is much better — he told me somethin' interestin'."

"What?"

"That he is using one of Barb's wisdoms tae keep himself calm about becomin' a king someday."

"The 'pay attention to the butterflies...' one?"

"Nae, the 'Do what makes the best story' one."

I looked up at the dappled light filtering through the canopy. "How does that apply?"

"He is thinkin' tae himself that the story is one he canna step out of, so he might as well make it good."

"I *love* that, Barb would be thrilled if she knew her great-grandson was living according to one of her maxims. Especially if she knew he was a prince. Her mind would be blown by all of this."

Magnus said, "He is growin' intae a fine boy. I believe she is lookin' down upon him, and warmly smilin'."

I said, "She had a beautiful smile." I turned and looked out at the woods. "She would have loved it here."

We walked for a bit, then he said, "Look at the trees."

I had been concentrating on my horse picking its path — the road was rocky, and somehow I thought my concentration was necessary, but Magnus was riding in front now, and my horse was content to follow him and was careful enough.

I didn't need to look up, we were as high as the canopy and it was lush and green and beautiful, as if we were nestled in the upper branches.

I said, "I would love to live in a treehouse."

He laughed. "Och nae, like a bird, mo reul-iuil? What... How...? I hae too many questions tae even begin."

"I know, I know, it doesn't make sense, but still..."

He said, "Twould be fun for about an hour, tops." Then he

twisted in his saddle to ask, "Are ye good, we are goin' higher still."

I said, "Yes, I'm good, and I love the air up here, it smells like flowers and trees and clean..."

"Aye, the air grows more fresh as we go." He arched to look up at a grouping of eight hawks swooping in the blue sky over the rise. "We hae been havin' some fine weather."

I said, "We deserve it, couldn't have happened to nicer people."

He said, "Aye, but the hawks above mean change is comin'."

"Does it? Uh oh. I don't like the sound of that. We have been winning, I don't want it to get scary again."

"Twill. Ye canna be the King of Scotland and expect the winds tae favor ye with calm, tis more likely tae bluster with ill-will, tis the way of the winds, ye canna fight them." He looked up again and back at the guards around us. "I daena want tae frighten ye, Kaitlyn, I just want ye tae ken. We hae a great deal of power, tis likely that we will be warrin' over it."

"The part that sucks about that is it's power you didn't really want."

"Aye, true."

"Is there something going on that you haven't told me about?"

"The King of England, Edward the First, has been threatenin' us, he is at our border."

"Oh? That sounds dire."

"Tis, he has a mighty army. Cailean and I sent word tae the French king, Philipe le Bel, askin' for his assistance. But I daena like askin' for it, Philipe le Bel's name stands for 'Philip the Fair'. He is verra young and I daena wish him tae think I am weak."

"But you're new to this, you only learned it, when... yesterday?"

"I think I hae known it for months, but also, I just learned it — time shifts, spins and rolls, and I must try tae stay atop of the wheel. Even though I am hearin' something for the first time, I must pretend tae hae known it already." He directed Dràgon around a boulder and back tae the path, and turned to make sure my horse was following well.

He shifted back in his seat and said, "But ye ken, I hae had tae do this most of m'life. I am practiced at the art of pretendin' tae ken what is goin' on. I was masterful with ye, ye had nae idea I was a time traveler—"

I teased, "I barely noticed you had no idea how to work the light switches or turn on the hot water."

"Ye saw me as competent, capable, and not needin' of yer help at all. Tis why ye kept offerin' tae drive me places."

"That's because you were so hot, *literally* — remember when you were sweltering in the house with no idea how to turn on the AC?"

He chuckled. "Tis not yer usual meanin' of the word 'hot' tae describe me."

"You were hot and you were also so very *hot*."

The climb grew steep, I went back to concentrating on my horse's path, but then I said, "But all kidding aside, so the English King is threatening?"

"Aye, he would like us tae bend the knee tae him. I winna, so there is likely tae be trouble."

"By trouble you mean, battles?"

He nodded.

I said, "What are we talking about: in a few years we might have to deal with him, or...?"

"He is amassin' troops on our border, tis likely tae be a pressin' problem." He turned to see my face. "Our messenger should return this evening, bringing us news. I will tell ye as soon as we ken."

"I'll be grateful when we have everyone under the same roof — when will Lochie and Quentin get here?"

"In the next few days they will arrive with the weapons. Then I will gather m'men and make some decisions—"

We both looked up at the sound of a hawk, cawing in the

wind. I watched it swoop and turn on the breeze, then we continued the climb to the highpoint for the view.

As we came upon the rise, two of the guards checked the area was safe. They gave us the all clear and Magnus and I climbed down from our horses and stood side by side on a large boulder for the view. It wasn't the widest view, the mountains behind us blocked the south, but we could see the north, a valley before us, the river snaking through, and to the right, the castle up on its high promontory.

He smiled appreciatively as his eyes scanned the landscape, then a flash of a scowl at the castle.

I said, "What?"

He said, "M'castle looks weak and defenseless, dost ye see the part of the wall that is built with timber? Twas built tae hold archers and defend against arrows, but armaments hae grown more powerful. We need the walls of Stirling tae be built of heavy granite, strong enough tae take blows by cannonballs."

"Sean is organizing that though."

"Aye he is meeting with the men of the quarry — the stone will come. The artisans will be hired, but until then I will scowl whenever I look in that direction."

I said, "I think we ought to turn this way then." I pushed his shoulders around so that we were facing southwest, with the castle behind us. Woods and mountains, stretching all the way to the—

Magnus cocked his head.

I asked, "Do you see something?"

"Aye, there is a group on horseback." Haggis, either seeing them, or sensing Magnus's interest, began to bark.

Magnus said, "That is enough, Haggis."

The dog sat down beside Magnus's legs and growled in that direction.

I saw a brief glimpse of a movement, very far away. I didn't see it as a group on horseback at all, just as a change in light, but Magnus and his guardsmen were all tense, watching. Magnus strode to the horses and retrieved his binoculars from a side bag.

I peered in that direction, but it seemed miles away. I saw nothing to my naked eye.

He trained the binoculars. There were hawks soaring above the place where we were focusing.

He said, "There are men there, at least six... not mine, the coat of arms is..." He quieted while he looked, then added, "English."

He watched through the binoculars for a long time, then said, "I daena see anything anymore."

I said, "I don't mean to sound like an idiot, but maybe it's just some English men out for a ride?"

He looked up at the hawks winging through the sky, then squeezed my hand. "Nae, I ken ye are tryin' tae set our minds at ease, mo reul-iuil, but if the English are journeyin' through Scotland, it is likely there is an enemy gathering strength. I haena met him yet, but I fear he is just over the horizon."

He called the guards over and they conferred. My husband's voice was low and rumbling, speaking in Gaelic, it was comforting though I didn't understand. Then he sent two men to investigate and we waited quietly, occasionally watching through his binoculars.

He said, "I am sorry this disrupted our ride."

I said, "It's fine, it was a good day, and I'm glad I was here. It's been a long time since we rode together — how about we pretend we weren't interrupted?"

"We can try." He reached out and brushed a strand of my hair blowing against my cheek and tucked it behind my ear. Then he kissed my temple, where the sun was warming my skin, his mouth lingered there.

I said, "Thank you."

"For what, mo reul-iuil?"

"That kiss, the view, the moment alone."

"Nae problem, I needed it as well." He checked his watch. "We ought tae get ye back, m'guards will catch up." He held my horse's reins so I could climb up, then he climbed on Dràgon and led us on the return path tae the castle.

After the guardsmen caught up and he spoke with them, I asked, "What did they find?"

"Naethin', m'men dinna see anything or anyone over there. They are probably scouts for the English King, but they daena hae permission tae be on my lands."

We continued on.

"What do we do? There's no phone, no way to call England and say 'Hey, we just saw your dudes here, that's an uncool thing to do, don't do it again.'"

"Aye, we daena hae phones, a lot could be solved with phones. Instead I will hae tae send m'own scouts out, tae ascertain where they are. Engage with them, demand an accountin' for the trespassing."

"At least he's an old school king and not involved in time travel."

"Aye, it gives me an upper hand."

Just as we were about to emerge from the forest at the wide fields, the guard behind us called, "Mag Mòr!"

We both slowed our horses and turned. He was pointing at the sky ahead of us. Through the canopy, between us and the castle, we had a glimpse of a large storm. The trees began to whip in the wind, a loud roar above us, thunder rumbling.

I said, "Isn't that the place that we jump in and out of? If it's Lochie, isn't he a day early?"

Magnus urged our horses to go faster.

CHAPTER 9 - KAITLYN

THE FIELD IN KING'S PARK - JUNE 16, 1291

*C*entered over the field, the winds were still strong, the cloud bank was high, there were thunder claps sounding, and lightning sparked from earth to sky.

We remained in the tree line watching, because it looked and sounded insane and was lasting much longer than usual, like it would not stop. Even though we were protected in the woods, I had to put my arm up to protect my face.

The gusts of wind were brutal.

The limbs above us whipped.

There was a loud crack above us and I shrieked.

Haggis barked at the sky.

Magnus yelled, "Stay here, get down from yer horse! I need tae go closer." I scrambled down as he jumped from Dràgon and passed me the reins.

I was holding the reins of two horses in a thunderstorm, while they stomped and neighed, wanting to get away from the storm. I commanded, "Stad! Stad!" The way Magnus had taught me, but though Dràgon listened, he still looked at me like I was an arse.

One of the guardsmen took the reins from me, because I did not look competent enough.

Far ahead of us in the field the wind was whipping up dirt and detritus, making it hard to see, and the storm clouds had turned the day into darkness. The clouds bulged down in the middle. I drew in breath, as Magnus and two of the guardsmen crept closer.

Oh no, this is going to be a full-blown tornado. But it didn't become one, instead the clouds bulged down, then rose back up, bulged down and rose back up again. A gust whipped in the other direction and I had to cover my face with my arm. *When will this end?*

But after a few more long moments, the next gust was less forceful. The next even less. The trees stopped whipping and went back to being tall and stationary. The wind was dying down.

Magnus glanced back at me, then headed out into the middle of the field.

When I was certain it was all clear, I went forward to get a better view — *who had arrived?*

But there was nobody there except my husband looking up at the dissipating storm with his sword drawn. Haggis was by his feet, also looking up. A memory flashed in my mind of Magnus when I had first met him: right after a kickball game a storm had hit and he had stood there as if he had wanted to fight the clouds.

We had never realized at the time — stupid modern people who had no idea that time travel existed — he hadn't been a lunatic wanting to fight storms, he was a hero drawing a sword against an enemy who could travel through time. An enemy who was brutal, and living and dying by long-ago rules.

Funny how much more I knew now.

From the direction of the castle I saw Hayley, Fraoch, Sean, and Zach on horseback headed across the fields to meet Magnus. One of the guardsmen followed me and one remained with the horses in the woods, and I walked across the mud-soaked field to meet them.

As I neared, they were conferring and looking up at the sky. I looked up too — wispy white clouds were swirling, then trailing away, leaving behind a high blue sky. Three hawks flew on the high wind.

I glanced at Magnus, looking up at them.

He was noting the hawks, thinking to himself, *change is coming,* I could see it in his eyes.

As I walked up, I heard Fraoch say, "Twas definitely someone, they just dinna land."

Magnus nodded. "I hae seen it before, and had it happen tae me once. I was traveling and I was pulled..." He used his hand to show being pulled at the waist to the side. "It feels as if ye are clawed aside, and forced in another direction. I daena ken if this is what it looked like when it happened tae me—"

Chef Zach said, "That's gotta be what it fucking looks like, that's totally what it looked like, the person—"

Hayley said, "Or persons."

"Or persons, were traveling, and it looked like they were being pulled away while trying to get here."

Hayley said, "Like a struggle."

We all nodded, because that was indeed what it had looked like.

I said, "Who do we think it was?"

Fraoch said, "I daena want tae think of anyone in our family goin' through it."

We all exhaled.

Magnus said, "On a different note, Kaitlyn and I were ridin' southwest of here and I saw a group of English men."

Sean said, "Och nae, the English are on yer lands now, Young Magnus?"

"Aye, I saw them. Kaitlyn and I were up on the hill there, and the English were near Meikle Bin."

Fraoch said, "How many men?"

"I saw six, they wore insignia."

Sean shook his head. "Och, it means they are part of a larger army."

Magnus said, "That is what I am thinkin' as well."

Sean said, "It must involve Longshanks."

Hayley whispered, "Who is Longshanks?"

Fraoch said, "Edward, the English King. He wants tae start trouble."

I gulped.

Zach said, "Wait, how far away were the English men?"

Magnus pointed, "Near that ben."

"Well, that's fucking formidable — I can see right over there, that's close."

Magnus said, "But remember, Chef Zach, the English King can threaten us, but we are time travelers. We hae time, power, and weapons beyond his imaginings." Then he looked over at Sean, chewing his lip, looking out at the mountains. "I am concerned, but I want tae set yer minds at ease, we hae dealt with worse things than a vexatious troll on a weak throne."

Sean said, "Ye think the English hae a weak throne?"

"Aye, or why else would they be scoutin' around in my bens? If he was a king with strength he would call a meeting. He would ask for a treaty. Instead, Scotland is allied with France, and who is he allied with? Nae one. He is sneakin' around, tryin' tae find out about what we are doing, and I saw his men, he has been found out — I can ready for any disquiet he brings."

Fraoch said, "Aye, Og Maggy, I agree, ye are king of time, surrounded by good men. Tomorrow Lochie will arrive. Two days later, Quentin will arrive with a large cache of weapons, James will come soon. And daena even get me started on Lady Mairead up in Riaghalbane, if she catches wind of the English scouting around she will become irritated. I wouldna want tae be in his shoes if Lady Mairead gets annoyed."

Magnus nodded. "Though I daena need m'mother tae fight the English King, I agree, tis good she is on our side."

I said, "I need to get back to the kids."

"Aye, I will accompany ye tae the castle. I will send scouts out lookin' for encroaching English. None of ye needs be overly worried, but if ye do go out, make certain tae hae guardsmen with ye."

CHAPTER 10 - LOCHINVAR

BALLOCH CASTLE COURTYARD - MAY 27, 1710

I jogged down the steps to the ground floor where I found the men of the castle, milling around the courtyard. Craigh saw me and sneered, then looked away. I once worked for him in the stables and he had been used tae antagonizin' me. It dawned on me that m'predicament was precarious — I was here without the protection of Magnus or Sean, and needed tae tread carefully.

I climbed up on a cask tae see over the crowd. Liam was at the gate, speaking tae five strangers on horseback.

I asked the man beside me, "Doest ye ken what is happening at the gate?"

He growled, "What do ye care about it, Lochie?"

I said, "I am one of Magnus's men, a guest of Sean, a mate of Liam — if I ask ye a question, ye ought tae answer —"

Craigh interrupted, "Ye causin' trouble, Lochie?"

"Nae, I want tae ken what is happenin' at the gate."

He scoffed. "Maybe it daena matter tae ye."

"Maybe it does, ye ken, Liam will tell me once he is done. It does nae harm tae tell me now so if Liam needs m'sword I am ready tae fight. Ye ken I am good with the sword, I would hae kicked yer arse that night if Magnus haena stopped me."

Craigh said, "Lochie, tis like ye wish for a painful death."

"I daena, I just want tae ken who is at the gate without havin' tae argue with the biggest bawbag for miles around."

"Fine, but only because listenin' tae ye be a big bairn causes m'head tae ache. Big Ham and Sneaky Simmin found the inner-lopes crossing the Earl's land and escorted them here, the inner-lopes claim tae bring a message from Edinburgh."

As he spoke I kept my eyes on the strangers. The leader looked agitated, and his horse stamped. I couldna make out what he was sayin'.

"Tis odd, daena the Earl hae his own messengers?"

I dinna wait for an answer, I pushed my way closer through the crowd, arrivin' at Liam's shoulder. I lowered m'voice and asked, "What pray tell is the messenger on about?"

"He says the Earl has arrived in Edinburgh but has fallen ill."

I said, "Tis an ordinary message though... Where are the Earl's messengers?"

He said, under his breath, "I daena ken, tis odd, our guardsmen are concerned—" Then he stepped fully in front of me and whispered, "Daena let them see ye, his eye is rovin'. I think they might be lookin' for ye."

Och nae. I stepped back behind the crowd and took cover in a shadow at the edge of the courtyard. The strangers did act as if they were lookin' for someone. They seemed shifty and were scanning the crowd.

Liam and the Balloch guards began usherin' the strangers from the castle, herdin' them toward the gate.

Craigh walked by. "Lochie, ye are goin' tae stand there, useless, or ye goin' tae help for once?"

"Liam told me tae step aside."

"Must be mighty fine tae be a favored guest. The rest of us hae tae see the innerlopes from the castle." He shoved through the crowd taeward the stables.

Liam met me at the wall. "What did Craigh want with ye?"

I shook m'head, irritated. "The usual — harassin' me for not helpin'."

"Lochie, ye ken tis his way. He thinks ye are a pain in his arse, he inna goin' tae change his mind unless ye give his arse a fine rubdown — ye willin' tae give the arse of Craigh a fine rubdown?"

I chuckled. "Nae, maybe an arse kickin'."

"Well, ye arna allowed tae — ye will bring trouble down on yer brother, and on Sean and me, because I am the only man left in the castle who cares a lick for ye."

"Aye, I will behave — what did ye think the strangers were about?"

"They were here scoutin' tae look for Magnus, I think, possibly ye and Fraoch as well. When dost ye think Master Cook and Black MacMagnus will return?"

"Sometime today, I canna tell."

"Och nae, I daena like that they are all away."

"Ye are the last man guardin' the castle, but I suppose twas good they dinna find Magnus here or see me in the crowd. There might hae been a battle in the courtyard."

He narrowed his eyes. "Dost ye think that is their aim, a battle?"

"I daena ken."

"What dost ye think they will do if they dinna find Magnus or his men here? Tis his trouble, nae mine — I am unsure how tae guard against a danger I daena understand."

I looked around at the men in the courtyard, most of them were going back tae their duties, completely unconcerned. Strangers were a common enough occurrence, they had nae idea of the danger the castle would be in if those strangers were time travelers and had been armed with modern weapons.

If they were time travelers it would be easy for them to have foreknowledge of who was here and how little we were protected.

Och nae. I looked around at the walls.

If the strangers were after Ash, there were not enough guards, this was not enough protection.

Every man in Balloch was not enough. And Sean wasna here. Liam was capable of guardin' against ordinary trouble, but Sean understood how tae deal with Magnus-level trouble.

I said, "If their aim was tae locate Magnus and they dinna see him, they might just leave. But if their aim was tae cause trouble with me... maybe they dinna see me. They dinna see Ash, that is good, but all they hae tae do is ask one man from Balloch at the local tavern, 'Is Lochinvar at the castle?' And they'll know."

"What dost ye think they would do with that information?"

"If they ken I am here, if they ken Sean and Magnus arna here, we ought tae prepare for an attack."

He exhaled. "Aye, we will double the guards and send men tae follow them, tae watch their movements, but Lochinvar, ye canna stay long, ye need tae go."

"Aye, I agree. As soon Quentin and James return, I will take Ash away. Speakin' of, I need tae go check on her."

"Will ye tell Lizbeth that all is well enough, I will see her at dinner."

I climbed the stairs tae the nursery.

CHAPTER 11 - ASH

THE NURSERY, BALLOCH CASTLE - MAY 27, 1710

We sat for a moment as the babies calmed, then to start a conversation, Lizbeth said, "Lady Ash—"

I said, "Would it be too much to ask that you call me simply Ash?"

"Of course, Ash, how is it ye haena married the lad Lochinvar yet?"

I said, "Oh, um... I..." It was an odd question, Lochie and I had literally just met, like there hadn't been enough time to marry him, and we had sort of decided to carry on as if we were... "I think Lochinvar believes we are married already, we just..."

"I daena ken much about where ye are from, Lady— I mean, *Ash*, and Kaitlyn assures me that tis verra different there, but Beaty and Sophie hae told me that there are some things which are constant — ye marry a man if ye want tae share yer life... for instance.... And I daena want tae offend, but how under the heavens does the lad Lochinvar believe he has married ye if ye daena ken if ye are married?"

I winced. "I don't know, he told me that we pressed our thumbs together and—"

She laughed merrily. "The lad Lochinvar has told ye that he

pressed his thumb tae yers? Twas covered in spittle?" She shook her head, frowning teasingly. "He told ye that was enough?"

I nodded. "I don't know, I thought that was how it was done."

"Och nae, sweet Ash, tis not the way, not for Ladies, not for Lairds, not for the brother of a king. What Young Lochinvar kens of the world is not much, but he ought tae ken this, ye hae tae marry in the church, be bound in front of God, and it must be marked in the record, or it daena *count*."

"Oh. I didn't think of it that way, I guess I thought the fact that we meant it was enough."

"How long hae ye known him?"

"Mere days."

"I hae known Lochinvar for a time, he is a handsome lad, and brave tae the point of foolhardiness. I thought him useless, but he is a champion of m'brother, Young Magnus, and over time, as he brawled and carried on in the courtyard of the castle, I watched him and learned that he is a loyal and gallant knight, but... he was an orphan. Ye canna forget it causes trouble in their minds, ye ken, Ash. Young Magnus was a bastard, it caused him a great deal of trouble. All of us are the children of Lady Mairead, och nae, that has caused us a great deal of turmoil. I wouldna wish that trouble on my enemies..." She paused and the corner of her mouth went up, "Well, *most* of my enemies. Some would deserve Lady Mairead and much more, but Lochinvar — he is an orphan, this is much farther beyond the trouble. He inna aware of his power, he wasna held tae his place, when he was first brought intae Magnus's fold he dinna understand his position in the family. At times he has caused a brawl with men three times his size and he won, but it canna rest easily upon him that he causes more turmoil than calm."

I gulped.

She said, "He is in many ways a big bairn, he needs direction and guidance, and ye seem tae be willin' tae take him on, and when he looks at ye — ye can see that he wants ye tae give him the guidance."

Beaty said, "He does love ye desperately."

I asked, "Really?"

Beaty said, "Aye, he looks at ye like a hungry man looks at a Saturday Feast."

"Wow, I hadn't noticed that. Wait, are you just having fun?"

Sophie said, "He does truly love ye, but tis also fun, here's one: he looks at ye like ye are the first challenge he has ever truly wanted, as if his soul longs for ye..."

Beaty said, "He looks at ye as if ye are a crystal vase that he must put upon his shelf, but he canna imagine how tae get ye there without breakin' ye and cuttin' himself in the act."

Beaty and Sophie high-fived and then did a long and elaborate modern-style handshake that made me laugh.

Then I said, "So basically he doesn't know how to handle me — this all sounds tricky, what do I do?"

Lizbeth said, "Well, Ash, he daena ken how tae be yer husband and so... I daena want tae overstep, but I would like tae advise ye."

Beaty said, "Ye ought tae allow her tae help, Ash. Lizbeth has the wisdom of Lady Mairead and the kindness of someone more kind than Lady Mairead."

I glanced at Sophie, she nodded.

I said, "Okay, tell me."

"My thought is Lochinvar needs guidance tae show him how tae be a husband. And so ye canna allow him tae think he has won ye with a thumb: this is the promise of a lad, ye need tae tell him tae make ye the promise of a grown man."

"Oh, yeah, that makes sense."

"Aye, he is known for running bravely intae battle and bein' impetuous and a wee bit wild. Ye will need tae smooth his brow, calm him, and tell him that ye will want him tae meet ye at the altar and tae promise ye tae be yer husband in front of God and tae care for ye like a laird and tae honor ye as his lady, like my

Liam — he is m'second husband, ye ken, but I knew he would honor me. Ye need tae expect Lochinvar tae honor ye, it means ye might hae tae demand it."

Sophie said, "Aye, also he wants the respect of Magnus and Fraoch, and daena ken how tae get it, because his nature is tae be much like a lad. If ye make him stand at the altar and promise himself tae ye, he will emerge a husband. It will gain their respect, the solemnity of the occasion will raise him in everyone's estimation."

Beaty said, "And he has never truly belonged tae a family, I think he wants tae belong tae ye, and for ye tae belong tae him. It might be the only belongin' he has ever had." She raised Noah up and rubbed her nose to his. "Inna that right, Noah? Uncle Lochie wants tae belong tae a family. If he marries ye, he will take his rightful place as one of the men."

She put Noah down on her lap again.

I smiled. "He will be sad if he doesn't get to sit with the kids in the back of the van."

Beaty said, "Just because he becomes yer husband daena mean he has tae always act like one of the men. He can still hang out with his nephews, Fraoch is a grown man with the heart of a bairn, sometimes that's just the way they are."

I said, "Thank you for the advice, I didn't think of any of that, but it makes sense."

Lizbeth nodded and folded her hands in her lap, "What do ye think Sean is doing?"

Beaty said, "I imagine he is up on the walls on guard duty about now."

"Och, truly, ye think — but Magnus is a king! Daena they hae guards for that...?" Then she said, "But aye, ye are probably right, if Sean is goin' tae stay in a castle he will want tae guard the walls, he canna trust other men tae it..." Then she said, "If he comes home will he do it at once? How long will it take?"

Beaty said, "It takes a long time accordin' tae yer soul, but accordin' tae a clock tis only a part of a day. Sean can come home, as soon as he decides."

"Good… I ken he goes on long hunts and sometimes tae Edinburgh and tae Kilchurn, but tis unsettlin' tae hae him gone tae a place I hae never seen. Maggie will be worried until he returns."

Sophie said, "Magnus and Fraoch will make certain he is safe."

Lizbeth nodded. "And yer husbands will be returned tomorrow?"

Sophie and Beaty said, "Aye."

CHAPTER 12 - MAGNUS

STIRLING CASTLE - JUNE 17, 1291

I sent men out tae scout for English trespassers and then I held meetings all mornin'. Sean and I met tae talk about the building project. Cailean and I discussed bringing more guards tae the castle, building and maintaining a larger standing army.

My soldiers returned — they hadna found any English, but they found the leavings from an encampment at the base of the ben, near where I had spotted the men yesterday.

The consensus was that the English had left the area already. But we carried on with plans anyway, strengthening the guard, protecting the castle. Anyone leavin' the gates needed a full guard. Messengers were sent tae the lairds at the borders, and more men were sent tae scout farther out.

Sean, Fraoch, and I met in my office at midday. "Och nae, Sean, I am sorry ye hae arrived in the middle of this — I would prefer tae take ye for a hunt."

He rubbed his hands together. "This is the kind of excitement a man relishes. King against king? This is stirrin'!"

I laughed. "Tis only stirrin' ye tae excitement because we arna outmatched."

"True. I do admire that m'brother is a powerful king."

"Did ye just say ye admired me, Sean?"

He said, "I admire yer *power*. Daena get full of yerself, Young Magnus, ye are m'wee weak brother. Everyone can see it."

I chuckled.

"And because of yer weakness, ye need me, and I daena mind buildin' yer walls — though I would enjoy ridin' out over the lands, marveling at an older Scotland. Tae see the power and wealth. The far-flung lands—"

"Tis my power and wealth! Tis my land!"

He rolled his eyes, and joked, "Alba belongs tae all Scotsmen in their hearts."

I said, "Och nae, ye will never give me m'due."

"Never. Tis m'duty as yer elder brother not tae allow ye tae think too highly of yerself." He drank from a mug of ale.

I said, "What dost ye think, Fraoch, this is the duty of an older brother?"

"Aye, tae kick yer arse, talk down tae ye, put ye in yer place, but all the while protectin' ye from yer enemies and helpin' build yer power. Tis a lot tae do, we are selfless. We daena even get tae hunt and fish, we must spend all our time helpin' our wee brother survive."

I exhaled. "Och, I feel verra put upon by ye gangin' up on me."

They both laughed.

Sean spun his mug. "I am only havin' fun, Young Magnus, I am impressed with yer power, tis a far cry from the lad kneeling in front of me, beggin' for m'forgiveness."

"Ye doled it out quite painfully."

"Aye, tis as older brothers hae always done. But all teasing aside, I would love tae go on a hunt, tae see with m'own eyes that Alba is yers. But my time is better spent helpin' ye build yer power than marveling in it. Replacin' the timber with stone on yer walls is crucial. The English King needs tae see he winna get through yer gates."

"Tis why ye came?"

"Aye, this is why I came — tae help ye hold yer crown. Might as well be here when the English King threatens ye, tis bound tae be much more interesting—"

"Ye think Eddie is threatenin' me?"

He and Fraoch both said, "Aye," at the same time.

Fraoch said, "Ye canna take Englishmen on yer lands any other way."

I nodded.

Sean said, "Och, and rudely — he haena given me enough time tae strengthen yer castle first."

"Aye, he is a craven tallow-faced sack of mold, I hae just begun m'rule and he is sendin' his men tae trod upon the m'lands and threaten the realm? Och nae, I am feelin' murderous — did I tell ye I met him at a tournament?"

"Aye, aye... ye won the joust — ye forget Young Magnus, ye hae told me of it numerous times. Ye are always boastin' on yerself — we might want a bit more humility."

I chuckled. "'We might want a bit more humility,' *Yer Majesty*."

He groaned and teased me, "Och, the wee man must be called 'yer majesty' or he will feel poorly."

"Aye, I will feel poorly, like I did the morning I awakened and prepared for the joust. I was already exhausted, havin' competed in many games already, yet I *still* beat the champion of the King of England."

Fraoch shook his head, "Och nae, ye are determined tae tell the story. I was there, I lived it!"

I laughed, leaned back, and continued, "...of course beatin' the King of England is worth the ridicule of m'brother — twas a proud moment and I will tell the tale of it again and again, the King of England is a be-slubberin' mule, and we must remind ourselves he can be beaten. I hae done it before, I will do it again. *Regardless* of the state of m'walls."

We nodded, but then Fraoch said, "I am certain we will prevail, but the state of the walls is dismal."

I said, "Aye, all it will take is a catapult and we are beaten."

Sean scowled. "The only savin' grace is twill take months tae bring a catapult up that terrain. It buys us time."

I nodded. "And ye forget that I can bring a catapult by time travel."

"Och, I dinna think of it — we could go get some fine cannons, though I am not certain if we hae the time."

I said, "All we hae is time. We can send someone for more weapons, I can send the women and children tae safety. Lochinvar arrives today. Colonel Quentin will arrive day after tomorrow. He will bring weapons and begin tae strategize. Master Cook will lend a hand with the build... there is a great deal tae do, but I need m'men around me afore I plan m'next step."

"What time will Lochinvar arrive?"

I looked out in the direction of the King's Park. "Any minute now."

Sean scoffed, "He is liable tae cause more trouble than he solves."

"Ye are verra hard on him for someone who caused all the trouble in the world when he was a young man. Ye used tae terrorize the auld men of the castle, especially the ones who stood in yer way, and here ye are, an auld man, standing in a young man's way."

He chuckled. "I ought tae kick yer arse for callin' me auld."

"'I ought tae kick yer arse for callin' me auld,' *Yer Majesty*."

He groaned. "Och nae."

I laughed. "Besides ye daena hae the strength or the army tae do it."

Sean said, "Fine, but ye helped me terrorize the auld men. Ye remember when we were working on the walls at Kilchurn? Ye would distract Baldie and I would move his tools a bit tae the left and he kept wondering why they were shifting—"

"We did it for days."

"He never caught on until I finally moved them across the room. He was furious, ye remember?

I said, "Aye, his face turned deep crimson, I thought we would hae tae revive him."

"He was yellin' that he would tell the Earl tae hae us both whipped!"

I stood and acted it out, "He stamped his foot! Remember how we laughed? And he stamped his foot again!"

I sank back intae my chair.

"He never would tell the Earl on us, he was too fond — he would strike us himself tae keep the larger trouble from our door."

I said, "Och, I miss that man."

"I do as well, a good man, the best we could hope for with a mother like Lady Mairead."

"Tis the truth."

CHAPTER 13 - KAITLYN

STIRLING CASTLE - JUNE 17, 1291

*T*he day grew long, Magnus was in meetings all afternoon, and I didn't see him. I just heard the castle was on alert and everyone needed guards if they went outside the gates.

Isla was oblivious. Archie grew worried. He whispered, "What is going on?"

"Your father figured out that the English King sent scouts to spy on us, this doesn't mean anything, this just means we need to be cautious—"

"Why would the English King spy on us?"

I chewed my lip. "I don't know why, maybe just to make sure we're not growing too strong—"

"The English King has a big army though, right, Mammy? He's very powerful?"

I nodded. "But your Da has a big army and he is very powerful, too. More so, because he can time travel. The English King won't want to start trouble with someone so powerful. Your Da will keep the trouble from starting, he's the smartest person I know."

"Even if he doesn't get how movies are made."

"He's smart in other ways, good point, and one of the ways

he's smart is he will know how to make the English King back off. Edward will get his men the heck out of Scotland and they'll stay away and we will breathe easier. Plus we are all together, so that's good."

He nodded and exhaled.

I said, "You seem bored."

"Kinda, I want to go out and explore."

I nodded, "We can't today, not until after Quentin gets here, so it will be boring for a few days, but... I need you and Ben to run an errand for me." I gave them a job, running across the castle to tell Hayley something. I told them it was 'very important.'

She sent them back with a message for me, keeping the boys busy was the goal, the messages were unimportant.

But Hayley and Emma and I were busy too, figuring out what we needed to do and organizing the King's House, our wardrobes, and our chambers, trying to distract ourselves from waiting for the arrival of our family, and worrying about a far-off threatening king.

Organizing was exhausting. I had the boys for running messages, and we had radios to talk to each other, but none of it stopped me from walking about ten thousand steps before midday — carrying loads from room to room and forgetting things, and occasionally getting lost.

When I met Hayley and Emma to go to lunch, Hayley said, "Remember when we lived in Kilchurn and we spent months preparing a safety plan?"

I nodded. "We ought to do that, tomorrow maybe, but when Quentin gets here he'll probably change it."

Emma said, "Yeah, I'm sure Quentin will have *ideas*."

Hayley said, "With a whole lot of weapons. But maybe Lochie is bringing a load. What is taking him so long? Can't believe he's not here yet." She looked at her watch.

I said, "You know how it is, it could be any minute now."

Magnus, Fraoch, and Zach went to the fields with a lot of guards to wait for Lochinvar and Ash to arrive.

In the afternoon I radioed. "There yet?"

"Nae, not yet."

"Can you come back for dinner? It's only the third night and the kids are worried. I think they need to see you."

There was quiet for a moment, then Magnus's voice: "Aye, Fraoch will stay with guards and Chef Zach and I will return for dinner, we will hae tae make it quick, but we will come."

"Thank you."

We were all settled in the Great Hall for our evening dinner. I was exhausted, leaned back in my chair, saying to Magnus, "I put in thousands of steps today. Yesterday we went on that long ride. I'm not used to this much. I guess what I'm saying is I've grown soft."

Magnus nodded, his eyes sweeping the room. Then he checked his watch.

I said, "You worried about them arriving while you're not there?"

"Aye, Lochie is tae come today — yet the day has grown long."

"They'll all be here soon enough."

"And then I can concentrate m'worry on the kingdom."

I glanced down the table at Archie, laughing with Ben, Isla, and Zoe.

Magnus asked, "How are they?"

"It's been easy to distract them from any worries. Archie's not feeling the existential dread anymore. He's a lot better than he was."

Isla got up on her chair and was pointing around at the other kids, "You and you and you and you!"

We had no idea why, but they laughed heartily.

Magnus chuckled. "Och nae, ye told me that the kids needed tae see me."

"Yeah, sorry about that, they're just goofing around like normal kids."

"Tis a sight tae behold. I needed tae see them as well, and goofin' is good." Haggis had jumped up into Archie's chair and was looking around at the kids like he was a part of the game.

Magnus laughed, then checked his watch again. "Chef Zach and I need tae return tae the field. Sean is on the walls. If ye need anythin' pressin' tell him."

I nodded. "You'll have plenty of guards with you?"

"Aye, definitely."

I said, "I wish I could go with you, I'm new around here, it feels desolate when you're outside the gate."

Magnus squeezed my hand and stood. "There are only four hours left in the day, they will be here soon — and call me on the walk-n-talk if ye need tae tell me anythin'."

I grinned "Like the olden days. Remember the night we were in the village, there were drones and Lizbeth was giving birth — it seems like a million years ago."

"Twas, we hae lived at least ten lives since then, but as long as we hae the walk-n-talk and ye can hear m'voice ye will be at ease." He grinned. "Ye can be overwrought and I will say through the radio, 'How are ye, mo reul-iuil?' and ye will be calmed."

"That is, basically, how I work."

Thirty minutes later I had the radio in my hand, sitting on a chair in front of the fire in my room. Isla was sleeping in Emma's room with Zoe. Chef Zach had gone to the clearing with Magnus. Ben and Archie were going back and forth between our rooms, but it had been a moment, they had probably fallen asleep in Emma's room.

Jack had fallen asleep in the bed we had set up near the hearth.

I said into the radio. "Are you all still awake?"

Magnus's voice came back, "Aye, tis quiet, and has been a long day, but we are up. Fraoch and Chef Zach say 'hello'."

"Hi." Then I asked, because I felt like I ought to. "He didn't come?"

"Not yet, but there is still time."

There was a soft knock on the door. Hayley, and Emma were there with the kids. They all came in, piled up on the little beds, and the women joined me in seats around the fire. Emma said, "I thought I wanted to sleep and not care that our friends were coming, to just see them in the morning, but then I realized I couldn't sleep and wanted to be near the radio."

I said, "I just spoke with Magnus, nothing yet, but there are still a few hours left in the day."

Archie sat down beside me, "Can I check in?"

"Of course." I pressed the button.

Archie said, "Hi Da, it's me, Archie."

"Aye, son, how ye holdin' up?"

In the dim room, lit by a small battery-powered lantern and the hearth, I could see Archie's face, full of responsibility, as he concentrated on his Da's voice. "I was hanging out in Ben's room, but now we're in Mammy's room, do you see Uncle Lochie yet?"

Magnus's voice: "Nae, not yet. We are in the field, ye ken the one we rode across yesterday?"

Archie hit the button to say: "Aye."

Magnus's voice emitted, "We hae a clear view of the sky from our place in the field and so we will see the storm right away. And ye ken what else I was thinkin'? This is a good Scottish night. There is a breeze and the trees are crackin' whenever the wind hits the upper branches. Tis verra comfortin'. When

Uncle Lochie arrives he will be welcomed by a familiar Scottish night, his favorite."

Archie nodded. "I'm kind of worried about Uncle Lochie because he really likes cookies, and he isn't that good at Scottish nights anymore. I think his favorites are Florida beach nights."

"Aye, that is probably true, and he inna alone, we all love the Florida beach and look forward tae goin' home. But the next best thing is havin' us all taegether. In two days Colonel Quentin, Madame Beaty, and Noah will arrive, possibly even Master Cook, Sophie, and wee Junior."

Isla said, "Push the button, Archie."

He pushed the button and Isla said, "I think Junior will be scared to jump, Da, I hope he won't be scared."

I heard the voice of my husband say to his children, "When he comes I will keep him safe, Isla, daena worry."

Isla said into the radio, "Good, then we know he will be alright."

Magnus said, "Keep the radio on, we will call as soon as the storm hits."

CHAPTER 14 - ASH

BALLOCH CASTLE - MAY 27, 1710

The nursery door opened and Lochinvar entered. "Tis all well, the disruption was merely a messenger bringin' word from Edinburgh, the Earl is ill."

Lizbeth said, "We went on alert for a messenger? Tis an unusual reaction!"

"Aye, Liam grew cautious as there was somethin' off about their behavior. They seemed tae be scoutin' the castle."

Lizbeth said, "Och nae, why would they?"

Lochinvar said, "We daena ken, but they hae been sent from the Earl's lands, Liam winna allow them tae rest here and I kept m'self hidden from view."

"That does seem wise."

Beaty asked, "Twill be safe when Quenny and James return?"

"Liam is sendin' guards tae wait for them, tae make certain of their safety. I will join them as soon as I can, but in the meantime, ye are all well tae leave the nursery."

Lizbeth said, "I think I will send yer meals tae yer rooms, as it has been harrowing, we winna want tae eat in the crowded Great Hall tonight. Would ye like yer dinner brought tae ye, Lochinvar?"

With a glance at me, he said, "Aye, thank you, Lizbeth."

He led me down the hall, up stone steps to the next floor, and along a cold dark passage to our room. He let us in. It was chilly. He went to the hearth and added a log to build up the fire, then brushed off his hands. "If we plan to eat here, we will need warmth."

Then he strode over to me and put his arms around me. "Now where were we when we—?"

I stepped back out of his arms.

"Och nae, what are ye...?"

I said, "I think, Lochie, that we need to slow down—"

"Slow down? Nae, ye canna — what dost ye mean, 'slow down'?"

"I mean we ought to—"

His handsome chiseled face drew down in a pout. "Are ye wantin' tae leave yer Lochie, och nae — are ye tired, Ash? Ye hae had a long day, ye need tae be fed. I will wait by the fire, give ye time tae rest. I winna bother ye or touch ye, I promise."

"Lochie, you ought to let me finish a sentence, it's not as dire as all of —"

"'Tis! Daena say it! Ye are the sun shinin' on me, the smile that lights m'heart, ye canna tell me terrible things—"

I huffed. "Lochie, I just want what is best for you."

His frown deepened. "Och, I think ye are goin' tae be cruel."

"I am not. I just have something I need to say."

He slumped down into the chair. "'Tis fine, ye can say it."

He looked despondent, kicked back, depressed, then he leaned forward with his elbows on his knees, his feet jiggling. Then he stood up. "'Tis just, Ash, ye ought not say anything hurtful, I want ye tae go back tae when ye said ye loved me."

I said, "Will you please sit down, Lochie, and let me speak?"

He slumped back down in the chair. "I daena understand what ye mean, 'slow down.'"

He exhaled with a huff.

I said, "You don't even understand, but here you are carrying on, well, my love, this is proving to me that what I'm about to say, *must* be said. It's important, you need to listen to me."

He nodded quietly.

I said, "You need to marry me, Lochie."

He looked into my eyes. His brow drew down. "But I did, I—"

I shook my head. "That doesn't count. I mean," I put my hand on my heart, "it counts here. But where it matters, in front of God and family, we aren't married—"

"I think God watched us make the thumb oath."

"If God watched us make the thumb oath then he likely saw the other stuff, that's disconcerting."

"Tis how it works. God sees all. He kens we made an oath."

I sighed, "That's not really the point, Lochie, but forget about God, we haven't married in front of your family, this is... we *need* to."

"Ye daena believe I married ye in m'heart?"

"I believe you did."

"What did they say tae ye — did Lady Lizbeth tell ye that I dinna mean it? She has never thought much of me. She saw me brawlin' when I first came, and I daena think she has ever forgiven me."

"It is not like that, Lochie, Lizbeth did speak to me, Beaty and Sophie agreed and—"

"Och, they hae ganged up on me, dost they think I hae taken advantage of ye?" His eyes went wide. "Dost they think me a scoundrel?"

I stepped closer and put a hand on each side of his jaw, "Lochie, this is the point, they don't think you're a scoundrel, they think well of you and want the best for you."

"Ye are the best for me, and I hae given ye m'oath that I winna beguile ye—"

I said, seriously, "You broke that oath, Lochie, you cannot deny it."

He set his jaw. "I thought ye forgave me."

"I did, but it doesn't help that the oath you made was broken and—"

He put his hand on his heart. "I feel a sharp pain through m'chest, Ash, ye are breaking me."

"I am not, stop being overdramatic."

He tried to look away but I held his face and made him look up at me. "This is a very simple point, if we got off on the wrong foot, with a broken oath—"

"I dinna mean tae break m'oath, I dinna ken what tae do..."

"Whether you meant it or not, we began with an oath broken—"

"Dost ye think I dinna mean it when I promised ye...? I mean tae always care for ye, tae protect ye. I ken ye were taken, but I searched for ye everywhere, I brought ye home, I fought for ye—"

I stroked the hair back from his face. "You did do all of that, it's not that you didn't promise me. I trust that you mean it, that you will do everything to protect me, and I know that you are heroic, but, this is important, Lochie, stop arguing with me about it... I want you to marry me."

He bit his lip. "'Tis not a bad thing?"

"No, this is a good thing. I want you to marry me in front of your family so that they *know*."

He nodded.

I said, "You said you didn't know what to do. I think you need to let me tell you in this, because I feel very clear that this is what we need to do. You need to marry me in front of your family so that *they* know you mean it. And if that isn't reason enough, you can do it for me. I am new around here, if you marry me, they will see me as important to you."

"Och, I never thought of it. Ye think it will matter tae their opinion of ye? I think they find ye verra fine already. Did someone say somethin' tae ye?"

"That isn't really what I meant, look, Lochie, I think that

when I stepped away it freaked you out and now you aren't able tae hear what I'm saying..."

"I canna hear ye over m'poundin' heart, I want tae run from the room and go brawl in the courtyard with Craigh. He crossed me earlier and it has all been terrible since."

I chuckled. "Well, that seems unnecessary."

"I think ye are, as Beaty would say, 'borrowin' flowers from the fae, and they arna yer friends.'"

I said, "Lochie, m'laird...?"

He looked up at me from his seat. "Aye?"

"Please take a deep breath, I have a question for you."

He took in a long breath and then when I rolled my hand he let it out.

I said, "Do you love me?"

"Aye, I—"

I said, "Shhhh, that's enough, 'Aye,' is what I wanted to know. Do you want to marry me?"

"I already hae in m'..." He met my eyes. "Aye."

"Will you ask me to marry you?"

He looked up at me and nodded. Then he rose from the chair and got down on his knees. He drew my hand up and he held it in his and pressed his lips to the back of it. "Aye."

His hands were big and strong, rough and calloused, very warm as they enclosed my hand. I waited, quietly. He said, "Ash... Madame Ash, would ye do me the honor of marryin' yer lowly servant, Lochinvar?" He looked up at me. "Please daena say nae."

I drew his hands up and kissed his finger tips. Then clutched his hands to my front. "Yes, Lochinvar, I will marry you."

"Ye will?"

I nodded. "Thank you for asking."

"I will never beguile ye..."

I let go of his hand to press a finger to his lips. "Shush, my love, I know, I know you will never. I have forgiven you, fully, in my heart."

"I am grateful for it."

"And we will be a team, a family, we will take care of each other and look out for each other, and so I know you won't beguile me, because to do it would be to beguile yourself, you know?"

"Aye, we are tied."

"Yes, we will be..." I looked down on him and tilted my head. "So how do we get married in front of your family?"

"We must meet them in the past, at Stirling castle."

"So, once we go see Don in Florida, then we can go, once I'm ready?"

"Aye, as we planned. Once Quentin and James are returned, sometime tomorrow, we will go tae Florida as planned. Then, as soon as ye are ready, we will gather our things and go back tae be with Magnus and the rest of m'family at Stirling."

I said, "Good, that seems right. Then we will get married, at Stirling."

"Aye. At Stirling."

I looked at the far wall. "Is there danger? Are we the cause of it?"

He said, "Aye, there is danger, but we arna the cause, tis more likely that Magnus's throne is the reason. But I daena ken what the danger is, so we ought tae do what we mean tae do, and ken that I will protect ye."

"I would never want to put all those kids in the nursery in danger—"

"Tis not yer problem, Ash. Liam and the guards of Balloch will protect their families, they hae been doing it for a long time. And none of it will be an issue once we leave for Magnus's castle."

"Good. And once we're there how long will it take to plan a wedding?"

"I daena ken, I hae never been married... I suppose we would hae tae call everyone taegether and—"

"Where I come from it can take months to plan."

"Och, I would think a good marriage could come taegether in an afternoon."

I smiled. "Do your knees hurt?"

"Aye, but I can stay here all day, tis easy tae override — ye are sayin' that when we go tae Stirling we will get married there. This is what ye are wantin'?"

"Yes, simple really, right? Not really at *all* a reason to be freaking out."

"Aye, I love ye, Ash."

"I love you too."

He stood up and brushed off his knees as there was a knock on the door. Three servants entered, bringing baskets and covered plates, a stack of dishes, and a tureen with soup, placing it on the small table in the room.

I said, "Thank you," and Lochie sent the servants from the room.

Lochinvar and I sat down at the table and ate some bread smeared with butter, dipped with jam, and barley soup along with white fish with gravy.

We ate hungrily and in good spirits, giving each other long lingering loving looks.

I said, "So we are going to get married?"

He grinned. "Aye, twill be official."

"Good, I like this idea, it will be really good, Lochie."

He leaned back in his chair and patted his stomach. "Och, I am well fed."

"Me too." I leaned back and we smiled happily at each other. "I really like you."

"I really like ye too, Ash, ye are the most bonny lass I hae ever laid eyes upon."

I grinned even wider.

He said, "Och, yer smile is the undoin' of me."

"You are very sweet."

He stood and strode to the door where the servants were

waiting just outside for our dishes, he asked them to come inside to clear our table.

We stood to the side until they had left again, then he said, "Good, now we can get back tae what we were doin'." He put his arms around me.

I stepped away from his embrace.

His eyes went wide. "Och nae!"

"Lochie, we can't, not until we are married!"

"Nae nae nae," he clutched his chest, "nae, ye canna mean it, not until we are...? Och nae."

"This is... this was the whole point of the conversation, Lochie, we aren't officially married in the eyes of your family, it will give me a bad reputation."

"Och nae," his mouth drew down in a pout. "But the thumb oath...?"

I shook my head.

"This is what comes of me deliverin' ye tae the nursery. Sittin' with the women and the bairns — they hae turned ye from m'bed."

I said, "Ha. It might seem that way, but it's not forever, Lochie. I'm not 'turned from your bed,' I actually think you've never been hotter. I've never wanted you more, even with all your pouting and moaning. It's just until we get married. Officially."

"Now I wish I haena said we would wait for Stirling, we could get married here, now, and tell Magnus we hae done it."

"That, my love, is not really the point."

"Fine."

He looked around the room. His pout was now fully comical. "Where am I tae sleep?"

I hadn't really thought of that, there was nowhere for a second person if we weren't stacked and making hot love. I bit my lip.

He said, "This is a tragedy."

"It's not meant to be, Lochinvar, it's meant to be romantic."

"My arse is goin' tae be romantic when it has sharp pains from sittin' on the floor in the passage outside yer door."

"You're going to sit outside my door?"

"Aye, if we are keepin' yer reputation, I canna lay on the floor by yer bed like a dog, it winna do any good. I would still be in yer room in the night. I will hae tae sleep elsewhere, but I canna leave ye alone at night in the castle, not when there is danger afoot, and besides, ye are like a bairn, ye canna go tae the garderobe by yerself and ye canna keep yer own fire burning—"

"I think I can build a fire."

He scoffed. "Ye canna do it right. And if I sleep in the barracks with the other men I will be worried on ye the whole night, so nae, I will sleep sitting outside yer door, keepin' watch over ye."

"I'm sorry, I didn't really think this through when I—"

"'Tis fine." He picked up my hand, bowed over it, and kissed it. "I bid ye a good night, my Mistress Ash, I will see ye in the morn."

"I will see you in the morning, Lochie."

He stalked to the door, opened it, and closed it behind him.

I sighed and looked around. I was going to be here all night by myself, with nothing to do.

My shoulder was sore so I took one of the pills for pain and peed in the pisspot, and then lay down on the bed. I watched the fire, thinking about Lochie, and how much I loved him, in all his silly, pouting, 'confused about what I was sayin' ways — but oh my, when he had gotten on his knees and asked me to marry him... wow. That had been amazing. He truly loved me, he would honestly do anything I asked of him, even if it 'almost killed him'. I chuckled. I had taken one step back and it had been enough to throw him into turmoil. I sighed. It was a wondrous thing to have the hot man, Lochinvar, sitting outside my door. I called. "Lochie, are you there?"

His voice came back to me, "Aye, Ash, I am here."

. . .

A few moments later, I heard him talking to a woman, then a knock on the door and Lizbeth entered.

"I came tae check on ye, why is young Lochinvar in the hall?"

"He isn't allowed in until he marries me."

Her eyes went wide. "Och nae, ye listened tae us?"

"Yes. You spoke to him, is he okay?"

"He is going tae hae a pained backside by morn." She patted my arm. "But twill be a good thing, Lady Ash, he will be glad of it by the time he is standin' in front of the altar beside ye."

I nodded. "I think you're right."

"I am always right." She smiled. "And ye are now one of my favorite new family members because ye agree. Can I get ye anything?"

"Television?"

She shook her head. "I daena ken what it is."

"How come you never time traveled?"

"Because I am auld and stuck in my ways and I think I would love it too much. I worry I would run off and leave everyone in my family behind, like my mother has done." She gave me a half smile. "A great deal of my life is tryin' tae not become my mother."

"Maybe the things your mother does are not connected to time travel. Maybe you can time travel without turning into her. But what do I know, I took some of the medicine and I'm feeling loopy again."

She nodded. "Tis good it helps ye tae feel better. But now I must go see tae the bairns, good night, Ash."

I said, "Good night."

She left the room, spoke quietly for a couple of minutes with Lochinvar, then he said through the door, "Good night, Ash, sleep well."

I said, "Thank you, m'laird, I hope you sleep well too." Then I lay there watching the fire as I slowly fell asleep.

I woke up in the middle of the night. It was dark and cool in the room and I thought, *this is what woke me up, the chill,* but then I heard a sound and my heart caught in my throat.

The door creaked open, and in the gloom of night I saw Lochie's profile as he crept to the hearth. He crouched and built up the fire. It was too dark to see anything but his dark form, and the faint outline of his face aglow from the small fire as he drew it forth.

I pulled the covers up to my ears and watched for a few moments. I said, "Lochie?"

He didn't turn, he only said, "Aye." Then he said, "I was worried ye were cold."

"It must be cold out in the hall."

He dinna answer, but I saw him put his hands toward the fire and rub them to warm them.

He stood. "Dost ye need anything?"

"My shoulder is really sore."

He came toward the bed, perched on the chair, picked up the pill bottle, and pushed and turned the lid for a moment til he got it open. Then he poured one pill into his palm and held it out. I picked it from his hand, popped it in my mouth, and took a sip of water from my cup.

I put the cup back. "Thank you."

"Y'are welcome, Ash."

"I'm sorry I banished you to the hallway, and that it's cold..."

"Tis okay, I understand the reason for it. I will marry ye, and once I do this will all be right."

He smoothed the hair back from my cheek, leaned forward and kissed me there. Then he went back to the hall to stand guard.

CHAPTER 15 - LOCHINVAR

BALLOCH CASTLE - MAY 28, 1710

*I*n the morning, Beaty and Sophie came tae our room tae help Ash dress and keep her company. I had been called tae meet with Liam; the guards who had sent the messengers away had returned carryin' news.

When I entered the Great Hall, there were ten men gathered. Liam told me, "They found their encampment."

"Were there more men, dost we ken who sent them?"

Craigh leveled his eyes. "What ye want tae ken for, Lochie?"

"Because I suspect they are here because of me and my wife."

"Yer wife!" Craigh began laughin'. "Lowly Lochinvar has taken a wife? Ye barely hae a beard upon yer bawbags yet, ye canna hae a wife!"

One of the other men, Amos, laughed, "Tis the bonny lass — the lass who was looking at Yarnoch with longin', ye ken? I could see by the look of her, she kens her way around her duties."

I stood, shovin' my chair back, and growled, "She inna a bonny lass, she is m'wife, ye get her from yer tongue or I will call ye outside."

Craigh said, "Now now, Lochie, watch yerself."

Amos laughed, maliciously. "She inna a bonny lass? Ye want me tae get my tongue from her? Ye want tae fight me, Lochie?"

"She is bonny, but ye daena get tae speak on her at all!"

Liam stepped between us. "Sit down, Lochinvar."

I sat down.

He continued, "Amos, nothing good comes from speaking on Lochinvar's lass, she is bonny, he is right in tellin' ye tae wheesht."

He turned, "Dost ye agree, Craigh, the men ought tae not speak about Lochinvar's wife, he ought not be antagonized?"

Craigh said, "I agree."

Amos folded his arms over his rounded stomach. "I am just wondering, *how* did Lowly Lochinvar manage tae get a bonny lass?"

Another man said, "I heard he was sleepin' in the passage last night."

I scowled.

One of the other men said, "His brother, Young Magnus, bought her for him."

They all laughed, heartily.

I stood up again. "I am callin' all of ye outside, I will fight every one of ye at once!"

Liam said, "Lochinvar, I am just tryin' tae get through a meeting with the guards, we arna goin' tae hae a brawl."

I said, "'Tis not on me, I am only wantin' tae hear about what they found last night. I daena want one more word about m'wife or I will call them out and fight all of them in the court-yard at *once.*"

Amos raised a hand. "Fine, daena be such a sparkin' idiot, Lowly Lochie. So ye won a lass with a bonny face, nae one cares. Give her ten years and she will look just as grievous as *all* our wives."

I scowled. "My wife was taken, stolen by a man named Asgall. We are worried Asgall might hae sent men tae spy on us, wantin' tae cause us harm. I daena hae time tae argue with ye about how ugly yer wives are, I will just agree — Amos has a verra ugly wife, as does Craigh and as do all of ye."

Amos shrugged, "For many men these would be fightin' words, but it daena bother me tae tell me what I already ken — she is a woman, a good mother, and she was cursed by the fae tae hae the face of a rodent, tis why I roll her over in the night."

Liam groaned, "Och nae, Amos, I am about tae call ye tae the courtyard m'self."

Amos laughed and waved his hand. "Pay nae mind, m'wife feels the same way about my looks and m'scent and m'wit and m'manner and..."

I clenched my jaw. "How many men were there?"

Craigh said, "The six only. They hae been forced from the Earl's lands."

Liam asked, "Did ye inquire about them in Aberfeldy?"

"Aye, we asked the man in the tavern, he said they werna sure where the men came from, twas as if they were just there all of a sudden."

Liam asked, "Hae there been storms?"

All the men said, "Aye."

I asked, "Hae ye heard the name Asgall?"

Amos said, "Aye, one of the men mentioned an Asgall, but tis a common name."

"Is it? I haena heard it much." I leaned back in my chair, I ought tae hae gone out with the guards last night and asked at the tavern. Amos was not givin' enough information and twas irritating that he haena asked the right questions. He wasna takin' any of this seriously enough.

Amos shrugged. "It daena matter, the men left, we told them nae tae come back. But now ye mentioned it, one man did ask if ye were here."

I said, "*Now* ye mention it?"

Craigh said, "Ye hae a high estimation of yerself for such a wee bitin' midge of a lad."

Amos said, "He's the carbuncle on Magnus's arse."

All the men laughed uproariously.

I chewed my lip. "Did he ask if my wife, Ash, was here?"

"Tis her name? Och, I thought he was speaking on something else. Aye, he asked about her, but I told him nae, I said 'I daena ken what ye are talking about and I am nae goin' tae give ye any information. Ye tell Asgall not tae come around Balloch, because the Campbells daena take kindly on strangers coming around causing trouble.' Tis what I said, I swear tae it."

Liam said, "That is a good answer, thank ye Amos for not givin' anything away."

I said, "But ye told them I was here?"

"Aye."

I exhaled, angrily.

The men all got up and left the hall and Liam and I remained tae speak privately. "Ash and I must run an errand afore we go tae Stirling, twill take a few days, while we are still here we need guards on the walls, we canna allow any strangers through the gate—"

Liam said, "I ken, Lochinvar, I ken how tae protect the castle, but we need tae send men with ye wherever—"

I scoffed, "Ye think those men will protect me, Amos and Craigh? I daena need them, I can protect m'own. Just put more men on the walls. Guard the gates, I will take care of m'self and Ash."

He chuckled. "Alright, but when are ye goin' tae get Black MacMagnus and Master James?"

"Now, I will wait for them in the clearin'."

"I want more men tae go with ye, or they will blame me for not sendin' enough men."

"Fine, I agree, but if the men ye send bother me I will kill them and blame it on the fae and I winna regret that I lied."

He said, "Lochinvar, how am I tae keep ye safe if ye threaten tae kill everyone who is tae guard ye?"

I shrugged, "I daena need a guard."

"Fine, but I will send extra guardsmen with ye, not Amos,

other men. Daena kill them, that is an order. I was told by Sean that I was allowed tae give ye orders and ye were tae understand they were direct from him, dost ye understand it?"

"Aye."

I left for the clearing with four guardsmen following me.

The guardsmen stood on the periphery, watching the path up tae the clearing, while I sat on the edge, waitin'. Twas boring work, especially after havin' spent the night in a cold passageway. I had barely slept. I was irritated by havin' been banished from Ash's bed, because I wanted her and felt I had made m'self clear. I had married her in m'heart, and felt as if m'word ought tae be good enough.

I dinna like that m'word was not good enough.

I wanted everyone tae accept m'oath, and I wanted her, I wanted tae bed her and was havin' trouble concentratin' on much else. I had risked m'life tae rescue her and thought I ought tae get the prize that I believed I was goin' tae get a few hours ago. I had been lookin' forward tae it, but now there was naething, nae prize, nae warm bed, just m'mind mutterin' about how I was not being rewarded well enough.

And taunted by her bonny smile… I had taken her on, as m'wife, and dinna think she ought tae send me from her bed.

Back in Dunscaith when I was growin' up I kent the older men were sent from their beds verra often, if they were covered in the sweat from brawling, or reekin' of drink, or with the rage of battle still upon them — they would be verra bitter. We would hae tae force them tae sleep or they would fight shadows. But the young men, with new wives, they got tae bed their wives.

They were welcomed.

And danger was followin' us, Asgall wanted Ash, and I stood in his way. Twas another reason why I ought tae hae woken up in the warm arms of the bonny lass.

I huffed.

I had made a comfortable place tae sit with my back leaned on a tree, beside the cart, waitin' in the clearin' tae drag the gear and supplies that Colonel Quentin and Master Cook would bring with them.

Och, they would tease me mercilessly when they heard that I had been sleepin' outside Ash's door.

Twas an affront tae me. I was never respected. It caused me discomfort that Ash was also disrespectin' me...

I took a deep breath and exhaled... on reflection though, Ash had been right in this... she was right tae hae sent me from our bed. She was right that nae one believed I had married her, they dinna take m'word, and by sleepin' in her room I was ruinin' her good name. She deserved better than tae be whispered about by a castle full of Campbell men.

The men of Balloch castle thought of me as a brainless lad, prone tae brawlin'. They thought I was only deservin' of respect because of m'proximity tae Og Maggy. How could I let m'failings tarnish the moral standin' of Ash? She was too bonny for such a fate. She was quick tae laugh and full of light, I couldna allow darkness tae settle upon her, not after the kidnappin'.

She had been kidnapped because of me, and she still loved me, she hadna left me.

She would marry me.

Magnus and Fraoch and Sean would bear witness tae my marriage, they would see me take the oath and they would ken that she gazes upon me with grace and love. It would raise me in the estimation of the family. I felt certain, but if nae, twould be all right. If they saw me make an oath tae Ash, twould raise her standin'. Twas honorable for me tae do it, and twas the least I could do for her, because she asked. I would hae tae suffer until I made it happen.

I waited, mutterin' for hours, until twilight was on us and finally a storm rose in the clearing and I stepped intae the woods tae wait it out.

CHAPTER 16 - LOCHINVAR

THE CLEARING NEAR BALLOCH CASTLE - MAY 28, 1710

*Q*uentin and James woke up at almost the same time. I was standin' above them, a light on m'forehead, blindin' them, and joked, "Och, ye are squealin' pigs in mud, look at ye."

James said, "Is this because Sean isn't here? You filling in as the smart-arsing Scottish dude?" He held up his arm tae block the beam. "And ouch, man, shine it somewhere else."

I pushed the light higher on my forehead so it wouldna blind them. "Aye, tis m'job tae jeer at ye, as one of the last funny Scottish dudes at the castle. I told Liam he could stay there, I am your greetin' party, I hae tae make ye feel welcome." I put out a hand and helped heave them both up. "But I need ye tae ken, there is danger afoot, I am here tae welcome ye, but I hae a full guard with me and we need tae get back tae the castle."

"What happened?"

"Asgall is sniffin' around."

James said, "Great, but Sophie and Beaty, the kids, they're safe?"

"Aye, Liam is guardin' over the castle. We are safe enough, but we will be better behind walls."

I directed the beam down and shined it around at all the

stuff they brought. "Tis a good thing we brought men tae help drag all of this tae the castle."

Quentin looked around, "Aye, it's a big load."

James said, "We already had to load this once, I'm frankly tired of moving it." They had a pile of boxes strapped tae a trailer, but also some boxes for the trailer we kept here in the clearing.

I set up a few lanterns and called the guards over to help us stack boxes.

James said, "We should have brought an ATV tae pull it."

Quentin said, "We should have brought earplugs so I don't have to listen to you bitch and moan."

"Fine, fine." James said, "How's Junior?" We began strapping loads tae the trailer.

"Good, he's well... Noah's well, our worries haena affected them."

Quentin asked, "So what happened exactly?"

"A group of men arrived last night, claimin' tae hae news from Edinburgh, but it seemed they were lookin' around, seein' who was home. I tried tae stay clear. The women hid in the nursery."

James tightened a strap over the load. "Crap, we need to get up there, I bet Sophie is freaking out."

Quentin said, "I think the sooner we get all of us together the better."

James nodded. He looked pensive.

Quentin said, "So, are you still going to Florida first before you go to Stirling castle?"

I nodded. "We hae tae, Ash needs tae speak tae Don. But as soon as we are done we should go tae the thirteenth century."

Quentin said, "I agree, we are drawin' Asgall here to Balloch. I think all of us need to get to the thirteenth century, sooner than later. When will you leave for Florida?"

"I planned tae once ye returned, but now tis dark, and Ash is at the castle and—"

Quentin nodded. "Wait for morning. Let's get inside the castle walls for the night."

I sighed like a huff. "Och nae... I wanted tae go sooner than later."

We were done harnessing the trailers, we began walkin' tae the castle, leadin' the horses, bein' mindful of the dark woods around us.

Quentin said, "We all armed?"

James and I said, "Aye."

We walked in silence for a moment, until James said, "So, what's going on with you, Lochie? You look uneasy. Beyond the danger, we always have danger — trouble in paradise? You look bothered, got relationship troubles?"

"I am just tired."

He laughed. "Been busy all night? I get ya, man, I do." Then his brow drew down. "But you don't look like a man who enjoyed himself. You look like a guy who slept on the floor in the barracks. Doesn't he, Quenny?"

Quentin said, "Yep, you got the 'I slept with one eye-open' look."

I trudged along with a sigh.

Quentin said, "Jeez, dude, seriously, what's going on?"

"I slept outside the room last night."

"Damn, boy, you got kicked out?"

"Aye."

Quentin said, "What did you do?"

"Wasna what I did, I dinna do anything, yer wives and Lizbeth told her I ought tae marry her first."

James said, "Oh shit, they didn't, did they?"

Quentin said, "Course they did."

"She told me that I had tae marry her in front of m'family or nae one would respect her."

James said, "Yet another reason why you want to get your Florida errand over and get to Stirling as fast as possible."

"Aye, there is danger about, but mostly because m'arse hurts and twas cold."

James said, "Did you tell them you already did that thumb thing? And they didn't believe you?"

"I told them, and nae, they dinna believe us."

James joked, "I'm shocked, *shocked* I tell you. Who would have thought women would want a wedding and not just a spit-thumb pressed together after fornicating."

I scowled. "'Tis not funny, we dinna fornicate. I married her. She agreed."

Quentin clapped me on the shoulder. "I know, Lochie, I get ya, you married a modern girl — they are much more casual about all this. Then you introduced her to a bunch of historic women and they got to her... now you have to wait until marriage. Sorry, this sounds... man, unintended consequences." He bit his lip tae keep from laughin'.

"I am verra glad Magnus and Fraoch arna here, they would be arses along with ye, and I daena hae the patience tae listen tae it. I rescued her from Asgall and I dinna even get a proper thank ye. Tis unfair."

Quentin and James both started laughing.

"Verra funny."

James said, "Damn, you rescued the maiden and she told you that you had to marry her first? That does sound unfair."

I scowled deeper.

Quentin said, "Look, Lochie, I know this is hard, but you are going to marry her, right?"

I nodded. "Of course, I asked her last night."

James said, "How?"

"I got down on m'knees and begged her because she told me tae."

James's eyes went wide. "Man, I *wish* Zach and Mags and

Frookie were here to hear this story. Okay, you got down on your knees, you begged her, she said yes?"

"Aye, she said yes."

"Good, then quit your bellyaching, you just have to make it happen."

"Tis why I wanted tae leave tonight."

Quentin said, "I know, it sucks, it's too dark, but if there's danger afoot none of us need to be out in it. At dawn you can go."

I nodded. "I ken, I am just irritated that I will sleep yet again in the passage outside her door."

CHAPTER 17 - ASH

THE GREAT HALL, BALLOCH CASTLE - MAY 28, 1710

*L*ochinvar sat beside me at dinner in the Great Hall. It was dark outside but there were candles burning on the table and the occasional battery-powered lantern to beat back the shadows. A warming fire in the hearth. Lochinvar was in a mood, overly polite and a bit cool. He also kept quiet, being a little bit sulky, but I forgave him. He was used to getting what he wanted, he was used to fighting and winning prizes, and he had come really close to a prize and then had it taken away.

His clenched jaw meant he was focused on winning it again, and struggling with keeping himself calm while going for it.

I was the prize, of course.

He brought me my meal and an ale — we knew danger was afoot but drinking one wouldn't hurt. And having Quentin and James back made the meal a bit jovial, even though the guards were on alert and everyone was taking the security of the castle very seriously.

Liam ate a quick meal, but then left for the walls.

It was unnerving to have this unspecified danger surrounding us. Men rushed around and were determined to protect us, but from what? From who? They were protecting me, mostly. And I didn't know any of them.

Beaty said, "Madame Ash, are yer eyes used tae the darkness?"

"Not yet, it's awful, so dark, like they haven't adjusted. And my breathing is really heavy sounding, it's giving me a headache. It's deafening."

She said, "Ye will grow used tae it, though twill take some time."

James said, "It's all stuff you get used to, but the shifts in light and the sound differences are jarring at first."

I said, "Especially if you don't know you time traveled."

Quentin said, "*That* must have sucked."

Lochinvar, quietly looking down at his plate said, "Och nae, I am sorry I dinna warn ye about the time travel."

I sighed, watching the side of his face. "It's okay Lochie, I lived through it, it's actually made me pretty badass, you know? Like I'm one of the most badass people I know, kidnapped to the thirteenth century! There was a firefight to rescue me, I dislocated my shoulder, barely cried — this is all going down in my heroic story... Wait! This gives me an idea, I should write an epic poem about it. Then when we go in bars I can recite my poem after yours."

He grinned. "Och, that is an excellent idea, an epic, heroic tale about Ash, named for the Tree of Life."

"I will talk about my trusty weapon, the spike I carried around. I never got to use it, but boy did I want to. I was so badass as I dragged it along the river when I escaped."

Quentin shook his head. "You must... and I can't stress this enough, carry a weapon on you, at all times, from now on. Don't be a Katie, she *never* has one when she needs it, don't do that."

"You won't have to tell me twice, there's no way I'm going anywhere unarmed. Though when I was taken I was armed — it was just in my purse, I couldn't get it out in time while I was driving."

Lochinvar said, "If ye had a blade ye might hae been able tae fight yer way from the mess. Ye need a gun and a blade."

Quentin said, "Lady Mairead is a perfect example, she never leaves home without a gun, three blades, and some surprise weapon, like a vial of poison or a razor blade."

Lizbeth said, "Och tis one thing about m'mother, she is always ready for some kind of intrigue or scandal."

I said, "I will model after her, without actually talking to her — no offense, Lady Lizbeth, but she's kind of scary."

"Nae offense taken, she is a formidable lady, not tae be crossed. Ye must be wary though ye want tae win her ontae yer side."

Lochinvar said, "Och, she is a gentle auld crone, verra sweet, ye just hae tae get tae ken her, and also, never trust her and never give her any information she can use against ye."

We all raised our glasses.

We finished our meal and then I glanced over at Lochie. He was thoughtful, looking down at his plate, guarded and quiet. I just wanted to roll up in his arms and tell him I had been wrong, this was stupid, let's go back to being 'married' and... because man, he was so hot — I could just take him to bed, make this all better... couldn't I?

What if I climbed in his lap and said, "Let's go up to our room." He would probably forget all of this, he would forgive me for last night, and we could actually have a 'night two' together, before we leapt into the great unknown. Because something could happen, anything might, you only lived once and... *I mean, night one was awesome, I bet night two would be amazing.*

I was eating and his hand was beside his plate, and mine was beside my plate, and he brushed the back of his hand along mine. An electric, static, charge, I sighed.

He nodded.

His nod acknowledged my sigh, but it meant a lot more, it meant this is good.

And I agreed.

He said, "Tell me when ye are tired, I will walk ye tae yer room, Ash."

"Where will you sleep tonight?"

"I will sleep in the passage outside yer door, Ash, but daena worry on it, I winna complain."

I frowned, and whispered, "I know you won't but I miss you, and wish I could invite you in."

"Ye changed yer mind?"

"Kinda, I'm nervous about what's going on and it would be nice to have you... You know."

"Ye are feelin' warm taeward yer Lochinvar?"

"Yes, warm." I sighed again.

"I miss ye as well, Ash, but ye ought not change yer mind on this, tis important, the long cold nights on the stone floor in the passage hae given me time tae think, I see it now." He drew my hand to his mouth and kissed my knuckles and then folded my hand in his, resting on his thigh.

"Besides I will need tae be on guard taenight, I canna spend the night holdin' ye, though I might want tae. I hae tae watch for trouble."

Quentin said, "And you're leaving for Florida first thing in the morning, Lochinvar?"

He nodded.

I winced.

He squeezed my hand, comfortingly.

I did not like the idea of time traveling again, it hurt, man, did it hurt. I had also been growing used to this, living in this dream castle of the dreamy past, it still didn't feel real, but it was as if I had become accustomed to the unreality of it. Like being on vacation I supposed, protected by high walls, and medieval looking guards, and now I was expected to time jump back to Florida, but as a visitor, to check in and say goodbye, then I would return to the thirteenth century.

Quentin said, "You're certain you don't need me to come help protect you?"

Lochie said, "Nae, Quennie, ye stay here Liam needs ye, I can protect us well enough."

"I have a few things I need you to pick up..." He tapped the pocket-sized spiral notebook beside him, but then shook his head. "You know, don't worry about it, I got the weapons, the biodegradable diapers, the compost stuff — we can always return later. You know where the safe house is in Yulee?"

Lochinvar nodded. "And I ken where the keys are."

James leaned forward. "You hear that, Ash? He's talking about the keys to the truck. That's my truck. Lochinvar doesn't get to drive my truck, you drive, he's not good enough at it."

"I am, I can do it."

Quentin said, "You don't have to, let Ash drive, that's an order. No one will be there to bail you out at the police station for driving without a license—"

James said, "Or any skill, *or* enough practice."

Lochinvar said, "Fine, I winna."

"Good, because the only person who could get you out of trouble is Lady Mairead."

Lochinvar shrugged. "Would like tae see the auld broad but I will let Ash drive if ye will stop houndin' me on it. We will be back day after tomorrow and then we'll all go tae Stirling tae meet Magnus taegether?"

James ran his hand through his hair. "Man, I am not ready to move Junior yet, he's still just days old. But yeah, we're going to sit tight until you're back and then we'll all go to Stirling."

Quentin said, "Shit, just remembered I forgot some things." He pulled a pen from his sporran, uncapped it in his teeth, opened the notebook, and began writing.

Beaty said, "Quennie, it canna hurt tae add more diapers."

He nodded, "I have a lot and *some* of these babies can potty train."

James said, "Dude, Junior is a few days old."

Quentin said, "I gotchu man, writing it on the list." He tore off the page and handed it to Lochinvar. "Don't fret it if you can't get to a store, but if you get a chance, it will save me a trip."

Lochinvar read the list with his mouth moving. "What does this word — yer handwritin' inna good."

Quentin said, "Mac and cheese."

Lochinvar nodded and tucked the list in his sporran.

I whispered, "Lochie, m'laird, I'm tired." I yawned loudly. "If they don't need you..."

He pushed out his chair and stood. "M'apologies, Mistress Ash is tired, I will accompany her tae her room." He bowed and took my elbow to help me up.

I said, "Thank you for the lovely meal."

Lizbeth said, "Ye are welcome, Mistress Ash."

And Lochie led me from the Great Hall up to our room.

In our room, Lochie crouched in front of the hearth to stir the coals, draw up the fire, and make it warm again.

I said, "I'm nervous about the jump tomorrow."

He stood up and brushed off his hands. "It helps tae remember that the bairns hae done it. Sophie has done it, Beaty has done it. The bairns hae a gold thread that keeps the pain away—"

"They do?"

"Aye. But we canna hae it, there arna enough for all, and we must have them for the bairns — we dinna hae enough the last jump and Archie went without. Twas verra brave, we canna expect the bairns tae hae that much courage every time."

"Wow, that *was* really brave of him."

"Aye, and if ye think how Archie's so brave and so wee, it will help *ye* find the courage tae do it."

"It does help."

He asked, "Need me tae assist ye in takin' off yer arm sling?"

I pulled the back of my hair to the side and he stepped close, untied it, and pulled it free. I held my shoulder and moved my arm around in a small circle, testing its limits. I said, "It feels a little better."

"Good." He kissed my shoulder. "Ye hae all ye need?"

I looked around: chamberpot, pitcher of water, wash pan, fire, bed. "Kinda, but I really wish there was a PlayStation."

"Och aye, tomorrow, all goes well, after we finish our meetin' with Don we ought tae go home, hook up the PlayStation, and play."

"I don't think we're allowed to, it's too dangerous."

He scowled. "I am of a mind not tae allow Asgall tae come between me and m'games."

I grinned. "That is the truth."

CHAPTER 18 - ASH

THE CLEARING NEAR BALLOCH CASTLE - MAY 29, 1710

*W*e left the castle at dawn. We needed to return the trailer to the clearing, so I rode on it, claiming that climbing on the horse was too difficult with my arm in a sling. Though as I watched James, Quentin, and Lochie climb on horses I could see that it was easy enough and I kind of felt like a loser in my big dress being pulled in a wagon like a child.

We were surrounded by ten guardsmen and they were watchful and cautious, looking out in all directions as they escorted us.

But we relaxed as we rode. Guardsmen rode ahead and reported back, there was no one around, no one trying to mess with us.

Quentin said, "Got your plan?"

Lochie smiled at me and said, "Aye, we are goin' tae the Palace Saloon, checkin' in with Don, a verra quick shopping trip for more diapers for the bairns, a game of GTA on the PlayStation, then come right back afore ye miss me."

Quentin's jaw clenched. "GTA? Where do you think this gaming is going to happen?"

"I daena ken, we could go tae the house? A hotel?"

"Lochie, you have no time for that at all."

"Och aye, I ken, but twould be verra nice."

"No, you're in and out. That's all and no more discussion."

Lochinvar was quiet as we traveled along the path, then he said, "Twould be good tae practice, I hae one of the high scores—"

James said, "Lochie, none of the rest of us can practice either, so your high score is safe."

"Fine, I winna, I just miss it, tis all. And I am only tryin' tae get a rise out of ye, I daena want tae waste any time. I want tae get tae Stirling castle as soon as possible."

James said, "Why such a — oh right," with a laugh.

Lochie glumly said, "Tis crucial we get married so I can think straight."

I chuckled while looking up at the tree limbs stretching over our path.

Then he asked, "What if Ash and I brought one of the things, ye ken, the flat thing on the wall, the PlayStation would plug intae it?"

Quentin said, "You want to bring a plug for the PlayStation back to medieval times?"

"Aye, ye must admit, the nephews would think I was the best uncle if I did."

I laughed, sitting in my shifting cart as it rolled down the path behind a big horse. "Now that I listen to you, Lochie, I can't believe I didn't realize you were a time traveler."

Quentin laughed. "You should have met Magnus, he was absolutely clueless."

James said, "Had never been in a strip club — remember when we took him to buy a Mustang? Can't believe we didn't see it."

I said, "You took him to a strip club and car shopping?"

James said, "Yep, he had been in town for less than a week, had not a bit of paperwork, no drivers license, it was like showing a caveman around. When I look back on it I feel like an idiot."

Quentin said, "In our defense, time travel doesn't exist."

James said, "True that."

Lochie said, "Ye dinna answer, though, could we bring the flat thing for the walls...?"

James said, "Nope, Lochie, you gotta have electricity to plug it in. Not as simple as bringing the plug."

Lochie nodded, then said, "Electricity can be made by that... I canna remember what they are called, the chargy things? The black shiny squares on the roof?"

"The solar panels?"

"Aye, if ye brought them, or a water wheel, we could plug in the PlayStation, tis how it works — daena it work that way?"

James said, "Yes, we could charge big batteries, then plug things in — we do plan to, Lochie. We plan to plug in some lights, here and there, to beat back that medieval darkness, but you don't really want a PS5 in the thirteenth century, it's just too much."

Quentin said, "You'd hear it for miles. You don't realize how quiet it is back here until you roar an ATV to life."

I said, "You brought ATVs back here?"

Quentin said, "We've fought many a battle with ATVs and drones."

"Ah yes, I met a drone in the thirteenth century. That was craziness."

Quentin said, "Balloch was attacked by drones, we called it the Battle for the Walls, we basically had an arms race."

James said, "Also helicopters, tanks, really any weapon, but it has to be able to maneuver the landscape. There aren't any roads. It'd be a pain in the ass to bring a big ol' truck, though it would be really freaking cool."

Quentin said, "Hayley and Katie were pretty effective on the e-bikes at the battle for the Vessels and the Bridge."

I said, "Whoa, you guys have had a lot of battles."

James chuckled. "That's not even the half of them."

"Aren't you worried about messing up history by having guns in a battle that should have been fought with spears?"

All three of the men said 'aye' or 'yes' at the same time.

Quentin said, "We do our damnedest to balance a need to keep history straight, with a need for survival. Sometimes survival reigns supreme."

James said, "Stay strapped."

Quentin said, "Yep."

I said, "I heard Lizbeth mention they were running low on the battery-powered candles, the kind that flicker."

Quentin said, "Oh good, thanks, I'll add them to your list. But only if you have time, don't sweat it if you don't have time." He stopped his horse, pulled the notebook from his pocket, and wrote, using the saddle for a surface.

James said, "Hey, Ash, did Quentin tell you about making sure the truck is gassed up after you're done?"

"He didn't, but yeah, that makes sense. Where's the money?"

"Petty cash in the glove compartment, more stashed in the safe. Lochie will know all of that."

"Got it."

Lochie said, "Ye daena hae tae think on any of this, Ash, I ken how tae do it."

I said, "I know, Lochie, I'm just being on your team."

He nodded. "Good, I am glad ye are, but daena worry, I ken how tae do it."

In the clearing, Lochie and I stood together, each carrying a bag, each with a weapon. Lochie and I looped our arms. Quentin passed us a vessel from his sporran. Lochie worked the device.

I said, "I hate this. I don't want to do it."

Lochie said, "I ken."

He tightened his hold around my back. I saw the machine

THE DAWN

twist in his hand. I stepped back and pushed him away. "Wait, hold on."

Lochie said, "Ash, ye canna let go, if I jump without ye, what would ye do — survive here by yerself?"

James joked, "Quentin and I are literally right over here!"

Quentin said, "That's not his point."

I said, "I know. I know. That was dumb, just hold on." I jiggled from foot to foot, rolled my neck in a circle, swung my uninjured arm.

"Okay, I'm ready— no, wait... hold on."

I got down into a one-armed plank and started doing push-ups. "One... two..."

James called over from his vantage behind the trees, "Lochie, ye gonna let your girl do one-armed push-ups while you stand there?"

Lochie said, "Nae." He dropped and started doing them too. I counted two more, it was hard to do with an injured arm. I sat up. Lochie finished twenty push-ups, saying, "Two-hundred seventy two." Then he jumped to his feet, put out a hand, and heaved me up. "Put yer arm through the crook of m'arm."

I did as I was told. He put his strong arm around me, and before I had a second to think, he twisted the vessel. Pain shot up my arm, spread through my body, and my brain filled with my own screams.

CHAPTER 19 - ASH

THE SAFE HOUSE, HIDDEN IN NASSAU COUNTY, FLORIDA - MAY 20, 2025

*L*ochie's face swam into view.

"I hate it. I hate it so much, I do not like it. At. All."

Lochie said, "I ken, Ash, I ken, tis terrible."

"But look, you're up, you're sitting there, like it's easy!"

"Nae, I am sittin' here as if tis dangerous. I had tae get up, I daena hae any choice."

I looked around and moaned because turning my head, using my eyes, effort, hurt. "What danger? Is there danger?"

"I daena want tae talk about all the danger, because I daena want tae scare ye, but I can think of thirteen dangerous things that might hae happened tae us during that jump."

I said, "Oh, yeah, maybe don't tell me, it's hard enough to do that without knowing how it could go wrong. How could it go wrong? Wait, don't tell me. Let's just call it a dragon attack. You got up early in case of a dragon attack."

"Aye, tis because of dragons. I was up so I could fight them off, while ye slept I fought two, valiantly, ye dinna see me?"

"No, I missed it."

"Och, ye slept through it, but I kept ye safe, that is the

important thing. Tis just as well ye dinna see me fight them, I stabbed one, the other I rode in a big loop through the air afore I slit his throat."

I sat up. "And where are these dragon bodies?"

"Och, when dragons die they disappear, everyone kens. And I am glad ye dinna see me as I prefer tae be more humble on m'wins."

We both laughed.

He put out a hand to heave me up.

"This is your job now, to heave me to my feet? I wonder if you're going to regret taking on the responsibility of me."

He grinned as he hoisted our bags to his shoulders. "First, I canna ever go back tae afore I met ye, I hae only gotten tae taste yer pie once. Och nae, how could I regret ye when I am dreamin' on ye constantly?"

I laughed. "And the second reason?"

"Even if I had tasted yer pie many times and I had grown used tae yer pie—"

"Lochie, don't say it, you would grow used to my pie? Like *bored?*"

"I canna imagine it, Ash, but even *if,* how could I go back tae only helpin' m'self stand? For one twould be lonely, but also tae go through life only lookin' out for yerself is too easy. I need more tae do, I want the hard things. When I heave m'self up after a jump, tis simple, I want tae say, is Ash well? Does she need help? Then I want tae say, is m'son up? Is m'daughter up? Is my...? And I will go down the list helpin' everyone up."

"You want more responsibility and complications?"

"Aye, of course I do, that is true happiness. I will be there all day heavin' people tae their feet, grinnin' like a fool."

I joked, "It's statements like that that prove you deserve another slice of pie, but alas, you haven't married me yet."

"Och nae, daena remind me, I am goin' as fast as I can."

. . .

He unlocked the door of the house. "I am bankin' all the good feelings ye hae, and when tis our wedding night, I will hae ye serve me all the pie. Do ye ken the recipe? Or do we need tae get it from here?"

I stopped on the entryway. "Lochie, are we talking about real pie?"

He laughed. "I canna remember. We dinna start with real pie, yet here we are, I am hungry for pie in all its forms."

"I can remember the recipe, but I would like to go by my place."

The safe house was a small ranch-style residence on a lot of land. They had a gassed-up truck and some ATVs in the garage, a gun vault, a 'money and valuable paperwork' safe, and toiletries in the bathrooms for showers. There were changes of clothes in assorted sizes in the closets.

Lochie walked me through to the master bedroom and stood at the door. "Ye can go through the drawers for clothes, anything ye want tae wear..."

"Good, and I can take a shower? I haven't had one in weeks."

"Aye, take a shower. I will take one in the other bathroom, unless..." He put out a hand.

I took it. "Unless what?"

"I daena ken... I wonder if ye need me tae shew ye how tae turn on the water. Dost ye need m'help tae get ye undressed?"

I looked down at my sling, "Oh... Maybe, but I also think this might be a trick."

His brow went up. "Ye think I might be trickin' ye tae see ye unclothed?"

I raised my brow. "Definitely."

His head jerked back a little. "But ye need m'help... aye?"

I nodded.

"Turn around. I will help, I winna take any liberties."

I turned around and he undid the sling at my shoulder. Then he stood quietly with his eyes averted while I loosened the laces in the front of my bodice. I said, "How do women back in the day get undressed without help?"

"They travel with other women and nae alone with a man they haena married."

"Oh, I guess you're right. This is shameful."

"I married ye in m'heart, I daena think tis shameful, I think ye need m'help undressing ye."

I said, "Okay, you can look, I need help with the laces at the bottom."

He stood in front of me and quietly concentrated on pulling the rest of the laces free.

I watched his face, but it was too close and intimate, he was so hot. I turned my head and looked away.

I sensed that he was glancing at my face as he worked.

He finally had the bodice free and pulled it off down my injured arm.

I grabbed a towel from a stack in the bathroom and wrapped it around me under my chemise. Then turned around, "Can you pull my chemise off? But don't look, you're not allowed to look."

He pulled the hem up and off my arms one at a time, until it was free. My back was exposed but I was mostly hidden. "You didn't look?"

"Nae, I promise."

I turned with the towel wrapped around me.

He stood there for a moment, emitting a deep exhale, holding the bundle of my chemise in his hands, stilled, staring at my shoulders.

I said, "I'm going to take a shower now."

"Aye."

"I'm sorry you're not invited."

He shook his head and put my chemise on the bed. "Aye, nae, I ken why, I will go out and get m'self cleaned as well."

I asked, "Are you okay, Lochie?"

"Nae, I canna think, m'mind went all foggy."

"By my shoulders?"

"And ye daena hae any clothes on under the cloth, Ash, tis mesmerizin' and causin' me dismay. It has taken all m'courage tae maintain m'composure."

I looked down. "That is a lot of power."

"Yer skin is so close, I could just reach out and all would be well." He lifted his hand but then dropped it again. "How long until we are married?"

I smiled. "I think it's like centuries."

"Och nae, I am the most courageous man who ever lived." He left the room and went down the hall.

I found a dresser in the main bedroom that held women's shirts, a pair of joggers, and a clean pair of socks.

I took a luxurious but quick shower, trying to really deeply experience it, because having warm water rolling down my face was amazing. There was shampoo and conditioner — I scrubbed and rinsed. Then I got dressed. I tried to fit into a pair of tennis shoes in the closet but they were way too big. So I would have to wear my boots again... *still*.

I looked down at them, my favorite boots. They looked beaten up and muddy. I sighed. It went against my nature to not have my boots in good condition, but I was so grateful I had been wearing good boots. What if I had been kidnapped wearing flip-flops? Ugh. I reminded myself why I liked a good pair of boots — *you never know when you will need to run from a zombie attack.* And at least now I was wearing clean socks.

When I emerged from the bedroom Lochinvar had dressed in jeans and a light blue button up shirt. He was bent over the gun box, and passed me a belly band holster with a handgun that I strapped on under the waistband.

I held out my arms. "Can you tell?"

"Nae, canna, can ye see mine?" He put out his arms.

I said, "Nope, is it there on your side?"

"Aye, and there is a knife here and here. Quentin says 'If

ye're close enough tae stick yer blade in someone you dinna use yer gun effectively.' But I feel naked without a blade."

I said, "Words to live by."

And we went to the garage to get in the truck to drive into town.

CHAPTER 20 - ASH

THE PALACE SALOON, FLORIDA - MAY 20, 2025

*L*ochinvar got in the passenger seat and put on his seatbelt. I paused for a moment with the keys in the ignition, "I'm sorry you're not driving. I'm following orders, you know?"

"I ken, tis fine. I ken how tae drive, tis just that James is verra particular..." The corner of his mouth went up. "He daena like it when I drive over the mailboxes."

I laughed. "Okay good, we have had enough excitement, I'm going to drive this big-ass truck very carefully." I loosened the sling. "Let me see. Yeah, this works. Doesn't hurt at all."

I backed out of the driveway and Lochinvar went through the glove compartment and pulled out a phone. I said, "A burner?"

"Aye, if we need it."

"I could call Don, but I don't know his number, hmmmm." I drove us out onto the road, checking the clock. "He'll be at work around the time we get there, I'll surprise him."

I got comfortable, but when I adjusted the rearview mirror I accidentally tapped the gas and the truck jerked forward. "Sorry, out of practice."

As I drove I marveled at the passing landscape, strip malls

and trees. "Florida looks weird now that I've been in medieval Scotland."

He said, "Scotland looks weird now that I hae lived in Florida."

I pulled into a drive-thru and ordered burgers and fries and large sodas for both of us. We paid with cash from a roll that was under a gun in the glove compartment.

I pulled to a space under a tree to eat, dipping fries in ketchup and moaning happily as I ate the burger. "Wow, this is amazing after being in the past for so long."

"Aye, a taste of modern food

I asked, "Can I tell Don about the time travel?"

Lochinvar said, "Tis against our rule, but naething good comes from secrecy. If ye trust him, ye ought tae tell him."

I nodded. "I just don't know how."

Lochie said, "It inna easy, I hae nae advice on it, but I wish I had just told ye, first thing."

"Then that's what I'll do."

We pulled up in front of the Palace Saloon and Lochie looked up and down the street. He got out, looked all around, then came around the truck and opened my door to let me out. He followed me up to the front door.

I peered through the glass and knocked seeing Don, inside, mouthing, "No shit! Ash! Ash, it's you?" He rushed to the door, unlocked it, and hugged me in the doorway.

Lochie said, "Ye alone, Don, nae one else?"

"No, just me."

Lochie said, "Good, lock the door after ye, I will keep watch outside."

He stood outside like a guard.

Don locked the door, saying, "What the hell, Ash? What happened — I was so freaking worried!" We hugged again.

"Oh man, I have so much to tell you, I'm sorry you were

worried. I came as fast as I could but I was injured and needed to recuperate first—"

His brow drew down, he looked at his watch. "Um... whatcha talking about, it just happened a few hours ago...?"

"Oh right."

He narrowed his eyes. "Is he in the mob? Is *that* what's going on?"

"No, got a minute? Can we sit down?" We went to the bar and he picked up his rag to wipe it down, as he always did. I said, "So... it's not the mob... I got kidnapped."

"By the mafia?"

"That's literally the mob, just a different name."

"Street gangs? International terrorism?"

"Dude, let me talk."

"I've been nervous, freaking out. Be nicer."

"I know. It's um... you need to brace yourself. Like *listen*, have an open mind. I'm going to tell you something that is hard to believe."

He rolled his hand. "Out with it."

"They're time travelers."

He scoffed. "Bullshit, Ash. Dammit. Come *on*. I'm your friend — aren't we friends? I mean... I get if you can't tell me, but don't bullshit me, at least respect me enough to say I can't tell you and we can just leave it at that."

"No, I won't bullshit you, and I won't lie to you, and the reason why I'm telling you is because we're friends. They time travel. I know it's crazy to hear it, they have a machine, they can jump into different places in time. Magnus, that man, Lochie's older brother? He's a king."

He shook his head.

I said, "You know the storms? The ones on the south end? That's them, time traveling in and out of here."

"No way."

"Yes way." I was turning my barstool back and forth a bit, as I thought about how to put it, so he would *get* it. "Magnus is in a big thing with this guy named Asgall, and for some reason he kidnapped me, not really sure why—"

"That guy who came here, who kidnapped you?"

"He worked for Asgall I think. I was snatched from my car and then woke up in a village compound in the year... can't remember, sometime in... 1296 I think."

"What the hell, Ash, I was not born yesterday."

"I know, but it's true. I was in Scotland, and there was a guy there calling himself a king."

"You hit your head or something. I've never known you to be crazy."

"I could call Lochie in, tell him to explain it, but think about it, why would I lie? And also why would Lochinvar be so damn weird? He's from centuries ago."

"He is pretty weird."

"Exactly."

"So let's say I believe you, I don't, but let's just say I do — how did you get out?"

"I was there for days."

He shook his head.

I said, "I *was*. Long enough to really despair that I might die there."

"In a compound in the 1200s?"

"Yep, I thought it was some bizarro cult."

"Maybe it was?" His eyes glanced at the door, with Lochie standing there looking up and down the street. "You're in a cult, you've got an armed guard now, making sure you don't get out of line."

"Except he's not worried that I'm out of line. He's out there. I could say anything I want to you."

He nodded. "So how did you get away from this cult compound?"

"Lochie and Magnus and Fraoch, you met all of them, they mounted a rescue. They sent a drone over the wall and shot missiles into the compound, they killed the guards. There was armed combat through the streets. It was *crazy*. They found me, and we raced out to their waiting horses."

He stopped wiping to say, "Horses *and* drones?"

"Yep, they can take weapons from now, back to then. They don't want to, they try not to mess up the history of the world, but sometimes they have to use modern weapons. For my rescue they used drones. Some of the guards holding me were armed too, that's what's so confusing about being there. At first I thought I had been kidnapped by a cult, because, one, time travel doesn't exist, and two, even though everything around me looked old, like living in a museum, the guys who kidnapped me were wearing modern clothes. A few of the guards carried modern weapons. It confused me. But then Asgall showed up and forced me to sign a contract, marrying him. I did, because I wanted to survive, I had to escape. I kind of thought I was somewhere in Florida, near by, you know, because I couldn't have gone far... but he told me I was in Scotland and that the year was 1296. It was a mind screwer."

"You thought it was Florida?"

"I mean not really... it just, none of it made sense. I couldn't believe my eyes."

"So Lochinvar and his brothers rescued you, brought you here?"

"No, they jumped with me to a castle in the eighteenth century."

"Bullshit."

I said, "It's not bullshit, have I ever bullshitted you?"

"You're generally pretty straight up, but we joke a lot. How are you not joking right now?"

"I'm not, why would I make any of this up? Why would I want you to think I'm crazy? They took me to a castle, I've been staying there while I recovered from my dislocated shoulder."

"How many days?"

"Another three. I've been gone for at least a week. Maybe

more." I counted on my fingers then said, "Can't remember, brain is fuzzy from the time jump."

He sat there for a moment, kind of huffing, looking down at the ground. Then he said, "Look, I want to take what you're saying as true, because we've been friends for years and I thought we were *good* friends. Please don't lie to me, please don't let me find out later that you developed a drug addiction and this is you hitting bottom. Or you're in some sister marriage cult and you're trying to recruit me."

"I promise, none of that. Being kidnapped in the thirteenth century almost turned me off alcohol altogether. They drank ale, barely any water—"

"That's not really my point. I'm just naming a couple of possibilities of *all* the ways you could be using this cockamamie tale to cover for something terrible going on with you — please don't."

"I won't. I promise. We are friends. You've been my closest friend for a long time. When I was recuperating in the castle all I wanted was to get back here to let you know I was okay. I was worried about you. I knew you were freaking out. If I was in a cult or a drug addict, I think I would have come up with a much better, more believable, excuse, you know?"

"Yeah, I know... you have a much better imagination..." He looked down at the ground for a long time then said, "Fine, I believe you."

"You do? What made you decide?"

"Your boots, actually. Those are your favorite boots and you usually have them shined and pretty. You were wearing them last night, at work. Now look at them, they look like they've been on a weeklong trek through a Scottish forest."

I looked down, "Huh, that's funny."

He ran his hand through his hair. "So what happens now? I take it you're not here for your shift?"

"No, don't think so, my days of slinging drinks are behind me, I think. I'm marrying Lochinvar."

CHAPTER 20 - ASH

"Damn girl."

"Yep, he's asked me, and I said yes."

"I guess it doesn't hurt that he's rich as hell."

"Doesn't hurt, but he's also desperately in love with me, and risked his life to rescue me."

"I guess your last boyfriend was more likely to fight over you than to fight for you."

"Yeah, there's a big difference there. Buck was a butt."

He said, "So I guess there's no chance for me? That's fine, don't answer it, you're not my type anyway."

I said, "Yeah, my bra size is too small."

He shrugged and the corner of his mouth went up. "It's true, a boy wants what he wants. I happen to want a girlfriend who can distract me from what she's droning on and on about."

I rolled my eyes and laughed. "Ugh, you are the worst, why are we friends?"

"Because you think I'm hilarious, and you know you can count on me."

"True, and that's... I need to ask you for a—"

"Here comes the recruitment."

I chuckled. "Yeah, kind of, you got my extra keys? I don't know where any of my stuff ended up."

He pulled the keys out and pushed them across the bar.

"Thanks. I'm going to go by to grab some of my things. But while I'm gone, can I get you to take care of my mail?"

He nodded. "And I'll get your car window replaced."

"Oh, I forgot about that."

I watched Lochie as he stood at the door, his wide shoulders stretching the back of his shirt, his feet planted, on edge, guarding me.

"I guess I need you to watch over my place too? We'll be back, I think we can come back whenever we want..."

"Yeah, no problem."

I asked, "This is weird right, a lot to take in at once...?"

"Yesterday I thought the world was normal, now it's a simulation with matrix-sensibilities. You say that they're the reason for all the storms? They change the weather with time travel? And I'm supposed to just work my job, knowing that this exists?"

"Yeah, it's blown my mind. But honestly, Don, it's good to have a reason for all those storms, am I right? That's been a mystery for *years*."

"Yeah... so you're sure you know what you're doing?"

I nodded. "I love him. I'm going to marry him. I'm going to live in some castle in the—"

He put his hands over his ears and said, "Blah blah blah, don't tell me, I shouldn't know. If I get kidnapped, Ash, by some asshat named Asgall, I warn you, I will sing like a bird. I'm not cut out to withstand torture."

I said, "I don't see why Asgall would bother with you, you don't know anything useful."

"Yeah, I'm just a bartender, I don't know nothin'. But still, y'all aren't doing anything illegal, right?"

"No, nothing, probably, but what do I know? I've only been around them for a little over a week."

"Damn you're a risk taker, you're really gonna marry someone you just met?"

I glanced at the door, Lochie's back.

"Yeah, I'm scared, this is a lot to take on, but also, I'm set in it — I know him, I never met someone like him before, he will take care of me, but also he needs me, like *really* needs me. I can't explain how he's both those things, but he is, and I adore him for it."

"He's pretty hot, all that other stuff is bullshit, you just like his ass."

I grinned. "Yeah, that's pretty great, it doesn't hurt."

"What else you need from me, your plants watered?"

"If you could clean out my fridge and take my plants to your place, that would be great. I'll owe you." I put the keys in my pocket. "I'll leave the keys in the mailbox."

"Gotcha, when will I see you again?"

"How about next Wednesday, the bar opens later, you're here earlier?"

"You can come back that quick?"

"You forget, with time travel I can stay away for years and come back at the same time."

"Damn, that's... that's absurd."

"Yep, if I wasn't doing it, there's no way I would believe it."

"So you don't blame me for not believing you — can you take me somewhere so I can see it for myself?"

"Where would you like to go?"

"I don't know, maybe to early nineties, to see Pearl—" Then he shook his head. "No, don't hold me to that, I can think of something better."

"Think on it this week, I'll come back on Wednesday, the fourth."

He uncapped a pen and circled it on the calendar. I gave him the phone number of our burner phone in case he needed it. As he wrote he said, "I'm going to not even mention that 'burner phone' is usually a sign of some illegal shit going down."

I shrugged. "Yep. Better not to mention it... But now I have to run." I stood up and he walked me to the door. He shook Lochie's hand and then returned to the saloon to finish setting up for work.

Lochie embraced me.

I held on tight. "That was hard. It's next to impossible to explain this to someone."

"Aye, tis why I couldna tell ye, tis good that ye told Don though." We walked to the truck and climbed in. I started the truck and drove toward my house.

First, I drove by it slowly, very slowly, while Lochie and I both peered out the windows. He said, "Notice anythin' off?"

"No, except the glass by my car. My landlady will be pissed, but she barely goes outside, maybe she hasn't noticed."

Next, I drove past, circling the block, scanning in all directions, and *then* pulled up in the driveway. I climbed from the truck and approached my car.

Someone had locked the doors, so I had to carefully reach my arm through the broken window to open it from the inside. I remembered being yanked through it, the man reaching in the car, scaring the heck out of me, dragging me out. So much had happened since then, but the memories hit me, fresh, especially the fear. I felt the fear all over again.

Lochie said, "Och nae, twas dire."

"I know, it looks scary — it was so scary. It's making me feel shaky."

I leaned against the car taking a deep breath, while Lochie crouched down and looked all around the floorboards and felt under the seats.

"There is nothin' here."

We went around the house to the front door.

I let myself in and listened for a moment, but then climbed the stairs, giving Lochie a funny look, pressing my finger to my lips. He grinned as he crept soundlessly behind me.

I opened the door with my key and Lochie went in first to look around. Then I followed. It was just how I had left it yesterday when I went to work. The weirdest thing to say, ever, because it seemed like a whole lifetime ago.

"Okay, what do I need...?" I pulled my suitcase from the closet under the eaves, opened it on the bed, and started pushing underwear and bras in. "What do I pack for a medieval castle?"

"I daena hae any idea, I simply put on what Madame Emma or Queen Kaitlyn tells me tae wear."

I held up some socks. "Wool?"

"Aye, bring wool socks. And yer comfortable boots. I hae seen some of the women wear layers under their skirts."

I rolled up some workout pants, placed them in the suitcase and all my wool socks. Then I held up my fanciest, tiniest, laciest pair of underwear and bra, in a bright pink color. "These?"

His eyes went wide. "They are yers?" He sounded breathless when he said it.

"I'll wear it for our honeymoon." I placed them in the case.

"Och aye, twould be... verra good."

I grinned.

He looked over at the bed. "Och, we had a verra fine time, ye ken, we were verra good at it, twould be a shame tae wait, I think. We ought tae be less concerned with what m'family thinks."

"You, m'laird, are changing your mind back and forth, agreeing with me, then disagreeing—"

"If ye kent how much I want tae bed ye, ye might disagree with yerself as well. We did it once, we could do it once more without harmin' our reputations, especially if we keep it verra quiet."

I sighed. "While a secret tryst does sound fun, I think we ought to keep to the plan. Think how hot you'll be for me by the time we're married. It'll be amazing."

"Unless I die first."

I playfully stamped my foot. "Lochie, you are not going to die, not from lack of—"

He looked crestfallen.

"Oh you mean because of danger..."

"Aye, ye hae given me somethin' tae live for."

"That is very sweet." I was holding a pair of boots and shoved them in the suitcase. "I'm sorry I was teasing you. It's just that sometimes we're talking about ordinary things, then next minute we're talking about life and death. It's jarring. And not funny."

He half-smiled. "Tis kind of funny, that I lay with ye right here, just a week ago, then risked m'life tae rescue ye, and now I must stare at the bed longingly, dreamin' of beddin' ye, and daena get tae because I must marry ye first. Tis like moving backwards, but I suppose time is a wheel, ye ken?"

"Is it? I always thought it was a line. And you're right, we are going backwards, but we can't stop now, we've come this far. We must carry on."

He nodded.

I went to the bathroom to get my perfume, makeup, toothbrush... I brushed the hell out of my teeth, and then did it again. I grabbed a mirror and my floss. My shampoo and conditioner, some hair products for making myself pretty. I put my best jewelry into a small bag. Then put all of that in a larger bag and shoved it into my suitcase. I had a favorite pillow: I rolled it up and put it in too.

When I looked up, Lochinvar was standing in front of the bookcase, holding a book.

I went over and glanced at the cover. "That was my favorite when I was younger, the Chronicles of Narnia. Do you think your nephews have heard it? I could read it to them, that would be fun."

"Ye would read a book tae the nephews?"

"Or you could read it to them, or I can read it to all of you."

"Aye, twould be verra good. I daena think they have read it."

I put the books in the suitcase.

He said, "Ye told me ye were goin' tae read me a book about... dost ye remember?"

"I think it was Twilight, do you want me to bring it?"

"Aye."

I brought that book and I pulled the Hobbit from the shelf. "This one has a dragon."

He asked, "Tis a true story?"

I stopped, my eyes went wide. "A true story — are dragons real, Lochie?"

He grinned.

"You're joking right? I swear, if you told me dragons were real right now I would be like, sure, I guess they are — really?"

"I hae never met one."

"That doesn't totally set my mind at ease."

I scrounged through my address book and found my parents' phone number. I called using the burner phone.

Mom of course hadn't noticed I was missing because she lived a few states away and I had only been officially gone for about fifteen hours. When she picked up she was excited to hear from me, but also busy, she asked if she could call me back.

At her voice, I got kind of overwhelmed, tears pooling in my eyes. I remembered walking down the riverbank in a medieval Scottish forest and how I had gone back to the compound because I hadn't wanted to disappear, I hadn't wanted to break her heart — I said, "No worries, Mom, I'm going out of town for a week, but I'll call you when I get back on Wednesday." My voice caught.

She said, "Are you okay, honey?"

"Yeah," I took a deep breath. "I'm good, just a late shift at the bar, my voice is cracking." I hated to lie to her, to not tell her that I was caught up in something big and dangerous, that I was going to get married.

I had been so caught up in getting married in front of Lochie's family that I forgot about my own. But then again, his family wondered why we were waiting — my family would be horrified that we were marrying so soon.

I said, "Mom, just really wanted to tell you I love you."

"What made you want to say that? And I love you too."

"I don't know, world events, tired, just wanted to tell you, I miss you and Dad."

She said, "I miss you too, desperately. When you get back on

Wednesday, call me, let's get a date on the calendar for you to visit, pronto."

"I'll try to come in the next few weeks, I promise."

"Perfect, good, very good—"

"Kiss Dad for me, okay?"

"Of course, honey, talk to you on Wednesday." Then we hung up. I stared at my phone for a moment, blinking back the tears. It felt weird and evasive to have so much going on and not tell her about it. I usually told her everything, mostly... but in this... no. Not yet. She would never understand. And I didn't have time to explain.

I looked over at Lochinvar, his nose in the fridge. He said, "Dost ye hae a bag for some groceries?"

I passed him a shopping bag. He placed three beers into it, a ziplock gallon-bag of flour and one of salt. I said, "Grab the salt and pepper too."

He put ketchup in the bag. I flipped through my recipe box. He said, "What is that?"

I pulled out a few cards. "My recipes for pies. Maybe I will make you one for our wedding day."

"That might be the greatest dream I ever had, dost ye think ye could?"

"Why not, we have sugar and flour, we just need fruit. Wait!"

I reached in the fridge and pulled out a bag with a dozen peaches in it. And two pie pans.

I put it all in the bag.

I zipped up the suitcase and he carried it.

As we went to the door I said, "Nothing happened, the whole time, we were cautious over nothing."

Lochie said, "I hae always learned, ye must be overly cautious, Ash, ye never ken when someone will time-travel at ye."

I laughed. "'Time travel at ye' I like that, it's funny."

"Aye, tis funny, but we ought tae go."

I nodded. "I'm ready, let's do this thing."

When we got downstairs I hid my keys, and then we got in the truck to drive back to the safe house.

I said, "Do we have time to stop at Target for the other things on the list?"

He pulled the notebook pages from his sporran, they were covered in Quentin's list. He read, "Tis more diapers, toilet paper, toothpaste, treats for the kids, and a—"

The burner phone vibrated.

Lochinvar read it, "Tis a text from Don. It says: Ye left yet? Ye see that storm?"

He turned the phone to show me. I took the phone, called Don, and put it on speaker.

"Where was the storm?"

"Centered directly east, near Egan's Creek."

"So, it wasn't just a thunderstorm, it was one of the strange ones, right? Big, sudden, brief? That's what you saw?"

"Yeah, that's what I saw. Where are you guys?"

I said, "We're off the Island, we were going to stop at Target, but I think we gotta get out of here."

"Alright, see you on Wednesday."

"See you then."

I hung up.

Lochinvar put the lists back in his sporran, shaking his head. "We will stop tae gas up the truck, but we canna shop for supplies." He looked over his shoulder out east.

I said, "Were they coming or going?"

"I daena ken."

I pulled the truck up at the gas pump, Lochinvar stood beside me, looking up and down the road while I filled it with gas.

Then we both went into the store because I needed to use the bathroom and couldn't wait. He said, "I will guard the store from inside, ye want a soda?"

"Yes, I'd love another Sprite, I need to store it up like a camel." He narrowed his eyes. "A camel, Lochie?"

"Och aye, a camel. C is for Camel. The bairns hae a book on it."

"They store water in their — you know, never mind. Next time we come back we'll all go to the zoo and I'll tell you all about it." I left for the bathroom.

When I came out he had a plastic shopping bag full of something and two Big Gulps.

He passed me my very large Sprite.

I asked, "What's in the bag?"

"I found the best things tae take back for everyone. The verra best."

We climbed in the truck and while I started it he opened the bag on his lap and showed me a pen. "Look, tis the verra best pen ye ever saw! This is a pen that will save yer life."

I laughed. "Show me, it looks just like an ordinary pen. How can that save your life?"

He gasped, comically. "Hae I *told* ye about how pens saved Magnus and Kaitlyn's life?"

"No, I heard pens were important, it's been mentioned, but I don't get how it happened."

"They were stuck verra far back in time, before history, almost, before anythin' was written down. Nae one knew where they were."

"Ugh, remind me not tae go back that far."

"Och, we are goin' *much* farther back."

I said, "Great... does this have a happy ending?"

"Aye, Magnus had pens. He signed contracts and leases and filled books with writin' with the modern pens. And then someone noticed, ye ken, that the writin' in the book was from a modern pen. Twas a mystery. Twas in a magazine. Emma showed it tae me, the headline said: The Mystery of the Modern Pen. That was how they found Magnus and Kaitlyn, the place, the date, and year."

"I'm impressed, that's amazing."

"Twill be even better with *this* pen, look at it." He fumbled with it. "There is a light!" He pulled off the lid revealing a flash-light on the top.

"Very cool."

"Tis not all..." He struggled for a moment, muttering that his fingers were too big, then he uncapped the other end. There was a tiny screw driver. He said, "A blade!"

I smiled. "Awesome. It's small though."

"Och," he joked, "tis like Fraoch says, 'Tis not the size of the blade but yer swing.'" He eyed the screwdriver. "I can think of three ways tae kill a man with it, right now." He capped it again, then pulled apart the middle to show me the pen. "*And* it writes, if ye are in dire straits in a dungeon in Balloch in a year before the vessels, ye will hae three tools tae get yerself free. Tis all one could ever need."

I said, "That is a great pen, how many did you get?"

"I bought all of them."

"Enough for the whole family?"

"Aye."

We pulled up at the safe house and parked the truck. He drew his gun as we moved from the garage into the house, and kept watch while I changed into my Balloch clothes. Then I kept watch while he dressed in his kilt. We met in the backyard.

I had my suitcase beside me, a grocery bag with stuff to make pies, Lochinvar had a bag of pens. We each had a Big Gulp in our hands. I joked, "It's not what we were told to buy but we did all we could. By the way, what's in that bag?"

I pointed with the big cup.

He opened the flap and showed me. It was an older PlayStation with the cord wrapped all around it, stuffed in his bag, and a couple of controllers. "You stole it out of the house?"

"Aye, seemed like we needed it."

"True, what games you got in there?"

He looked through three games. "Call of Duty, Gran Turismo, and Golf."

I said, "Smart thinking. Either we are going to have so much fun or Quentin will never send us on a supply run again. It's a win-win."

He laughed. "When he sees m'bag of pens he is goin' tae send me on all the supply runs."

I laughed too.

He pulled a vessel from his pocket, then narrowed his eyes. "I ken we are headed back tae Balloch, but..."

I slurped some of my Sprite. "But what?"

Lochie said, "I am in a hurry tae get ye tae Stirling."

I asked, "Is that so that we can get married?"

He nodded, "I daena think I can wait any longer."

I nodded looking up in his eyes. "But didn't we tell them we were coming straight—"

Lochie said, "I daena think ye understand, Ash, how desperate I am tae marry ye. M'mind inna workin' anymore. I canna think over m'thoughts on... ye ken, and I told ye, tis dangerous tae jump, what if something happens tae us and we are unmarried? And... now I hae seen yer pink underwear and we ought tae be married — then ye are m'wife. I am yer husband, twill give us more protection."

I smiled. "You are really desperate, I am close to saying yes, but... I really don't like the idea of disappointing anyone, especially Quentin." I looked around at the stuff we brought, it was a poor showing. I sipped from my Big Gulp.

He said, "We could go meet Magnus at Stirling, get married, then return tae Balloch — we time travel, we wouldna even be late. If ye think about it, Ash, we ought tae do it that way or yer peaches will become too ripe and yer pie winna taste as good."

"Oh this is about my peach pie, huh?"

"Aye, Ash, everythin' is about yer pie. Tis all there is in the whole world."

I sighed. "This is very sweet. Okay, I've put you off long enough, let's go to Stirling and get married."

Lochinvar grinned then began working the vessel.

I narrowed my eyes. "You know how to set it?"

"Aye, tis just..." His voice trailed off, I saw him pause and it seemed like he was counting in his head, it was disconcerting, but then finally he said, "Aye, tis right..." He looked down on it, then said, "Och, ye need this as well." He twisted it and did one more thing. Then he nodded.

I felt alarmed. "It's set? You're sure, we could go to Balloch first."

"Tis set, trust me, Ash, we are goin' tae the agreed upon date tae meet Og Maggy at King's Park, Stirling. Ye are armed?"

I jokingly held up the Big Gulp.

He chuckled.

I said, "We're going to time travel with our Big Gulps so that when we wake up we can immediately drink some."

He said, "We haena ever tried it, tis a genius idea."

"Good, we make a good team. And yes, I am armed. But we're going to Stirling — Magnus will be there to meet us, right?"

He pulled his gun and checked it was loaded, then returned it to his holster. "He will, but we must always be ready for a chance of melee."

I gulped. "Melee, huh?"

"Daena worry on it, Ash, grab m'arm." He checked his watch, "Och nae, we hae been here a long time, we need tae go."

He looked down on the vessel, he was about to twist it.

I didn't want him to twist it.

I stepped away, shaking my head. "Nope. Don't want to."

Lochie said, "Och nae."

"We could... I don't know. Live here. Right? There's a house, it's called a *safe* house, we could just... not go."

"It inna what it means, Ash, ye ken?"

"I know, but it has a PlayStation, it has all we need."

"I am takin' the PlayStation with us..."

"I know, I get it, I just don't want to get on the swooshy storm machine. Sometimes I need to talk myself into things. Sometimes I need to be bossy about it."

"Ash, ye are the love of m'life and ye are also a pain in m'arse. Ye hae tae go because I said tis time tae go."

I swung my good arm around in a circle, then I jogged in place. Looking at him the whole time.

He repeated himself, pretending to be stern, "Tis time to go."

I said, continuing to jog. "You bossing me, Lochie?"

"Aye, ye are goin' tae be m'wife, I am tellin' ye tis time tae go."

I kept jogging. "You're telling me I have to put my hand on yer arm so that pain can shoot up my arm and drag me into the past?"

"Aye, right now, because I told ye ye hae tae."

"Fine," I swung my arm around in a circle while saying, "but only because I will, not because you're being—"

I put my hand on his arm. He put his arm around me with his chin on the top of my head, holding me in a big bear hug. And the ripping, searing pain began to fill me again.

CHAPTER 21 - MAGNUS

THE FIELD IN KING'S PARK - JUNE 17, 1291

*J*ust afore midnight the wind began tae rise fast and brutal. I yelled over the roar, "Get tae the trees!" Fraoch, Chef Zach, and I grappled with horse reins, pullin' them tae the side as the thunderclouds grew overhead. Wind whipped in a large circle. We found cover behind a large oak. Our headlamps were spotting the field with small beams that were nae match against the darkness of the storm. The branches were whipping. Chef Zach put his arms up tae block the wind.

"Wish I had brought the monitor, this better be Lochinvar."

A thunderclap boomed. A gust overhead caused the branches tae crack dangerously.

Chef Zach yelled, "I don't know whether to cover my head or watch in case something happens!"

Fraoch said, "I ken! We must be ready tae run!"

Lightning arced from the clouds to the ground and then as suddenly as it began, the storm began tae dissipate, gusts became erratic but lessening, and then we were able tae ascertain with our weak beams, two lumps in the field.

I made my way taeward them, tae see Lochinvar and Ash. I hit the button on my radio: "Mo reul-iuil, he and Ash arrived."

Her voice emitted, in a whisper because the bairns were likely asleep. "Finally, tell them I said hi."

I said, "Go tae sleep, we will be there soon."

CHAPTER 22 - LOCHINVAR

THE FIELD IN KING'S PARK - JUNE 17, 1291

I could hear men's voices. I pulled m'self awake. It smelled like Scotland, the air felt like Scotland, I felt damp. "Och nae, did we make it?" I blinked my eyes, there was a blazin' light makin' it difficult tae see.

Fraoch's voice said, "Och, tis good tae see ye, Og Lochie, ye made it!"

Chef Zach said, "I've never seen that tried before."

"What?" I looked down, I had a Big Gulp drink poured on me, the cup, lid, and straw tossed around. I glanced over at Ash, she was wakin' up, shifting and moving. She had her Big Gulp turned over on her stomach, soda spilled everywhere.

I moaned, "Och, this was not a verra good idea." I added, "Yer lights are too bright."

Chef Zach said, "Oh, shit, right." He and Fraoch pushed their lamps up so they lit the sky.

Magnus said, "I ken ye need a moment tae recover, but tis the middle of the night—"

Fraoch said, "Och, tis the middle of the night in King's Park, we hae all the time in the world." He smacked a bug on his cheek.

I said, "And what a fine Scottish night. But alas I am covered in soda — Ash?"

She mumbled, "Yeah?"

"We need tae get up tae go. We are covered in soda."

She sat up and pushed the hair from her eyes, blearily. "That *sucks*, I'm furious my Sprite spilled. Are the peaches okay?"

I looked in the shopping bag. "Aye." I stood and heaved her up. We met each other's eyes at the moment — her thought, *You will always heave me to my feet?* My thought, *Aye, always.*

Magnus said, "I am verra glad ye are here, but where're m'supplies, Lochinvar? We need weapons."

"Nae worries, they are comin' in the next load."

"But we hae the English King threatenin' us. He sent scouts ontae my lands."

I groaned. "Och nae, truly?"

"Aye, ye ought tae hae brought the weapons."

"I am sorry, Magnus." I shook my head. "I regret it, they remain at Balloch, Colonel Quentin will bring them when he comes—"

Magnus interrupted, "Day after tomorrow, Lochinvar, a great deal could happen afore then."

I groaned again. "I ken, I am sorry, I just... I came directly from Florida, because... I wanted tae get married."

Fraoch narrowed his eyes. "Ye dinna bring the weapons, Og Lochie, because ye wanted tae get married?"

"Aye, tis not m'best decision makin', Fraoch, I will agree, but tis what I hae done. I wanted tae marry Ash first thing."

Fraoch shook his head. "Och nae, ye are goin' tae be the death of me."

Magnus said, "We hope he winna be the death of anyone — but Lochinvar, ye are goin' tae get married? Tis good news, verra good news."

Zach brought their horses near and guards surrounded us.

Fraoch said, "Och ye are a softy in yer auld age, Og Maggy, the lad dinna bring yer weapons and ye are goin' tae be joyful?"

Magnus said, "Aye, daena misunderstand, I am verra disappointed he dinna bring the weapons. He dinna even bring his horse, tis as if he has forgotten everything."

A guardsman gave us a horse, I helped Ash up, she whispered, "I have to?"

I whispered back, "Wheesht — aye, ye must, Ash, ye canna walk. Put yer hand here."

I pushed her up and climbed intae the saddle behind her. A look of amusement passed between Magnus and Fraoch.

I held her around the middle and directed our horse tae follow behind Dràgon. "In m'defense, I dinna ken the English King was threatenin' ye."

Fraoch said, "Chef Zach, dost ye hear him makin' his excuses?"

Chef Zach chuckled, "Leave me out of it, no one would trust me with bringing the weapons."

Fraoch said, "True, we wouldna ask ye tae, but we would trust ye tae do it if asked."

I said, "Och nae, Fraoch, I wanted tae come get married, I dinna consider the rest of it. I will ride Ash up tae the castle and then go get the weapons, I will leave before dawn."

Magnus said, "Ye canna, the turn around is too tight, ye need the three-day window..."

I exhaled. "I dinna think about that... but I daena hae tae. I could risk it."

Magnus said, "Tis fine, Quentin will bring them, we might as well accept they arna here now. We will make do."

Ash said, "I am so sorry, I'm the one who talked Lochie into all of this, I just had no idea."

I said, "Ash, tis not yer fault, twas my responsibility."

She said, under her breath, "But we were supposed to be a team. I forced you to marry me, you haven't slept in days, I feel really bad about it."

"Tis fine, Ash, daena worry, they are just harassin' me, tis a normal occurrence."

I saw Magnus, able tae hear us, nod his head, then he said, "But ye ken, Fraoch, a weddin' is always a good thing, ye ken tis."

Fraoch was riding along behind us. "Aye, tis, a verra fine thing. When I am not so irritated I will tell Og Lochie that I am verra pleased about it."

Magnus chuckled and said, "When dost ye want tae hae the ceremony, Lochinvar?"

I scowled, "I hoped as soon as I arrived, but tis as dark as a bear's arse at midnight. What time is it?"

Chef Zach said, "Midnight."

I huffed. "I suppose tis too late."

Magnus said, "On the morrow we will plan it, we will hae a verra big feast, the priest will marry ye, if we wait for the followin' day Colonel Quentin will be here, twould be good tae hae the full family—"

"I would like tae do it first thing in the morn—"

Magnus turned in his saddle. "In the morn! What is yer hurry?"

I chewed my lip. "Tis important that I marry her in front of m'family afore we continue on with each other... ye ken?"

Magnus nodded and turned back around. "Aye, I see, ye must be married."

"Aye."

"Then, naething else matters, all else will wait, first thing in the morn we will gather in the chapel."

Fraoch said, "But what of the feast? I was promised a feast."

Chef Zach said, "One minute ago!"

"I was already looking forward tae it."

Ash said, "I brought peaches and flour to make some peach pies."

Fraoch said, "Tis official, I hae forgiven Lochinvar for everything."

Chef Zach asked, "You ever made peach pies in a medieval kitchen before?"

Ash shook her head.

He said, "Me neither, I haven't figured out how the hell the kitchen works yet—"

Magnus said, "Ye daena hae tae cook here, Chef Zach, but I would appreciate if ye oversaw the work. Just give the ingredients tae the cook, tell him what ye want."

Chef Zach said, "Have you met me, Magnus? That seems unlikely."

Magnus laughed.

The castle was in front of us, our path inclined as we rode up the hill. Sean emerged from the gates tae welcome us.

I asked Magnus as we rode through the gates. "Has there been a room set aside for us?"

Magnus said, "Aye, I will hae ye shewn tae—"

"Ash needs the room, I will sleep in the barracks for the night."

Magnus said, "Och, I see, Lochie, aye."

CHAPTER 23 - MAGNUS

MIDDLE OF THE NIGHT, STIRLING CASTLE - JUNE 18, 1291

*L*ochinvar said goodnight tae Ash at the stair. She was led up tae her room by a maid and he stood watchin' her go.

Fraoch, Sean, and I were standing nearby. Sean said, "I think the lad is tormented. What happened?"

Fraoch said, "Aye, fully tormented — I think she has denied him until he marries her."

Sean shook his head. "Och, the lad called her his wife and here he stands corrected. I suspect tis the work of Lizbeth, for the first time I feel sorry for him."

Lochinvar returned tae where we stood. "Dost ye think Ash will be well? Ought I go up and see that her room is comfortable enough?"

Fraoch said, "Og Lochie, twill be fine, but explain what has happened — ye arna invited tae her room, she has refused ye?"

"Aye, we must be married first."

Fraoch chuckled. "She dinna think yer thumb oath was enough? Ye assured me ye were married and she believed it as well."

"The ladies Lizbeth, Beaty, and Sophie dinna think twas

enough, they told her tae refuse me until I married her in front of ye."

Sean looked amused. "I *knew* twas Lizbeth's doin'."

Lochinvar said, "That is why we came afore I thought of doin' anything else. Tis why I forgot tae get the weapons, because I hae not slept in days, sittin' guardin' her door every night since."

Fraoch bit his lip to hold back a smile. "She is torturin' ye, by the looks of it."

I watched Lochinvar's face, he was torn between fury at his circumstances and worry over his lass, and looked as if he might decide tae brawl.

I clapped him on the back. "We hae another room near mine, ye can sleep there, I daena want ye in the barracks."

"Thank ye, Magnus. Twould be good, it has been a long time since I slept."

~

I climbed intae m'bed verra late at night. Kaitlyn wrapped her arms around me, "You're cold."

"Twas cool out taenight and tis late."

"No sign of trouble?"

"Nae, twas a calm Scottish night, not a sign of trouble anywhere."

She raised her thigh up across m'hip. "You showed Lochie and Ash to their room?"

"We hae shown them each tae separate rooms, they winna share a bed until they are married in the morn."

Her quiet voice in the darkness, "Very interesting... and that's nice, our Lochie is going to get married."

"Aye, twill be an important step for him, I am proud he is takin' it."

~

Far too soon there was a soft knock on the door of our outer room.

I rose and shuffled tae see who was there at the cusp of dawn.

Twas Lochinvar. "Magnus, I was wonderin' if we could prepare for the ceremony."

I chuckled. "So early, ye must hae barely slept."

"Aye, twas troubled in m'mind about not bringing ye the weapons, and I ken I disappointed ye, it weighed heavy on my thoughts... And I want tae marry Ash. I hae a verra strong feelin' that all will be well once I do."

I said, "I also hae a strong feeling all will be well once ye do—"

Kaitlyn emerged from our room, "Who is it — Lochie?"

He said, "Aye, Queen Kaitlyn, m'apologies for wakin' ye, I wanted tae ready for the ceremony."

Kaitlyn said sleepily. "That's fine, I *love* weddings, we might as well get up and get ready."

She sent maids tae Ash's room tae help her ready for the ceremony.

CHAPTER 24 - MAGNUS

DAWN, STIRLING CASTLE - JUNE 18, 1291

*L*ochinvar had bathed and I had given him a fine tunic and cloak for the occasion. Fraoch, Sean, and I were speakin' with him as he sat in a chair and pulled on his boots.

Fraoch said, "So what is the longer explanation of what transpired with ye and the lass that ye are here tae get married?"

Lochinvar leaned back with a sigh. "Ye ken how I rescued her?"

Fraoch laughed. "Aye, we were there."

Sean said, "I heard the story."

"Just when I thought I was goin' tae bed her again, which we haena done in a verra long time, a verra verra long time — we were interrupted. Strangers arrived at Balloch, a group of six men, the guards allowed them intae the courtyard."

Sean said, "Och nae, I told Liam tae be careful with the security."

Lochinvar said, "He was reasonably careful, but the men said they were carryin' a message from the Earl of Breadalbane in Edinburgh."

I said, "Were they messengers?"

"They claimed the Earl was ill, but why would he send

strangers tae tell us? Liam regretted allowin' them through the gate."

Sean said, "Tis too late once the danger has been invited inside."

"Aye, and they were lookin' around in a way that — twas suspicious. Liam told me tae keep hidden, he thought they were looking for us."

I said, "Och nae, I daena like the sound of it, ye think Arsegall sent them?"

"Aye, they were sent by Arsegall. We found out they were askin' about us in the village afore they came tae the castle."

Sean said, "I ought tae get back."

I nodded. "We will send ye home, we can send ye home by the end of the day."

He said, "Yet I am meetin' with the quarry master tomorrow afternoon, I could go right after?"

"And ye will arrive on the same day, we are time travelers. We can do whatever ye want."

Fraoch said, "Lochie, continue yer story."

"Ash waited in the nursery, and after, when I returned her tae our chamber, she had all sorts of new ideas about our oath tae each other — she said we ought tae be officially married, she told me my family wouldna respect her without it, she said ye dinna respect me enough."

I looked around tae see all of us shakin' our heads in commiseration.

Fraoch said, "Och nae, what did the ladies say tae her?"

He looked sullen. "They told her she ought tae make me marry her afore we carried on — they dinna believe me on my thumb oath…"

Fraoch bit his lip tae keep from laughin'.

Lochinvar continued, "Twas an oath, but tae them twas not enough, they advised Ash tae banish me from her bed."

Fraoch said, "Och nae, this is a tragedy. How long has it been since she has been denyin' ye?"

"It has been days without… I believed I deserved some grati-tude — daena ye agree? I rescued her! I ought tae hae some solace in a warm bed." He was fully pouting.

I said, "Tis true, ye rescued yer wife, it would seem customary for yer wife tae offer ye gratitude. But, Lochinvar, therein is the rub."

Lochinvar put his hand on his forehead and rubbed the spot between his brow. "She wasna my wife."

"Aye," I asked, "And ye hae been sleepin' outside her door?"

"In the passage tae guard over her."

Fraoch said, "Och nae, I hae been there before — tis a dark and desolate time, nae wonder ye are as ornery as a bear."

"I had tae build her fire tae keep her warm! Tis nae sense in any of it!"

I said, "Finish puttin' on yer boots, ye will be married afore God, then all of this will be behind ye."

Fraoch said, "Aye, ye will hae yer wife, yer warm bed, and if ye satisfy her none of the women will be capable of advisin' her against ye."

"*If* I satisfy her! What does *that* mean?"

"Tae be stern but kind, tae be funny yet strong, tae be a good provider and tae listen tae their endless conversations about things they care about, ye ken. Hayley tells me tis what *all* ladies want, and especially tae clean all around yer undercarriage, tis crucial in satisfyin' her. Then when ladies in the nursery speak poorly on ye, she will say," he raised his pitch tae sound like a woman, "'Och nae, not a poor word on m'husband, he smells like an angel and has the temperament of a godly man, and he makes me laugh with his jokes about fishin'.'"

Lochie stood up and I stood in front of him tae straighten his collar, brooch, and the shoulder of his cloak.

I asked, "Lochie, dost ye ken any jokes about fishin'?"

"Just this one: Why do auld men always clean their tackle-boxes?"

Fraoch said, "I daena ken, why?"

"Because their tackle drags in the dirt when they walk."

We laughed heartily.

Fraoch said, "Tis verra good, she will be a happy wife."

I said, "Ye ready tae go tae the chapel?"

Lochie said, "Aye."

CHAPTER 25 - KAITLYN

DAWN, STIRLING CASTLE - JUNE 18, 1291

*A*sh was bathed in sweet-smelling floral water, dressed in her bright pink underpants and bra, while we picked out a fine tunic dress in a pale blue for her, it was the closest I could find to white. Her sleeves were long, and the inside color was a deep blue, the edges were embroidered with intricate floral patterns. She looked really beautiful. We pinned her short hair back with bobby pins and put a white veil over her hair, a small pretty gold pin holding it on.

While she readied, Emma asked, "So what happened, Ash? I thought you and Lochie were settled, as good as married."

She was looking down at her dress as we draped a pale blue cloak on her shoulders. "Well, I don't want to piss anyone off, I promise this is not meant that way, but *sometimes*, the people around Lochie—"

I said, "Meaning us?"

"Yes, *sometimes* you don't take him seriously. Lady Lizbeth told me I ought to marry him in front of Magnus so that he would know that Lochinvar was *serious* about being responsible."

I said, "Ah, so it was Lizbeth…"

Emma said, "Classic Lizbeth."

I pinned a pretty gold brooch at her collar. "I don't know if I can agree that we don't take him seriously... Magnus owes Lochie his life, so does Fraoch—"

Hayley said, "But they all tease him mercilessly."

I said, "They love him, he's their brother. They just treat him like that because they think he's young."

Ash said, "It's sort of the same thing, you know?"

"I suppose it is, and yeah, I think it matters a lot to Magnus that there will be a church wedding, it will likely raise Lochie in their respect to witness him married."

I appraised her. "That is really wise, you know, I just hope you understand, he needs someone to be wise. He's strong and capable, but also what we might call a 'handful.' He can be impetuous. This life is so... it's difficult. There's danger and near death experiences—"

Hayley said, "Daily."

I nodded. "Right now the English King is being a threat. This could mean war, the kind with attacks on a castle, and this is just our newest danger, this whole life you've chosen is likely to be really hard. I hope you understand what you're signing up for... but then again you were a soldier, right? You get it."

She nodded. "Yeah, I think I get it. I served in the Army, it was really hard, but I wouldn't trade it."

I dug through the makeup bag for some powder.

I said, "So you're going to marry Lochinvar. Got any worries besides... you know, impending war?"

"I'm worried that I can barely survive a horse ride. I'm actually kind of freaked out about embarrassing myself around the horses."

"Been there, no worries, you'll learn to ride, I'm sure of it. Necessity alone will force you to learn, but also, there is a positive aspect, way beyond transportation: it is really hot riding alongside them."

I dusted powder on Ash's nose.

Hayley said, her eyes dreamy and faraway, "I look at Fraoch's knee, sticking out of his kilt, against his horse, and it *slays* me."

She fanned herself. "How do modern women even like their husbands without seeing their knees like that on a horse?"

We laughed.

Emma said, "Just smile at him with those dimples, Ash, and Lochie will forgive you for not being good with riding."

She nodded. "Okay, good advice, I won't sweat the horses."

Emma smeared a little bit of pale pink on Ash's lips and then held up a mirror for her. "You look really beautiful."

"Thank you."

Hayley said, "But since we've been pretty positive, maybe we need to talk some sense too, you sure you're ready for this? You're about to tie yourself to *Lochinvar* for good or bad, you're going to become his ride or die. You'll be his make or break—"

Emma said, "She understands, Haylcy, no need to go negative, you're going to freak her out."

I said, "Lochinvar was an orphan growing up in a medieval castle who found out that he's the brother of a king. And *still*, Ash is going to be the best thing that ever happened to him."

Ash gulped. "You have a lot of faith in me, how do you know?"

"Because this decision, making him marry you was so good, it portends for a good future."

Hayley said, "Yeah, you'll be able to guide him, but if I could ask for a favor, if you could guide him into not taking Fraoch's seat all the time, that would be great. Fraoch hates it when Lochie takes his chair."

I laughed, "I don't think any of us can stop the Campbell brothers from arguing."

Hayley said, "Speaking of brothers, have you heard about Finch Mac?"

"Who, Finch Mac the musician... What about him?"

Hayley said, "He's a brother."

"Jeez Louise, no, really?"

Hayley nodded. "So what we're saying is it will be really

hard, full of danger, you gotta keep him in fighting shape, keep him from arguing with his elders, but also free concert tickets."

"That's some trade off."

"Yeah. Worth it. Finch Mac is great."

"What you're saying is their dad got around."

"All of them have different mothers, yep. We don't talk about Donnan, the dad, if we can help it." I gulped, I hated even saying his name. "They all had a claim to the throne, but it was Lady Mairead who made it happen for Magnus. She's formidable."

Hayley said, "You met her, she's a Queen bitch. Don't cross her, I do my best to never even talk to her, just don't."

Ash said, "Lochie thinks she's a funny old broad."

I groaned. "Your first job in civilizing him is to gently remind him to never say that in front of her."

Ash asked, "Where is Fraoch's mother?"

Hayley, Emma, and I all said, "Dead."

Ash nodded and put out her arms. "So what do you think, do I look good for a wedding?"

I said, "You look beautiful. Lochie is going to lose his mind."

She giggled, "That's not hard, he's desperate."

Emma joked, "What's it been, a whole week while he waited to make an honest woman of you? The poor guy."

Hayley laughed. "Have you just been beating his hands off you all night?"

"I made him sleep in the hall."

We all laughed. I said, "Man, Magnus and Fraoch would have loved to see that."

"Don't tell them, please. He's barely holding it together."

Emma said, "You *are* good at this."

"Making him miserable?"

Emma said, "No, making him grow up and do the right thing. He needs you, desperately. I think you're going to be good for him."

Hayley said, "I agree, he's lucky he found you."

I nodded. "Definitely."

"Awesome, thank you."

Ash looked really beautiful, we put the final touches on her dress making sure she looked perfect.

I said, "You ready?"

"Well, I've been kidnapped, injured, I was in a battle, learned about time travel, have almost died like fifteen times, so many times. I thought I just met a hot guy in a bar and so far it's been one long near-death experience. So I don't know if I'm ready, but I do love him and I really believe he loves me too, and what do we really ever know about our future? We have today, we hope for tomorrow."

I said, "Time is a wheel, hold on, we're rolling."

She smiled. "You guys keep saying that — time is a wheel."

"It is, we learned the hard way."

She sighed. "Okay then, yeah, I'm ready."

We swept from the room to meet the men outside of the chapel.

CHAPTER 26 - ASH

THE COURTYARD, STIRLING CASTLE - JUNE 18, 1291

*A*s my foot hit the courtyard after coming down the steps I saw Lochie, he was so handsome, clean and wearing a pale blue tunic that matched mine and we hadn't even planned it. He also wore a long deep blue cloak that accentuated his gray eyes. His ginger hair was brushed back, the curls laying on his collar, his jawline had a close-cropped beard emphasizing the angles of his face. He was standing with his nieces and nephews. Archie and Ben were talking excitedly. Isla and Zoe were looking up at him adoringly. He was holding Jack in his arms and laughing at something Ben had said, but then he turned and his eyes fell on me. Even from across the courtyard I could see him take a deep breath. Then he smiled.

I smiled back.

He put his hand over his heart.

That was really really really... he was so big and hot, and he loved me so much, he had rescued me, he was my hero, about to be my husband. I had a million things to be afraid of, but it was all gone, looking at him as he stood in the courtyard of a castle in the bright morning dawn of a day in medieval Scotland. He was all mine. And the way he looked at me, it was as if I, Ash, a waitress who worked at the Palace Saloon, were the prize. If I could ask for one thing in this life, it was that Lochinvar would look at me like that to the end of my days.

He passed Jack to Magnus, and said something to his nieces and nephews, then strode toward me and met me halfway.

He said, his voice low and rumbling, "Ye are beautiful Ash, I am the most grateful man that ye are tae be mine."

I smiled.

He put out his fingers to touch my cheek at my dimple, to lift my chin. He was going to kiss me — he leaned in, but then paused, his fingers brushing away. He straightened and put his hands behind him.

He said, "I look forward tae it."

Fraoch clapped Lochie on the back and smiled at me. "Lady Ash, are ye ready tae marry our brother, Og Lochie? He's a bit scrawny, he daena like tae fish, he daena hae a full beard yet, but he makes up for all his many failings with enthusiasm."

Lochie laughed as red spread up his cheeks.

I met Lochie's eyes. "Yes, I'm ready."

He took my hand, enveloping it in his warmth and led me toward the chapel with his family following behind.

CHAPTER 27 - KAITLYN

THE CHAPEL AT STIRLING CASTLE - JUNE 18, 1291

*M*agnus held the door, beaming at us as we entered. I whispered, "Are you happy?"

"Aye, tis a verra good thing, all thoughts of danger are gone when we hae such a blessin' upon us."

Magnus stood beside Lochie and the priest asked him who speaks for Lochinvar. Magnus said, "I, Mag Mòr."

Then Magnus was asked a series of questions that I didn't understand. He answered, "Of the age." Then he answered, "Nae." Then he said, "I, Mag Mòr, hae permitted the marriage between Lochinvar and his bride."

Then Magnus came to sit beside me in the front row. He picked up my hand and held it on his thigh, while we watched Lochie marry Ash at the altar. Lochie shook with nervousness, she trembled. Lochinvar repeated an oath, promising to "...have and tae hold her, in bed and at the table, whether she be fair or ugly, and for better or worse, in sickness and in health, until death do us part."

And then he gave her a ring and said, "With this ring, I thee wed."

Two young men came in and held a canopy over Lochinvar and Ash's head while the bride and groom knelt in front of the priest. He said a very long Mass. So long that I began to worry about Ash's knees. I didn't worry about Lochie's, he was Magnus's brother, he could probably kneel for a long time if he felt he had to.

It was very sweet seeing Ash's hand resting on Lochie's as the priest prayed over them. I was filled with happiness watching the love they had for each other. I was so proud of Lochie, he had done really well.

The priest asked them to stand, had us all bow our heads in prayer, and then the wedding was over with a kiss.

I put my head on Magnus's shoulder.

"Ye overcome, mo reul-iuil?"

"Yes, I'm just..." A tear slid down my cheek. "It's just beautiful."

"Aye, young love, we are blessed tae witness it. It means a great deal tae me that Lochinvar honored me by doin' it here."

CHAPTER 28 - ASH

LOCHINVAR AND ASH'S BEDCHAMBER, STIRLING CASTLE - JUNE 18, 1291

"So, how did this happen, that we are going to bed at ten in the morning?"

He pulled my gown off over my head. I had already put the veil and my belt on the small table in the room. My boots had been kicked off to the side in a pile beside his.

"I dinna sleep last night, too excited, did ye sleep?"

"Barely, too excited, too."

Our room was small but nice, a good rug on the floor, lots of lush bedding, a canopy, and a good fire roaring in the hearth.

We had wine and some bread and cheese on a table for a snack, but we weren't hungry though we had barely eaten breakfast — it felt like being jet lagged, *this had to have been a full day already, wasn't it?*

I unbuckled his belt and let it fall away. He carefully pulled my chemise over my arms and head and then stood breathless looking at me in my pink underwear and bra. "Och, ye promised me, and here tis, centuries later."

I said, "It was yesterday."

"It feels like forever ago."

I giggled and began pulling his tunic up over his arms and

off, leaving him in a shirt that went to the top of his thighs. I teased, "I'm in my underwear and you're still in a dress."

"Aye, but I am naked under this dress, ye still hae..." He ran his hand through his hair. "Ye hae the pink garments on, tis verra fine, I canna remember what we were talking about."

I giggled again and began pulling his shirt up over and off and he was standing there, absolutely glorious and completely nude, ready to go.

"Oh my."

He scooped me up, lifted me from the ground and carried me to the bed. He carefully put me down in the middle, then all but lunged onto me. Then he was pulling my bra off then fumbling with the latch, and then trying to pull it again. He finally got it off then lay on my breasts, fondling and kissing them, driving me wild. I arched toward him and he looked in my eyes, "Ye like it?"

I nodded. His breaths were bullish, I could tell he was torn between giving me more pleasure, but needing to take me, now, then, there — he kissed me on my breast once, then shook his head and broke away. He began shoving down my panties and climbed on me and entered me, and with his shoulder against my mouth, sweet heat rising, his breaths warm against my ear, he rode me hard.

It was a lovely morning, being ravaged in our medieval honeymoon suite, desperate and hot. In our thoughts we might have wanted to be slow and deliberate, but we lost our minds in the excitement.

Afterwards, he nuzzled his face against my cheek. "M'apologies, m'wife, twas fast."

"Twas perfect." Then I giggled as I raised my foot to show him my pink underwear still looped around my left ankle.

He laughed, crawled down my body, pulled my underwear off my foot, crawled back up, and lay on me, clutching the pink fabric in his hand.

He said, "I am torn, m'wife, tae let ye wear them again, or

tae keep them in m'sporran so I will hae them tae remember the sight of ye on our weddin' morn."

I kissed his forehead, and with my lips pressed there, said, "You will have to follow your heart on that, Lochie, they're yours now, it's your wedding gift from me, do what you want with them."

"Och aye..." He kissed my chest and grew quiet. Then he said, "Ashy, daena tell Magnus that I stole the games from the safe house, I changed m'mind on it."

I nodded. "Yeah, I agree, I changed my mind about it too."

He kissed me again, then grew heavy, he mumbled, "I am verra tired."

"You haven't been sleeping for nights on end." I ran my fingers through his hair, once, twice...

He said, "We hae a lot tae do..."

"There's time to sleep..." I kissed his forehead again, and felt him fully relax and fall asleep.

We woke up and although I had slept deeply, and for what seemed like hours, it was still daylight. Lochie kissed my chest, waking up just after I did. "Och, I am famished."

"Me too." He looked at the pink underwear, clutched in his hand. "I would like tae partake of another delightful stroll through yer gardens, but..." His stomach growled, loudly.

I said, "I was thinking..."

"'Tis about food? Because I am thinking the same thing."

He had his chin on my chest and looked down at me with a merry expression.

"No, I was thinking about how to make it up to Magnus that we showed up without the weapons."

"Ah." He rolled onto his back, with my underwear on his chest. "What is yer idea?"

"I'm new to this, but if we left today—"

"After food. I heard there would be pie."

"Yes, *after* food, after pie, we could go to Balloch and help Quentin move the weapons and supplies here. He has a kid and the animals, I don't think it will be easy, if James is coming with Sophie... I don't know how they manage it, we could help. If we leave today, we come back tomorrow, that's how it works."

He said, "Aye, I agree."

I raised my head. "You agree, just like that?"

"Just like that, tis a good idea." He rolled back on me, kissed my lips, and said, "Let's dress for the meal."

CHAPTER 29 - KAITLYN

THE WEDDING FEAST IN THE GREAT HALL, STIRLING CASTLE - JUNE 18, 1291

*L*ochinvar and Ash came down for the feast. They looked flushed with excitement, blushing about what they had been up to, and deeply in love, as honeymooners should. The feast was grand, and then we had peach pies. Two.

Chef Zach lamented, "I worked on them for hours, it's like baking while camping. Not easy. Followed your recipe though, they look delicious."

Ash blushed, "I'm sure they're perfect. I'm glad you were able to bake them, I promised Lochinvar but we were um... napping."

Hayley laughed.

Lochinvar kissed Ash's cheek and rubbed his hands together excitedly.

Chef Zach handed Ash the knife, and as she sliced the pie, Lochinvar looked delighted. She served him a piece first, a bit of cream poured beside it, and he had the look on his face of someone whose dreams had come true.

I glanced at Magnus and Fraoch, who were beaming proudly on their younger brother.

Ash took a piece and then Chef Zach cut the rest and passed

them out, performing his magic trick of somehow getting the perfect amount of slices out of the pies so that everyone had one, even a teensy bit for Jack.

Cailean loved it, he said, "I hae never tasted such fruit, Mag Mòr, tis wondrously sweet."

We all ate. I said, "Ash, I am very glad you're in the family now, we needed a dedicated pie baker."

Chef Zach said, "I am not going to argue on that."

Magnus pushed back his chair and raised his mug.

Fraoch said, "Och nae, here we go again with the auld man givin' a toast."

Magnus said, "Put up yer mug, stop bellyachin'." We all raised our mugs.

Magnus said, "Lochinvar, I see ye are verra pleased with yer match and I want ye tae ken we are verra proud of ye — May ye both be bless'd with the fortitude of heaven, the full bright shine and heat of the dawnin' sun, the guidance of stars, and the leading glow of the waxin' moon. May ye hae the magnificence of a fire warm in yer hearth, the pleasure of a cool breeze, a firm ground, and a strong foundation for yer home. May yer joys be as sweet as the blossoms in spring and as radiant as the summer heat. May the shower of autumn leaves bring ye faith and fortune, and may yer love be resilient amidst the long winter nights."

We all said, "Slàinte!"

Fraoch said, "Twas lovely as always and especially because twas short."

Magnus laughed as he sat down.

Fraoch said, "... and I agree with every word of it, except he dinna say a word about providin' for yer wife, so I will add, 'May ye hae the good fortune of a fish on yer line at the end of every day."

We all raised our glasses and said, "Hear hear!"

Chef Zach raised his glass. "May your larder be full with cookies, your house filled with the scent of them."

The kids all cheered.

Sean raised his mug. "May yer halls ring with the voices of yer sons."

We said, "Slàinte!"

Isla said, "And daughters!"

Sean raised his glass toward her, "And the bonny daughters as well."

Lochie raised his mug. "Tae my wife, thank ye for takin' me on. I am not always the best man, nor the wisest of men, but I am yers tae my final day and I am verra grateful tae ye for the taste of yer pie."

The kids cheered, we all said, "Slàinte!"

Ash had tears rolling down her face.

He put his arm around her and they kissed.

Once we had calmed, Chef Zach leaned back and patted his stomach, "*Now* what do we do?"

Lochie stood and pulled up a plastic bag from near his feet. The kind of bag that came from a convenience store. "First, I hae presents for all."

He went around passing out a pen to each person at the table, including Jack.

Then he said, "Tis a pen! And a weapon, and a light!" He began unscrewing it to show everyone and the entire table went quiet as we were investigating, and the kids were excitedly opening theirs up and then they cheered when they found all the parts.

Then the kids stood on their chairs and gave a round of applause.

Lochie said, "Och, tis verra grand, I hoped ye would love it."

He looked at Ash proudly. Then he said, "Ash and I are going tae return tae Balloch."

Magnus raised his brow. "When — now?"

Lochie said, "Aye, Ash and I discussed it, we regret not

bringing the weapons, we will return tae Balloch and help Quentin bring them on the morrow."

Magnus nodded. "Aye, Lochinvar, thank ye."

"Ye're welcome."

I said, "Ash, you want to go? You don't want to stay here with us?"

She said, "No, I'm going to go with him, I'm on my honeymoon. We need to stick together while we run the king's guns."

Magnus asked, "Dost anyone else want tae return tae more modern days?"

Archie said, "Not me!" All the kids yelled, "Not me too!"

I said, "I think we're decided, we're happy, English scouts or not, to be together."

Zach looked at Emma, "We're staying too. We'll leave if shit goes down, but for now we'll stick together. It's like Kilchurn, back in 1707, except even fewer comforts."

Magnus joked, "Och nae, Chef Zach, ye calling my castle uncomfortable?"

Zach leaned forward with a fork in his fist. "We had to bring our own utensils."

Magnus nodded. "Aye, I canna deny it, we want for some basic comforts." He grinned, "Tis the *royal* we."

CHAPTER 30 - LOCHINVAR

THE FIELD IN THE KING'S PARK - JUNE 18, 1291

*W*e had many guards around us as we rode tae the field in King's Park.

Magnus put his hands on m'shoulders, looked about tae say somethin', then patted m'shoulders, and dinna say a word.

Fraoch said, "What happened, Og Maggy, ye speechless for once?"

"Aye, he kens what I mean tae say."

Fraoch said, "Og Lochie, ye ken what he wanted tae say tae ye?"

I said, "He wanted tae say he thinks I am braw."

Fraoch said, "Tis what it was, Og Maggy?"

"Aye, verra braw, but also, I meant tae say, if he returns without m'weapons I will put him in a dungeon, and not think anything of it."

I chuckled. "Alright, we are goin' tae get yer weapons, stop bellyachin'."

Magnus said, "I am verra glad of yer wedding, I appreciate ye let me be a part of the ceremony."

I said, "I ken."

Fraoch said, "Och nae, I am surrounded by men who hae gone too soft."

Magnus said, "Ye daena hae anythin' nice tae say on yer younger brother?"

Fraoch waved his hands. "All of ye ken how I feel about ye, I daena hae tae get all misty-eyed."

I joked, "I hope not, I will return on the morrow, tis embarrassin' tae think on ye both weepin' that I went away."

Fraoch patted me on the back.

Magnus pressed the reins of the horse he was givin' me for m'journey, intae my hand, "His name is Finny. Make certain ye bring him back, his favored mare is here."

"Aye, I will get Cookie from Balloch and bring them both home." I patted Finny on his withers. "Ye a good lad, Finny?"

Finny neighed in answer.

Magnus passed me the vessel. He and Fraoch moved their horses tae the side.

I asked, "Ash, ye ready tae go?"

She said, "Uh uh, not at all."

I said, "We goin' tae go through this again?"

"Apparently yes, because I can't motivate myself without being bossed around."

I exhaled. "Put yer hand on m'arm."

"Nope, not yet. I will not, not until I'm ready." She began dancing, stepping side tae side and snappin' her fingers, looking straight at me, dancin'. "I need to distract myself."

Fraoch called over, "What ye doin', Lochinvar? Ye ought tae dance with yer wife."

I huffed, put the vessel under m'arm, and began dancing with her. Finny weaved and bounced his head along with us.

I said, "I will give ye one minute of dancing, Ash, then ye are goin' tae put yer hand on my arm. Dost ye understand?"

She twirled around. "What if I argue?"

"Ye are not allowed tae, five, four, three, daena argue, everyone is watching, two, one."

I stopped dancing. She put her hand on my arm, I twisted the vessel and our jump tae Balloch began.

CHAPTER 31 - JAMES

BALLOCH CASTLE - MAY 29, 1710

*S*ophie was pacing the room, trying to get Junior to calm down. She said, "Och, he is fretful,"

I ran my hand through my hair. "Has been for hours, do you think Lizbeth will come settle him down like she did last night?"

Sophie said, "We canna expect it, she is likely at the opposite end of the castle for peace and quiet."

"Damn this is hard."

She walked across the room to the other window, I was sitting by the hearth, my feet jiggling as if they wanted to run from the room without me having a say in it. I said, loudly, to be heard over his cries. "He's got good lungs!"

"Aye!"

"He's not sick, right? We aren't worried? There's not a real doctor for centuries, but we could jump, if he's sick we can jump."

"Nae, he is well." Junior started really bellowing.

Sophie shifted him to her other arm and he stopped for a moment. She said quickly, "He is just visited with the colic. Tis a common state in bairns."

He began wailing again.

She turned at the wall and paced across the room the other way.

I said, "It's really hard to listen to! He echoes off the walls of this castle."

"M'laird, ye could go up tae the castle walls, or go for a ride, I can go tae the nursery, ye need yer mind cleared."

"Oh hell no, not leaving. Zach didn't leave when Zoe was wailing, I remember — he was all in. I ain't no quitter."

She yelled, "What did ye say, m'laird?"

"Never mind!" I stood up, and began pacing with her, going the opposite way. As I walked to one wall she walked to the other.

She said, "We are going tae wear a tread through the middle of the rug."

"We might." We met at the middle of the room, and I put out my elbow, she hooked hers in mine and we turned around each other, then let go and walked to the corners of the room. The turn quieted him.

I said, "Damn, that worked! Junior likes line dancing! I ought to turn on some music but—"

He wailed again, we turned at the opposite walls and walked toward the middle again.

I put out my elbow and turned Sophie around, then put my arm around her back and rocked her back and forth, starting a two-step with Junior held between us. "Two-steps, one two three. Swing, sway, rock."

Sophie laughed. "He's quiet!"

"Yep, my hot dance moves quieted him down." I spun her around and we looked down at Junior, his eyes big and quiet, calmed, looking up at us as we walked and rolled and rocked and stepped. "If he would give me one second to turn on my music, this would be fun." I danced her around. Then, our arms around each other, we rocked back and forth and she laughed quietly.

"I believe he might be asleep."

"Nah, really?"

I pulled the edge of the blanket away from his face, his face screwed up to cry again. "Nope, not gonna cry, Junior, we are dancing the wails away." I rushed over to my bag and rustled through it for my phone, while he got cranked up again. I turned on my downloaded playlist and I put my arms around her again, "A one-two-three, a one-two-three." We moved around the room rocking and dancing to the song. I hummed along.

Then Sophie said, "I am goin' tae look down tae see if he's sleeping."

"Don't stop moving, we hae to keep dancing."

She looked down. "He's asleep."

I said, "But we have to finish the song."

I rocked her back and forth and continued humming the song about red clay and rolling rivers... Junior finally slept.

Once they were settled in our bed, I whispered, "I'm going to the walls."

"Aye, m'laird, will ye leave me the radio?"

"One is under your pillow, the other in my pocket."

"Good..."

"I'm just going for an hour, I wanted to speak to Quentin, I'll be back long before dawn." I kissed her on the cheek and went up to the walls.

The night was clear and the stars were flung across the sky, it was cool out. Quentin was at the end of the wall. I strolled down the parapet, asking one of the guards I knew by name, "Have you seen Liam tonight?"

"Nae, he ought tae come soon, we had a visitor arrive, he is seein' tae his horse, showin' him tae a room."

"Oh, who?"

He shrugged, but he was notoriously a man of few words, so I met Quentin at the other end of the wall near the stairwell. "You heard why Liam isn't here?"

"Yep, he's showing—"

I heard Liam's voice as he emerged from the closest stairwell. "James! Yer squallin' bairn has quieted enough that ye can come get some peace?"

"You heard him?"

He clapped me on the shoulder. "The whole castle heard him, my Lizbeth said he has good lungs because he is from the magical land of Florida where everyone is verra loud."

A man climbed up the stairwell behind him.

I said, "Robbie! Rob Roy MacGregor!"

Quentin said, "That's what I was about to tell you."

"Well well, if it inna James Raw-Bottom Cook, ye hae returned from yer lands? M'lads and I were cattle drovin', just last month, and I was speakin' on ye — 'Dost ye ken what we need?' I asked m'lads, and they replied, 'What dost we need?' I said, 'We need Raw-Bottom Cook tae drove with us, his tales and songs kept us company on our long rides and his complainin' about the blisters on his arse gave us a reason tae continue on, we had tae get ye tae a soft bed so ye would quit yer squawking."

Quentin laughed. "Oh man, James, I'm glad I was here for this. Rob Roy calls you 'Raw-Bottom'? That's hilarious."

"Very funny, Quennie, it was a long ride, your arse would have been raw too."

Robbie said, "I'm certain yer arse inna chapped anymore, yer wee bum want tae come for another drove?"

Liam said, "He canna go with ye, he has a new bairn, and I winna permit him tae leave us here listening tae his bairn, och nae, ye haena heard squawkin' until ye hae heard the bairn of James Cook — the castle rings with his wails."

"'Tis what I heard when I arrived? Och nae, I bet ye want tae get some rest, the snorin' of Bone MacUilliam would be a fine trade over the shrill shrieks of a bairn — is he a fine son?"

I nodded. "He's a big strong bairn."

"Good, I am glad for ye, when ye dinna hae a bairn at yer auld age I thought perhaps the fae had cursed ye."

I chuckled and nodded. "I used to think I was lucky, but now he's here I want about five more sons."

He said, "Tis a fine idea. Ye hae tae remember tae thrust from the west or ye will end up with daughters." He scowled.

Liam asked, "How many daughters do ye hae?"

"None, because I thrust from the west, do as I tell ye!" He pulled the cork from his bottle of whisky and did a hip-thrust and a hip swirl, three times. "Tis the movement, ye hae tae do it. I heard Magnus had a daughter, ye need tae tell him next ye see him. Daena face yer arse tae the east or ye will hae more lassies and naething but trouble."

Liam said, "Ye can marry yer daughters tae other sons, twill expand yer family all the same and might grow yer lands."

Robbie shrugged, chugged from his bottle, corked it, and stuffed it in his pocket. He said, "How about ye, Black Mac, want tae drove with us?"

Quentin chuckled. "No thank you. I have things to do, though it's an interesting offer — a black guy droving with a bunch of wild notorious Scotsmen in the middle of long ago Scotland, testing my ability to survive — what could go wrong?"

"Drovin' is the best way tae find yer true mettle."

Quentin said, "It's not *my* mettle I'm worried about."

Liam asked Robbie, "So ye told me why ye are here, why daena ye tell Master Cook and Black Mac?"

"I was asked tae take a journey, tae deliver a message tae the Earl, but he inna here, come tae find out, he's in Edinburgh."

Quentin said, "Who asked you to be a messenger?"

"A man I met in a tavern last evenin', he asked about Magnus and Lochinvar, he dinna ask about Fraoch or Sean, and I haena even met Lochinvar, so it struck me as interestin'. Why did this man want tae ken about Magnus and his younger brother's whereabouts? I wondered why he dinna ride up and ask himself, ye ken?"

Liam's brow raised. "Aye, I ken."

Quentin and I looked at each other. Quentin said, "I don't like the sound of this."

Liam said, "We had messengers from Edinburgh here, just yesterday. We chased them off the Earl's lands. Tis the same men?"

He shrugged. "I daena ken, he seemed like the kind of man who wanted the particulars and was used tae gettin' what he wants. I think he wants tae cause trouble with the Earl's family and I knew when the Earl heard of it he would offer a sizable reward for the knowledge."

Liam said, "What was the man's name?"

"He wanted me tae report back tae the tavern after I had ascertained where Magnus and Lochinvar were. Where is Sean?"

Liam scowled. "I am not answerin' ye on anyone's whereabouts."

Robbie took his bottle of whisky from his pocket again. "I am only askin' because Sean would ken the worth of this information. He pays me handsomely, if warranted." He raised the bottle and swigged, capped it, and stuffed it back in his pocket.

I said, "When you report back, tell him, 'Magnus is here, he's in his room, sleeping before his guard duty, Lochinvar is probably brawling down in the courtyard, and Sean is sharpenin' his sword. All the Campbell men are here,' right Liam?"

"Aye, the Earl is away in Edinburgh, but we are protectin' the castle in his stead."

Robbie nodded. He pulled an envelope from his coat pocket, it was sealed with wax. "He wanted me tae give this message tae the Earl." He tapped it against his hand. "He offered me a bag of silver for m'trouble. Are ye certain Sean inna here?"

Liam stuck out his hand. "I will take it, I will see ye given a reward."

Robbie kept the envelope. "Tis tae be closely held, he told me not tae allow anyone else tae open it."

Quentin said, under his breath, "Hold on, I'll go get some coin for Rob Roy." He strode down the parapet.

Meanwhile Liam nodded slowly, he had a familiar look in his eyes, biding his time, moving slowly to his point. "It seems there are many strangers wanting tae speak tae the Earl, comin' around the castle, wantin' tae start trouble."

"Aye, tis the way — once ye find peace and wealth, they are certain tae draw near, lookin' tae exploit yer weakness. That is why I came tae tell ye of m'meetin' with him as soon as I could."

Liam nodded. "Ye can never be too cautious."

"Aye."

Liam eyed the envelope and said, as if nonchalantly, "Who did ye say was tae open it?"

"The Earl."

"But the Earl inna here, dost it mean ye will hae tae go tae Edinburgh? Or will ye pass it tae one of the eldest relatives of the Earl, the man charged with watching over the walls of the castle?"

Robbie looked down on the envelope. "I had a sense of the man, he wanted me tae see the message intae the Earl's hands. I hae a reputation tae uphold."

Liam laughed. "Yer reputation? Dost ye consider yerself of good character, Rob Roy MacGregor? Ye spend more time in extortion than gainin' yer wages in honorable ways. Just a few months ago ye came askin' for money tae keep the reivers from the Earl's cattle, but the only reivers workin' these lands hail from Clan MacGregor."

Robbie chuckled. "Tis true. I keep company with scoundrels, yet... tis often the best way tae ken the measure of a man. Tis why I am here, first thing."

Quentin returned and stood beside me.

Liam put out his hand. "Robbie, I will take the message."

Robbie held up his hands with the envelope in it. "Liam, I

am here tae be helpful, but I will need the silver I was promised. It seems fair. I need it for m'lands. That is why I drove, ye ken, because of the taxes — ye see this is fair." He waved his hands from right to left as he spoke. "I brought ye news, ye give me the silver I am owed. I will give ye the message, and ye will ken all about the man in the tavern. I work for ye, ye are friendly with me. Dost ye agree, Raw-Bottom Cook, Black Mac, we ought tae remain friendly?"

Quentin said, "We *should* remain friendly. I will pay you for the information." He pulled a small bag from his sporran and passed it to Robbie.

He smiled, weighing the bag in his hand. "It has a fine heft."

Liam said, "The *envelope*, Robbie."

He passed Liam the message. It was pale white, the wax seal had a tree on it. Liam asked, "Recognize it?"

It might have been Asgall's seal, but I assumed trees were commonplace.

Liam broke the seal and opened the letter at the fold. Inside was a small device, wires, and a small mic.

Liam said, "What is it?"

Quentin pressed his hands over the mic, and whispered, "The man who gave him the message has been listening to our discussions."

Robbie backed up a step. "Tis the work of demons?"

Liam and Quentin both said, "Enemies of Magnus's kingdom."

I said, "Thank you for bringing it."

He shook his head. "I canna believe I carried it."

Quentin asked, "Was it Asgall? Is that who you got the message from?" He dropped the mic to the ground and stepped on it, crushing it under his heel.

"I think he... aye, he mentioned Asgall. Tis all I know."

Liam said, "Och nae, what did we say, did we say anything of importance?"

I shook my head, "We said that Magnus and Lochinvar were here."

Liam said, "So the man at the other end of the message was listenin' in? Lochinvar returns when?"

Quentin said, "In a couple of days.." He looked up at the stars then said, "James, I want to take you and Sophie and Beaty back home, to one of the safe houses. Then I'll turn around and meet Lochinvar here. Then I'll deliver the weapons to Magnus."

I nodded. "That's a lot of jumping."

"I don't mind. You know how it is. I'm worried about everyone, this gives me something to do."

"Okay, yeah, let's do that. Tomorrow we'll leave. Let's go through the boxes in the morning though, I hate leaving you with a big mess. We can do some packing in the morning, make sure you're ready to take the load to Magnus. I don't like the idea of jumping, but yeah, hell yeah, this dude is all up in our business around here. Should we go to Maine or North Carolina?"

Quentin said, "I think the one in Highlands, North Carolina. We haven't used that yet, close enough to town to get supplies. Once Lochinvar and I take the weapons to Magnus I'll meet you there."

I said, "Beaty and Sophie will be disappointed that they're not meeting up with the rest of the family."

Quentin said, "Yeah, I have a feeling the rest of the family will be meeting up with us very soon."

CHAPTER 32 - JAMES

BALLOCH CASTLE - MAY 30, 1710

I called as I walked up the next morning. "What's going on, Quennie, you started without me?"

"Yep, after the wailing last night, I thought I'd let you sleep in."

I yawned.

He laughed, looking down at his clipboard, placing a check on his notes.

I said, "You got enough weapons? All Magnus really needs is weapons, and toilet paper."

He nodded, looking down, "Maybe Lochinvar will bring more, but I doubt it. I've got these crates full." He pointed at the stack. "We could always use more, I think, not enough. Plenty of the biodegradable diapers here." He tapped those boxes. "Saving some for us, here." He pointed to a box to the side. "This is toilet paper." He tapped another box. "Those boxes have some food, but alas no mac and cheese, I hope Lochie brings it. The more I think of it the more I want it for the kids."

"You'll win World's Greatest Uncle, for sure. Wish I could see their faces."

"You'll be in North Carolina, eating as much as you want."

I yawned, long and loud. "I got more sleep last night, but I'm still on a deficit."

He chuckled. "Ah yes, I remember those days well — Junior actually slept through?"

"Yep, line dancing." He laughed. "Who knows what will work tonight… Night before he went to sleep because of Lizbeth."

"How so?"

"He had gotten cranked up and she knocked on our door, came in, and said, 'Madame Sophie, may I speak tae the bairn?' And Sophie said, 'Aye,' and Lizbeth looked him right in the eyes and focused on him until he stopped. He looked surprised. She said, 'Ye are not a wolf pup, ye are a human with a soul that requires dignity, ye must be more resolute.'" I shook my head, laughing. "He quieted down and went right to sleep. Lizbeth patted Sophie on the shoulder and said to me, 'Get some rest.'"

"Wow, I would have liked to have seen that."

"So what we're learning is Homeboy needs something weirdly different to calm him down. He gets crying like that in North Carolina, I'm going to take him bowling. Man, speaking of bowling, I can't wait to have a grilled steak."

"You'll get it soon enough, though I'm not sure you should leave the safe house for a bowling alley. Is Sophie packing up?"

"Yeah, she wishes she didn't have to go but I convinced her that she misses the fruit."

"You hungry, man?"

"Absolutely."

Quentin wrote on the list, then made a pronounced dot, as if it was final. "That's it, nothing more."

"I don't think that is true, I think you can always think of more. Sucks I'm not going to be there — you got a solar charger for the phones? Zach and Magsy need music."

He rolled his eyes. "We have chargers, they're in…" He pointed at the bottom box, labeled: Juice.

"What about barbecue sauce? You taking some?"

"Your mind is all over the place."

"Sleep deprivation."

He looked at his watch. "Alright, as soon as everyone's packed we'll go to the clearing and take you to the Highlands House."

"Key in the lockbox on the door?"

"Ayup. Money in the safe in the guest room, couple guns in the closet."

I cracked my knuckles. "Sounds like I've got what I need."

"Good." He checked his watch again. "Don't forget your wallet, phone."

"Yeah, I got everything, except the vessel."

"I got that."

CHAPTER 33 - KAITLYN

STIRLING CASTLE - JUNE 19, 1291

*E*arly the following morning, we were in the courtyard, when there was a commotion up on the walls. Magnus turned to look up. Sean looked up. Fraoch told the guard beside us, "Go see what is happenin'."

We all watched and listened.

Then Magnus turned to me, "They are signaling a messenger has arrived, gather the bairns in the nursery tae be safe."

I said, "Keep your radio on. Let me know what's happening."

Magnus, Fraoch, and Sean rushed away.

We herded all the children into the nursery and sat near the fire. The windows looked out on the wrong part of the courtyard. I hated not knowing what was going on.

My hands shook, as I held Jack on my lap, bouncing him up and down like my knees were a horsey.

Emma whispered, "What do you think it is?"

"I don't know."

"Do you think Zach knows we're up here, he was in the kitchen."

I shook my head. "I don't know that either—"

Archie said, "Mammy, what is going on?"

I jiggled Jack on my knee, he squealed with joy. "A messenger has arrived, we have to stay here until we have an all-clear from your da."

He huffed. "You'll tell me if it's more?"

I nodded. Isla sat beside me, put her head on my shoulder, swinging her little legs under the chair.

"Just the mailman, Mammy?"

"Something like that."

Archie narrowed his eyes.

I said, "Any minute now we'll get to go back to usual."

Archie sat down beside Ben on the ground, they leaned back on their arms. Archie said, "What is usual? This sucks."

Ben said, "This is so boring." Then in the next breath he said, "When it's over, want to build a pulley on the west tower?"

Archie jumped up. "Yeah, definitely. There's a basket with a handle on the back wall." They both pulled out the pens Lochie had given them and asked for a piece of paper. I tore two pages from my small notebook for lists, and they both lay on their stomachs and drew their plans.

While the rest of us waited.

CHAPTER 34 - MAGNUS

THE COURTYARD, STIRLING CASTLE - JUNE 19, 1291

*F*our men were ushered in, patted down, and relieved of their weapons tae speak tae me.

I received them in the center of the courtyard, surrounded by my men and guards. Cailean, Fraoch, and Sean stood just behind me. I was irritated at havin' my mornin' interrupted: we were waitin' for Quentin and Lochinvar, we had plans tae make.

Cailean looked pensive.

Chef Zach rushed up, tugging his sleeves down over his tattoos. He had a questionin' look, Fraoch shook his head so he stepped near enough tae listen, keeping a watchful distance.

I said tae the men, "What business have ye? Ye told the guard that ye needed tae speak tae me and hae interrupted my day."

The leader claimed tae be an envoy of the English King, Edward. "I am carrying a message for the Scottish Lord, Magnus—"

He held out a scrolled paper.

"—who has stationed himself in Stirling Castle and must submit himself to the English Crown."

"Nae, there will be nae submitting. I am Mag Mòr, King of Scotland, I am not a mere lord, I daena answer tae any crown."

"Then I am to inform you that Edward would like to meet you at the fields of Kippen—"

Cailean looked shocked. "This is a call tae battle? Ye are askin' the Scottish King tae fight on Scottish lands? Kippen is mere miles away!"

Fraoch said, "This is madness. Tell Eddie that he must come tae Stirling at once tae seek permission tae be on Mag Mòr's lands."

"No, no, there will be no battle... King Edward demands your presence at a peaceful negotiation, one that will benefit England and Scotland, mutually."

I narrowed my eyes. "Continue with the message."

He continued, "At the fields of Kippen on June 20, 1291—"

Chef Zach checked his watch and whispered, "That's tomorrow."

Fraoch said, "I am busy on the morrow, we will hae tae plan it for later in the week."

The messenger continued, "—while Edward looks forward to a beneficial and peaceful treaty with the Scottish Lord Magnus, he will remain encamped and will gather forces until Lord Magnus complies to the request."

I huffed. "If I meet Edward and we come tae an agreement, he will remove himself and his army from the lands of Scotland?"

"He offers his deepest assurances that he will remove his armies after the successful completion of the negotiation." He shoved one of his men forward. "To that end we offer Thomas Harden, second cousin of King Edward, to accompany your entourage and ensure your safety."

I scoffed.

Fraoch said, "A second cousin? If I wanted m'second cousin dead, this is just what I would do with him."

The messenger continued, "King Edward also gives you this holy relic as proof of his steadfast commitment to the peaceful negotiations to come." He handed me a silk-wrapped bundle. I untied the cord and drew the silk open tae see a gold cross.

I said, "Tomorrow?"

The man nodded, "Yes, my lord. I also have this letter, it provides his promise of safe passage." He passed me a scroll.

I scoffed again. "He wants tae give the rightful King of Scotland safe passage on his own lands? This whole thing is ridiculous, I am Mag Mòr, I say who steps foot on my lands — what exactly does Eddie believe we are negotiating? It seems Eddie is trespassin' upon the lands of Scotland, without permission."

Fraoch said, "Instead of negotiating ye ought tae tell him tae get off yer lawn."

"I agree."

The messenger said, "Is that the message you want me to carry to King Edward?"

I shook my head. "Nae, let me speak tae m'men."

I drew my men tae the side and asked, "What dost ye think?"

Cailean said, "'Tis outrageous that he is standin' on yer land, but we daena hae time tae build our army. Kippen is close by, if he has men with him, they could be in our park by sundown."

I nodded, "Aye."

Zach said, "You're a time traveler, maybe you should go to London and make the same demands there."

I chuckled. "Walk up and demand a negotiation with the king at his castle in London? Tis an interesting idea."

Fraoch said, "We will hae our weapons later today, that will give me more confidence. We could tell him we will meet him next week, that will give us time tae prepare."

I said, "But he could grow an army in the meantime. He will be more intractable." I looked at Sean, "What dost ye think, brother?"

"He is a king, wanting tae negotiate with another king, I think ye ought tae meet him. Ye hae more power — he is campin' in a field, ye hae a castle on a hill. By the end of the day ye will hae weapons. Tomorrow ye will hae strength and we can raise an army if ye need it."

I said, "What if this is a trap?"

"He has given ye a hostage and an oath, he sounds desperate tae my ears. I think ye hae the upper hand."

I nodded. I looked around at the rest of the men. "Ye agree with Sean?"

Zach said, "I don't know, I guess it doesn't hurt to talk."

Fraoch said, "We talk, fine. But I daena hae tae be nice."

Cailean said, "I will kill the second cousin at the first sign of trouble."

I smiled. "I ken ye will, Cailean, ye are in charge of the cousin." I added, "Alright, we are decided." I stalked over tae the messenger and said, "Tell Eddie that Mag Mòr will meet him on the morrow for a peaceful meeting about our mutual benefits."

The messenger said, "Yes, Lord Magnus."

"Och nae, this is disrespectful. I am Mag Mòr." I glared. "Ye ken, I hae grown irritable, ye think this is how tis done? Ye walk right up tae my castle and tell *Mag Mòr* tae attend a meetin' on yer command?" I made m'self laugh, heartily.

My guards stepped closer tae the men.

I said tae Sean, "Did ye ken, Sean, that this is a thing ye can do? Ye could gather two men, and ride tae another kingdom, England, for instance, ride right up tae their castle and demand a meeting?"

Sean said, "I dinna realize twas possible, but now I ken."

I said, "Ye could do it, with m'blessing, go command kings tae meet ye. Spain, France, ye could go anywhere and demand kings do what ye say. And who are ye?" I looked at the messenger. "A nobody bringing a message from a nobody king."

Sean chuckled, "If I were doin' it I would at least be the *brother* of the king."

I said to the messenger. "Who are ye?"

"The king's first cousin on his wife's side."

"A nobody for a nobody king. Dost ye remember, Fraoch, that we met King Edward?"

"I do, twas after a day of games. I was verra good at the—"

The messenger interrupted, "What is the point of this?"

I ignored him. "Aye, Fraoch, and what was our impression of the English King?"

"Ye thought he was the blusterin' wind from the back-side of a loch frog."

The man growled. "Daena speak ill of the king."

I said, "He is not *my* king. In Alba I am the only king, Mag Mòr."

The man glared.

I raised my chin and glared back, then said, "Ye can go, tell Eddie I will be there on the morrow."

He turned on his heels and I watched him leave.

Cailean sent a guard tae take the second cousin down to the dungeon.

Fraoch took some of the guards to follow the messenger away from the castle.

I took Sean tae the fields in King's Park tae wait for Colonel Quentin and Lochinvar. We waited all day. Then Sean returned tae the castle for guard duty and Fraoch and Chef Zach met me in the fields for more waiting.

But Colonel Quentin and Lochinvar and m'cache of weapons never arrived.

PART II

CHAPTER 35 - ASH

???? - ????

I slowly woke up to Lochinvar sitting above me again. Finny the horse beside him.

I watched him for a moment, his strong back stretching his shirt, the deep draw of inhale and exhale. I put my arm across his lap, my face against his kilt.

I could go back to sleep. Then I noticed his head swivel left and right.

He whispered, "Ye awake, Ash?"

I mumbled, "Yeah, starting to be."

"Good, because I daena ken where we are."

My heart sank. I scrambled up to sit by him. "What on earth do you mean?"

"It daena look like the clearing and Quentin and James arna here, they ought tae be arrivin', but listen... there is nothing." He stood and peered around in all directions. "And I daena fully recognize the bens on the horizon, we are somewhere odd — did ye feel it?"

"What, the searing pain? Yes."

"There was a tug, it hit me about halfway through, twas like changin' direction."

"I don't know, I just felt like it hurt and kept hurting."

He scanned the horizon and picked up the vessel. "I think we might need tae jump again. I daena ken how we ended up with the wrong location." He held the vessel close to his eyes.

"Is this a thing that can happen?"

"I think so, but I ken I had it set right, ye ken that Magnus looked at it as well, we all knew the vessel was set correctly for Balloch, yet here we are..." He looked all around again. "Och nae, we are in the wrong place."

"I don't want to do it again, let's just live here."

"Here, in this forest, in the middle of naewhere?"

"Sure, this looks great, I love camping."

He grimaced. "Ye love campin'? A tent in the woods — dost ye like campin' when there is a cooler of food? Some drinks? Because we dinna bring anythin', only some bread and a horse we just met."

"I think it would be fine, we can make do. You're hardy and resourceful."

He scoffed. "Aye, but ye canna live in nothing, Ash, ye are a modern lass, ye need *much* more than a plot of land and a stand of trees. There is not one pizza, not for miles. Nae refrigerator, how would ye live without one? Ye would never accept it."

"I'm pretty adaptable."

"I would feed ye rabbit for a week, while we travel tae the nearest loch—"

"It would take a week?"

"Aye, and then once there I would build ye a shack tae live in, and I will hae tae fish for our dinner, Ash, ye will hae all the fish ye want, fish for breakfast and lunch and then dinner, twill be all ye could hope for and ye ken what ye will say?"

"No, what will I say?"

"Ye will say, Lochie, ye are the love of m'life, but if ye feed me fish or rabbit for one more meal I will steal the vessel and go tae Florida on m'own."

I screwed up my face. "Rabbit?"

"Aye."

"Fine, maybe I'm not that resourceful."

He nodded. "I believe we are north of Stirling, but I am nae certain of the year. But I do ken one thing, we will hae tae jump once more, are ye able tae?"

I shook my head. "I need to pee first."

He looked around at the horizon. "Can ye go right there? I daena want ye too far out of m'sight."

"Yeah." I stepped to the other side of the clearing pulled my skirts up and squatted behind a bush. My shoulder felt a lot better, I moved it gingerly in a circle while I urinated, a long stream, splashing on my ankles and shoes which was exasperating. I wiggled my hips in an attempt to dry myself. Not successfully.

He stood there for a second then huffed. "Now I need tae go as well. Stand guard."

I looked out at the woods, sideways glancing at the big horse, while I heard Lochie piss behind another bush.

Something about the loudness of it made me think about how we were alone here, and — *where was here?* I turned and looked in all directions, and it dawned on me, we were alone and lost. "Lochie, we really don't know where we are?"

He was quiet as he finished and returned to stand beside me. "Aye, but tis nae matter. Daena worry on it."

He was looking at the vessel again.

"Should I look, I might have an idea?"

He said, "Nae, I hae this figured out, twas a mistake, I will fix it." He twisted the vessel once more, chewing his lip. Then he showed me. "Dost it make sense tae ye?"

I looked. It was a weird device I had never really looked at before. A string of numbers, a few shapes, a form that felt alive, thrumming with life.

I was scared to touch it.

I shook my head.

He said, "Tis nae matter, I ken tis right. Daena be worried, Ash, I will get ye tae safety."

I said, "I know you will."

He nodded.

"But... I can't believe we have to do it again. I am putting my foot down, no."

He said, "Nae, ye canna say nae, ye hae tae come, och nae, ye are a pain about this, ye ken the bairns daena complain this much about it."

"They have the gold threads, you told me about it, so I know why the kids don't complain." I spoke to the horse, "What do you think, Finny, this is bull-caboodle, right? We shouldn't have to go if we don't want to go."

Finny neighed.

"I winna stand for ye two gangin' up on me, this is not a democracy, ye hae tae come because I am the laird of ye both."

I began doing one-armed jumping jacks.

He said, "Och nae, ye are goin' tae be the death of us." He began doing jumping jacks with me, his kilt flapping, his boots stomping, his hair flying around.

He said, "Five, four, three, ye better do as ye are told—"

"Fine, two, and one."

I put my hand on his arm, clamped my eyes tight and pressed my forehead to his shoulder as the pain began.

CHAPTER 36 - MAGNUS

THE FIELD IN KING'S PARK - JUNE 19, 1291

I said, "Och tis a good night tonight."

Fraoch said, "Tis better outside than in yer drafty castle."

"Och nae, ye are calling it drafty? That is rude."

Fraoch scoffed, "Ye goin' tae argue the point, while we are out in the fields waitin', ye want tae argue during it?"

"Nae... ye are right, tis verra drafty, in most rooms the wind blows right through the timbers."

Fraoch said, "It winna once Sean oversees buildin' the stone walls. All yer troubles will be solved with a good strong wall."

I looked in the direction of the castle, seein' only darkness against the night sky. "Twill be verra good, I canna look up at the walls without feelin' scorn for the last king for the oversight."

Fraoch said, picking at his fingernails in the beam from his headlamp. "When Quentin and James get here they will be lookin' at the Big Picture, while *I* will be overseein' the kickin' of Arsegall's arse. I daena like how we were treated when we rescued Ash, I demand a reckoning."

Zach said, "Excellent use of the term 'Big Picture'."

"Tis a good phrase, it tells ye what ye need tae ken. Colonel Quentin will think on the overall strategy. I will be concentratin' on the death of Arsegall, bleeding out on the dirt by my feet, gaspin' for—"

I said, "Why is he dying at *yer* feet? He ought tae die at Lochinvar's feet, *he* was the one wronged."

Zach said, "The case could be made he should die at Ash's feet, she was the most wronged."

Fraoch shrugged, "Och, twould be fair, and I ken she could do it and she has the training — I hae modern views on ladies as ye hae observed, but I daena ken, Zach, it seems likely it ought tae be Lochinvar *for* Ash. Or myself, because Arsegall is the reason I hae had tae move tae the thirteenth century, it makes me feel ornery. I would like him tae pay for m'mood." He checked his watch. "They ought tae be here any moment, aye?"

I scanned the sky. "Aye, any minute now."

Fraoch nodded and scuffed his foot through pebbles. "I canna wait tae discuss our strategy and pass out the weapons. I am certain Lochinvar must hae thought of ten ways tae kill him by now."

I said, "How come ye arna mentionin' Mag Mòr? I think tis as likely tae be me as anyone."

Fraoch said, "Arsegall kidnapped Og Lochie's wife, I daena think anyone else gets tae murder him but let's agree tae disagree, one of the Brothers Campbell are goin' tae kill him, that is the plan."

We all grew quiet and sat waiting for the storm.

～

Finally, I glanced at my watch in a pool of light from a flashlight. Twas midnight. "I canna believe they dinna come."

Fraoch said, "Aye, we hae waited all day, och nae, what has happened? We need tae assume tis somethin' dire. We hae tae mount a rescue."

I said, "Aye, I canna understand how Colonel Quentin inna

where he said he would be. Tis unsettling, something must hae happened. He haena ever not done what he said he would do."

Fraoch said, "I will go get them from Balloch."

I exhaled, long. "Och, but I need ye, Fraoch, with the English King just miles away... Could I send Sean back, he could...?"

Fraoch said, "Ye ken the answer tae it, Sean canna. He has only ridden a vessel once, he wouldna ken what tae do if he got there and Quentin and Lochinvar werna there."

"Where might they be?"

Fraoch shrugged.

Chef Zach said, "So we're all going to ignore that I'm sitting right here? I can go."

I shook my head, "Nae, ye canna."

Chef Zach said, "Of course I can go, why 'nae, ye canna'? Name one good reason why not. I've ridden these blasted vessels numerous times. I can shoot, I'll be armed. My family is here, safe."

"We daena ken what is happening, and I daena want tae separate any families right now. Emma is likely tae never forgive me." I shook my head looking in the far distance, thinking. Finally I said, "Ye are right, Fraoch, ye will go. Ye can try tae return the followin' day, ye will miss the meeting. But Sean will be here — he and Cailean and I can handle parleying with Eddie."

Fraoch scowled.

"Tis fine, Fraoch, the negotiations are goin' tae be peaceful. If they are nae I will shut them down and set them for another day when ye are returned."

Fraoch said, "I guess twill be alright. And Sean and Cailean are able tae speak medieval arsewipe better than I, I hae forgotten how tae converse as I am almost fully a modern man now, from m'tooth down tae my boots. They will advise ye well, I will go be the hero and rescue Quentin and Lochinvar."

I said, "Maybe ye ought tae take Madame Hayley with ye, then ye will hae two who ken how tae use the vessels."

Fraoch thought for a moment and nodded. "Aye, she will be glad for somethin' tae do. She daena like sitting around a castle much."

I said, "But please daena tell Madame Hayley that I offered her tae go."

"But ye did! What, Og Maggy, are ye afraid of m'wife?"

I chuckled, "Nae, not at all, but all the same, daena tell her twas my idea."

Then I looked down on the radio. "I suppose I hae tae tell Kaitlyn that Quentin dinna arrive, that Lochinvar and Ash dinna return."

Zach said, "Radio ahead so they'll be used to it by the time I get back. They're going to freak out. Man, if I ever needed a kitchen to cook some comfort food it would be now."

Fraoch said, "I am glad ye canna cook here, I would hate tae miss it while I am on m'mission."

I pushed the button on the radio.

Kaitlyn answered.

I said, "None of them came."

She whispered, "Ugh, Magnus, what happened to them?"

I said, "We daena ken."

"What about the weapons? Oh no, you need the weapons!"

Fraoch pulled the radio from m'hand and said, "Will ye tell Hayley tae ready herself tae go? Tell her we leave in an hour."

We had been standin' in a tight circle, usin' the ambient light from the moon tae see enough of each other while we discussed, but now twas time tae return tae the castle. Zach turned on his headlamp and we gathered our horses. But then I stopped, my hand on m'saddle and listened. "Dost ye hear it...?" I turned tae the southeast.

Fraoch stilled. "What...?" Then he said, "Och, ye are speakin' metaphorically."

"Aye, I hear the rumble of an army."

Zach said, "Metaphorically speaking, that freaks me out." He switched off his headlamp.

Fraoch said, "Aye, verra far away, but tis gatherin', dost ye hear it? It sounds like the winds of war."

I climbed on my horse. "Now tis just a breeze, but by the day after the morrow we need tae be expectin' a full-force gale."

Zach said, "I do not like the idea of that. The only storm I like these days are the ones that carry our family."

Fraoch said, "Hear hear." We all mounted our horses and rode toward the castle.

Hayley met us in the courtyard. "Where are we going first?"

He said, "Balloch."

She looked down, "Okay, dressed well enough, I have some modern clothes in case we go to Florida."

I said, "I hope it winna be necessary—"

Sean walked up, "What are ye plannin', Young Magnus? Nae one else arrived?"

I shook my head.

Fraoch said, "They dinna come, Hayley and I are goin' tae check on the family and make sure all are well."

Sean winced. "Och nae, they are certain tae need my protection."

I chewed my lip. "Aye, Sean, though I could use yer help here, the meetin' with the English King is tomorrow—"

Fraoch looked at his watch and said, "Today now, tis after midnight."

I said, "Och aye, tis a terrible time for Fraoch tae leave. I relented because I knew ye would be here for at least a few more days."

He stared off at the walls. "I ken, ye need me, but I am worried on Maggie and m'sons. I want tae see if Lizbeth is well. Liam might need m'help. I understand, Young Magnus, but this is concernin'..." He shook his head. "Nae, I must go see tae them. I can come back, canna I come back once I check on them?"

I watched him, calculating, thinking of the promise made tae Lizbeth, who was worried on him. I had drawn him away from his family intae m'life, twas nae fair... I nodded. "Aye, ye can go tae Balloch, then ye can come back as soon as ye ken they are well. Then ye will build the walls."

Fraoch chewed his lip. "Ye wanted Sean tae be here while I was gone."

"I changed m'mind. He needs tae ken if his wife and bairns are well, there is too much unknown—"

Fraoch said, "I could loop, I could try tae come back later taeday, ye could stall Edward. I could time travel intae the middle of the field and interrupt yer meeting. Och that would be a sight!"

"While that would be extraordinary, the last thing we need is looping, *or* for the King of England tae learn of time travel. Yer presence would be helpful, but perhaps tis not so critical. I am goin' tae tell the English King he is an arse and tae get off my lawn, nae one needs tae be here for it."

Sean said, "Daena start a war."

I said, "A war? A war canna start now, the walls haena been built. The walls need tae be built first or the world inna fair."

Fraoch said, "Probably the world inna fair, and ye ken it." He checked his watch, then said, "Och, I wish there were more hours in a day and the ability tae return on the same day."

I shrugged tae show I was more assured than I felt. "I will meet the English King with Cailean and Chef Zach at m'side. This is the way it will go. I winna argue about—"

Kaitlyn's voice squawked over the radio. "Hey, you home?"

I spoke intae it. "I returned, aye, I am in the courtyard, but now must return tae the field with Fraoch, Hayley, and Sean, I am sending them tae Balloch."

Her voice sounded sleepy. "Oh, Sean too?"

"Aye, he would like tae check on his family and I am makin' decisions in the middle of the night."

Her voice: "On very little sleep."

"'Tis fine, mo reul-iuil, sleep for both of us, I winna be back for a couple of hours."

"Good night, my love."

I turned tae everyone, "Ye ready tae leave?"

CHAPTER 37- JAMES

THE CLEARING NEAR BALLOCH - MAY 30, 1710

a few hours later, with Liam and surrounded by Balloch guards, we were unloading the trailer in the clearing.

I said, "I thought of something Magnus needs—"

Quentin said, "You'll be near stores, start your own list for next time."

Beaty said, "Is this everyone? Ye all hae yer gold bands on the back of yer heads?"

She checked Noah's head for the third time. Sophie checked Junior's head.

Beaty peeked in the bag on her shoulder, at her chicken, Saddle. She also had a leash draped over her arm that was hooked to Mookie's rhinestone collar. She said, "We are all ready, Quennie."

Quentin said, "Liam, I will return long before Lochinvar, but just in case he gets here early, tell him I'm coming back day after tomorrow. Tell him to go ahead and take the weapons if he can, I'll meet him there... I... I'm not sure that this is the right thing to do, but I want to get Beaty and Sophie out of here."

Liam said, "I understand, Black Mac, tis a good plan, I will see ye soon, and I will give Lochinvar the message."

"Tell him we have gone to the North Carolina house."

Liam said, "I hae nae idea where tis."

"He'll know."

I said, "Stay safe, Liam. Give Lizbeth our love, tell her we are sorry about all the drama."

"Och she daena think a bit on it, it fills her heart tae hae ye here, she will miss ye, but I will tell her ye are safely off. Her only sadness will be that the castle will be too quiet from now on."

We all gathered in a circle, I put my arm around Sophie and Junior, and watched as Quentin worked on the vessel. "Man, I hate long awkward goodbyes, we already said it, we need to go."

He twisted the vessel. "It's not working."

"What the hell do you mean, not working? No way."

"Yes, way, it's not working. I'm twisting and nothing is happening, but it also feels dead. Like it's not on."

Beaty's eyes went wide. "Tis out of batteries?"

Quentin said, "That's what it feels like, but… it doesn't have batteries."

I took the vessel and began twisting it and working it.

He asked, "You don't trust me?"

"It's not that, you know how it is, I just have to see."

Nothing happened. I shook it and banged it against my palm.

Liam called, "Is everything well?"

I passed it to Quentin. "Our vessel isn't working!"

He twisted it and then lowered it by his side, exasperated. "I'm supposed to get you to safety and then deliver a pile of weapons and supplies to Magnus and the freaking vessel isn't working."

"But what if we need to get out of here? We're stuck?"

He nodded. "In the eighteenth century, but look at the bright side, at least we're not in the thirteenth century. Magnus isn't going to get his delivery of weapons." He sighed. "He needs the weapons."

I said, "But probably Lochinvar's vessel will work, when he gets here you can use his."

"You think his is working?"

I shook my head. "I have no idea."

He said, "Let's think this through, if ours isn't working, what could go wrong because of this — so much could go wrong."

I said, "First thing, most importantly, we're not getting the weapons to Magnus, he's probably going to need them."

Quentin joked, "Glad he's got a chill temper."

I laughed. "Hide his sword — was there anything he was expecting besides weapons?"

Quentin calculated. "Diapers, toilet paper, I have everything a man needs to stay in a good mood, I just have to get it there."

"Maybe it will work tomorrow."

He narrowed his eyes. "Who did this?"

I said, "Shit, I don't know, could it be Arsewipe? Damn." I looked around at everyone. "I guess it's good we have the weapons now."

Quentin said, "At least Lochie is coming, day after tomorrow. No panic, not yet."

"Unless he's stuck."

"We ought to get back."

We all returned to Balloch.

CHAPTER 38 - LOCHINVAR

AN UNKNOWN CLEARING - AN UNKNOWN TIME

I was up, crouched above her, m'gun in m'hand. We werna in the right place again. I had felt the tug in m'middle — we had been pulled. I dinna ken where or when we were. A different forest, a different mountain in the distance.

I looked over m'shoulder and around in every direction. Nae one was coming, nae one was here tae greet us. Finny was grazing without a care in the world.

The vessel had been set for the right place and time, I ken twas. I dinna hae as much experience as the rest of the men in m'family, but I kent enough. I knew how tae get where I meant tae be, and I had Ash with me. I was being cautious. I was serious about fixing this issue, certain that I knew where and how tae go.

I looked up and saw a streak of a cloud — but twas natural, not caused by airplanes.

Ash was still, her eyes closed, her mouth drawn down intae a deep frown.

I said, "Ash, are ye angry?"

Without openin' her eyes she said, "I'm furious."

I said, "At yer Lochinvar?"

"Yes, at my Lochinvar, you bossed me around again."

"Och, ye told me tae!"

"Doesn't mean it was okay."

"Ye are bellyachin' because I told ye tae listen tae me and we were goin' tae jump. Would ye hae jumped if I haena? Nae, ye would be standin' in the field still."

"You would have left me?"

"Nae, of course not. I would hae stayed, but och, tis not manly for me tae stay and cajole ye tae come, ye must come when ye are told tae."

"I am not okay with taking orders, just so you..." Her voice trailed off. "Why are you so ornery?"

I exhaled, checking behind us again. "Somehow we ended up in the wrong place again."

She said, "But you were sure we were going to the right place!" She sat up, running her fingers around in her hair to set it tae rights.

I asked, "Did ye feel the tug?"

She nodded. "Yes, I did, actually, it felt like I was being forced in another direction, who would do that... ?" She whispered, "Asgall?"

"I am not certain but we must get tae a secluded place in the trees, can ye rise?"

She put out a hand and I heaved her up. I led her tae the cover of the trees. "Pull yer gun, I want ye tae remain here, guard well, I am goin' tae grab Finny."

I pulled my gun from my holster and jogged out, gave a quick glance around as I picked up Finny's reins, and led him tae the woods.

Ash said, "Sorry I didn't help." She patted her cheeks. "Need to wake up."

"Nae, tis fine, we need tae be on guard, but it seems as if nae one else is here." I added, "Och I need a tent."

"Why do we need a tent?"

"'Tis about tae rain."

She looked around at the trees and up at the sky. "Ugh."

We sat down on a log. Ash had opened the flap on Finny's saddle bag, pulled out a piece of bread and tore it in two. She gave me the biggest piece and we sat chewing. "Could the vessel be broken?"

"I hae never heard of it. But I do remember hearin' a story of someone in the family bein' pulled against their will, I canna remember who told the story. I wish I had paid attention tae it."

"We have to jump again?"

"I canna decide. We might need tae search for a village tae find out where we are. Unless..." I dug through the pack until I found a phone tucked in the back. I passed it tae her. "Can ye see if it will work here?"

She worked on the phone for a few moments then said, "It's not picking up any wifi or signals at all. Clock is..." She banged it and held it tae her ear. "I think we must be pre-phone." She climbed tae her feet and stepped away from the tree line tae look up at the sky. "It doesn't feel medieval, right? Do you notice that?"

"Aye, but I canna place why — m'thinking inna as muddled, tis not as dark as it would be."

"I agree. It was really dark when we went to Stirling. This, not so much, but maybe we are used to it... We ought to get higher."

I said, "Aye, tae do it, ye will need tae ride, without complaint, on Finny."

"Without complaint? I reserve the right to complain about anything."

"Fine, ye can complain, I daena mind, but ye will hae tae ride and *he* might mind."

She put her hands on her hips and huffed. "I don't think he likes me."

"Aye, he likes ye, because I like ye, I spoke tae him about it while ye were sleepin'. He just has an expression of dismay because ye daena trust him. He has assured me he is a verra good horse, he just wants yer respect. Ye dinna even say hello now that ye are up, ye forgot tae ask if he was well."

"He needs me to be polite — that is why he looks at me like that?"

"Aye, sort of, tis also just the way his face looks. Tis a horse face. He daena mean anything by it, but he told me if ye are polite he will be accommodatin'."

"Fine." She looked at the horse. "My apologies, Mr. Finny, I should have been more polite. How are you today? I am sorry about the jump, it feels terrible. I'm sure you agree."

Finny raised his head and whinnied. She smiled. "Does he understand me?"

"Aye, every word ye say. Horses ken, they just canna answer because their mouth inna the right shape. That is what Beaty told me about my horse, Cookie. Cookie would answer me if he could, so would Finny. I hae learned tae listen tae what a horse *means* tae say."

"Mr. Finny, I take back everything, I didn't realize I was hurting your feelings. My apologies. I think we are about to ride you now."

Finny nuzzled his muzzle against her shoulder.

She frowned. "Yes, it was ouchy, but it is feeling much better now, Sir Finny, thank you for asking." He stomped his feet and turned so his side was tae us.

I said, "Ye ready tae climb on, Ash?"

She nodded. "Yes."

I pushed her up with my shoulder and held her thigh while she lay there for a moment getting her balance, holding on with her one strong arm, then twisting around and sliding her leg across and finally coming down in the saddle.

"Ye good?"

She nodded, she looked frightened, but said, "Very good, this is fine, not worried at all."

I grasped the reins, fit my boot to the stirrup, and pushed myself up, swingin' intae the saddle behind her. I raised her hips a bit, pushing her forward, so I could fit. She settled down between my legs.

She asked, "Is this good?"

I joked, "Ye mean the way ye are positioned? Or the feel of m'wife between m'thighs?"

"Both."

"Aye, both are good."

I turned Finny tae the path and we left for higher ground and a view.

CHAPTER 39 - MAGNUS

THE FIELD IN KING'S PARK - JUNE 20, 1291

*T*was the middle of the night and we were headed back tae the field tae send Fraoch, Hayley, and Sean tae Balloch. The rumble of our horses and the shifts and movements of the other riders surrounded me, lulled me almost tae sleep.

Sean pulled his horse beside mine, "Wake up, King."

I jerked m'self awake. "I am not sleepin', I never sleep on a horse."

"Och, when ye were a bairn ye slept all the time on horses. I used tae hae tae pinch ye tae keep ye from slumpin' off tae the ground — we would ride taegether and I would be blamed if ye fell."

I chuckled. "Of course ye would be blamed — twould be yer fault, I was younger."

He said, "Maybe I pinched ye because I wanted tae. I canna remember, twas a long time ago, travelin' from Balloch tae Kilchurn — dost ye remember, Young Magnus, the name of the horse?"

"Aye, twas Fiadh." The image of him flashed in m'mind, a verra fine horse. "Ye say he was the regular size of a horse, yet I remember him a giant, large enough tae carry the largest most heroic men across the harsh highlands of Alba. But yet he carried us, wee lads, and seemed proud tae do it. Och, he was fine. I am glad I was livin' in London when he passed, it might hae broken m'heart."

"Ye were always soft toward the horses and Fiadh was one of the best." Sean was quiet then said, "I am sorry I am leavin' ye, Young Magnus, I ken tis a difficult time..." His voice trailed off. He pulled the horse off the path and slowed tae allow me tae pass.

I said, "Daena worry, Sean, tis not something ye need tae dwell on, I agree with ye, ye hae tae go home, ye must make certain Maggie and yer sons are well. We need tae ken of Lizbeth." He pulled his horse behind mine.

I added, "If ye daena check on Lizbeth she will hold it against us."

"Aye, that she will. Tis the whole reason tae do anything, tae keep our good names with Lizbeth."

We continued on.

We came tae the field and settled around the boulder. They were going tae leave the horses with me, we would need all we had tae move men tae the meeting with Eddie.

They were taking a gun each and some small supplies, but they dinna need much because they were going to Balloch. That castle would hae what they needed, and Liam would meet them in the clearing.

Fraoch said, "I hate leavin' ye at a time like this, Og Maggy, it goes against m'better judgement."

"I ken, but we decided already — ye will return on the morrow, without the three day buffer, I will regale ye with stories about my meeting with Eddie in Kippen. I will hardly miss ye, tis only a parley with the English King, he is an arse, but nae match for me."

Sean said, "I ken ye think high on yerself—"

I joked, "'I ken ye think high on yerself, Yer *Highness.*'"

He chuckled. "Yer arrogance might be yer undoing. I wish ye would demand tae speak tae him on *yer* terms, Young Magnus, ye could send a messenger, refuse tae parley until we return."

Fraoch said, "I agree with Sean. Ye could refuse."

I said, "Och, this sounds like yer arrogance, not mine. Dost ye think me incompetent tae negotiate on a battlefield? Ye think I need m'older brothers around me for a good outcome? Ye think I might fail!"

Fraoch and Sean looked at each other and nodded.

I scoffed.

Sean joked, "Tis not that we daena trust ye, Young Magnus, tis that we think ye are but a wee lad who needs our wisdom and guidance."

Fraoch grinned. "Aye, Og Maggy, daena fret over it. We arna insultin' ye, we just daena think ye can do it without our help."

I scoffed louder. I said, "Madame Hayley, what dost ye think?"

"I don't want to get in the middle of it — between my husband and the king and his older brother? Nope. But I will say this, we'll be back tomorrow. It'll be more helpful to have us here, and the sooner we go, the sooner we get back."

I reached in the saddlebag on Dràgon, pulled out a vessel, and passed it tae Fraoch.

He looked down on it while Hayley and Sean drew around him. Hayley slung her bag over her arm.

Fraoch flashed a light beam on the vessel, and asked, "Tis set?"

"Aye, tae Balloch."

"Are ye certain — it feels odd."

"I am certain." I dug through the saddlebag for another vessel. I turned on a small penlight, held it in m'mouth pointed down on the vessel in my hands, looking it over. "This one is set tae Florida, that one is..."

I held the vessel up tae his. "Aye, see, that one is set tae Balloch. I ken it, I set it earlier in the day."

"Feel it though, it daena hae the heft. It feels dead."

I felt the one in my hand, it also felt dead. He placed his vessel in my palm, I weighed them both. "They feel the same, but tis not... they daena feel right."

Hayley poked it, nothin' changed.

I was tired, and grew exasperated. I shook my head. "Tis fine, tis ready tae go. I am goin' tae draw the horses over there, then ye will twist it."

I passed the vessel tae Fraoch and drew the horses tae the side.

I chewed my lip as I watched.

Sean clamped his hand on Fraoch's elbow, Hayley had her hands around Fraoch's other arm. Fraoch was looking down on the vessel.

I called across tae them, "Why arna ye goin'?"

Fraoch said, "I daena want tae say—"

"Why not?"

"Because ye are crossed."

I huffed. "Why inna it goin'? Ye ken how tae do it? Daena ye ken?"

"Aye."

"But och nae, nothin'?"

"Nothin', tis dead."

Sean said, "What does this mean?"

I stalked across the field tae them, put out m'hand, and throwin' caution tae the wind, twisted and turned the vessel. It remained idle, without any stir, still and lifeless.

Sean said, "I canna go home?"

Without answering I twisted the other vessel, then I shook my head. "Nae, we are all stuck. This has happened before. It involved Lady Mairead, controllin' us. But I am certain she wouldna block us from travelin', tis unsafe tae block a man from his free passage."

Fraoch said, "As well as bein' infuriatin'."

"Aye, tis. I daena like tae set out on a voyage and hae m'vessel break down."

The sound of horse hooves rumbled, growing closer through the forest. I drew my gun and turned Dràgon tae meet the men as a large group of them came at a fast clip across the field.

Sean tensely asked, "Who is it?"

I watched for a moment, then relieved, answered, "My soldiers, I sent them tae scout."

The leader pulled up in front of me. "Yer Majesty, we are returnin' from Kippen."

I asked, "What did ye find?"

"Their encampment, they hae raised a tent for yer parley with Longshanks."

"How many men?"

A different soldier said, "I counted fifty."

Sean said, "Young Magnus, ye will need tae take seventy-five."

I said, "That is a great many men tae peacefully negotiate."

The men said, "Aye."

I said, "Return and keep watch, report tae me if ye see him gainin' more troops."

The soldier turned his horse tae his men and began directing them, while I said tae Fraoch and Sean. "We need tae return tae the castle, prepare for the meeting."

Fraoch said, "That is the one fortunate part of this, Sean and I will be here for the parley."

Sean said, "Aye, at least there is one good thing…"

∼

We crossed the damp field, cool in the darkness.

Fraoch said, "Och, we are goin' tae be doused with rain, the weather is turning."

Sean said, "Change is upon us."

I had been quiet.

Fraoch said, "What ye thinkin' on, Og Maggy?"

I chuckled. "I think I fell asleep again."

Sean laughed.

I ran my hand up and down on my face, tryin' tae reinvigorate m'self.

Fraoch said, "Maybe the vessel not workin' was by chance—"

I said, gruffly, "Two vessels."

Fraoch said, "'Two vessels' not workin' was by chance, *maybe*. I will try it again in a few hours, perhaps twill start workin' again."

I said, "By chance."

Fraoch said, "Och, ye are in a mood. I am sayin' we need tae keep checkin'."

Hayley said, "Man, I hope everyone is okay."

Fraoch said, "Aye, we are the rescuers and we are stuck, I hope someone is out there preparin' tae rescue us."

The thing that kept turnin' in m'mind is that somehow I had lost m'upper hand.

CHAPTER 40 - ASH

CRIEFF, SCOTLAND - OCTOBER, 1683

*W*e rode to the top of a hill and looked out over the valley. I said, "It's not modern."

"Aye, but tis not as old as we hoped." He shifted in the saddle, looking around. "We are north of Stirling, Balloch ought tae be over there."

He pointed behind us.

"So what should we do?"

"I see a village there. See it?" He pointed. "I believe tis Crieff, there is a market. We will go there, get some information, some food. We can spend the night if we need tae, there is... ought tae be, an inn." He turned our horse and we rode down the path through the woods, headed in that direction.

I actually loved the ride, the gentle sway of Finny as he picked his path, rocking beneath me as Lochie's arms were around me, holding the reins. I looked down on Lochie's hands, bound muscles and powerful strength held in his tendons and the veins traversing them. I felt an almost electric charge when his forearm rested on my thigh, and my back rocked against this chest.

The woods were close but then opened up onto a road, and

there were low stone walls marking fields. Peppered throughout were cows and sheep grazing and farmers working near low, long, pale houses with bushy thatched roofs.

Cattle meandered along the road, sometimes blocking our way. A cart rolled past us. Lochie stopped the driver and briefly conversed. I tried to tell by the surroundings what the time period was, but everything just looked old.

I was no help at all.

Then the man drove the cart away and Lochie urged Finny into a walk. He shifted and looked around in all directions and said, "He dinna ken the exact date, but he believed the year tae be 1683." His eyes drew away and he looked thoughtful.

I said, "Does that date mean anything?"

"I canna think of any reason why we would be here. Tis... not a usual time. If Magnus has been born he is likely verra young, tis likely there inna time travel here."

He counted on his fingers. "I daena even ken if Lady Mairead is around. Hae Sean and Lizbeth been born?"

He added, "I dinna ken... *But* he did tell me we are close tae the time of the big market gathering, drovers from all across Scotland come tae sell their cattle, twill be likely crowded and rowdy in town."

"Should we try to jump again?"

He looked over his shoulder. "We are verra close tae the village. I need a meal and tae think this through. I think we ought tae continue on."

I nodded and we grew quiet again as Finny headed toward the village.

I finally asked, "So as far as you know this doesn't happen... like, *usually* when you want to time jump it takes you where you mean to go?"

"Aye, it always has before."

"Damn it. That's not good."

We left Finny in the stables behind the village inn and went around to the front entrance.

Moving from the bright outdoors to the dark interior, it took a moment for my eyes to adjust. The downstairs of the inn smelled like smoke and that sweet sickly breath of a hangover day. The wood floor was sticky with old ale. The carved chairs looked rickety. There was a surly man behind the bar, and a woman carrying a plate of food from a darker room in the back. It looked like every dive bar I'd ever been in, but with an ancient vibe. Men were packed around some long tables through the middle of the room, being boisterous and loud. But near the hearth was a small open table.

Lochie nodded toward it. "Grab us two stools, I will get some ale and a meal."

He went to the bar while I found two stools and dragged them to the table. Using my peripheral vision to watch the men in the room, while not making any eye-contact. The two men at the next table sized me up, narrowing their eyes, and elbowin' each other, speaking in whispers.

I ignored them, directing my gaze at the fire, heat drawing up my face. I wasn't dressed right, I hadn't covered my head, I didn't know much but I knew my hair was too short.

Lochie returned with two ales. He snarled at the men and they turned away. Lochie sat down, ran his hands through his hair, then took my hand in his. "I am sorry Ash, I will get us from this place, but I needed sustenance tae be able tae think through our predicament."

"Me too, Lochie. But this is okay, I've been in a dive bar, and I worked at the Palace Saloon, I know my way around drunks."

"Good, so here is the issue, we dinna make it tae the eighteenth century. I believe we are in the seventeenth — what did the man say?"

"I think you said it was 1683."

"Aye, that sounds right, though tis the wrong date. We are

not in Stirling or Balloch, but halfway between. And we felt the pull — ye said ye felt the pull, dinna ye?"

I nodded. "It's like someone dragged us to another place. But why here?"

He said, "This is a small town in the middle of nowhere, a couple of weeks afore the big market convenes. It daena make sense. But we must be on guard, whoever brought us here might be layin' in wait."

"But wouldn't they have picked us up when we first landed? Or when we were alone on the path? We've been alone most of the day, if someone wanted us they could have just taken us. Now that we're in an inn it seems like we are safer, you know? At least there are witnesses."

"'Tis true."

"Maybe someone just moved us out of the way?"

He narrowed his eyes. "Out of the way from what...?"

"I don't know... like who do you think? Who would know how to do this?"

"Perhaps Magnus, though he's never mentioned it, definitely Lady Mairead."

"And where is Lady Mairead?"

"She's in Magnus's kingdom."

"The one in the future?"

"Aye, his *other* kingdom, though with two we might need tae call it an empire."

He was holding my hand, stroking the back of it with his thumb. Then he let go to lift the ale to his lips.

I asked, "So are we going to stay here tonight?"

"Aye, I procured a room."

"It's a honeymoon."

He chuckled. "Aye, I hae been makin' excellent decisions, I am verra glad we got married. Ye would feel so sorry for me if I had tae sleep out in the hall in this terrible inn."

I nodded. "And I'm so hot after riding with you, I don't know if I could bear it."

He chuckled. "Och, m'wife is enjoyin' horse ridin', I knew she would."

A loud banging sounded behind us. Men raised their voices. Lochie laughed, shaking his head, slowly. "Yet when the tavern is full of drunks I daena think I will be able tae sleep with ye, even if I wanted tae—" He looked around the room, a cacophony of shouting and laughing, two guys drunkenly singing. "I will hae tae take watch in the hall. This is a rough inn, and the drovers are fillin' the town with their stench and cattle."

I pouted. "Darn it, I was looking forward to a hotel room and a nice bed."

He joked, "And I paid extra for the private room so we winna hae tae share the bed with Old Sleaze-bag there, fartin' and snorin' all night."

I gulped. "Ugh, sharing *rooms* is a thing? I'm relieved you're rich."

He looked around at the rafters and the walls. "This is rich? Och nae, I would hate tae see poor."

Another loud bang. "When ye met me I was well-rested and comfortable, not a care in the world, and now look at me, I must sleep upright in passages with one eye open." He turned his head, with one eye open, and glared at the men beside us, they abruptly looked away.

I laughed.

Food was brought to our table, wooden bowls with a gravy spooned over a type of fowl. A hunk of bread on the side. We were given spoons. Lochie pulled a switch blade from his sporran to cut the bread into smaller bits and we shared it to spear the meat and lift it to our mouths. "Like pirates."

He said, "Aargh."

I asked, "Do you know any pirates?"

He said, "Aye, Jack Sparrow, Barbossa, Turner—"

I laughed, "I meant real life pirates, those are from *Pirates of the Caribbean!*"

He shrugged. "I hae spent many hours watchin' the movies with the nephews, I feel as if I ken them."

When we were finished eating, he pushed away his plate and rubbed his ear. "The crowd is growin' louder and even more rowdy, we ought tae go up tae the room afore the brawlin' starts."

Carrying a candle he walked me up the creaky stairs to our room under the eaves of the thatched roof. There was a bed in the middle of the floor, covered in a ratty blanket, a small table beside it, a chamber pot. I pulled a small flashlight from my bag and used it to light my way to the dark corner where I pissed in a loud stream while Lochinvar put our bag down and searched through it. My pee was so loud I started giggling, hysterically. Downstairs the drunk men began to really belt out a song.

He began to laugh with me. "Tis a verra fine establishment, aye?"

"Four stars. No notes." I hiccuped and shook my hips, trying to dry myself. I let my skirts down, smoothed them, and placed the flashlight on the bedside stand with the beam illuminating a small bit of the space. I sat on the bed while he peed in the pot. His stream of piss being quite loud made me giggle again. I said, "Now, *this* is the height of luxury."

I wiped my tears of laughter. "Has anyone noticed we're lost do you think?"

He shook himself to dry and dropped his kilt. "Ye can return the day after ye left, nae one would even notice we are gone unless we canna fix it... I daena ken, but they will notice eventually."

I kicked off my shoes and lay down on the bed. I shifted to make a soft place under my shoulder, but the mattress was thin in spots, bunched in others. I struggled to fluff it. "Because I think I should start my..." My voice trailed off.

I had left my menstrual cup back in Stirling in my suitcase, because I was only going to be on this errand for a day, two days tops. What if I was here for longer? I couldn't even imagine how to deal with getting my period back here. What would I even do...? There wasn't underwear, apparently. I had never been offered anything to wear underneath my skirts and hadn't asked the women of the family how it would work. It was fine, most days, there was all this fabric. I had grown used to no underwear, frankly it was better than wearing an uncomfortable pair that stuck in my craw or were too tight, but without underwear or my menstrual cup I had no way to deal with my period.

Lochie sat down on the bed as another chorus started downstairs, louder than the first. He asked, "What dost ye mean, ye should start yer what...?"

"My period?"

He looked at me blankly.

I whispered for some reason, "Menstruation, the... you know my monthly flow?"

His eyes went wide. "Och, yer curse?"

"Yes, my curse, I don't know what... or how..."

He grimaced comically. "We will need tae get ye tae Stirling so ye can ask Kaitlyn tae advise ye. Ye canna ask anyone here, they are medieval, twill be terrible advice."

A loud ruckus came through the floorboards to our ears. He listened. "The brawlin' has begun. We need tae remain dressed." He pulled the blanket up over my legs.

"We might hae gotten more rest sleeping in the woods."

He nodded. He was sitting on the edge of the bed, his elbows on his knees, in thought.

I said, "My main point is how many days have I been gone?

I'm trying to calculate how long it's been since I got my... um *last* curse."

He shook his head.

I counted on my fingers. "I think it's been three days in the compound, maybe four, but then two days before I left, three days in Balloch... half day in Florida, our wedding, it all feels like two months — with time travel, does the menstrual cycle last the same amount of time? Do the days still count the same?"

"I canna say."

I grinned up at him. "I am borrowing way too much trouble. We will be back in Stirling long before I start. I'll have my supplies, for sure. Kaitlyn will be able to advise me, she's a Queen, she is *not* going to go caveman-style."

I pulled the covers up to my chin and looked up at him sitting there on the side of the bed. "You sure you don't want to come to bed?" The singing from downstairs grew even louder.

His brow went up. "Aye, I verra much want tae, my randy wife, but I—"

Loud stomping footsteps passed by our room. "...I winna be able tae enjoy m'self. I must guard yer door." His hand stroked down the blanket on my hip. "I canna imagine what m'brothers would say if they heard I was accosted with my pants down in an inn full of drunken drovers."

"You, m'laird, don't wear pants."

He smiled.

Another man stomped down the hall. There was a bang on a door near ours.

He clapped his hand down on my hip. "I will sleep on the morrow. I will guard ye, m'lady, and we will leave at first light."

He leaned down and kissed me, pausing there for a moment, his mouth against mine. Then he climbed onto the bed, on his knees, and kissed me long and deep and lingeringly...

Until there was more banging. His head dropped to my shoulder.

"Och nae."

I said, "I'm so sorry you have to protect me, promise you won't get tired of it? It's our honeymoon and it seems like, I don't know, such a *bother* to have to take care of me."

"Ye are my heart, Ash of the Tree of Life. I am won. Daena worry, I am goin' tae go guard yer door."

"I feel terrible that you'll be awake while I'm sleeping."

"What will ye dream of?"

"You, m'laird."

He smiled. "See, tis all worth it."

He drew away and slipped from our room. I heard him, leaning against the door out in the tight passage. Footsteps went by, he grunted, menacingly.

CHAPTER 41 - MAGNUS

ON THE WAY TO KIPPEN - JUNE 20, 1291

I climbed the steps tae m'chamber and entered. I put a log on tae beat back the chill and then I crept tae our bed. Kaitlyn was asleep, Jack was sprawled in the middle of the bed with his arm thrown out looking verra pleased with his comfortable position. I knelt beside the bed and smoothed back Kaitlyn's hair tae wake her up.

She mumbled, "Hi... you're back?"

"Aye, and I still hae Sean, Fraoch, and Hayley with me. They couldna leave, the vessels arna working."

"Oh no." She raised her head and peered around in the darkness, "It's late at night, are you coming to bed?"

"Nae, I hae tae meet with the English King. I will leave at dawn, tis only a few hours away. I will sit up and take a guardsman's nap."

Her face drew down in a frown. "What is a guardsman's nap?"

"'Tis when ye sleep sittin' up with yer eyes open."

"Ah... you'll be tired."

"I will be, but there is too much tae do, I must be ready. Where are Archie and Isla?"

"Sleeping with Ben and Zoe."

I leaned over and kissed her, then went tae the hearth in the outer room. I sat, leaned back, watching the fire. My elbow rested on the arm of the chair, my chin restin' in my hand. I watched the fire and considered what I was goin' tae do.

I might have slept... though I felt like I dinna at all. But then there was a soft rap on the outer door. I got up as my page entered tae help me dress. I washed m'face in the bowl and toweled off, while the page passed me a fresh shirt. I pulled it on over m'head and brushed m'teeth while he tied the back of my hair. We worked quietly in candlelight.

I had recently shaved, so my beard was close cropped, and twas too dark tae do it again, anyway. I pulled my arms intae the sleeves of a coat and the page buckled my sword belt around my waist. I pulled on my boots. He helped me put on the cloak. "There will be rain, Yer Majesty."

"Aye, the weather has turned."

I returned tae the bed and kissed a sleeping Kaitlyn on the cheek. I kissed Jack on his forehead, then shuffled down the hall tae relieve m'self in the garderobe.

I wondered if I ought tae wake Archie and Isla, but the castle was verra quiet, and I dinna want tae bother nor needlessly frighten them. I was certain this would be the first of many negotiations with the English King. He had been interferin' in Scottish succession for years, and I doubted he would remove his troop from m'lands after one meeting. But I would threaten him. Twould be a good start. Then I would use my power as a time traveler tae...

Why dinna the vessels work?

Twas unsettling, I had been strong, just yesterday, and now I was weakened.

I left the stairwell tae find a large contingent of m'men in the courtyard, gathered near the stables, preparing tae go. Fraoch and Sean met me and Cailean passed me a bundle of cloth wrapped around a bread and a sausage. "For yer breakfast Magnus."

I said, "Nae coffee?"

He said, "Nae, though tis needed this morn. Instead ye hae ale."

I sighed. "Coffee is one of the things Colonel Quentin had promised tae bring."

"I will pray for his arrival, Yer Majesty, I hae acquired a taste for the bitter drink with a bit of white sugar."

I asked, "Tis one of the greatest things in the world. Where is Chef Zach?"

Fraoch said, "I expect him down any minute now."

We gathered our men and horses and moved toward the gate when suddenly I heard Kaitlyn's voice, "Magnus!"

I turned tae see her with Jack in her arms, leading Archie and Isla, rushing across the courtyard, wearin' a robe and lookin' disheveled yet beautiful. "You were leaving without saying anything!"

I swept her intae m'arms. and kissed her ear. "My apologies, mo reul-iuil, I am not thinking straight, twas tired... a great deal on my mind."

She nodded. "I understand." She kissed me. "Jack wanted to say goodbye."

Jack put out his arms and climbed into mine. He waved at Kaitlyn. "Bye-bye."

I said, "Jack, ye canna come, ye must stay here with yer ma."

Archie said, "Can I come, Da?"

I narrowed my eyes, considering, as Isla hugged me around the waist.

I ruffled her hair and said tae her, "Ye hae a good day, I will see ye at dinner, wee bairn."

Archie said, "You didn't answer, does that mean I can come?"

Kaitlyn raised her brow. "Are you considering taking him with you?"

I nodded, thinking... He was only eight, but he had been consumed with worry. I dinna want him tae spend the day worryin' about this. The ride tae Kippen was a ride he could do. He could watch the meetin' and the negotiation... Twould be a lesson in ruling.

I said, "Twill be a long ride, then a longer meetin'. Twill be verra borin' and ye winna hae Ben with ye."

Just then Chef Zach came up with Ben following him. "Sorry Magnus, slow getting going, but I'm ready. Let's go kick some English ass."

"We arna kickin' ass, we are *discussin'* with arses."

"Damnit, that doesn't sound nearly as fun."

Archie ignored us, his gaze directed at me, earnestly. "Da, I still want to come, can Ben come too? Me and Ben. I won't bother you, I promise."

I considered. Then I looked at Chef Zach. He shrugged.

I nodded. "Okay, ye and Ben can come, but ye hae tae listen, ye canna speak up, ye hae neither the vocabulary nor the accent, and twould be dangerous. Ye must not cause any trouble, ye ken?"

Kaitlyn asked, "Are you sure?"

"Aye, I am sure, twill be a good lesson for the lads tae see kings speak. And we will hae many guards." I said tae Archie, "But twill likely be cold and wet, both of ye grab cloaks and nae complainin' on the rain."

Ben said, "Complain about the rain? This sounds awesome!"

Chef Zach said, "Alright boys, let's go get cloaks and your horse. Katie, you'll tell Emma I took Ben with us?"

She said, "Yes, but be careful, bring them back if it's... if it's too much."

Archie hugged Kaitlyn goodbye. And then we took our leave and went tae the men gathered near the gates. Fraoch put out his fist and he and Archie and then Ben fist-bumped.

We all climbed on our horses to go as the first beams of dawn emerged on the east horizon, with Haggis joggin' along beside us.

I had gathered around me an army of men, most were from this century. Fraoch and Sean were from the eighteenth century — Chef Zach was tae be my only modern advisor, traveling with two young lads who had been raised on chicken nuggets and Fortnite. I watched them riding on the same horse, cloak hoods pulled over their heads as it was beginning to mist. They were pointing around at cool things they saw in the fields as we crossed King's Park under the gray sky of a moody dawn, promisin' an unrelentin' day of rain.

The lads were goin' tae learn a lesson about long cold wet rides and medieval treaties. Twould likely be a verra boring day.

I asked, "Did ye get a lot of sleep, Chef Zach? I am livin' vicariously through ye."

"I got a lot, though I was nervous about today. You get any?"

"None, except a moment here and there while ridin'."

"Why do you think the vessels aren't working?"

Archie said, "Da, the vessels aren't working?"

Ben said, "Uh oh."

I said, "I daena ken, but I think it has something tae do with Arsegall."

Fraoch said, "Aye, tis definitely his arsery."

I said, "But I canna focus on it right now, *now* we hae Edward tae deal with."

Fraoch said, "Eddie *loves* tae be the center of attention."

Zach rubbed his hands together causing his horse to veer. "Whoa, oh… whoa!" He pretended tae almost fall off while he directed the horse back to the path. "Phew, that was close. Follow the army, horse! Come on now, you have one job, follow all the other horses."

The boys laughed.

Ben said, "Dad! You have to hold the reins with both hands!"

Chef Zach held the reins in both hands up high. "Like this?"

The boys giggled again. "No Dad, you look ridiculous."

Haggis barked as if he were insulting Chef Zach too.

Chef Zach laughed. "I know how to do it, Haggis!" He held the reins in one hand, looking like a pro. "What I was going to say, before the boys started micromanaging my driving, was I can't wait to watch you school the English King. Then I can't wait to watch you deal with Asgall."

"Aye, first, I hae tae deal with a medieval king — there will be a medieval solution, then I will deal with the time traveler with a time travel solution. First one, then the other." I pretended tae snore.

The boys giggled again.

Fraoch said, "Og Maggy, ye need a nap already? We just left the castle!"

I rubbed my hands up and down on my face again tae wake m'self up. Then pulled my hood over my head, so the drips of rain didn't roll down my face.

Sean said, "Except yer time travel vessels are broken, Young Magnus — twill be difficult tae find a time travel solution without a working vessel."

Fraoch said, "This is true."

I remained quiet as we rode.

Archie and Ben rode well on the same horse, talking and laughing with each other, and sometimes talkin' tae Haggis. There were moments when it was easy tae forget what we were doin'. We knew it had tae be past sunrise, but the sky was covered in fat gray clouds, weighty in the sky. A drizzle greened the forest. Quiet all around, damp and soggy, the air was heavy with the fresh scent of rain.

. . .

I had drawn back tae ask Cailean a question, now I sped my horse tae pull up beside the boys, "Ye stayin' dry?"

Archie said, "This is fun!"

I chuckled and drew ahead of them on the path.

I loved ridin' on a rainy morning. But then m'eyes settled on my surroundin' soldiers, dressed as if for battle. Twas jarrin'. We were meeting an adversary, the men depended on me tae negotiate well, tae stop a battle afore it had a chance tae begin.

There were long periods of quiet, and as we drew near we began tae hear the noise of a large encampment.

Some of my soldiers returned from scouting ahead. "The camp spreads well beyond the field where ye will be meetin', Yer Majesty."

How did it grow so large without notice?

"Still fifty men, ye counted?"

"Aye, seems that way. Though there may be more in the tents."

"Let me ken if ye hear anything more."

They rode on ahead.

I pulled my horse alongside Archie. "Archibald, I want ye tae ken, ye are tae be quiet and tae stand in the back, daena draw attention tae yerself. Dost ye understand?"

He nodded. "Yes, Da."

I said, "Ben, ye understand?"

"Yes, Uncle Magnus."

"Good, ye are about tae meet the English King. He is full of self-importance, but I will do m'best tae prove him unimportant. Ye are tae watch and listen."

Chef Zach said, "You got this Mags!"

"Thank ye, Chef Zach, did I tell ye I hae met him before?"

Archie asked, "When?"

"At a tournament. Yer Uncle Fraoch competed in the sword fighting, I partook of the joust."

Archie said, breathlessly, "You *jousted?*"

"Aye, I won the day, and then Edward called me tae dinner and wanted me tae bow in front of him and I refused. I told him that I was goin' tae be the Scottish King and I wouldna bow in front of any Englishman."

Chef Zach said, "Hoowee, I would have liked to have seen that."

Fraoch rode up, and brushed rain off his face. "Ye tellin' stories again, Og Maggy?"

"Aye, I am tellin' about m'meetin' with Edward after the joust."

"Och, I thought ye were goin' tae get us killed, Og Maggy. Boys, tis rarely good tae bad mouth yer betters, but in this case twas Og Maggy, standin' before the King of England, who inna his better at all, and deserved every bit of grief that Og Maggy piled upon him. Twas a sight tae behold! *Except* we had tae high-tail it out of there without havin' one bite of dinner. I was terribly disappointed."

The boys laughed.

~

We came tae the meeting place, a wide field along the River Forth. A large impressive tent had been erected, but in the terrible weather it stood soggy in the middle of the field. The Edward's standard had been raised tae the tallest center pole, but it hung dripping. The bottom of the tent was mud-splattered. I wondered if the canvas was keepin' the interior dry, or if there would be rivulets runnin' from the canvas roof down the walls. The whole scene was rain-soaked, and too dreary for a king — for *two* kings.

I ordered my soldiers tae line up along the edge of the field. His men lined up along the opposite side.

Up and down the line m'men were tense, eyeing the soldiers across the field, prepared tae fight if it came tae it.

The rain became a dampening downpour.

Fraoch grumbled, "Och, I canna lay m'eyes upon a medieval tent without rain pourin' from the sky. It inna fair."

My line parted as my royal guard rode forward carryin' m'standard tae the tent.

I rode behind the flag bearer. Archie and Ben were riding behind me. Chef Zach rode beside them, watching over them. On my right hand I had Fraoch, on my left was Sean. Cailean rode beside Fraoch, keepin' his eyes on all of us and especially helpin' tae guard my son.

CHAPTER 42 - ASH

CRIEFF, SCOTLAND - OCTOBER 1683

I didn't think I would ever be able to sleep but then I must have, because suddenly there was a nudge on my shoulder. A whisper, "Ash, tis time tae arise."

It was black in the room.

I sat up. "Is something wrong?"

"Nae, but more men are comin', we ought tae leave while tis safe."

While he spoke he was rolling our stuff up and shoving the rolls into our bag. I shuffled over to the chamberpot, blinking, and pissed, trying to wake up. I needed to be fresh. I had gotten sleep, he had been guarding out in the hall.

I needed to be helpful. I returned to the middle of the room and finished packing our things while he pissed in the chamberpot, now totally disgusting.

He put our bag across his shoulder, and led me from the room, creeping down the steps so we wouldn't wake anyone. We snuck through the now quiet 'dive bar,' empty but for a dozen men sleeping in front of the fire.

No one was aware we were leaving. Lochie pressed his finger to his lips.

But I already knew — stealth.

If *one* of these drunk guys woke up we could have an issue. If more than one woke up we could be in real danger.

Once out, we rushed to the stables. Lochie paid for our horse while I waited in the dim light, looking around at the sleeping village. There was not a light to be seen in any direction, just the glow of the moon softly giving us a bit of light to see by.

Lochie hurriedly tied our bags to the saddle, then wordlessly helped me up on the horse. He climbed on behind me. The same shift of my hips as he slid into the saddle, right up against me. His strong hands took the reins and pulled Finny around. His thigh shifted alongside mine.

We rode down the main lane but then Lochie pulled Finny onto a side path, and urged him to go faster. We rode across a field at a quick clip until Lochie pulled Finny to a stop behind a building.

Lochie shifted in the saddle and watched behind us, tense and worried. "We are bein' followed."

He swung his leg back and dropped to the ground, then helped me down.

I hadn't been able to see anyone coming, but now I heard horse hooves. Lochie jammed his hand into a bag, rummaged around, and pulled out our vessel. Wrapping Finny's reins around his arm, he said, "Tis too dark tae see the vessel, we are jumpin' blind."

I nodded.

A man's voice from inside the building was yelling in Gaelic at us.

Lochie whispered, "Wheesht!"

The men following us gained ground.

Lochie said, "Hold ontae me."

I threw my arm around him, he clutched me to his chest, and twisted the vessel.

Nothing happened.

He shook it, he banged it on his hip.

I was frightened.

A man emerged from inside the building, yelling and waving his arms. Lochie banged the vessel, saying to the man, "I ken... we just needed tae... we will get off yer croft, we are tryin' tae..." He glanced around the building. "Och nae, they are almost here."

He shoved the vessel under his arm. "Climb back up." I stepped on his knee and heaved myself up, but the man from the house grabbed at Finny's reins. Lochinvar pulled Finny away, with me dangling off the side trying to get my foot in the stirrup or anything useful.

Lochie somehow managed to hold the vessel, hold the reins, keep Finny calm, argue with the man, and heave me up. He yelled, "Daena come close, or I will shoot ye!" as he swung himself up, and urged Finny into action — we raced across the field. I held onto the saddle horn. Not quite on, one side of my skirts caught up under Lochie's leg, pulling me off center. I gripped with my thighs, my eyes closed tight, but *that* seemed stupid — I forced them open but it was hard to see in the darkness, the wind rushing past. Lochie folded his shoulders forward, pressing against my back, his elbows clamped on my sides, his knees holding my skirts. Finny had a rhythm, gallop gallop gallop. We came to a stone wall, followed it until we came to a gap, crossed the lane, and raced into the woods.

We pulled Finny in behind trees in the darkness. Lochie slid off, held up a hand, meaning 'stay,' and crept away.

I hoped Finny was listening.

The horse was breathing heavily. I peered through the darkness. I could see the faint glow of the open field, but I couldn't see Lochinvar. He had crept closer to the road to watch out. What if he had to fire his gun? The idea scared me — if he fired it, couldn't it scare the horse?

I was on a horse, I had no idea what I was doing on a horse. I was terrified to stay on him, scared to get off him. I was stuck, heart racing. Facing the wrong direction.

Just sit.

I stared at the horse's ear as it quietly flicked.

It was like he understood to be quiet, to remain still.

A few minutes later I heard Lochinvar's footsteps. He put a hand on my hip, stroked his other hand down Finny's neck, and whispered, "Thank ye, boy, ye did good."

He looked up at me, "Were ye frightened?"

I nodded. "Where did they go?"

"They turned around and went back tae the village."

"Were they time travelers?"

"Nae, they wanted tae rob us, but we were too much hassle."

"Good, that's a relief... but why won't the vessel work?"

"I daena ken, tis broken." He exhaled.

Then he climbed up on the back of Finny and settled down behind me in the saddle. He turned Finny toward the path and looked left and right as if making a decision. Then he said, "We will ride north tae Balloch."

I said, "So, what... are we stranded?"

"Aye." We began the ride.

A little while down the path, I asked, "What year is it again?"

"I believe tis 1683."

"I've been in like four different centuries now, can't say I'm a fan. Most of my visits have not been by choice."

He stiffened in the saddle behind me. "Dost ye regret it...?"

"No, not like that, but I don't like the time travel aspect of it, the actual jumping, and now that I know how dangerous it is—"

"Aye, tis verra dangerous."

"Especially when your vessel doesn't behave."

"It has become a menace." He yawned loudly, and joked, "M'kingdom for a tent."

I said, "That is the truth. You exhausted, m'laird?"

"Aye, but we canna stop now. We'll be in need of a bed by tonight."

The sun was high, warm, the day lovely, quiet and calm.

"But if I fall asleep, nudge me with yer elbow."

I laughed. "Just promise that if I *do,* you won't fall off. I don't know what I'm doing up here."

"Ye think yer girly nudge would knock me tae the ground? Ye hae a verra fine idea of yer elbow."

"Hey, my elbow went to bootcamp, it can nudge like crazy."

A while later I felt him shift in the saddle looking in all directions. He pulled Finny off the path into the woods. "I canna go any farther. I hae tae sleep."

He dismounted, tied Finny to a tree, and helped me down. He swept his foot through some leaves, spreading them out, and then dropped to his butt. "I think I am already asleep."

"Do I need to keep watch?"

"I need ye tae be aware. Watch the path. But sit here. I want yer lap for m'pillow."

I sat down on the ground with my back against a tree. He slumped over, put his head on my thigh, fluffed my skirts a bit, put his hands to the side, and muttered, "M'gun is here in m'holster, wake me if anyone comes up the…"

"Yes, no worries." I ran my fingers down the side of his cheek, pushing his red locks back from his face. He exhaled like a sigh, and fell fast asleep.

It was a strange experience to be sitting in the woods, in a past century, with my newly married husband, in long-ago Scotland… I had no idea where. I needed to orient myself, but for now I was just lost. I was entirely dependent on this man, my Lochinvar. It was scary if I thought about it too much, so instead

I focused on what was here — his wide shoulder under my hand, the side of his face, his strong jaw, his ginger hair. Fully relaxed, he was asleep on my lap, entrusted to me. I was his and he was mine.

We were in this together.

A bird sang above me and I watched as the sunlight filtered down through the leaves, dappling my skin. I worked my sore shoulder around in a circle, slowly, a low circle, but still, it was so much better.

I felt better, stronger, and filled with love for him. I wanted to protect him, keep him safe. He had guarded me while I slept and kept me safe, rescued me from that maniac. His heart was protective and it made me want to take care of him. Funny how that worked.

I relaxed and daydreamed, a dream of Lochie and me on a comfortable couch, laughing. I was on one end, he was on the other, our feet in the middle. In my daydream I said, "Lochie, if you make me laugh I'm going to wake the baby."

Then I thought, *what baby?*

And everything went dark and cool as I looked down, there was a baby there in my arms, *whose baby is this...?*

Lochie's voice whispering, "My baby."

I blinked and looked around.

The sun was shining. The only explanation for that moment of darkness was that a cloud had crossed the sun.

The explanation for the waking dream was that I had Lochie in my lap, and was feeling love for him, that was all it was.

I counted on my fingers how many days it was until my next period, unable to shake the weird feeling I had that I ought to be getting close.

· · ·

He shifted and turned and looked up at me with a smile that spread. "Ye are a verra fine sight when I wake up."

"Glad you think so, my love. But that wasn't long at all, a half hour, tops."

"'Tis fine." He raised up on one arm and put his hand on my face and steadied me and kissed my lips. "Enough sleep, we need tae get m'lady under a shelter before nightfall. But first, we ought tae try the vessel once more."

We stood in a clearing, my arm on his, Finny standing behind me with his head over my shoulder, looking at Lochie as he tried to twist and turn it.

I asked, "Does it run on batteries?"

He shrugged. "Might as well be magic, I daena ken, but I hae never been told that I need tae charge it or put batteries intae it."

"If it's magic, do we need a fairy?"

"Could be, we can ask the Dragon at the next stop where the fairies are."

I said, "I know you're making this all up, but I do wonder if you might be telling the truth."

CHAPTER 43 - MAGNUS

ROYAL TENT IN THE MIDDLE OF KIPPEN
FIELD - JUNE 20, 1291

*M*y men and I climbed down from our horses and stalked toward the tent. Haggis was covered in mud and spattered as he walked.

I held the flap up on the side and paused before entering — twas dark but I could sense there were many men, making this a dangerous situation. My men filed past me intae the shelter, one pushing our hostage, Thomas Hayden, tae the side. I nodded Archibald toward the back wall.

I ducked my head, the last tae enter.

It took a moment for m'eyes tae adjust — tae see the English King, Edward, sitting on a carved throne with about fifteen men behind him. Beside him was a table, and on the table was a battery-powered lamp.

When I noted it, I met his eyes, and he smirked.

My eyes traveled across the other men. I dinna recognize any of them, twas dark in the tent and they looked shadowy, the look of men who had been livin' in an encampment for a long time. I couldna tell if any of them were time travelers, but Edward's lamp was meant tae signal tae me that this was not an ordinary medieval negotiation.

I glanced at Fraoch, he sneered, his battle face on.

Cailean looked around irritatedly. "Where is Mag Mòr's chair?" Without waiting for an answer he told one of my men tae draw a chair over from their side.

Edward spoke. "I'll say when he gets a chair, first, this man must bow tae me."

"I hae told ye, when I was but a lowly man putting forth a claim tae be a king, and I will say it only once more — I am a king. I winna bow tae ye, Eddie, I am Mag Mòr, cousin tae Cailean Campbell of Loch Awe, of the lineage of Normand the First, son of Donnan the Second, winner of the jousts in yer games, and I was foretold tae be the next King of Scotland by Morag, the Seer of Glencoe. She was correct, by the by, I am king. Crowned at Scone, in the year of our Lord one thousand two hundred ninety, King of all Alba, Magnus the First. Ye are on my lands, in the shadow of m'castle, ye ought tae bow tae me."

"Never."

I nodded. "Tis what it is then, we both sit."

Cailean nodded at m'man, he dragged the chair across the mud-covered rug, and set it behind me. I lowered myself into it. Haggis sat down beside my feet. I raised my brow. "And tis amusin', Eddie, that ye believe ye can offer yer opinion on *anythin'* we do with our kingdom."

I watched him shift.

I saw his eyes go tae the lamp.

I said, "Ye hae learned some things about the world since I saw ye last."

He narrowed his eyes. "Have you been to the world where these lamps are made?"

I leaned back in my chair, sprawling my legs. "I am a *king* in the world where those lamps are made."

I kept my eyes on Edward, but in the periphery I watched the faces of the men behind him, looking for the time traveler. He must be here. But where?

Then I realized that I *did* recognize one of the men. I said, over m'shoulder, "Fraoch, dost ye see who is there in the back?"

"Nae, I daena recognize anyone."

"Tis William Wallace."

The young man set his jaw.

Fraoch said, "The scoundrel who cut ye?"

"Aye, he was younger then—" I said, louder, "Take yer hood down, Wallace. Let me see ye."

The man shook his hood off and glared.

I said, "Ye are a son of Alba! What are ye doin' on that side of the tent?"

He grunted.

I said, "I am yer king and I asked ye a direct question."

He said, with youthful righteousness, "I am on the side of King Edward."

I shook my head. "Ye hae become a traitor." I asked Fraoch, "What think ye on the young William Wallace becomin' a traitor?"

Fraoch said, "I think we hae a problem."

I muttered, "Aye, a big historical problem." I said tae Wallace, "Ye ought tae step away from the English King. He inna yer friend. He is buyin' yer allegiance with weapons and tales of yer future glory but ye are on the wrong side of this... I warn ye."

He grunted again, but I saw him falter.

"I once met ye in combat — dost ye remember meetin' me, striking me with a sword?"

He shook his head.

Edward said, "We order you to cease addressing Wallace—"

"Nae, I winna, he is a young man, a young *Scotsman*, unclear on what he is doin'."

Tae Wallace I said, "Tis just as well ye daena remember strikin' me, ye dinna kill me, and ye gained nothin' but m'disdain, but I will forget all of it as well. Tis behind us, time is a wheel, ye ken, Wallace — I will give ye a chance, right now, tae step away from Eddie and yer current treasonous path and cross over tae my side. I am the rightfully crowned Scottish King, Mag Mòr, and I will forgive yer traitorous impulses as long as ye join me."

Fraoch said, "Think carefully, lad, yer king is givin' ye a chance tae live."

The rain grew louder, the deluge drowning out any chance of a conversation. I waited for a moment, watching him, quietly.

Then he shook his head.

"Fine."

The burst of loud rain calmed and I focused on Edward. "Good Scottish weather we are havin', daena ye think?"

He said, "Scotland is a miserable curs'd land, and the weather is nigh insufferable. We are only here to offer our assistance in—"

"We daena need assistance. Ye are mistaken in it. Therefore ye can remove yerself from our lands. Take yer traitors with ye."

He cocked his head tae the side, a habit he had when tryin' tae gain the upper hand. Twas as if he were ingratiatin' himself, but it came tae my eyes as weak.

I leveled m'gaze. "Ye are usin' Berwick as if it is yers, yet tis part of Scotland. I command ye tae remove yerself and yer men from the properties ye hae seized. I demand yer army depart from the lands around it. Once yer soldiers hae fallen back tae the other side of the borders, *then* we will speak."

A slithery smile across his lips. "Yet we rather like Berwick-Upon-Tweed and we want to keep it."

Fraoch, standin' by my right shoulder, muttered, "Och, the royal we, tis irksome tae hear it in use."

I said, under m'breath, "Aye, tis not nearly as endearin' as when we use it on the deck in Florida for fun."

I said, louder, "Eddie, are ye disputin' that Berwick belongs tae Scotland?"

He said, "Yes."

"Ye will not pull back, ye will not accept that I am king, and ye will not stop meddlin' in Scottish affairs?"

He pointed in the air. "No, no, and no."

I shook my head. "Then, as ye are unreasonable, I hae decided that I will be meeting with Philip of France tae form an alliance."

He cocked his head. "You would ally with the French? It would be a mistake. England will frown upon the decision."

I shrugged. "Frown all ye want, cousin, Berwick belongs tae me, and ye are bein' unreasonable. I will see ye removed. Either ye will gather yer men and leave out of self-preservation and good will. Or I will force ye south. Which will ye prefer?"

"We would prefer for the man in front of us to stop being so insolent."

"I am a king. My bloodline demands the throne. God placed the crown upon my head. I am more than a mere man — daena forget yerself."

"Yet once you begged us to back your claim to the throne."

I scoffed. "Fraoch, dost ye remember any beggin'?"

Fraoch, his thumbs hooked in his belt, said, "Nae, as I remember it, ye won the joust then ye looked Eddie right in the eyes and demanded he back yer cause. When he refused, ye won the throne anyway."

Cailean added, "Mag Mòr fought many a-battle against the men ye backed, and won them all."

I said, "I laid waste tae the armies of Ormr and Domnall, who, I will remind ye, ye backed for the Scottish throne."

Fraoch added, "Then m'brother Lochinvar and I killed them in the arena."

From behind Edward, in the crowd, a man's voice sounded, "And how is Lochinvar? He is well?" Whoever it was, I couldna tell as he was cloaked and shrouded in darkness.

Edward commanded over his shoulder. "Quiet, no speaking."

Fraoch narrowed his eyes. "Who said that? Show yerself."

I scanned the crowd, narrowing it down tae one man. I glanced at Fraoch, he had followed my eyes.

He nodded.

I glanced at Sean, his gaze was directed on the same man.

I returned my attention tae Edward. "Why are ye here, attemptin' tae intimidate us?"

Haggis beside me growled low and deep.

Sean tapped my shoulder. I followed his eyes to the man I suspected, I couldna make out his face, yet I felt certain he was the time traveler — twas Asgall? It could be, though I had only seen one photo of him.

But the lamp made it clear, Edward was fraternizin' with time travelers.

"...We have come north because we believe you have forgotten that you sit on a throne because we have allowed you to possess it."

I said, keepin' my voice steady, "Ye are not our overlord, ye must remove yerself from our land. If ye remain I will meet ye in the battlefield."

He said, "We will not continue this conversation. You have already lost, Mag Mòr, king of the medieval Scots. We lead a mighty force. We understand you are not used to being told what to do, but we demand you surrender your throne. Now."

The man who I had been watching pushed through the crowd to the back of the tent, ducked under the canvas, and left.

I met Sean's eyes. He nodded, and left the tent tae follow him.

Then Edward said, "We see you have brought your son."

Haggis growled.

I narrowed my eyes. "Daena speak on him — where is yer man goin'?"

"Which man?"

"The man who was behind ye, over there."

He said, "He is not *our* man." His voice sent a chill down my spine.

I said, "I hae had enough of ye, Edward. Ye will gather yer men and leave the way ye hae come, or I will bring down a force upon ye that will—"

There was a scuffle outside, men yellin'.

Cailean whispered, "I will go see about the uproar, Mag Mòr."

I glanced behind me, Zach had pulled the boys close. Haggis was behind them, facing the wall of the tent, growling. *Had someone been sneaking up on my son?*

Fraoch took a step back and drew a gun.

I stood.

The disturbance outside grew louder, it sounded like a brawl.

I blocked the boys, drawin' my gun.

Edward stood, his guards fell around him to protect him, drawing swords. I counted three who had drawn guns.

Then I heard Sean's voice, yelling in fear and anger.

"Och nae."

I rushed in the direction, but the flap raised, and three men barged through, with a struggling Sean between them. Everyone drew their weapons. We were in a standoff, guns pointing, tension as my eyes swept the men in the room.

Then a shot fired behind me. I ducked and turned tae see Zach holdin' a smokin' gun, standing over Thomas Hayden on the ground.

Zach yelled, "He was lunging at the boys!"

I turned back and saw Sean struggling. I yelled, "Unhand him!"

Fraoch fired, killing a man. I fired, killing another. But before we could kill them, a man reached down, pulled back Sean's head, and slit his throat there on the ground. "Nae!"

All I could see was red and horror, the sound of m'brother dying in the mud of the field. I fired, killing that man. Fraoch fired, killing another.

There were gunshots everywhere, a huge melee, and some of

my men lying on the ground, and reaching my ears, as if from far away — the sound of Haggis barking.

Edward was leavin' the tent surrounded by his guards. The whole crowd was in disarray. Some of the men who had murdered Sean were down, but others had escaped intae the mayhem and fled the tent. The time traveler who I had been watchin' was long gone — my heart was poundin'. My sight turned crimson. The bloom of blood from Sean soaked the rug. I was frozen in horror...

Fraoch grabbed my arm and pulled me back. But I had trouble pullin' my focus from the lifeless body of m'brother, dyin' alone. "Nae!"

He shoved me through the canvas flap intae the rain, the colorless landscape drained of life, the rain-soaked muddy ground. My men on horseback ready tae fight, their horses stampin' in the mud, earth and steel and storm — *Archie!*

I swept the crowd tae see him — Cailean pushin' Archie and Ben up ontae their horse. Zach getting on another. I saw a glimpse of Archie's eyes, terror and despair, a great deal of fear.

I had to get them away from the battle.

I asked Fraoch as I was pushed toward Dràgon, "Where is Edward?"

"He left, but Og Maggy, we hae tae decide — do we stand and fight or flee? I must tell the men—"

"We canna flee—!"

A large rumbling sound shook the earth. We turned tae see a verra large modern military tank, shoving against the tent, collapsing it with a crash, and rollin' up ontae it. The tank stopped in the middle, the turret turned, and it aimed at me.

Fraoch pulled me hard, stumbling tae the horse, yellin', "Retreat!"

A voice from the war machine counted down, "Ten! Nine! Eight..."

We had never mounted our horses so fast — we raced intae the woods, crashing through the trees. Ahead of me, Archie and

Ben were bent over, ridin' fast, with Haggis runnin' alongside. Cailean was leadin' the way, Chef Zach was followin' them.

The war machine fired.

I looked back, but the blast missed. They werena shootin' at the woods, but behind us — as if it were missing on purpose. *Or we would all be dead.*

We were outgunned, outmaneuvered, fleein' for our lives through a medieval forest.

My son just ahead of me.

I had tae get him tae safety.

Dràgon galloped, I rode low, my sight leveled on Archie, keeping him safe through pure will.

Thinkin' over and over — *m'brother is dead.*

CHAPTER 44 - ASH

BALLOCH CASTLE - OCTOBER 1683

We arrived near sunset at Balloch castle. The tense guards met us at the gate. Lochie spoke to a man there, and then we were passed through to the middle of the courtyard. He helped me down from Finny and quickly loosened our bag from the saddle and passed our horse to the stableboy.

Then we were shown up to a room.

Lochie said, "I need tae leave ye here, Ash, while I go speak tae the Earl, explain why we are here, and... ye will be alright, we will get fed as soon as this part is done."

"What are you going to tell him?"

He grinned. "I have nae idea — who am I? The young brother of Magnus, he is verra young at this time. I canna be the ward of Lady Mairead, she must be verra young as well..." He stopped, "Dost ye think m'father might be here?"

"Who is that?"

He blinked looking at a far off wall. "Donnan... I am not certain if he ever lived here... nae one speaks on him much." He shook his head, then smoothed down his coat. "Dost I look good? I am not prepared tae meet him."

"You look good. Yeah, you look good enough to meet him. Did you ever know your father?"

He shook his head. "I was raised at Dunscaith, the closest person I ever had tae a father was Auld Man Lister. He was an arse, he trained me tae be a warrior by takin' away everything I cared about." He scowled. "Then when I turned against him, he told me it dinna much matter, he told me I was useless, worthless. Dost ye ken, Ash, tis verra hard tae hear the man who raised ye call ye useless? Tis hard tae bear."

I said, "That sounds awful. But... and I know I'm new around here, but I think you might say Magnus is a father figure for you."

He nodded. "Aye, and Fraoch, tis why I am fiercely loyal. They haena once called me useless." He chuckled. "Well, if they did, they dinna mean it. I am a young man, sometimes I need tae be told tae grow up."

I smiled. "I think you do a good job of taking care of me. If you weren't with me I would have already died twelve different times."

He joked, "At *least*. Ye were in the military? What on earth did they teach ye? It dinna involve how tae get through the Ancient Scottish countryside. Seems they lacked foresight."

I shrugged. "The United States isn't planning on going to war with Ancient Scotland any time soon."

He said, "Lack of foresight *and* imagination, speaking of, I must go speak tae the Earl."

I adjusted his coat shoulders, and wiped a smudge off his cheek. "A little rumpled, like your last good rest was a while ago, but... I think you'll do well. What's your end goal?"

"Tae convince him I am a laird who he wants tae keep comfortable. Magnus told me tae hae yer way against the Earl ye must wave money at him."

"We have enough money?"

"Aye."

"Good," I grinned. "Go convince him you're a lord. I'll get cleaned up to pretend I'm a lady."

He left the room and I washed my hands and arms, ran a wet rag over myself, and smoothed down my hair. There were no mirrors in the room, so I had no idea how I looked. I assumed it was not my usual level and my pits smelled gross. Luckily for me there was a general reek of everything — dust and must and smoke.

Thick.

I sat in the only chair and waited for my husband to return.

In the past few weeks I had passed so many hours of sitting quietly with nothing to do — *like living in the dark ages,* I chuckled to myself.

Then the door opened and Lochinvar strode in with a smile. A lady's maid followed him, carrying a dress for me.

I said, "It must have gone well!"

"Aye, I was persuasive." He bowed. "I will stand in the hall while ye are dressed."

Somehow I had managed to get a little luxury from his one meeting. I was awfully proud of him. I put my arms out, oddly growing used to letting other people dress me.

I pretended to be a lady, but my stomach growled loudly.

The maid bit her lip to keep from laughing.

I would need to be fed soon.

Finally I was done: I was much cleaner. My bodice was tight, the fabric heavy, the stitch work was fine. My sleeves were full and puffy and my skirts were wide. My hair was pinned back with a tiny twist to hide that it was so short.

Even with the embroidery on the sleeve edges though, I could tell the dress was plain. Especially compared to some of the fancy dresses I had seen Lady Mairead, Lizbeth, and

Kaitlyn wearing in the... when had that been? The eighteenth century?

This was the seventeenth century. That might explain the plainness, or more likely I was given the basic model.

I had perfume spritzed on me and I was ready.

Lochie entered and stopped still. "Och, ye are beautiful, Ashy, m'wife."

I grinned. "Did you just call me Ashy?"

He ran a hand through his hair. "Aye, tis short for Ash of the Tree of life."

I said, "Good. I like that. Now, you must dress, fast, because I'm starving."

I turned my back on him, taking furtive glances, while he washed and dressed. A fine form, total hotness.

By the time he had dressed for dinner I was excited, hot, fanning myself.

He ran his hands through his hair again and put out an elbow. I placed my hand on his sleeve, and he led me down to the Great Hall.

We were seated at the main table, pretty far down from the Earl of Breadalbane, but it was nerve-racking anyway. The Earl was opulent, wearing a really high wig, and had rouge on his cheeks. His clothes were colored in gold and cream, he wore a high collar with lace. Everyone was exquisite looking, all the men were rouged, wearing long curly wigs, except Lochinvar who was fresh-faced, wearing his natural red hair tied back with a piece of lace. Lochie and I definitely looked like the poor relations, except he was very handsome. The most handsome man in the room, by far.

Lochie held out the chair for me. I sat. He whispered, "Ye are the most beautiful woman in the Great Hall."

I blushed.

Then I recognized Lady Mairead seated near the Earl. She was much younger, early twenties, but it was unmistakable, she was beautiful and had the same haughty lift to her chin. Her eyes swept the table and landed on Lochinvar and me. Her eyes narrowed, then she quickly looked away.

Lochinvar whispered, "We must be careful, she canna ken anythin'."

We were served our meal and I glanced around to make sure I mimicked the manners of the high-born people at the table. I did my best, enjoying the wine and the delicious food.

We mostly listened, as casual conversation was made at the high end of the table. Then I overheard the Earl say, "...ye ought tae consider him, Mairead, Young Magnus needs the name..."

Lochinvar sprayed his ale, then coughed to try to cover it up.

He wiped his mouth with a cloth napkin and said to everyone staring, "M'apologies, I drank up instead of down."

Lady Mairead narrowed her eyes again. Then addressed the Earl. "Ye ken, I am not interested in marrying again. That is the end of it. Magnus has a name. His father is Donnan. I winna hear another word."

The Earl tossed down his napkin, irritated.

Lady Mairead raised her chin.

Then she turned to our end of the table and looked directly at Lochinvar. "I am Lady Mairead, ye look familiar. How do I know ye?"

"Nae, I daena believe we hae met."

"Ye hae a verra familiar look about yer eyes, ye remind me of someone, dost ye ken a man named Donnan?"

He shook his head. "Nae, Lady Mairead." He shifted in his seat uncomfortably.

She sipped from her wine. "Ye are a Campbell?"

"Aye, Lady Mairead."

Then she set her sights on me. "And yer lands are...?"

I stammered. "Um...Florida...?"

"The New World? Are ye a Spaniard?"

"No, um..." I said, "My last name is MacNeil."

From the corner of my eye I saw Lochinvar bite his lip.

The Earl said, "Dost ye ken Neil Og MacNeil? I met him in Edinburgh last summer."

"Neil... no, I don't know... not certain." Everyone was staring, I should have been more careful, but I decided that the best way to get the attention off was to dig the hole deeper. "My father's name is Tom MacNeil, maybe you met him at... um... he likes to golf...?"

"Golf! Och aye, I love tae golf. I play whenever I am at Stirling."

Lady Mairead leaned forward. "Ye hae a verra interesting accent, does everyone speak like that from the New World?"

I nodded, but was uncertain what to say so I mumbled, "Yes."

"And how much land does yer family hae and what is their primary source of income?"

I said, "A great deal of... um... land, they now spend most of their time in a place called, um, North Carolina..."

She said, "I hae just heard of the naming of Carolina, fascinating — I heard twas a wilderness though, and ye seem tae hae fine manners, how does such a fine lady hail from Carolina?"

"I... um...."

"Yer father must hae a great deal of wealth tae live in the New World with his young daughter."

The Earl asked, "Why would ye think so, Mairead?"

"Because ye must hae wealth tae hae safety." She all but rolled her eyes. "Ye hold yer wealth, brother, and are safe because of the strength of yer walls, and the men who are loyal tae ye. Everyone kens it."

She turned to me, blinking, waiting for an answer.

I said, "He was... I mean, *is* a doctor."

She blinked some more, then her mouth drew down. "A physician? A physician who went tae the New World — whatever on earth for?"

I smiled. "The beaches?"

She continued blinking.

Lochie said, "I hae seen the beaches of the New World, they are verra beautiful, Lady Mairead. Ye can stand on the sand and look across the ocean and ye ken there is Scotland on the other end of the water. Tis thrilling. The sky is always blue, and there are riches beyond yer imagination."

She said, "Really? Och, it does sound lovely, is the sea voyage verra grueling?"

Lochinvar nodded. "The vessels are harrowing, the voyage is terrible, but tis worth it for the food."

She leaned back in her chair. "Dost they hae… I believe tis called 'chocolate'?"

I nodded. "They have wonderful chocolate where I come from, my favorite is a chocolate bar with salted caramel."

"Someday I would like tae try that."

Her attention was drawn down to the Earl's end of the table, and I spoke to Lochie in whispers, "Phew, I had no idea what to say."

He said, "Aye, twas difficult."

"It was."

We finished our meal and I began eating my dessert. He whispered, "My wife, ye ought tae eat quickly, we need tae return tae our room."

I said, "Aye, m'laird, that sounds perfect."

He raised his brow. "What sounds perfect? I dinna even mention what we would do in the room."

I smiled and batted my eyes. "Oh I know what we will do in the room."

He said, "Och, yer smile is the undoin' of me, I canna look or I winna make it tae the room. Even though we are stuck, I am verra glad we were married first, or we would be discussin' right now where I would be sleepin'. I daena think I could bear it."

"I am very hot for you, I would be trying to talk you into sleeping on me or under me…"

"Lady Ash would be drawin' me intae a sin?"

I sighed. "Yes, I would, because I would totally regret putting you off — I *did* totally regret it, though I'm glad we are married now. And relieved I didn't need to steal a time machine and go back to that moment in Balloch when I told you that the thumb oath didn't count."

"What would ye say tae yerself?"

"I would tell myself to hush up."

"I told ye, I told ye ye were causing trouble where it dinna need tae happen."

"Well, I was sure I was right, it's very hard to turn me from an opinion once I believe it is rightly made. One of my drawbacks, I'm glad you married me before you got to know so many of my drawbacks."

"Och, ye are opinionated… ye are certain of yerself, these are not drawbacks. I tell ye, Ashy, the men of m'clan are always tellin' me, 'Lochie, ye canna be such a braggart, tis causin' trouble.' But I tell them 'It is better tae be certain than uncertain.' I hae confidence, so do ye, I winna hold it against ye."

"You say that but I haven't argued with you about anything yet."

"Ye argued with me about gettin' married! Ye won the argument! I had tae live with the consequences of it! I had tae shift time tae marry ye in a medieval church in front of a king, och nae, I think we hae argued plenty."

"True. And I suppose you still like me."

"Aye, I do, verra much. I am verra glad I winna hae tae sleep on the floor."

"That must have been really uncomfortable."

He chuckled. "Twas torturous. Hae ye seen yer face when ye sleep, Ashy? Ye are the most beautiful thing I hae ever seen, tae hae ye within reach, but telling me I couldna touch ye, drove me senseless..."

I said, "Then we better get to it."

He grinned, asked permission of the Earl that we leave, then, once granted, he stood, pulled out my chair so I could stand, and said his goodbye to the Earl and his guests. We left for our room.

CHAPTER 45 - MAGNUS

THE FOREST BETWEEN KIPPEN AND STIRLING - JUNE 20, 1291

I raced Dràgon through the dense underbrush. I caught up tae Archie and Ben, and rode right behind Chef Zach. I yelled over m'shoulder, "Fraoch, are they chasin' us?"

He dinna answer.

I yelled, "Archie, pull tae the side! I want ye on m'horse! Ben get on yer Da's!"

They pulled their horse to the side.

All around us men on foot or on horseback were barreling through the trees, running and stumbling and careening and passing us by.

I grasped hold of the boys' horse's reins. "Archie hold on, Zach, pull Ben tae yer horse."

Zach dragged Ben from one horse tae the other.

"Now, Archie, cross tae me." His face was streaked with rain, dirt, and tears as he dove intae my arms. After a quick hug I helped him turn and sit in front of me as Fraoch pulled his horse up beside us. "They arna followin'! But it looks like a storm behind us!"

"How many men did we lose…?"

"I canna tell."

"Are they followin'?"

"It daena seem like it, but they are time travelin', we hae tae go."

Suddenly a man came crashing through the trees toward us, on foot.

Fraoch brought his horse between us, and said, "Och nae, tis William Wallace."

When he saw who we were, Wallace dropped tae his knees. "Mag Mòr, I beg yer forgiveness..." He was out of breath, struggling tae speak. "I dinna ken... och nae!"

Fraoch said, "Lose yer sword."

Wallace pulled his sword from its sheath and tossed it in front of him. "From this moment forward I will only draw m'sword for Mag Mòr, the rightful King of Scots."

Fraoch asked, "What should we do with him, Og Maggy?"

I said, "Wallace, ye dinna cross the tent when given the chance — how dost I ken ye are bein' truthful now?"

He said, "I will go back and fight, I will kill the man who ordered yer brother tae be killed or I will die fighting—"

"Dost ye ken the name of this man?"

"Aye, twas Asgall, he is villainous and contemptible."

Fraoch said, "And he has the ear of the English King..."

"Asgall is armin' him."

Chef Zach said, "Damn, that's dire."

I said, "I must get tae the castle."

He said, "They are already headed that way. If ye let me come with ye, I will lay down m'life tae protect ye."

I said, "Fraoch, what dost ye think?"

Fraoch climbed down from his horse, stalked over, and punched Wallace hard in the face.

Wallace fell over.

Fraoch said, "Get up, bawbags, take it like a man."

Wallace pulled himself up and Fraoch punched him again. He slumped tae the side, but then righted himself.

Fraoch grabbed him by the hair.

"Og Maggy, I think he is a traitorous creep and I think ye ought tae kill him out of revenge for yer brother."

I said, "What dost ye think, Chef Zach?"

"It's fucking William Wallace, he's kinda important."

I exhaled.

My son was shakin' in fear. I had tae get from the woods. I dinna hae time tae decide William Wallace's fate.

Fraoch punched him in the face again — Wallace cried out in pain. Haggis circled them, barking.

Archie hid his face in my shirt and clamped his hand over his ear.

Fraoch hit him again and again, yet Wallace never raised a hand against him.

Finally, I said, "Tis enough, Fraoch, daena kill him."

"He would deserve it."

"I ken he would."

I said tae Wallace, "I would kill ye, but I will spare ye yer life. I demand yer allegiance tae myself, tae Prince Archibald, tae my men, but most importantly tae Scotland. Ye must always take the side of Scotland. Ye canna allow yerself tae be swayed by the promises of an English King."

He bowed over, his face swollen and bloody.

"Aye Mag Mòr, I give ye my oath. I will lay down m'life for ye and yer son, and Scotland."

"I canna give ye back yer sword, but ye can ride with us, take the horse."

He scrambled tae his feet and climbed on the boys' horse.

Fraoch picked up Wallace's sword. "Tis against my better judgment. Ye will ride in the front so I can keep m'eye on ye."

He climbed on his own horse and drew it behind ours.

Wallace led us tae a path and kept a fast pace, Zach just behind him, I was next, and Fraoch brought up the rear. I occasionally checked behind us.

There was nae one following us.

. . .

A while later Cailean rode up, he asked, "Are ye all well? What is William Wallace doin' with ye?"

I said, "Aye, we are well, Wallace has deserted the English and sworn his allegiance tae Mag Mòr."

"Wallace, tis good ye had yer arse kicked, because I want tae do it as well, but I daena hae time, we must ride."

Wallace said, "Aye, sire."

Cailean fell in behind me tae guard our rear flank, Fraoch rode behind Wallace and we moved through the forest, with Haggis racin' along beside us, toward King's Park and Stirling Castle beyond.

Archie said, "Da, did Uncle Sean...?"

"Aye, Archibald, he is nae more."

We rode at a fast clip, and we were quiet, Archie occasionally wipin' at his face with his sleeve.

I put my arm around him and tightened my hold tae comfort him. My eyes on Chef Zach's back, willin' him tae be a good enough rider while protectin' his young son from the danger chasing us.

Fraoch drew his horse to a stop. "Och nae, dost ye see it? There is a storm ahead in the field of the park!"

Wallace said, "That is how Asgall travels!"

I said, "Aye, I ken, ye hae seen it?"

"Aye, and he carries terrifyin' machines with him."

Zach asked me, "Does that storm carry friends or foes?"

I said, "I assume a foe, but we canna look, we hae tae get the boys tae safety."

Fraoch said, "I will go check, ye go on tae the castle. Wallace, come with me, twill be yer chance tae prove yer loyalty."

I said, "Before ye go, we ought tae check if our vessels will work."

I fished through the saddle bag until I found one of the

vessels. It felt dead. I passed it tae Fraoch, he boldly twisted and turned it, mutterin', "Och nae."

I brought out the other. He tossed me the first, I tossed him the second. He twisted it as well. "Ours daena work, but how come there are storms, is Asgall able tae travel? Tis much like he is the one who has stranded us."

I shoved both the vessels intae the bag.

"If ye find him, kill him. Get his vessel."

Fraoch said, "On it," as he and Wallace rode away toward the park and the storm.

Cailean took the head of the line, leading us around the park toward the castle. Along the way we caught up with many of m'men who were fleeing Kippen. By the time we came tae Stirling hill, we had about thirty men around us. Twas a relief. There was safety in numbers.

I looked over m'left shoulder tae see in the distance that there was a storm billowing above King's Park, but then it began tae collapse on itself.

The castle gates were opened and we rode through.

CHAPTER 46 - ASH

BALLOCH CASTLE - SATURDAY AFORE THE
DROVERS ARRIVE AT CLEIF - OCTOBER, 1683

I used the garderobe, then Lochie accompanied me to our room, leaving me there with the maid undressing me, while he returned to the garderobe himself.

The maid left me with my hair undone, wearing a big billowy chemise. My shoes and socks were off for the first time in what felt like days, my bare feet on the stone floor were wonderfully cool, but then too cold. I was shivering, standing on the rug when he returned.

He glanced at me, ran his hand through his hair nervously, and took off his coat. "I canna look at ye too closely, or I will forget tae be civilized."

I fluffed out the chemise. "Even with all this fabric?"

"Och aye. Look at ye, in m'mind ye are naked under the... dress, tis easy tae tell, tis givin' me the..."

I laughed. "The what?"

"Ye ken, I canna think, and now ye are smiling. I am barely strong enough tae bear it while I undress."

He placed his coat on the trunk at the end of the bed, and then he worked on the buttons on his shirt. He worked on loosening his collar, then asked, "Can ye do it, Ashy? M'fingers are large for it."

I stood in front of him and unbuttoned the two top buttons at his neck, concentrating, which wasn't easy with his eyes on my face, he was inches away.

He put his arms around me and pulled my hips close, his breathing had grown heavy.

"This is all it takes?"

"Aye, I canna wait, I need tae take yer clothes off." He scooped my chemise up over my head and off. He smiled widely.

I crossed my arms across my chest and shivered. "Too cold, we need to get into the bed, or warm the room."

He picked up the chemise and put it down over my head and held it so I could put my arms back in. "I will build the fire, but ye canna distract me with yer body or I winna be able tae."

I put my arms out. "Is this distracting?"

"Aye, verra, I deeply regret puttin' yer chemise back on ye." He ran his hand through his hair again. "Och I would greatly like tae pull yer hem up and peek underneath, just a small peek."

I crossed my arms across my chest. "No peeking. You, m'laird, were going to build the fire. Do you want me to build the fire?"

He said, "Och, tae watch ye kneel by the hearth, yer arse right there — twould end me."

I turned around with my hand blocking my rear. "Is this better?"

"Nae," he loudly sighed. "I can see yer wrist, Ashy, I would like tae kiss ye, right there on yer pulse, ye ken, and yer elbow just above it, and then just beyond…"

"Very funny, Lochie, but it's freezing in here."

"Right. Tis. I am buildin' the fire." He crouched beside the hearth and began poking the coals and adding logs.

I went to the bed and climbed on it, my knee bonking on the board where no mattress covered it. "Ow!"

He said, "Och nae, twas yer knee?"

I fake cried, "There's barely any mattress!"

He frowned, comically, "Tis a poor treatment, but not

directed at us specifically. I daena think there is a good mattress for years."

I patted around on the bed, "It's lumpy!" I started kneading the soft parts out to cover the bare.

He stood there with his hands on his hips. "Och now ye are crawlin' around on the bed."

"And you are done building the fire." I said, "If me, in a giant chemise, crawling on an uncomfortable bed, covered from head to toe in billowing fabric, is getting your engine roaring, you better get over here."

He laughed, "My engine roaring!"

"You never heard that before?"

"Nae." He kicked his shoes off while I pulled the blanket over me.

"Ye are drivin' me wild, ye are verra sexy." He crawled onto the bed and lay down on me.

His face was dimly illuminated by a flashlight on the edge of the table.

I watched his expression as we looked deeply in each other's eyes. "Lochie, what happens if we don't get out of here before the flashlight batteries run down?"

He kissed me. Then said, "Tis borrowin' trouble, in the morn we will attempt tae use the vessel again."

I pushed him to the side and squiggled to the table and turned off the flashlight. "Just in case."

I lay back down and he climbed on me again. He kissed me deeply, stirring me to excitement, but then through the heat and passion of the moment, I heard a small whirr sound.

I stilled.

Whirrrr.

"Lochie, what is that?" It was electric, out of place.

He had his eyes directed at the window.

I raised my head and listened, it was faint but definitely something.... Whirrrrr. It almost sounded like a... *was it a drone?*

A big very bright light beam rose up from under the sill, and swept across the other end of our room.

My heart raced.

Lochie pressed his finger to his lips and stealthily rolled off me.

The beam of light swung around the interior of our room, so bright it stung my eyes. The circle of light illuminated the end of our bed, and then traveled up the covers. I slowly pulled the bedding over our heads and lay in darkness, listening. Lochinvar was still, but tense, about to spring from the bed — I didn't breathe.

After the searchlight traveled over our bed, it illuminated the headboard, and then traveled back down and swung around the room again. Then it turned off.

The room went pitch black.

The whirring sound slowly faded.

Lochinvar jumped from the bed. He whispered, "Get up, we hae tae go." He turned on the flashlight.

I jumped up and started pulling on my socks and boots. "That was a drone!"

"Aye, twas."

"That was so scary…" I tied my boots and then started pulling on a skirt. "What was a drone doing here?"

"Someone is lookin' for us."

He pulled on his kilt, and buckled his belt, and tucked in his shirt. "Dost ye hae paper, pens?"

I jammed my arms into the bodice and hastily tied the front. "I don't know, do I? Yeah, I have a notebook, I have pens, I definitely have my wedding pen you gave me… where is it?" I yanked open my messenger bag and rummaged through it for the small notebook and the wedding pen. "What do you want me to write?"

He tucked in his shirt, his eyes focused on the window. "I want ye tae write: I, Lochinvar Campbell, and ye, m'wife, Ash, hae arrived here, at Balloch Castle in the year 1683. Tis October, write that, I believe tis the Saturday afore the drovers arrive at Crieff tae sell their cattle."

I was scribbling furiously, writing it all out as he spoke even though it was slow as he tried to figure out what to say. "Our vessel inna working. Make sure ye say that part well. It is not working—"

"I'm underlining that."

"Good, and tell them we are tryin' tae find our way home tae the kingdom of Riaghalbane."

"Should I say the century?"

"Nae, if someone comes across it, they ought tae be confused by it. That way twill be noticed." He added, "Put down that there are drones here. Dost ye hae room tae write it?"

I nodded as I wrote.

He repeated, "Our vessel inna working."

I said, "Is that all?"

"I think so. Finish dressin'."

I put down the pen and stood, adjusting my breasts in the bodice, and tightening the laces, while he pissed in the chamber pot in the corner of the room.

Then I heard the whirring sound again.

I whispered, "It's back!" realizing that I had left the flashlight on, laying on the table.

He finished pissing, dropped his kilt, rushed to join me where I had pressed up against the wall. We both stood there with our backs to the stone, watching as the drone hovered at our window, the searchlight sweeping around the room.

The strong beam settled on our flashlight and paused.

Then the light began sweeping around the room again. I clutched Lochie's hand and bent my knees, sliding down the wall to the floor, pulling him after me. We were hidden in a shadow behind the headboard of the bed.

We kept still, hoping it wouldn't see us, trying not to breathe.

Finally it withdrew from the window.

. . .

We stayed quiet listening, then he said, "I think tis gone."

"Lochie, what is happening?"

He looked right and left. "I daena ken." He stood up, put out his hand to help me up, but the drone quickly rose up and flew over the window sill. The light beam directly on us, I was frozen in fear.

An amplified voice came from the drone:

"Lochinvar Campbell, you are under arrest. Ash MacNeil, you are under—"

Lochie demanded, "Under what authority?"

"By the authority of Emperor Asgall of the Chronum Empire."

Lochie said, "An empire, what dost ye mean, an *empire?*"

"Lochinvar Campbell you are under arrest by the authority of Emperor Asgall of the Chronum Emp—"

Lochinvar said, under his breath, "Gather yer things, Ash." Louder, he said, "I winna comply."

I gathered all my stuff, turned off the flashlight and shoved it in the bag. Then I dug through for a gun. I wasn't exactly sure it was loaded, I hadn't been the one to pack it, but I didn't have a lot to lose. I kept my back to the drone, counted to three, then spun around, yelling, "Lochie, Down!" and shot at the drone. I hit a rotor. The drone shot back, firing a staccato of bullets at the wall, but I had hit it.

It sank in the air, nearly crashing, then rose off-kilter, turning in a slow circle. It flew out the window, banging the sill as it cleared it.

Men were running down the halls toward our room. Lochie said, "Stow the gun, be ready tae go."

We left the room, holding our bags. Lochie spoke animatedly with the men in the hall. Lochie described what he had witnessed, while others went into the room to investigate.

Lochie said, "I daena ken, there was a loud monstrous sound, twas like a cannon went off!"

I held onto Lochie's sleeve as we backed away. Men were rushing up and down the stairwell, stalking up and down the passageway. Lochie explained what we had seen, while keeping the truth of it hidden, until we made it to the stairs and rushed down. I dragged my hand along the stone to keep my balance as we jogged down the uneven steps. We made it to the courtyard and raced to the stables, and waited with our back to the wooden wall while the stableboy saddled Finny. Lochie grew irritated and took over the job, working at top speed.

He shoved my bag into the saddlebag on the side of the horse, while I frantically looked out — the whirring sound was happening again.

I grabbed his arm. "What are we doing? We can't! Where are we going?"

The drone flew over the wall and neared us, saying, "You are under arrest."

The stableboy covered his ears and hid behind the horse stalls.

I pulled Lochie by the arm down the wall to hide behind a shadow. "They're going to follow us, we can't leave, oh no! Lochie, how many people are out there, waiting for us? They'll capture us! I don't want to get kidnapped again!"

Lochinvar said, "Aye, ye are right, Ashy, we canna leave."

The drone pulled back.

Lochie stood up and peered around, then asked, "How does it ken where we are?"

"It might have a heat sensor."

"'Tis what exactly?"

"It can see through walls, it can see what we're doing, where we're going. We can't leave, they'll just take us." I frowned. "Finny has my gun!"

"Och nae, we need it. Tis on Finny's saddle?"

I nodded. "Right side."

He raced around the stable and made it to Finny, unclipped the bag from the horse's saddle, and told the stableboy, "We changed our mind, return him tae the stall."

Then Lochie raced toward me with the drone swooping behind him in chase. It pulled up short as Lochie reached me and pulled me behind him.

The searchlight beam shone brightly on his face.

The voice from the drone said: "By the power vested in me by Asgall, Emperor of Chronum, lay down your arms and—"

He whispered, "Dost ye hae a clean shot?"

"No, plus it will fire on us, we're unprotected."

"Give me the sack."

I passed it to him.

Completely still, hefting my bag in his right hand, he whispered, "Behind ye… the stairwell. Count of three."

I tapped on his back: one, two, three.

He leapt, swinging the bag at the drone, catching the corner and making it careen. But I couldn't watch, I was scrambling to the open stairwell door, and descending into the darkness all by myself.

My last glimpse, Lochie running in the opposite direction.

It was a little like falling — the steps were inconsistent and worn, steeper than I expected. It was exactly falling, I tripped and fell on my knees at the bottom. It hurt, badly, but I forced myself up and feeling with my hands on the cold stone, I moved farther into the tunnel.

I was in such pitch darkness that when I looked back at the opening at the top of the stairs I could barely tell where it was.

I immediately felt frightened and a bit claustrophobic. I had given Lochie my bag, I had no flashlight, no nothing but the clothes on my back. I was panting, having trouble getting on top of my breath. I stared at the opening, thinking of my last freedom, from down in a medieval hole, trying to convince myself that I was safe.

No one will close the hatch. No one would do that.

No one would lock me down here — this was not a big deal, at all. Probably in the day this was just a regular underground passage. Definitely not some crazy rat-infested medieval torture chamber.

Could there be rats?

I gulped.

With my two hands on the wall I tried to breathe down my rising panic.

CHAPTER 47 - LADY MAIREAD

THE KINGDOM OF RIAGHALBANE - 24TH CENTURY

I was eating the last few bites of my chocolate cake and then I glanced around the table as I chewed and swallowed the last one. M'staff had been irritatingly slow today, nae one was paying me any mind. I put my fork down, paused... nae one took it. *How long was I tae sit with an empty plate in front of me?* Another moment passed. I pushed the plate away and a servant rushed over and whisked it away.

It had been a long day, I had nae patience for anyone not doing their job. If Magnus was here they would tighten up, but he hadna been here in a while. The day had grown long, time was passing. I had been busy in meetings — *but hadna he promised tae come soon?*

We had left his return date open, because there was a great deal he had tae accomplish.

My job was tae run everything and check in on him through the historical record, he was doing well. A king in the middle ages, enjoying a fine time in the thirteenth century surrounded by his family, I supposed. All had gone tae plan.

I thought about visiting him. I would like tae see the age. I had always wanted tae, but never had because I dinna like the idea of doing it alone. The long ago past was unstable. I had always been worried about becoming lost. What if I became stuck? Who would come for me? Nae one.

But with Magnus there, twould be a good time tae visit...

I dinna like being the only person who hadna been there.

I lifted my wine glass tae my lips and sipped the last of it. I put the empty glass down and waited for it tae be noticed.

If I went tae visit Magnus though, I would certainly hae tae suffer a tour. I *despised* tours. Havin' tae smile and nod while someone beneath me explained tae me about the layout and workings of a place — the idea of it was enough tae keep me away.

Though I was certain twould be interesting. I would verra much like tae meet Robert the Bruce.

Also, I thought William Wallace would be fine company.

I had been busy all day in meetings with the generals, I really wished I had a fine young man tae rub my feet.

I sighed. I did miss Pablo. I had meant tae go visit him but hadna had the chance. I would go, as soon as Magnus was back.

I waved my hand for more wine. Nae one had noticed my empty glass.

Of course they probably expected me tae go tae my chamber now that the meal was done...

When Magnus returned I would meet him on the roof, tell him that he needed tae take his staff tae account with a firm hand because I was *done* with the empty glasses and havin' tae ask for what I wanted.

Then I would twist my vessel and just go. Tae Belle Epoque Paris or Manhattan or anywhere but here.

Wine was brought near and my glass filled.

I took a sip.

What did I have on my schedule, anything?

I considered... two days with nothing much, a meeting with the head of transportation... twas unimportant. I could put him off. I could take a couple of days and go see Pablo. Magnus would never even know.

I glanced at my watch. It was 9:30 pm. If I left now I could return on the morrow. The chances of Magnus arrivin' in the next twenty-four hours was verra small.

And what did I care — he might be the King but I was the Queen Mother, *everyone* knew the Queen Mother trumped the King. Everyone.

I drained my wine and pushed my chair back from the table as the servant rushed over tae help. I leveled my gaze on him. "I hae been considering yer fate most of my dinner — in the future ken this, when I dine with company I might not notice, but when I dine alone ye must be more responsive. I hae had ample time tae stew upon yer lack of qualifications."

"Yes, Yer Highness."

I raised my chin and left the dining room.

I went upstairs tae my room and changed intae my best Parisian clothes, a tight corset, a long red velvet dress, a wide hat. From the safe behind the Picasso painting I retrieved my vessel and put it in my always packed overnight bag. I left my rooms.

I would go and come right back before I was missed, in and out. Just enough time tae relax. I would return rested and able tae run the kingdom.

I passed my household manager in the passage on the way tae the landing pad. "Where are you off to, Your Highness?"

"I hae decided tae spend the night with a friend, I will return on the morrow."

"Would you like me to send a guardsman with you?"

"Nae, it winna be necessary. I will take precautions. Please contact Marshall and tell him our meeting must be pushed, and let Hilda ken I winna need breakfast in the morn. Also, watch over everything in my absence and if for some reason, King Magnus returns while I am away, which winna happen, he inna expected, but if he *does*—"

"...I will tell him you had pressing business and you will return in a few hours, Your Highness."

"Perfect."

A guard pushed the door open and I stepped out ontae the landing pad. It was night, all around the castle were the wide lawns, and lush gardens, dark and mysterious in the moonlight, with wee lights twinkling along the walking paths. In the distance were roads with headlights moving along them, and overhead there was a sprinkling of stars, but in the distance, in the direction of the city, a sky filled with air traffic: helicopters, planes, and drones.

I strode out intae the middle of the pad and pulled the vessel from my bag and looked down on it, blinking. What was wrong?

It felt odd, as if it werna working.

I twisted the ends, checked the numbers, even recited them out loud as I used tae do — *what could have caused this?* Naething worked.

I had done this before tae Magnus, grounded him. I had the device for it, but this had never been done tae me.

This was outrageous.

I was very very unsettled by this happening. I stamped my foot. I had been looking forward tae a visit with Pablo and I had been also thinking about visiting Flora and Cully. They were going tae introduce me tae Liz and Jock Whitney at the races...

Who had done this tae me?

. . .

I stalked back intae the castle and rushed down the passage tae the elevators. The Household Manager met me in a hurry. "I thought you left, Your Highness!"

"I wasna able tae, I hae had tae change my plans." I pressed my hand tae the pad for the elevator tae take me down tae the vault.

He said, "Would you still like me to tell Hilda that you will want no breakfast?"

"Of course not, tell her that there must be a grand breakfast, and if I am not here for it, then I am not here for it — tis what it is." The doors slid open. I stepped in.

He said, "So if the King arrives — have you been called away?"

I rolled my eyes as the doors slid closed.

I rode the elevator down tae our underground vault. The outer room was filled with ancient and expensive weapons and other artifacts, behind it was a room where some of my most expensive art was stored — the pieces with complicated provenance, that were impossible tae explain how I came tae possess them. I passed through another sliding door that I accessed once again with my handprint.

This was the interior vault for the vessels and other devices. I overlooked the boxes that I knew held vessels — I had taken a recent inventory, and had nae patience right now. If I was stranded I wanted tae go tae bed and not think about it. If I found out that our vault had been robbed I would not be able to sleep.

I opened the chest that held a Trailblazer — right where it was supposed tae be. In another chest there was a Bridge where it was supposed tae be as well.

Then I went tae the far wall where there hung a painting by

Turner, titled *A Ship Against the Mewstone, at the Entrance to Plymouth Sound*. It had been Donnan's favorite and was a fine example of Turner's work, hanging in a prominent place on Donnan's gallery wall and I had admired it, until one day Donnan had corrected me with his fists, blackening my eye, and causing me a great deal of pain and fear. I had clamped my eyes closed tae keep from crying, yet Donnan had demanded, "Open yer eyes and apologize tae yer King!"

I had opened my eyes tae see over Donnan's shoulder: this painting. It was majestic, a lone ship on rough seas, overcoming the storm tae get tae a farther shore, the shore of the New World. I had focused on this painting as I had said, 'Aye, sire, my apologies, sire, I winna do it again.'

Now I hated this painting, even as I knew that brewing hatred had inspired me tae keep going, and as soon as I found myself the mother of a king, as soon as Donnan was dead, I pulled that painting off the gallery wall and moved it down here. 'Twas verra valuable and reminded me of my strength but I only wanted tae see it when I was in the vault, counting my spoils. Because I had won.

I pushed the painting aside and unlocked the door of a small hidden safe with my handprint, and removed an antique jeweled box. I unclasped the latch and opened the lid to find it empty. It ought to have contained what Donnan had called the Darner. It changed the course of the vessels and could draw someone tae ye, or repel them away.

The Darner was also able tae strand someone.

I used tae hae at least one Darner, *how many did I hae last week?* I shook my head. Perhaps two — I couldna remember. I pulled my newest book from my pocket, and flipped through the pages looking for my last inventory.

I went back about two weeks, and found one — *had it been that long?*

I had never allowed that much time tae lapse afore.

Was it on account of my complacency or despondence? I

had been out of sorts. I knew it. But would I have let ennui hinder me from taking an inventory?

I drew my finger down the page looking for the correct number of Darners, but the last time I had taken an inventory I hadna counted them, I had to go back tae one of the first pages of the book tae find a full inventory.

Then, I had one.

Now I had none.

I swore tae myself I would keep better track and flipped through tae the first clean page and wrote a quick, partial inventory:

> *Three chests, I did not count the vessels as I have a great deal on my mind, a Trailblazer and the Bridge are here, and safe: the box with the Darner (Darners?) is empty. They are missing.*

I dated it.

Under that I wrote:

> *My vessel is not working.*

I opened the closest chest and dug through the straw for a vessel and held it, it felt lifeless. Och nae. Another and another. It took twenty minutes to go through all the boxes and check all the vessels. I had all that I remembered, none of them were missing, but none of them seemed to be ready tae work.

I left the vault with two more vessels tae test them out on the landing pad, traveling up the elevator tae the rooftop once more. I pulled all three of the vessels from my bag and twisted and turned them, growing more and more irritated, until the door opened behind me. "Your Highness! I thought you were not leaving! Are you planning to leave once more?"

I exhaled, exasperated. "Nae, I am nae."

He said, "So I will tell Hilda that you still want breakfast."

"Aye."

I wanted tae scream. But I put the vessels back in the bag, raised my chin and stalked past him. "I am retiring."

"Yes, Your Highness."

CHAPTER 48 - JAMES

BALLOCH CASTLE - MAY 30, 1710

As we rode through the front gate Lizbeth was waiting for Liam, and surprised to see us all. "Why haena ye gone?"

Quentin said, "I don't want to alarm anyone but our vessel isn't working."

Lizbeth said, "Och nae, consider me alarmed! Is this a thing that regularly happens?"

I said, "Nope, I heard tales, but can't remember the facts of them, usually it's diabolical — most of the time I think they involved your mother."

She said, "Well, this must be related tae the issue I wanted tae speak tae ye on." She held out a folded piece of lined paper. "This was in a book on my private shelf, they are books given tae me from Lady Mairead, mostly, and I hae looked through them all, many times afore, but as I was looking for one in particular I found this within the leaves."

I opened the paper and read:

I, Lochinvar Campbell, and Ash, are here in

*Balloch Castle in the year 1683 October the
Saturday before the*

it said drivers, but the word was scratched out and replaced with the word 'drovers' then continued:

*arrived at creeve to sell cattle.
Our vessel stopped working.
There are drones here. Attacking us
Our vessel doesn't work*

and then nothing.

Quentin, reading over my shoulder, said, "Okay, this sucks, what is happening?"

"They got stuck in the year 1683? How the hell are they in 1683? but then... What does drovers and 'creeve to sell cattle' mean?"

Lizbeth said, "The drovers go tae Crieff tae sell cattle in October, usually the third week." She counted on her fingers. "This might mean tis the second Saturday if tis afore the cattle market."

I said, "With some time and calculations I can probably figure out what day of the month this is, I'm just not thinking straight." I leaned over and kissed Junior on the head while he was cradled in Sophie's arms.

Quentin said, "That means none of the vessels are working, right?"

"At least ours aren't."

"And no weapons to Magnus — is he going to be okay?"

I said, "If the vessels aren't working are we missing our rendezvous date?"

Lizbeth said, "What of Sean? Is he stranded in medieval times? Och nae, Maggie will be frantic with worry."

I put out my hands. "Look, it's all going to be okay, this *never* happens. We are just in a glitch in the matrix—"

Lizbeth said, "A glitch, what is a glitch?"

All the women looked at me, blinking.

Quentin raised his brow. "Yeah, James, how bout you explain a glitch in the matrix to the ladies here."

"Um... A glitch is like there is a... like there is a wheel of time, but it's got a nail stuck in the tire, so it's gone—"

Sophie said, "A flat tire sounds dangerous, tis a terrible thing, inna it?"

"Yeah, but *this* isn't, this is just a hiccup. That's a better explanation. We'll try again tomorrow and it will work by then, you'll see. We will all go to the past, and then we will send Sean back. He needs to be home, there's too much worry."

Beaty said, "But Lochie and Ash are trapped — they say there are drones. It sounds as if tis dangerous."

I nodded, "Yeah, um... I suppose it could be. We need to get a message forward in time to Lady Mairead. If she's done this before, she will know how to undo it."

Lizbeth said, "How will ye get the message tae her?"

Quentin said, "We'll add to this letter, and put it back in the book. She will find it in the time she is um... living."

Sophie was rocking Junior and patting him comfortingly, she said, "It sounds tae me as if that would take a long time. A great deal could go wrong."

I said, "Nah, Soph, it's easy, it sits in a book, and then in no time, as long as the book exists and she looks in it, voila! But the letter better be good."

We followed Lizbeth up to her room to use her writing desk. Quentin and I both pulled out pens at the same time.

"I have five pens."

He looked in his sporran. "Seven, I win."

"But do you have the best handwriting? I don't want to be an ass, but it seems like handwriting is going to be a dealbreaker with Lady Mairead. Imagine if she said, 'I'm not reading that.'"

Quentin nodded. "Good point. I agree. I have terrible writing, I'll dictate."

I tore a piece of paper from a notebook and began to write, but Lizbeth interrupted, "Ye must start with 'Dear Lady Mairead', and then tell her ye 'hope she is well.'"

I crumpled up the paper and tore out a new one from the notebook and wrote:

> Dear Lady Mairead,
> I hope you are well. We are with Madame Beaty and Madame Sophie and our bairns and we are stuck at Balloch castle in the year 1710 on May 28. Our vessels are not working, they were working yesterday, but now they do not work. We also think there are men around who are working for Asgall and are spying on us.

"Should I write 'spying on us'?" I reread it and then scratched through it and wrote:

> They are keeping track of us. We were planning to take a load of weapons and goods to Magnus in 1291 but we can't.

"How should I sign it?"
Lizbeth said, "Verra sincerely yours..."
I wrote that and then signed my name:

> Master James Cook

I passed the pen to Quentin and he signed:

Colonel Quentin Peters

I folded the paper and gave it to Lizbeth. She put both the letters, the one from Lochie and Ash, and the one from us, inside the book's pages.

I said, "What book is it?"

She said, "Tis Harry Potter, dost ye ken it?"

I chuckled. "Yeah, it's a favorite where we're from."

"The boys love it a great deal." She replaced the book on the shelf.

Sophie said, "What dost we do now?"

I said, "We wait."

CHAPTER 49 - MAGNUS

THE SIEGE OF STIRLING CASTLE - JUNE 20, 1291

*K*aitlyn was racing across the courtyard. "I saw you coming up the incline! It looked like you were running, Archie, are you okay?" She held up her arms and he slid down off the horse into them. She fell back on the ground holding him. "Are you okay? Is everyone okay? What happened?"

He said, "Mammy, Uncle Sean is—" He burst into tears sobbing into her shoulder, she looked up at me as I dismounted from m'horse.

I shook my head.

"Oh no!"

I handed Dràgon tae the stableboy. Emma took Ben from Zach and they were huddled, comforting each other.

Cailean yelled, "All able-bodied men must go tae the battlements!"

Hayley rushed up, "Where is Fraoch?"

"He ought tae return any moment..."

She started to run tae the stairs tae look for him but I grabbed her by the sleeve. "Wait, Hayley, we need... there is an army comin', we canna hae ye up on the walls."

Cailean raised his voice, "We need the women and children

tae go tae the cellars!"

Everyone began rushing around herdin' people from the courtyard.

Kaitlyn clamored tae her feet. "Where should we be?"

"Gather the bairns, go with them tae the cellars."

"Oh, not the nursery? Is it this dire?"

"Aye, tis dire, during a meeting with the English King Sean was murdered in front of me — the English King refused tae leave m'lands. He had a lamp, mo reul-iuil, he is time traveling, and then there is a verra large modern war machine — they are travelin' by storm."

Her eyes went wide. "And our vessels don't work?"

"If they did, Sean would be alive right now." I looked down on Archie's face. He looked terribly frightened. I said, "Archie help yer Mammy get Jack and Isla down tae the cellar. Stay there, daena leave, not until I come tae get ye."

"Da, you won't die?"

"Nae, I winna die, but when I tell ye that I need ye tae get yer Mammy and Jack and Isla tae the cellar, what ought ye tae say tae set m'mind at ease?"

"Aye... yes sir."

"Good, thank ye." I passed him the bag with the vessels and he slung it over his shoulder, took Kaitlyn by the hand, and they raced away. Emma, Zoe, Ben, and Hayley followed them tae the stairwell tae go find his siblings.

I said, "Haggis, go with Archie, follow him, stay with him."

Haggis ran off.

I turned, my eyes taking in the courtyard of m'castle— the weak walls, the warriors in disarray. We had fled, everyone was exhausted from the flight. Now we were tae come up with a strong defense, when everywhere I looked we were nae prepared for an attack, especially one led by a modern war machine.

'Twas evening, I looked tae the southeast and saw the high clouds of yet another storm.

Och nae, we were goin' tae be attacked by weapons much better than m'own.

I hadna gotten the munitions from Colonel Quentin. We hadna even begun tae build the stronger walls.

We were unprepared for the scale of this attack.

Men were calling for the gates tae be opened and Fraoch barreled through, followed by William Wallace, and ten more of my men who Fraoch had gathered as they fled. He pulled his horse tae a stop. "The lads are back safe?"

"Aye, what did ye find?"

"Wallace was right, Asgall and the English King are travelin' by storm, amassin' troops in King's Park, and..." His horse stamped and stomped. "He has brought giant war machines with—"

There was a screeching sound, distant, then growing louder — then a missile crashed intae my east wall. The explosion was intensely loud. It hurt m'ears and rocked the stone cliffs beneath us. The evening sky was marred by the sudden, harsh light of an explosion, breakin' the wood with a blast that sent men flyin' through the air tae their certain death. Timber cracked and crashed tae the ground. Flames leapt from the timber battlements, now splintered and ablaze.

I yelled tae Chef Zach, "Run tae my office, grab all the guns ye can find!"

He raced away.

My men-at-arms, clad in armor and wielding swords, were bravely rushin' up another flight of stairs tae defend the walls.

Wallace yelled, "Mag Mòr, I need m'sword, I canna fight the English without it."

I asked Fraoch, "What dost ye think? Ye trust him tae be armed?"

"Aye, we can return it." He raised his voice, "But if he does anythin' alarmin' I will run him through with my own."

Wallace said, "I swear m'allegiance tae Mag Mòr."

I nodded.

Fraoch tossed Wallace his sword, then they rushed away tae wave men tae other positions. Archers lined along the battlement, drew and shot, when my Marshal yelled, "Fire!"

The roar of the tank's engine had a guttural growl that filled the air, the gun's report was like a thunderclap, echoing off the cliffs. Another screech, growing in magnitude, and another deafening blast, leaving a gaping hole, and wind and fire and fury. All it took were two blasts and the castle was exposed tae our enemies.

Cailean rushed up, "Mag Mòr! What kind of a machine is this?"

"'Tis called a tank!" Another screeching sound. Another blast. Timber, stone, and rubble flew from the wall, a whole wide section was useless — a stair hung off, men were jumping from the broken span of wall tae another as parts of my fortress succumbed tae the onslaught.

Cailean coughed from smoke, then said, "We canna fight against it! Our arrows do nothing! We daena hae the right armaments. What do we—?"

Another whistling screech and a massive explosion on the wall that the men had just crossed tae — the screams and shouts of m'men as some fell off down the side of the cliff face. There was a man holdin' on, scrambling tae survive. Men raced tae save him, but he plunged tae his death.

Fraoch said, "We need tae pull them back from the walls! We are losin' too many men!"

The air was thick with the acrid stench of gunpowder, a sharp, biting scent that stung my nostrils. I coughed tae clear my chest and Cailean and I began directin' our men down, wavin' them tae the opposite side of the castle. There was another long whistle and a blast, more than half of my wall gaped open tae Edward's advance.

Men stood on the side of the courtyard, armed with swords and bows. Fraoch and I were armed with handguns, nae match for the scale of armaments built up against us. The stone keep, my last bastion, stood stark against the fiery backdrop. Cailean grabbed my sleeve and pointed behind us — another storm.

Fraoch groaned. "Och nae."

Cailean said, "We need tae get up in the Keep."

I said, "Ye stay here with a radio — I will go up."

Cailean said, "Mag Mòr, ye are goin' tae fight on the walls?"

"Aye, the Keep is the King's Tower, tis mine tae hold!"

We raced to the Keep with Wallace following, passing Chef Zach emerging from the stairwell with a bag of guns. Those guns were all we had in firepower. It made me deeply uneasy — we were massively outgunned.

Fraoch slung the gun bag over his shoulder and we took the stairs up two at a time.

I yelled, "How many grenades do ye think we hae?"

"Four?"

I said, "We need tae make every shot count."

At the top floor we stepped out ontae the battlement. We could barely see through the thick smoke of m'burning timber walls. The Keep had been protected by its height, the walls ringing it, and its location, towering over the cliffs of Stirling. But now the walls had gaping holes, the Keep looked precarious and exposed.

If I were siegin' this castle, I would put a cannon ball right here on the upper floor.

I blinked through the smoke and peered over at the gaping holes in my castle's curtain wall, as Fraoch and Zach unzipped the bag and pulled out our grenade launcher. They handed us each a rifle. They opened my munitions box and loaded the launcher.

My stinging smoke-filled eyes spanned the horizon in all directions — the tank in the west had beaten m'walls down, and now a tank in the east, ominously swiveled its turret and aimed right at the wall below us.

There was the thunderclap, a flash. The whistling scream.

Wallace yelled down at the men in the courtyard below, "Move! Move! Move!" Wavin' them away from the target.

That missile hit a wall made of stone, causing rubble, dust, and smoke tae fill the air. It took a long moment for the air tae clear enough that I could see what was left: piles of rubble, a wooden stair hanging precariously, and the beginning of yet another gash in my walls.

Fraoch stood with the launcher on his shoulder, "Get down!"

Wallace, Zach, and I crouched with our hands over our ears. With a loud boom he fired a missile, speedin' across the sky tae the second tank, exploding against the back end, causin' it tae rock.

The turret turned. Zach yelled, "Down! Get down!" There was a loud clap and a flash and the horrible whistlin' screech and a missile exploded against the wall in front of us. Dust and smoke filled the air again, rubble slid down the pile, men were yelling.

I crouched below the parapet, aimin' my gun in the direction of that tank, but there wasna anyone tae shoot. I watched through the sight, tryin' tae find any enemy... when from behind us there was another thunderous clap, a whistling screech, and a missile hit the Keep, farther down. We all ducked. Everything shook.

Fraoch looked at me. "Twill hold?"

"Aye, of course twill. It has tae."

"Which tank should I shoot?"

Zach pointed. "I know I'm not the boss, but that one is pissing me off."

Fraoch loaded another grenade in the launcher. We crouched, clamping our hands over our ears once more. He fired, hitting that tank, liftin' it from the earth for a moment, it landed billowing dirt and dust. We were quiet, scopes tae our eyes, watchin' and waitin' while the dust settled.

Wallace said, "Did we get it?"

Nae one answered.

But then we saw the gun turn, aim, the flash and the thundering clap, a missile whistling through the air, and the explosion against another section of the wall.

Zach said, "Fuck," and aimed his rifle at the tank. He fired off some bullets but it changed nothing. He sat down, dropping his back to the stone parapet. "Fuck, I just want a bigger gun."

He looked back around the stone. "Try it again, Fraoch, aim a few feet to the right."

"I hae two more tae go." Fraoch fired twice, once at each of the tanks. We shot our guns. But the two tanks fired round after round at m'walls until I was left with naething but two corner towers, one leaning precariously. My castle was fully exposed, the walls beaten, holes in the side of the main building. The brewery was on fire. Black smoke billowed from the kitchens.

Fraoch said, "At least this Keep is still standin'."

Zach groaned. "Don't say it, that can't be good—"

The tank turret rotated and then a loud clap, flash, blast, and a whistle screech. A missile struck the side of the Keep just under us. Zach yelled, "Go go go!"

We raced, ducking, while we ran tae the stairwell.

The Keep was rocking, the stone crumbling under us. We descended the stairwell, the steps underneath, shakin' and shimmying as we careened down. Fraoch stumbled behind Zach, I grabbed him by the shirt and heaved him back tae his feet.

Wallace was behind me. He called, "We daena hae any more weapons?"

"Nae, I had a great many comin' but they never arrived — our vessel daena work."

CHAPTER 49 - MAGNUS 301

"Twas Asgall's plan!"

We raced from the stairwell out intae the courtyard.

I stopped, havin' tae yell tae be heard over the roar of war.

"He did it? Dost ye ken how?"

He shook his head. "Nae, I just overheard it!"

I heard a squawk from the radio clipped tae Zach's belt. A man's voice said something unintelligible.

Zach was doubled over, pantin', fumblin' with the radio, when it squawked again.

He pressed the button. A voice emitted:

Had Enough, Yer Highness?

Zach drew his hands back in shock, "What the fu—?"

He unclipped the radio and passed it tae me.

I pressed the button: "Who is it?"

Is this His Royal Highness, Mag Mòr?

"Aye, and ye are...?"

My name is Asgall.

"Alright, Arsegall, ye murdered m'brother, I want ye tae ken, I will kill ye for it." While I spoke, my eyes looked out over the bleak ruin of my castle, still ablaze. The sky was dark with thick smoke, the world smelled of death.

The voice emitted from the radio:

I would expect nothing less. I *hoped* Mag Mòr would fill his heart with hate and seek revenge until his last dying breath. This is delightful.

I tried tae control m'breathin'. Tae keep m'voice steady, but I wanted tae race down the hill with m'guns drawn. "Ye are a madman, ye brought modern war machines tae a medieval firefight, and hae destroyed an important Scottish castle. How did ye get the English King tae submit tae ye?"

Asgall's voice:

He was easy tae convince. He does like his toys. I usually am not one tae move objects through time, I prefer tae keep the historical record intact, but *ultimately*, I wanted tae get the upper hand on

Mag Mòr... as ye remember, ye destroyed m'compound and stole m'wife—

I pushed the button and said, "She was not yer wife, she is my sister-in-law, married tae Young Lochinvar."

It sounded as if he chuckled, then said:

She married me first, Mag Mòr, the marriage tae Lochinvar is fraudulent.

I pressed the button again. "I will repeat, why hae ye brought the English King tae m'walls?"

His voice:

Mag Mòr, from my perspective ye daena hae any walls.

Fraoch was turning in all directions. He whispered, "Where is he? I am goin' tae kill him."

Zach said, "Get in line, we all want him dead."

The radio squawked and Asgall said:

Tell Wallace he is a deserter and I will see him drawn and quartered.

I glanced at Wallace, he set his jaw.

I asked, "What is yer plan, Arsegall?"

There was a moment of silence, then he said:

Edward wants ye off the throne. He plans tae place his own man upon it, someone beholden tae himself. Ye ken, Mag Mòr, that ye are illegitimate because ye are not of this time—

"I ken nae such thing. I was crowned at Scone, I am the legitimate King of Scotland — who does he want tae replace me, John Balliol, Toom Tabard?" I scoffed, turning around, lookin' out over the destruction. *Where was he?* "I want tae ken what side of the castle ye are on."

His voice was low:

I might not even be there, Mag Mòr, I might be *anywhere* else, but yet... I ken right where ye are.

From behind me I heard the thunderous clap, the whistle and screech, and before I could fully turn around, a missile blasted against the stone wall beside me. The wall exploded, the blast threw me ontae the ground, and then the rubble of my stone walls rained down on me.

My ears rang from the shock and I couldna see from the smoke. I came to as stones were lifted.

Pain coursed through my body as I was freed from the rocks, pinnin' me down. My face was wet. There was a sharp pain in m'knee. Once m'arm was free, I wiped m'face and saw a large swath of blood. "Och nae." Fraoch put out a hand and hefted me tae my feet. I staggered and swayed.

The radio, lyin' on the ground, squawked.

Fraoch scooped it up and yelled intae it. "Tell me where ye are, I am going tae kill ye!"

Asgall's voice said:

Tell Mag Mòr I want him tae surrender.

Fraoch said, "Never!"

Both the tanks fired from different directions. Their report rang off my cliffs, echoing throughout the valley. I clamped my hands tae my ears, the whistlin' screech sounded, and then the missiles exploded on the Keep. Smoke and fire billowed out, obliterating the view. I watched the top floor, willin' it tae stand, havin' trouble catching my breath.

But then the smoke cleared, the top had collapsed, the upper rooms were exposed tae the sky.

I stood there, swayin' on m'feet as one of the tanks fired another round aimed at the wall of the stable. It slammed intae the side of it, horses inside screamed.

Twas difficult tae think over the sound of screaming horses, flashes in my mind of Sonny, and I doubled over.

Fraoch was talkin' furiously intae the radio — the world had gone slow. Men were racing tae save the horses, their shouts interminglin' with the horses' cries. I couldna see through the smoke billowin' out, and I feared the horses were gravely injured. *What of Dràgon? Mario? Would they survive?*

I heard my marshal call, "Ready, aim!" And there was a row

of my men-at-arms drawing their bows, aimed at the tanks, but without a chance tae win against the machines of war. My walls were rubble. The castle collapsed. He had accomplished it all with two tanks, methodically, strategically —

Cailean yelled over the roar and fury, "What dost he want?"

Chef Zach yelled back, "To fuck with us, sounds like!"

Fraoch looked down on the radio. "Tis a great deal of fuckery!"

I couldna hear what Fraoch was saying tae Asgall on the radio, Asgall spoke and I saw fury in Fraoch's eyes.

I wiped blood from my head and swayed a bit on m'feet. "What is he saying?"

He held the radio closer tae me, Asgall's voice sayin':

...wife and children are in the cellar, the entrance is behind the kitchens at the north corner of the...

"He is threatenin' m'family?"

Another thunderclap, and the whistle-scream as a missile whizzed past, aimed at the kitchens, near the cellars where I had sent Kaitlyn and the bairns.

CHAPTER 50 - ASH

A CELLAR UNDER BALLOCH CASTLE - OCTOBER 9, 1683

I was in that pitch black dark for about twenty minutes, when, coming from further down the tunnel I heard footsteps.

Who was it?

Someone was running toward me, there was a swinging beam of light, coming closer. I froze, waiting.

But then it was Lochinvar. He pulled me into his arms. "Och nae, twas menacin' — are ye well?"

I nodded my head against his shoulder.

"I raced tae the other stairwell, I wasna sure if I could get here from that side."

"Thank God."

We both turned toward the opening at the top of the steps.

He said, "Did the drone find ye?"

"No, not yet, maybe it can't see us under here."

"Perhaps."

I said, "Where are we?"

"Near the store rooms."

"What are we going to do, wait for morning? Will we be able to leave?"

"The drone must grow tired eventually, then we will sneak out with the market day crowds."

"Is tomorrow a market day?"

He chuckled. "We pray so." Then he said, "Did ye bring the letter?"

"No, darn it, I left it lying on the table in our room."

He sat down on the floor and raised an arm. I sat down beside him with his arm comfortingly around me, my head on his shoulder.

We were quiet, then he said, "Och, now I wish we had said where we were headed... We ought tae get out of here. Our presence is bringing danger on these people, and they daena hae good enough weapons."

"Where would we go?"

"We could go tae... we could go tae Edinburgh. I would be able tae leave notes that way — och nae." He opened his sporran and dug through it. "Och, I hae yer pink undergarmies but I daena hae a pen. Did ye bring yer pen?"

"You have my panties in there?"

"Aye."

"But no pens?"

"I hae, as Fraoch would say, 'questionable priorities.'"

I frowned. "Well, *I* left my wedding pen on the table. But..." I dug through my bag, and found pens. I held up a small handful in my fist. "I do have these."

"Good. But daena tell Magnus or Fraoch I dinna hae one... Daena tell Quentin either."

"Your secret is safe with me — but you did have one, Lochinvar, because you have me, and so *we*, you and I, have one in our bag that just so happens to be on my shoulder. We are a team now, you're not the one that has to do everything. I'm the one that left my amazing wedding pen on the table, that's on me, and I'm not saying you shouldn't have at least ten pens on you, along with my pink underwear, I'm not exactly sure why you need so many pens, but it sounds like they are incredibly important—"

"They are verra useful."

"So…" I passed him three pens, and he stuck them in his sporran.

"Thank ye, Ash, that is a relief."

"To have pens?"

"Aye, but also tae hae ye, I need—"

"I imagine I am a huge pain in the ass sometimes, but also, I give you something to do — imagine how bored you would be if you never had met me."

He chuckled, "I canna barely remember life without ye, twas endless feasts in beautiful Florida and I hadna had tae kill someone in months."

"Now murderous rage is happening on the regular. What do we do?"

"Nothing tae do but wait for the morn."

I thought I felt something. "Can I click on my flashlight?"

"Aye."

I dug through my bag.

"Shoot, I left it on the table upstairs with the letter and our wedding pen."

Lochie reached in his sporran and pulled out a penlight. He waved it around. I saw rats scurry away.

"Ugh, rats, this sucks!" I shivered.

He put the penlight in my hand. "Tae keep them at bay."

I said, "See, you have stuff in your pockets too."

He tightened his hold on my shoulder.

I shone the light in a circle, seeing shifts of movement in the darkness. I gulped. "What can we talk about? I wish I had a book…"

"Recite tae me the story of Twilight."

I laughed. "First, though I read the series three times and watched the movies a *lot*, I can't recite it from memory. But I can tell you what it was about, the young woman, Bella—"

"She is verra beautiful?"

"Yes. She meets a vampire in school."

He said, "Wait, how old is she?"

"Like 18."

He said, "Okay, I thought ye meant the wee school for the bairns. But what is a vampire?"

"A mythical being who feasts on blood and lives forever."

"Tis in the form of a man?"

"Yes, a *very* handsome young man."

He said, "I hae never heard of vampires, we hae the baobhan sith, tis a female who will distract ye with beauty and dancing and then drains ye of yer blood."

"That's grim. But sort of similar, Bella falls for Edward the Vampire and—"

"Yet he daena feast on her blood?"

"No, because he is hot and wonderful and sexy and he loves her."

"He seems suspect. Inna he hungry?"

"He feasts on the blood of animals instead."

"So what happens tae her?"

"She loves him, but he is too dangerous for her, so she begins to rely on Jacob."

"Who is Jacob?"

"He is a wolf some of the time, but most of the time he's a man, a really hot and handsome man."

"She is hangin' around with the wrong sort of men, they are all monsters. She inna safe."

I giggled. "So true, but she has to decide which of the two men she will—"

"Why must she decide between two, there arna any other men in the world?"

I laughed again. "Good point, but these are the two hottest men around. And they both love her, but they are both dangerous so—"

"Because they are monsters. I bet if she goes tae Scotland she can meet a verra handsome man and not worry about monsters drinking her blood or eatin' her for dinner. Ye like this book?"

"I *love* this book, the point is that she has to decide who she loves."

"Is the blood thirsty man always a man?"

"Yes, and he lives forever. His is a sad story because he is lonely. Everyone he loves will die of old age, unless he drinks their blood and turns them into a monster, too."

He said, "Ye said the wolf is sometimes a man other times a wolf?"

"Yes, he can shape-shift at will. Unless... when he's angry he becomes a wolf—"

"Then he might eat her?"

I nodded. "Either way it's a tragedy."

"Aye, but the decision is easy, if she has tae choose it must be the wolf man."

"It must be? Why?"

"Aye, because a man who is a monster, who will drink yer blood, how can ye trust him? If he canna die, if he is not a part of the circle of life, then he is not a part of the natural order—"

"The case could be made that your family of time travelers aren't a part of the natural order either."

"Nae, we age, we feel all the pain and horror of life. We are on the wheel. We are just spinning differently than most, but we arna monsters. Ye canna want tae live with a... what did ye call it?"

"A vampire."

"Aye, a vampire would be terrible. Ye would hae tae sleep with one eye open, worried about him drinkin' yer blood. If he was lonely or he thought he might lose ye tae time, he'd just... how would he get yer blood?"

"Use his teeth to prick holes in your neck and suck yer blood out."

"Och nae, Ash, tis a horror story."

"Yes, it is, but it's also very romantic. But you think you can trust a wolf man?"

"Aye, he is a man or a monster. Tis more natural I think. If he daena get angry he might never be the monster at all."

I put my head on his shoulder. "I never thought of it that way."

"And wolves are good beasts. They live in dens with their family. They hunt in a pack. They are protective and smart. And they are the grandfathers of dogs."

"That is true."

"One is a bloodsuckin' monster, the other is a wolf — I think the wolf."

"I heard once that the reason why humans have been so successful in creating a world is because of the domestication of dogs. They helped us hunt, protected us while we slept, lived alongside us. I've always liked that about dogs."

"So ye would pick the wolf man as well. We are wishin' we had a dog right now tae beat back these rats."

I swung the light beam around again, watching the shifts and scurries of vermin rushing away.

"Can we get out of here, soon?"

He said, "Wait here." He crawled up the stairs and peeked out. He was still and quiet. I hoped he would say, 'come on,' but instead he crept back down, and resumed his seat. "We must wait."

I put my head on his shoulder. "Am I too heavy?"

"Nae, tis alright. Tis the good kind of heavy. Are ye scared or cold?"

"Why?"

"Ye are shakin'."

"Both."

He tightened his hold. "Daena worry, I will keep ye safe."

CHAPTER 51 - MAGNUS

THE SIEGE OF STIRLING CASTLE - JUNE 20, 1291

M'head spun. I had nac weapons, I could nae time travel, and I had nae idea if Lady Mairead was on her way tae rescue us. Was anyone able tae rescue us? My family and all the people of the castle were at risk.

Fraoch yelled intae the radio, "What are ye sayin'?"

Asgall's voice:

I am saying that if Mag Mòr daena surrender, the next bomb will be aimed at the stairs of the cellar—

Zach said, "Get them out! We have to get them out!"

Fraoch yelled, "Go, go get them!" But Zach and Cailean were already running across the courtyard toward the stairs that led down tae the cellars.

My head pounded. *How had I allowed this tae happen?*

The voice, emittin' from the radio:

Ye daena hae enough time.

My knees buckled, I dropped tae all fours on the ground and threw up.

I wiped my arm over across m'mouth as a helicopter rose in the air from King's Park.

It flew through the air toward us.

Behind me I could hear Haggis as he emerged from the cellars, barking and angry. He was goin' tae get hurt. We had nae protection, nae chance tae fight, Asgall's modern weapons were too advanced for us.

I was on my knees. "I surrender!" I put m'hands behind my head, facin' in the direction of the helicopter as it approached, shining its spotlight directly at me.

Fraoch said, "Nae, Og Maggy!"

"We hae nae choice—"

"He will kill ye!"

"Tell him I surrender."

"Nae, we will hae some other plan!"

The helicopter was ridin' closer.

"Fraoch, tell him!"

He was speakin' intae the radio.

The winds buffeted me as the helicopter hovered, then lowered and landed in the courtyard.

Three men, wearin' black military-style uniforms and carryin' rifles, descended from the helicopter and rushed towards me.

Fraoch tried tae block their way. "Where are ye goin'?"

One man shoved him, another raised his gun tae Fraoch's face.

Fraoch raised his hands.

Behind me I heard Kaitlyn shriek. She had emerged from the cellars. She was a witness tae this... *Och nae, this would frighten the bairns.*

One of the soldiers put his hands on me and Haggis lunged, barking and snapping.

I yelled, "Fraoch, grab Haggis!"

He pulled Haggis away as the dog snarled and twisted in his grip.

The soldier grabbed m'arms. He took my gun and my knives, and tossed them tae one of his other men.

I asked, "Are ye Asgall? Who here is Asgall?"

The man wrenched m'arm as he zip-tied m'wrists in front of me. "He's in the copter."

Fraoch said, "Where are ye takin' him?"

My captor dragged me tae m'feet. "Tae a meeting."

Kaitlyn yelled, "Magnus, Magnus!"

"Aye...?" I turned tae look over m'shoulder.

She was holdin' Jack, surrounded by Isla and Archie. "Magnus, don't let them take you!"

I tried tae smile, tae make it seem less frightening. I said, "'Tis alright, Kaitlyn, I haena met Arsegall yet. I canna fight someone I haena met, daena worry — I will be back afore ye miss me."

The soldier put his hand tae his ear as if he were listening to the radio. Then he said, "Is that your wife?"

"What...? Nae!"

He jerked his head toward Kaitlyn.

A soldier stalked toward her.

"Nae!!" I tried tae climb tae my feet, but I was shoved back down. "Nae!"

They were struggling, Kaitlyn and Jack were being dragged taeward me. Archie and Isla holdin' ontae her waist.

"Let them go! Ye daena need them, let them go!"

The soldier beside me laughed and spoke tae the other soldier — twas impossible tae hear over my frantic breaths.

The soldier who had been conferring on the radio commanded, "He daena want the children, leave them. Bring the Queen."

I saw Emma drag Jack from Kaitlyn's arms. Zach was pullin' Isla and Archie from around her waist. My kids were held back and Kaitlyn was shoved toward me. "Nae, nae, ye daena need her! I surrendered!"

The soldier yanked me up and shoved me tae the helicopter. "I get extra for a king *and* a queen."

Kaitlyn was being shoved behind me. She was yelling, "No! No no no no!"

Isla shrieked. Jack was wailin'. Haggis was barking. Kaitlyn was sobbing behind me. My heartbeat was loud in my chest.

But then Archie yelled, "Da!"

I looked over m'shoulder, he said, "Da! Take care of Mammy!"

"I will, son! Take care of Isla and Jack!"

Then Archie howled, "Arh-ooooooh!" He howled long and loud, "Arh-oooohoooooooh!" And then another person joined him and another, but I couldna tell who because I was shoved intae the helicopter, and although I tried tae stop the fall, my bound wrists were nae match tae gravity. I landed flat on m'face on the floor.

Kaitlyn cried out in pain as she was shoved in behind me and landed on my back. This was not m'first time being forced intae one of these god-awful machines, not even my first time being in one of these machines with Kaitlyn captured alongside — still, there was never goin' tae be any gettin' used tae it.

The soldiers jumped in around us, strappin' intae their belts. The helicopter lifted off from the courtyard of m'thirteenth century castle. I managed tae push Kaitlyn up with m'shoulder and flipped myself over ontae m'back. I lifted my bound arms so she could put her head on my chest. She sobbed. "I'm sorry, Magnus, I'm so sorry!"

"I ken, mo reul-iuil, we will get back tae them."

"My poor babies!"

"I ken... I ken mo reul-iuil. I ken." I put my arms around her.

"What are we going to do?"

"Survive and then kick some arse, not necessarily in that order."

She nodded her head.

We were headed somewhere I dinna ken. We both raised our

heads tae look down as we left — Kaitlyn said, "Oh no, oh no, oh no..." as the helicopter swooped out over the land.

My castle was destroyed. The walls torn down, our bairns were standing in the desolate courtyard watching the sky as we were taken away.

CHAPTER 52 - BLAKELY

LIAM AND BLAKELY CAMPBELL, NEWLY ARRIVED FROM THE US TO BECOME CARETAKERS OF TAYMOUTH (BALLOCH) CASTLE - PRESENT DAY

I woke up and usually I would partake of some hot, hot Liam-loving to go back to sleep, but instead I stared blearily up at the ceiling of this grand bedroom. It was unfamiliar, ornate and gilded. And I was seriously jet-lagged. Also I had forgotten to turn off all the lights, so the room was lit up, making sleep difficult.

I took stock of everything: the carved four-poster bed, the velvet bedspread and luxurious sheets. The antiques. The sweeping windows and long drapes. The mural on the ceiling, the carving over the door.

I had lived in nice homes before. I had been quite rich back in Los Angeles, an agent to the stars, used to luxury, but this was a palace.

I pulled a pillow over and tucked it under my leg, it was all so comfortable. *Why couldn't I sleep?* I focused on the victorian-style desk, imagining the people who had written letters there through history... I would need to research who had lived here. The doorway was so wide, tall double doors... *was that for the big skirts and the tall wigs?* Would there have been guards stationed outside for the kings who lived here?

But not kings, this castle had housed the Earl of Breadalbane, I had looked him up on Wikipedia. I was amazed that an Earl had lived in this much opulence...

That was an exquisitely painted door handle... I needed to bring my best-friend Jess soon, she needed to see this place. She would never believe it until she saw it for real.

Our suitcases were wide open on the furniture, clothes strewn around on the floor, as if we were the American Hillbillies from near Asheville, North Carolina, come to Scotland to rule the palace.

Liam had been sleeping like he often did on his stomach, his big wide rugby playing shoulders stretching his shirt, his face scrunched into the pillow. He mumbled. "Ye are awake, Woodshee?"

I ran my fingers along his back, feeling the warmth of his skin. "Yeah, sorry I tossed and turned, I have a hard time sleeping in a new bed."

"Me as well, daena let the snorin' fool ye, tis hard tae get used tae our new home."

"This is all ours?"

"Aye, courtesy of m'mysterious cousins."

We rolled onto our sides and faced each other. "What are we going to do first?"

He grinned and his big rugby hand pulled my hip closer to his. "First we might want tae welcome ourselves tae our new home."

I wrapped my arms around his head and kissed his forehead. He tucked his head to my chest.

We were fully entwined as he stroked his hand up and down my thigh.

"That sounds good, because it's the middle of the night. I'm all turned upside down."

He chuckled against my neck, "I will turn ye upside down."

I laughed. "One minute ago you were fast asleep, your face all smushed, and now you're ready to go?"

He bounced his hips against me, he was indeed ready to go.

I said,"Oooh, you're pokey."

"Ha! I daena ken if pokey is the way ye ought t'describe me. I prefer tae prod than poke, it sounds more substantial — or better yet plow. Och aye," he pulled my hips even closer, "I am goin' tae plow ye in our fine bed, with our fancy beddin'."

"You, sir, sound all kingly."

He pulled my shirt up and kissed my breast. "I feel like one, livin' in this fancy castle. Ye heard the manager, what was her name? Nae, daena answer that, I daena want tae think on her. I am thinking of ye, and yer panties comin' down yer legs, and how I am like a king of... what am I king of...? I am distracted by yer..."

I kicked my underpants off and his fingers played between my legs. I moaned, "What are you distracted by...?"

"Ye ken," he breathed deeply against my ear, "yer lovely field. I am goin' tae score a goal down here by yer..." He rolled me over, pulled my shirt off, and kissed and sucked on my breasts and then his mouth against my neck, in that lovely oh so sensitive place, he pushed up into me, big and heavy, hard and powerful — a gasp of my breath as it caught, and then an exhale... as I pressed my lips to his shoulder and held on. We rocked and pushed and pulled against each other for a long deliriously delicious time, and then he rose up above me and plowed into me, over and over, driving me to a climax as he finished.

With a low moan, he collapsed on me, heavy and spent...

He raised his head and shook his hair.

I looked up at him, God, I loved him, such a beautiful man. I tightened my grip around his back and held on, a bear hug kind of holding on, then I let go, with a long exhale, relaxing, fully, releasing him...

He kissed me on the bridge of my nose. "Och, Woodshee, twas a fine way tae start the morn."

I reached over to the bedside table and fumbled around until

I found my watch. I pulled it to my bleary eyes. "I can't see what time it is."

He turned his head to the digital clock on the other side of the room that I had forgotten was there. "Three a.m."

I joked, "Och nae."

"Dost ye think our hired help will bring us a sandwich?"

"I think, before you ask, you need to make sure you remember her name. She gave us an hour-long tour yesterday."

"Ye remember her name?"

"Yep, Martha."

"Och, right, Madame Martha of the Medieval Castle, I remember the joke I made last night. Twas not m'best work. I was worn from the flight and there had been a bit of whisky at dinner. I am not in my right mind, tis why I couldna finish m'metaphor about the try I was goin' tae score by touchin' down in yer zone."

"So sexy."

He joked, "Tis my way."

He rolled onto his back and raised his head to look around for... then he got up and walked naked, showing off his incredibly nicely rounded ass, as he went to the bathroom and returned with a towel. He jumped on the bed and we dried me off, then I tossed the towel off the bed and immediately regretted it. "Ugh, what was that? That's really... not classy." I peeked over the edge of the bed at the fancy hand towel lying crumpled on the ornate rug. "Someone should really pick that up..."

I lay back. "But what are you going to do, you know? That seems like a lot of work. I'm just going to have to accept I am not classy. I thought I was, but compared to this castle... this is a whole 'nother thing."

He returned to the bed, put out his arm, and I curled up alongside him. "So how long was this castle empty?"

He said, "For years, they hae done a fine job of makin' it

nice again. When I was a lad we would sneak ontae the property and peer intae the windows."

"You never broke in and messed around in here?"

He raised his head looking around and then joked, grinning, "Wheesht, Woodshee, daena let Martha overhear ye. I would *never* break intae this fine castle." He nodded his head, then shook it. "Never ever, it dinna belong tae me."

I laughed. "Now it does."

"Aye, but I daena want Martha tae think me crass. She is a fine upstandin' woman she must think me kingly."

"Again, I regret the hand towel on the floor."

He looked up at the ceiling, then said, "I canna sleep, let's dress and go down tae the kitchen for some food."

My eyes went wide. "Are we allowed to?"

"Tis my castle! Of *course* we are allowed tae, at least we ought tae begin as we mean tae carry on — gettin' food at all hours." He sat up, pulled on his boxers, pulled a t-shirt on, then dug through his suitcase for pants.

I got up and put on clean underwear and a pale blue sundress. If I was going to wander around a palace, post-coital, sneaking food from the kitchen, I was going to wear a dress, as if I were civilized.

He said, "Och, I love the color on ye, Woodshee."

"Thank you, Liam."

We snuck from the room. Outside the door, I asked, "Did you remember the way?"

He whispered, "Almost certain tis this way." He led me down the hallway to a wide grand staircase.

We descended to the foyer. "I'm glad you remembered, I'm totally lost. "

He said, "Follow me," and led me through two very grand rooms until we came to the double-swinging doors of the restaurant-sized kitchen.

Liam felt along the wall and finally flicked on the overhead lights. I was blinded for a moment. They were so bright.

Suddenly Martha stuck her head in through the door on the other side of the kitchen. She looked alarmed and like we had woken her from a deep sleep. "Sir! Did ye need something?"

"Nae, Martha, I wanted somethin' tae eat."

"Ye want me tae get ye something tae eat at this hour?"

"Nae, I am good with gettin' it for m'self, ye ken, I will make some breakfast for Woodshee— I mean, Blakely, and me."

Her eyes were wide with surprise, shaking her head as he spoke, seeming at a loss for words.

He added, "We arna allowed tae get food from the kitchen?"

"Ye hae a kitchen in yer apartment! Tis stocked with food!"

I bit my lips to keep from laughing.

He said, "Och nae, I dinna ken, tis... my apologies, Martha. I dinna realize. I am nae used tae the house yet."

"Well, as the Laird of Taymouth, ye hae yer verra own kitchen. Tis stocked with food and drink."

I said, "My apologies, Martha, we are sorry we woke you — jet lag, it's... hard to think straight. I am so sorry. We will go straight to our room."

"Tis fine, Lady Blakely, ye hae the run of the house, but yer kitchen has been stocked for ye and the Laird. Ye ought tae eat there and not allow the trouble of it tae go tae waste."

Liam awkwardly bowed and we backed out of the room. As soon as the doors swung behind us we immediately started laughing. I whispered, "I think we got in trouble!"

"Aye, she is wonderin' how I am a laird and yet so uncivilized."

"I will have to put on some much better behavior. Do my hair, actually put on makeup so I look respectable."

As we walked back along through the grand rooms to the stairs,

I noticed the library. I pulled his arm and we went in. I switched on a lamp.

The walls were covered from floor to ceiling with shelves holding ancient books. There were ladders to reach the upper shelves. A big desk at one end of the room, a fireplace at the other, two fine leather chairs in front of the hearth, a footstool, lamps on end tables... I wondered who were the historic people who had sat in this library, reading.

Liam had told me about a woman named Lady Mairead who had once lived here, centuries ago, the sister of the Earl. Were some of these her books? I ran my fingers along the shiny wooden desk top. There was a plumed quill pen on the blotter. In front of it, an inkwell. The inkwell had the initials MC on them. Did that stand for Mairead Campbell?

Who had written letters here?

Of all the beautiful rooms and galleries of this palace, I knew this would be my favorite. I was speechless.

Liam said, "Ye like this room, Woodshee?"

I nodded. "I'm already planning to sit there in that chair with my feet up on your lap, while we read books together."

"Already plannin' it?"

I walked over to a shelf of books. "Absolutely. Do you think there's a secret passage behind the shelves? I would love that."

He said, "I daena ken, we will need tae explore."

I ran my fingers down the spines, but then my eyes were drawn to a copy of Harry Potter and the Philosopher's Stone. I pulled it out. "I love that this book is here." I looked it over. "It looks so ancient, but it was just published... what...? A couple decades ago? Maybe it's a first edition."

He said, "Woodshee, I am so hungry — can we go tae the room? I canna leave ye here, ye will become lost, and we might not find each other for weeks."

"That does seem likely. I'm taking this book though, it's fascinating. How's it so old?" I tucked it under my arm and followed him out. "And I don't know if I'll ever find this library again."

He led me to our room.

When we were in our apartment, I said, "I'm so impressed you remembered how to get here."

He said, "I am too hungry tae forget. M'stomach led the way, I was smellin' the larder." He pointed. "Look Woodshee! We hae a kitchen counter over there."

He stalked over and bent down, I heard doors open. "We hae a bar and a refrigerator full of food."

He pulled out a charcuterie tray, pulled the plastic off it and placed it on the counter. He looked behind himself for glassware. He got down a can of smoked almonds and a bottle of wine.

I said, "I think I forgot it wasn't a hotel, that this is where we live now, and we are rich apparently."

"Verra rich."

He poured us each a glass and pulled the lid off the peanuts.

We began to eat, sitting on barstools, facing each other with my feet on the rungs of his stool. I piled salami and cheese on a cracker and ate it happily.

He groaned with pleasure while chewing.

While we ate I had the book in my lap. "Isn't it weird, Liam? It's Harry Potter, but it looks a hundred years old, at least."

"Aye, but all the books looked like that." He wadded up a piece of salami and stuck it in his mouth.

"But most of them were old books. It's odd that an old book and a new book would be in the same condition, especially in such a nice library, one that is trying to keep it temperature-controlled, you know?"

I opened the front cover to look for the copyright, finding a bookplate, it said:

To my daughter, love, Lady Mairead

"Wait, when was she alive?" I showed that to Liam.

"Long time ago."

Then I turned to the title page where it said,

To Mairead, Love, J K Rowling

"It's signed, it must be worth a lot." I flipped to the next page. "The copyright is 1997, and it's a first edition." I did some quick counting. "Twenty-six years old. Weird. Have you read it?"

"Aye, the whole series when I was young. Ye ken I went tae the book store in the middle o'the night for the release party o' the last book."

"Me too! Aren't we meant to be?"

"Aye, though I think everyone in the world went tae the release party."

"True." I flipped through the pages carefully, because it seemed like it was fragile and noticed there was a gap in the middle, as if there were a bookmark between the pages. I pried my finger inside and flipped it open on the counter. There were two very old pieces of folded paper.

They were once white with pale blue lines, a torn edge, as if they came from a spiral notebook, but yellowed with age.

"This is so mysterious! I wonder what they say!" I picked them up and began to unfold them.

Liam said, "Och, I hope they say somethin' good and no' just a utility bill.." He looked around at the ceiling and the room. "Speaking of, what do ye think the utility bill is on this place?"

I pressed the paper open. "I have no idea, it's gotta cost a fortune."

He sipped from his wine. "Thankfully m'cousins pay it, I think."

I nodded. "Yes they do..." I read the papers.

Then I read them again.

Liam popped a peanut in his mouth. "What's it say, Woodshee?"

I raised my brow. "You sure you're ready?"

"Aye, lay it on me."

I read, "It says, 'I, Lochinvar Campbell, and Ash, are here in Balloch Castle in the year 1683 October the Saturday before the...' this is hard to tell, it looks like drivers but crossed out to say 'drovers arrive at creeve to sell cattle. Our vessel stopped working. There are drones here. Attacking us. Our vessel doesn't work'"

His brow drew down. "That is an odd thing..."

I put that first paper to the side and read the second, "'Dear Lady Mairead, I hope you are well. We are with Madame Beaty and Madame Sophie and our bairns and we are stuck at Balloch Castle in the year 1710 on May 28. Our vessels are not working, they were working yesterday, but now they do not work. We also think there are men around who are working for Asgall and are...' it looks like it says spying on us, but then it is changed to 'They are keeping track of us. We were planning to take a load of weapons and goods to Magnus in 1291 but we can't. Very sincerely yours,' it's signed, 'Master James Cook' and 'Colonel Quentin'."

Liam said, "Och nae, what does it mean?"

"I don't want to sound crazy, but it sounds like time travelers are stuck here in the palace somewhere." I looked around and whispered, "Have I been drinking too much?"

"Ye only had a sip of wine, Woodshee, and time travel is no'real. Tis just a prank, likely."

I flipped the paper over and read the other side out loud, "But check this out. 'For Lady Mairead's eyes only.'" I said, "This warning might bother me, but this is *historical*, right? Who cares, *except*, it's a modern book, maybe they need someone to find it and get the message to her— except you told me Lady Mairead is a historical person, right? She is long gone."

"Aye, but could be a namesake, ye ken."

"Yeah, right, true, but get this, 'the Kingdom of Riaghalbane,' where the heck is that? Then it says, 'If this letter is found, please direct it to Lady Mairead on the secure crypto chain: bc1pw508d2...' and so on, blah blah blah." I put the paper down on the other. "This is *wild*, what should we do?"

"We hae tae send it tae Lady Mairead on the alphabet blockchain."

I raised my brow. "Like... take the letter at face value and send it to a person named Lady Mairead? Like, 'Hey Lady Mairead, we are Liam and Blakely, we are from the U S of A and we are living in a Scottish castle now because of some cousins who gave it to us to caretake and while we were snooping around, barefoot in the middle of the night, not understanding protocol and decorum, we found a book and some messages, they sound like a hoax, or like a murder-mystery game, but we decided to go ahead and bother you with it because we're not sure how to behave.' Like that?"

Liam popped another peanut in his mouth. "*Exactly* like that."

I laughed. "Okay, let's send it to Lady Mairead." I got out my laptop and keyed in the wifi code.

He said, "Ye ken how tae send an encrypted message on the blockchain?"

I laughed. "Don't you?"

"Nae, while the other rugby players were becomin' crypto boys I was wonderin' if I would bother with getting a cell phone."

I said, "Ha! Well, I lived in LA, I have crypto. It was all the rage. I'll send it. Do you want to write it? You're the guy who runs the place."

"Aye." He spun my laptop around and began typing.

I poured us two more glasses of wine and then used my phone to take photos of the two letters and shared them with the laptop so I could send them all with the message.

He continued striking the keys until he tapped three with a flourish. "Done!"

"What did you say?"

"I wrote, 'Dear Lady Mairead, Ye daena ken me, I am Liam Campbell, a direct descendant of Sean Campbell, born in 1675. I believe ye and I are somehow cousins. I am the caretaker of Taymouth Castle. I found a book in the library here with two letters. There were instructions tae send them tae ye, so I am includin' them. I hope this helps and my apologies for the interruption...' How dost ye think I ought tae end it?"

"Yours sincerely."

He typed. Then read, "Yers sincerely, Liam Campbell."

He narrowed his eyes and read it again. "Does it sound good?"

I read over his shoulder. "Yeah, that sounds good. Whatever, right, anyway? She's nobody to us."

"She's a 'Lady.'"

"Oh right." I read it again. "No, I think it's great, plus, you're the lord of the castle now, right? Don't worry, we'll just send it."

I took the laptop, added the two images to it then said, "Maybe we should add a phone number too—"

"Add yers. Ye ken I never carry mine."

I typed my phone number with a note that said in parenthesis:

(My wife, Blakely Campbell's, phone number...)

I drank some wine, arranged the message, typed in the chain address, and hit send. I closed the laptop. "There. We've done it. I don't know what it is, but we got a message and we followed through. I mean, if you think about it, she doesn't even need to respond. She could just ignore it, if it's dumb, or send us a reply if it's useless. We probably won't hear from her at all—"

My phone rang.

CHAPTER 53 - LADY MAIREAD

THE KINGDOM OF RIAGHALBANE - 24TH CENTURY

I went tae my room and collapsed on my settee. The voice in the room greeted me and asked if I needed anything. I requested a nightcap and then asked the room tae show me a soothing video of aerial footage of the Scottish Highlands. I watched the familiar and calming video and tried tae relax in front of the fire, but I was unsettled — it seemed as if time were changing again and I needed tae discover the reason.

But I was at a loss.

Nae one had informed me of trouble brewing. Was I simply imagining it?

I had an entire system set tae warn me of historical discrepancies, it was a system that usually worked. Yet somehow this time I hadna been given a warning.

It had been a surprise tae find my vessel not working, tae find the Darner missing. I dinna like surprises on principle.

I was loathe tae ask the system tae investigate though, because I dinna want tae become unsettled.

I sighed. I dinna want tae investigate — what might I find?

And why was it up tae *me* tae look for historical discrepancies, the system should find them. The system should warn me. The system should be better than this.

And ultimately I had learned, nothing good came from looking for historical discrepancies right before I went tae bed.

I needed my sleep.

I couldna put my mind tae rest whenever I wanted, not anymore, too many people relied upon me.

I sipped from my drink and watched the video landscape, the camera soaring over the bens — *but maybe I ought tae look, something might be... something was likely going on...*

My deliberation was interrupted by the computers voice:

Your Highness, we have discovered a discrepancy.

I muttered, "Och nae," sipped from my glass, and put it down on the table in front of me. I smoothed down my skirts and turned on the lamp beside me. "Of *course* ye hae discovered a discrepancy at the last possible moment when I hae already been inconvenienced and just on the verge of asking for the information. *Now* ye tell me."

The voice said:

My apologies, Your Highness.

Apologies from a computer were never verra satisfying. It dinna grovel quite like it ought.

I said, "Tell me what ye found."

There were flashes and lines of text, scrolling down the wall.

The voice said:

We have found historical discrepancies in three distinct time periods, in four historical figures, and in two people who are related to Your Highness. Would you like the list first or the summary?

"Related to me? Who?"

Magnus the First and Sean Campbell.

My stomach dropped. "Start with the summary, begin with Magnus, then tell me about Sean — wait, I daena ken..." I took a deep breath, having a distinct sense of foreboding. "Tell me what happened tae Sean."

The computer said:

The date of his death has been added into the historical record.

I blinked. "What did ye say…?"

The computer:

Sean Campbell died during the English assault on the King of Scotland's men during a negotiation on the Field of Kippen, on June 20 in the year 1291.

I blinked again, my breath quickening. "I daena understand… it canna possibly be true… who killed him?"

The computer:

He was killed under the orders of Edward the First of England. Mag Mòr, the King of Scotland, was meeting with King Edward at Kippen to negotiate a treaty. King Edward's men attacked Mag Mòr's men. Sean Campbell was killed in battle.

"Nae. It canna be true… Magnus would never allow for it."

There was a date on the wall that I couldna bear tae look at so I stood and paced across the room. Thinking tae myself, *Why am I alone? Why is nae one here tae assist me?*

I felt shame for thinking on myself, but couldna get past the fact that I had been alone for a long time while my son had died and I hadna even been given the news. Magnus ought tae hae come directly tae tell me.

But instead I was here and there was nothing I could do — I couldna control it, and I was receiving the news while I was desperately lonely.

I then sank in the chair again. And focused on the date: June 20, 1291. Grief overwhelmed me —*Sean is gone.*

Nae, tis nae fair.

Sean is gone. Fionn's son. Gone. He is nae more…

I dabbed at my tears with a tissue. "Where is he buried?"

A pause, then the computer said:

That record does not exist, Your Highness. His body was not recovered from the battleground.

I gulped down my tears. "That is outrageous."

The computer said:

It is common with historical records from medieval times.

I scowled. "Daena back-talk the Queen Mother."

I thought of Sean's wife, Maggie, and his bairns.

And how he had wanted tae time travel with his brother, Magnus, and now he was gone.

I had kept Fionn in my heart by looking upon our son... he had resembled his father and the alikeness had given me solace. His voice had taken the same cadence, his personality had been so similar, it had given me comfort through the years. Looking on Sean, I felt that somehow Fionn was still in the world.

Tae lose him was tae be reminded of how much I had lost.

Maggie would be inconsolable. His sons were tae grow up without a father... *och nae.*

But I couldna mourn. I couldna collapse intae a heap and bemoan the loss.

I dried my eyes. I was alone receiving news that my first born son was dead and I had nae time tae cry. There was nae one tae console me. I had tae straighten my back and raise my chin. I couldna lament that our family had yet *more* fatherless sons — twas a curse upon us, brought upon us by my brother, the Earl.

I blamed him.

For *all* of it.

Why was I alone? Because my brother had widowed me, imprisoned me, married me off against my will, *and* brought upon our family a curse that meant my sons would be fatherless. My grandsons too—

Och nae. I dinna want tae ask, but I had tae — I clamped my eyes shut and asked, "What is the discrepancy involving Magnus?"

The computer spoke:

On the same day, after the death of Sean Campbell, Mag Mòr and his son, Prince Archibald, fled the meeting with the English King. They were—

"How old was the Prince at this time?"

The computer answered:

Eight years old.

I huffed, irritated that Archibald's life had been risked in that way.

I rolled my hand. "Go on."

The computer reported:

The record shows that Mag Mòr and his son, Prince Archibald, fled to Stirling Castle—

"They arrived safely?"

The computer said:

Yes, but the King of England attacked in what is now called the Siege of Stirling Castle, 1291—

My eyes went wide. "What do ye mean, attacked? He laid *siege*? With Magnus and Kaitlyn and their bairns inside the castle? Did they survive?"

The computer answered:

According to the record, Stirling Castle sustained heavy damage, the princes and princess survived the onslaught, Mag Mòr surrendered to King Edward. He and Queen Kaitlyn were captured—

"What? This is unbelievable!"

I stood, picked up my glass and drank the rest of my wine, slamming the glass back down on the coffee table. "What dost ye *mean*, he 'surrendered'? How can this be?" I began pacing again. "Magnus is a time traveler! He has all the weapons in the world and kens modern warfare! How could he *possibly* surrender tae the Medieval English King?"

The computer said:

This is one of the discrepancies, Your Highness, the historical record is inconsistent. The bombardment of Stirling Castle went beyond contemporaneous thirteenth-century warfare. The destruction of Stirling Castle was near total. The medieval historian, John of Fordun, described Edward's weapons as being 'a glistening trebuchet of racket and roar' and a 'mighty bird direct from the heavens who captured the Scottish King and took him away.'

"Those must be modern weapons."

The computer said:

The historical account seems consistent with modern weapons. That was one of the flags for this report.

I said, "So, Magnus has surrendered tae the English King. Where was he taken?"

The computer said:

That is inconclusive.

"Nae one has bothered tae rescue him?"

The computer answered:

We have no reports on—

"Daena answer that, I ken how this works — of *course* nae one has rescued him because *I* am just now hearing about this." I huffed. *Why hadn't I been told about any of this when I could have solved it?* It had all happened so quickly, behind the scenes, like a takeover in secret. King Edward wasn't capable of this villainy.

Who had introduced him tae modern weaponry?

Then I thought, this must involve Asgall.

I returned tae my chair. *Why hadna Colonel Quentin solved this?* Magnus was surrounded by good men who would lay down their lives for him. Modern men who knew how tae fight and were capable of providing him with security and firepower. How had they allowed him tae be captured?

I exhaled. I was certain that if Colonel Quentin dinna protect Magnus he either wasna there, or… Had something dire happened tae him?

Something dire had happened tae my son, Sean…

I shook my head tae keep the grief from settling there.

How could Magnus and his men have allowed this tae happen? Usually I would ken first thing. *This* was the trouble of them being so far back in the past. Twas not natural. News from the thirteenth century making it tae the twenty-fourth century took time.

It was a disadvantage

There were a great many things that could interfere with gathering information over those many centuries. That was why

Magnus never wanted kingdoms at both ends of time, twas too much like an empire, easier tae gain than tae hold.

He wasna suited tae be an emperor. He was much better at protecting his lands as a king. And though I wanted him tae amass as much power as possible, I was a realist — I wanted him tae wield power *and* control. Empires were difficult tae control.

Perhaps when I had been younger...

In my advanced age it all sounded like a great deal of work, lonely work.

I said tae the computer, "You mentioned more historical discrepancies — list them. I am growing tired and need sleep."

I poured more wine in my glass and took a sip.

The computer responded:

The discrepancies in historical time periods.

One: the siege of Stirling Castle. There are conflicting dates, it is listed as taking place in the years 1291, 1292, and 1304. There is a mention of a trebuchet used called the Warwolf, but in only one record. Contemporaneous records do not call the weapon a trebuchet. In most of the records the weapon is called a War Machine.

Two: In the year 1775, at Staunton, Virginia, there is a battle that took place, that has only one—

I waved my hand. "All of that is unimportant, I daena want tae hear of unimportant things or we will be here all night. Only tell me of what is directly related tae Magnus and Scotland. Tell me about the discrepancies with the historical figures."

The computer voice said:

One, The King of England, Edward the First, had an advisor by the name of Asgall. He was present at the negotiation at Kippen where Sean Campbell was slain.

I nodded. "Then there is proof. He is the one who has done it. Do we ken anything else about Asgall?"

The computer responded:

The alert you set for 'Asgall' has listed him as a frequenter of brothels in Staunton, Virginia.

I said, "Och nae…" I sighed. "Is this all? Hae ye told me—"

An alert appeared, projected on the wall, warning me that I had a message on my secure channel. I answered it with my code and a letter appeared. It read:

Dear Lady Mairead,

You do not know me, I am Liam Campbell, a direct descendant of Sean Campbell, born in 1675.

I believe you and I are somehow cousins. I am the caretaker of Taymouth Castle. I found a book in the library here with two letters. There were instructions to send the letters to you, so I am including them.

I hope this helps and my apologies for the interruption.

Yours sincerely,
Liam Campbell

I opened and read the attached letters, then read all of them again — Lochinvar was stranded in 1683. Quentin and James were stranded in 1710. I was stranded in the twenty-fourth century. Magnus had surrendered in 1291. Sean was dead. *Och nae.*

My eyes settled on Asgall's name in the letter from Master James Cook and Colonel Quentin.

Asgall was winning.

He was building an empire by conquering ours.

The bottom of the letter gave me a phone number tae call. Twas for Liam Campbell's wife, Blakely.

I asked the room tae shew me their files and read through

CHAPTER 53 - LADY MAIREAD 337

the information. Liam Campbell was my great-great-great-great-grandson through Sean. I asked for the computer tae shew me a photo of him. It came tae me, a photo of Liam in his rugby uniform, young and handsome. I marveled at the likeness, he looked much like Fionn, his great-great-great-great-great-grandfather.

I felt comforted by finding him, after discovering that Sean was dead.

It seemed like a miracle.

Then I wondered who they thought I was... did they know about time travel?

Liam was living at Balloch. I read through the titles and leases of Taymouth Castle. Then I asked the computer, "Is this true? A consortium called the Riaghalbane Royal Company bought Balloch and gave it tae Liam Campbell?"

The computer voice said:

Yes, Your Highness.

"List the name of the owners of the consortium."

The computer said:

Yes, Your Highness, the Riaghalbane Royal Company Consortium is made up of Magnus Campbell, Fraoch MacDonald, James Cook, Zach Greene, and Quentin Peters. They met with Liam Campbell and signed the contracts at the Och Nae Pub in North Carolina. Liam Campbell and his wife, Blakely, moved to Balloch, now called Taymouth Castle, a few months later.

I exhaled long. "Tis odd, I daena remember any of this. Why was it kept from me?" This was yet another decision that my son, the king, hadna informed me about. How was I tae handle everything for him — if I dinna hae all the details?

I looked at the image of Liam Campbell again. Fionn would be proud of his descendant.

I asked the computer tae call the number.

CHAPTER 54 - LIAM

LIAM AND BLAKELY CAMPBELL, CARETAKERS OF TAYMOUTH (BALLOCH) CASTLE - PRESENT DAY

*B*lakely's laptop began tae ring, she answered the video call. "Hello?"

An older woman, who looked very wealthy, her hair up, jewels at her neck, a sophisticated air, appeared and said, "My name is Lady Mairead, I am the Queen Mother tae Magnus the First, the King of Riaghalbane. I am tae be addressed as 'Your Highness' — I wish tae speak tae Liam Campbell, caretaker of Taymouth Castle."

Blakely said, "Yes, um... Your Highness, here's Liam." She pushed a button tae turn off the microphone, put her hand over the camera, and whispered, "It's Lady Mairead, she wants to speak to you."

I joked, "Och nae, what do I say tae a Lady, 'hullo, I am Liam, I live in a castle'?"

"It's a place to start." She turned the laptop toward me.

I said, "Aye, Liam here."

"Liam Campbell, please explain tae me *exactly* what ye found."

"Aye, ma'am, I mean Yer Highness." He held up the book. "Blakely found this book as we were wanderin' through the—"

"What do ye mean, ye 'were wandering'?"

"We arrived here yesterday—"

"This is yer first night at Balloch?"

"Taymouth castle, aye."

"And ye were looking through the library, go on."

"Blakely found the Harry Potter book, she thought it looked too old for its age."

"Can ye look upon the inside cover and tell me if there is a book plate that says 'Tae my daughter, Love, Lady Mairead'?"

Blakely flipped tae the front of the book, and turned it around tae shew Lady Mairead.

She bit her lip and took a deep breath and nodded. "It once belonged tae Lizbeth."

Blakely said, "Lizbeth is also the name of the sister of Sean Campbell — we've been looking up Liam's ancestors on Ancestry Dot Com."

Lady Mairead was quiet, then said, "Aye, that is a book from her library."

Blakely said, "Wait... that doesn't make sense, how did Lizbeth get a Harry Potter book?"

Lady Mairead was quiet and dinna answer.

I asked, "Lady Mairead, Yer Highness, are ye still there?"

"Aye."

Blakely said, "Oh, I thought..." Her voice trailed off.

I opened up the first letter and held it in front of the camera.

She said, "Does it say anything else?"

"Nae, just that—"

"What year does it say?"

I read out the year and watched her head bow over a book as she took notes with a verra fine pen.

"...and what was the month?"

I read the part about the drovers. She wrote a bit, then said out loud, not speaking tae us, "Shew me the month of the drovers in Crieff in the year 1683."

Her attention was away from the screen.

Blakely and I glanced at each other.

Lady Mairead said, "October 9, 1683." She wrote some more.

Then she said, "Shew me the other."

I unfolded it and held it up for her.

She peered at the screen and began writing again. She wrote for longer. Then she put down the pen. "Thank ye verra much."

I folded the papers up and placed them back in the book.

She said, "I would like tae pay ye for the trouble."

Blakely said, "Oh, that's not necessary, we already—"

"Hae ye been given a title?"

I said, "Nae, I daena — this is no' expected."

"I think ye ought tae be the new Earl of Breadalbane... the title is dormant. I will begin on it in the morning, in the meantime I will set up a new account for ye tae run yer lands and the castle."

Blakely said, "Oh, I didn't realize... we get money for our living expenses, but—"

"As if ye are glorified caretakers? Nae, that is not acceptable. Ye are the laird and lady of the castle, a direct descendant of Sean. The castle is yers. Ye will need a title as well. Write this down."

Blakely rushed tae grab a pen and a scrap paper. She looked frantic and when she sat down she brushed hair from her face.

Lady Mairead continued, "Ye will hae an account at C. Hoare & Co. Contact the Honorable Theodore Russell, esquire, he will help ye access the funds." She paused as if she were choosing her words carefully, "All I ask in return is that ye contact me just as ye did today, tae tell me what ye find in the books, or in the back of paintings, or perhaps carved intae the walls or under the furniture."

I said, "Ye want us t'look over all the furniture?"

"Under all the furniture, aye, just tae be certain. And look within *all* the books. Let me ken what ye find."

I nodded. "Alright, I will."

Lady Mairead narrowed her eyes. "Also, ye will be looking for vessels…"

"What is a vessel? Like a boat?"

She shook her head. "Nae, never mind, but if ye find anything else that seems odd or unnerving, just send me a message. This is verra helpful."

Blakely said, "I'm glad sending the message helped you, I just don't really understand *how* it helped."

Lady Mairead said, "Tis because ye daena need tae ken anything else about it. This is private historical business, life and death historical business. Ye must let me ken as soon as ye learn anything."

She hung up, without sayin' goodby.

Blakely turned tae me with her eyes wide. "What in the world is going on?"

I ran my hand through my hair. "How does Lizbeth from… when was she livin'?"

"Few hundred years ago, at *least*, unless… is there a more recent Lizbeth and Sean? Do you remember?"

"I daena think so, but I wasna looking."

"This is the weirdest job. Now you're going to have a title?"

"I canna believe it. She wants me tae be an earl? I daena think she understands who I am."

Blakely said, "You'll make a great earl, I think… but then again I'm American, I don't really know what that is."

"An earl is third rank from a king, I was a groundskeeper just last year."

"And she's giving us a whole new bank account? She barely even knows us."

She typed on her laptop.

I asked, "What ye lookin' up?"

"The bank where she said there was a… Damn, look at this bank. It's the oldest bank in the UK."

"It daena look like the kind of bank where ye log in and check yer balance. The chairs are too expensive."

Her laptop dinged.

There was another incoming video call from Lady Mairead.

Blakely answered.

Lady Mairead said, "I wanted tae clarify something with ye. Are we alone, nae one will overhear?"

I said, "Aye, we are alone."

"Good, I will be absolutely truthful with ye. We are time travelers."

She paused and we were quiet.

Then I broke the silence. "What dost ye mean, time travelers? Like ye go around in costumes, pretending tae live in the past?"

"Nae, we hae vessels that take us forward and back through time."

Blakely said, "That's not true."

"I assure ye tis as true as I am speaking tae ye from m'desk in the year 2391, yet I was born in 1660."

Blakely said, "I need some kind of proof."

"Ye are holding proof in yer hand, the book is from me, tae my daughter Lizabeth, who lived in Balloch — I mean, Taymouth Castle, three hundred years prior tae ye. Her brother was Sean. If ye go intae the library ye will see on the shelf Marcus Aurelius's, *Meditations*. Twas written in the second century, but the copy on the shelf was published in the twentieth century and specially bound and engraved for Sean at a publishing house in Paris. I gave him the book on his twenty-seventh birthday. The year was 1702. Should I go on?"

"No, I get it, sort of…"

She said, "The letters ye found are from my family who are stuck in time. We are at war with a man named Asgall. Hae ye met a man named Asgall?"

Blakely's eyes went wide. "I did! I met a man named Asgall at the airport lounge in Heathrow, yesterday. I told him we were moving here to be caretakers of the castle."

Lady Mairead put her fingers on her temple and rubbed

briefly. "Och nae." She exhaled. "Ye canna trust him, be guarded and watchful. He is verra dangerous."

Blakely nodded.

I said, "This is a great deal tae take in, how are we... so ye mean that the men who came tae the pub, Quentin and James, this is *their* letter?" I unfolded it and looked at it again. "They were with Magnus and Fraoch, they're all involved?"

"Magnus is my son. He is the King of Riaghalbane. He is also King of Scotland in the thirteenth century. Ye can look him up in the historical record. Fraoch is his brother, he is with him at Stirling Castle in the year 1291. And aye, the Colonel Quentin and James Cook who are stuck in time are the same men ye met. I must help them. But my vessel inna working..." Her voice trailed off. "I need for ye tae do me a favor."

CHAPTER 55 - FRAOCH

THE AFTERMATH OF THE SIEGE OF STIRLING CASTLE - JUNE 20, 1291

I watched as the helicopter lifted from the castle grounds and flew away. Time stood still and m'heart raced. *Och nae, there wasna anything we could do.*

I would hae tae keep his bairns safe.

I turned tae take in the scope of the castle, it had been destroyed by the English King and Asgall.

Jack was wailing.

Archie was despondent.

Isla was hanging ontae Emma sobbing.

They had seen their parents taken captive — *what would I do?*

I met Hayley's eyes. She said, "We can't stay here, there's no place to sleep, it's a ruin."

I swept m'gaze along the horizon. I would hae tae make decisions: I was in charge of the castle, of Magnus's bairns, of a kingdom.

Cailean said, "Fraoch, we ought tae get the prince tae a protected place. He is in the open."

"Aye, though it seems as if the army is withdrawin'."

All around the castle were storms, a vision of disaster and horror, but we were a distance away. We could watch without harm as storms whisked the War Machines away. This was just an army havin' accomplished what it wanted tae do, leavin' tae cause trouble somewhere else.

But the bairns were terrified.

"Take them tae the chapel, we will set up beds for them tae sleep."

There was the rumble of horses galloping up the hill, the standard they carried in front belonged tae the English King.

Cailean ushered everyone away. "Tae the chapel!" Hayley, Zach and Emma herded the bairns as Edward and his men arrived at the gate and entered and milled around in m'courtyard as if they owned the place.

I planted m'feet in front of them. "Ye canna enter."

Edward spoke down tae me from his horse. "We can, we will, and we accept your surrender."

I scowled. "Nae."

"Your surrender, now! It is the only way the prince survives. We are of a mind to arrest both the sons of Mag Mòr for the overthrow of the rightful King of Scotland."

Wallace spit in the dirt. "What rightful King of Scotland? Mag Mòr was crowned King at Scone, in 1290."

"We have been determined to be the administrator of the court, and therefore *we* have declared that action to be treason."

Wallace said, "Ye are on Scottish lands, an illegitimate English usurper! Ye hae nae say in the Scottish throne, I will kill ye!" Wallace fumbled as he unsheathed his sword, but Edward's guards lunged forward, knocked him over, and held him down. He struggled as they pinned his arms behind his back.

I said, "Unhand Wallace."

"He must drop his sword at our feet and bow."

"He winna bow tae the English King when ye hae just conspired tae overthrow the Scottish crown. He will sheath his sword and he will quiet down while we discuss this matter." I spoke over my shoulder. "Dost ye hear me, Wallace? And next time twill save ye trouble if ye kill first and *then* say ye are goin' tae kill a man. Ye waste valuable time with yer youthful tongue."

The guards let him go and Wallace sullenly sheathed his sword.

The English guardsmen stood around him threateningly.

Wallace sneered.

I asked Edward, "Where hae ye taken the king?"

"We cannot say, Asgall has taken him. He did not tell us his plans, only provided assistance in our own pursuits in exchange for Mag Mòr."

"Ye expect us tae stand for this? Ye hae unlawfully taken the king, and his wife, the queen, and removed them from their seat, Stirling castle. Yer armies hae destroyed our walls, and ye stand here threatening the crown prince?"

"Yes, it does seem that way." A slithery smile spread across his face. "We command that you surrender."

Behind him more men rode up the hill.

There was nae way we could fight them all.

Edward said, "We are convening the Scottish Magnates to plan the succession."

Cailean said, "We will call on the French! We will bring their ships tae our shores, we will call up an army and chase ye from our lands!"

William Wallace yelled, "Hear hear!"

Edward said, "I am placing Prince Archibald and Prince Jack under arrest for high crimes against the throne of England—"

I said, "Ye hae nae authority tae arrest the sons of Mag Mòr on Scottish sovereign lands."

"Mag Mòr surrendered, he has given up his castle — his last man is standing in the courtyard arguing with us and risking the lives of his sons. But we will be benevolent. The English Crown will give you an hour to remove yourself from this castle. Whoever is left will be arrested. On the way to the tower, we will parade the sons of Mag Mòr through the streets of London as a warning — the line of Mag Mòr is no more."

Wallace said, "Och nae, ye are an arse. English pigswill of the kind that needs tae learn a lesson."

I nodded.

Edward said, "Who would be teaching us a lesson? Mag Mòr? His men? You have all been beaten."

Wallace said, "It will be me, maybe not taeday, but someday soon."

Edward chuckled. "What are ye waiting for?" His horse stamped. "If you want to survive to—" He made his voice falsetto tae mock Wallace, "'teach us a lesson' you will need to leave this castle, the time is counting down."

He turned his horse and moved his men tae the gate.

Cailean and Wallace drew near, the men of the castle gathered around. Cailean said, so all could hear, "Make haste tae depart!"

There were groans, and some of the men yelled, "Nae!"

One of the men answered, "But we canna remain! We are nae match for the dragons. They hae destroyed the castle!"

I said, "If we want tae live tae fight another day we must leave. I hae tae get the prince tae safe lands."

A man said, "My men will ride along tae protect yer passage."

One of the men in the back said, "I will take m'men tae the south, send men tae the west, we will gather an army."

Cailean said tae me, "We will take the princes and princess tae Innis Chonnell, my son is there, he has men, tis protected."

I said, "I was thinkin' the same thing, Magnus will ken tae find them there."

"Aye, he will ken, he would expect it I think. If I am alive he kens I will take his bairns home tae keep them safe."

Wallace said, "I will ride with ye, Cailean and Fraoch, I will lend m'sword tae the prince's cause."

Chef Zach and Hayley emerged from the chapel. She asked, "What are we going to do, Fraoch?"

"We need tae gather all we can carry, we must get the bairns tae safety."

Zach said, "Fuck, that sounds dire, he would hurt a bairn?"

"A bairn in line for the Scottish throne? Aye."

Zach looked up at the ruined Keep. "I'll go see what I can salvage from upstairs."

I said, "Hayley, go with him, grab whatever ye can carry. I'm goin' tae get the horses readied. Tell Emma tae gather the bairns. We hae a long night of travel ahead of us."

Cailean yelled, "Gather any blankets ye can find, as we will be sleepin' along the way."

I announced tae the group, "load them up!"

The courtyard and castle were rushin' and chaos as we loaded horses with all we were able tae collect. We got the bairns up intae saddles; Ben and Archie on a horse, Isla rode with Emma, Zoe rode with Zach. Hayley had Jack wrapped tae her front. He had cried so hard he fell asleep and missed all the activity. Isla was exhausted from weepin'. Archie looked terribly frightened.

He asked, "Uncle Frookie, what are we doing?"

I said, "We are gettin' on horses, goin' tae stay with Cailean's family."

"Will Da know where we are?"

"Aye, he will ken where we are. He will come right there as soon as he can."

When we were in the big group, about tae go, I saw him looking around everywhere, a look of panic on his face.

I rode up. "Ye well, Archie?"

He asked, "I daena see them — where is Isla? Where is Jack?"

"Isla is with Aunt Emma, dost ye see? And Aunt Hayley has Jack. We are goin' tae ride slow, and all stick together. As soon as we leave the gates, it will be easier to see them."

"I wish you were holding them."

"I ken, Archie, but I hae tae ride guard — nae worries, we hae this. I winna allow anything tae happen tae ye or yer brother and sister. Ye will ride in the middle of a large guard. Twill be slow, but all will be safe."

He nodded, anxiously.

I was on m'horse on one side of the gate, Wallace was on the other as the large group rode from the castle en masse. Archie said, "You're coming?"

"Aye, I will be right in the back, with m'eye upon ye. I will catch up as soon as I ken tis safe."

We watched them go, then I said tae the English King and his men, "Daena follow us, or we will kill ye."

"We will not follow you, but do not return. If we discover that the son of Mag Mòr is returning for the throne his father lost, then we will have him executed in London for all to—"

Wallace said, "I ken, I heard yer diabolical threats — I am sick of listenin' tae ye goin' on and on. Ye would threaten the son of the Scottish King? Truly? Then I will see yer head taken from yer shoulders."

Edward said, "When fleeing a stronghold that has been destroyed by forces from England, ought you insult and threaten the King on your way from the gates?"

Wallace glared.

I rode my horse between them. "Come on, Wallace, we hae a journey ahead of us and yer whole lifetime tae solve this dispute."

CHAPTER 56 - KAITLYN

STAUNTON, VIRGINIA - SOMETIME IN 1775

*T*he helicopter was swooping over the landscape, it was soul-shakingly loud, and freezing with the air rushing in through the open sides. I tucked my head against Magnus's chest and clamped down, trying to keep myself from shaking apart with cold and fear.

I felt him tense as he raised his head to look around, then put his head back down and was quiet for a while. We couldn't talk, it was way too loud for talking.

Then he raised his head up again and watched. "Och nae!" He yelled, "Hold on! They are twistin' a vessel!"

"While we're in flight? In a helicopter?"

Magnus shoved his back against the wall and jammed his feet against another wall. I was pulled partly under a seat, gripping the legs. I held my feet clamped around a bar, as I felt the wind grab and buffet the helicopter, swinging back and forth in the air.

I screamed as the pain shot up my arm and I held on for my life.

～

We weren't flying anymore.

Everything was still.

The helicopter rested at an angle.

I opened my eyes to see Magnus's face, still and...

way too still.

I tummy crawled across the floor of the helicopter and grabbed his face in both hands. "Magnus! Magnus are you okay?"

He nodded without opening his eyes. Then they fluttered open. He groaned. "Och nae, twas a horror."

Behind me a man was laughing, loudly. "Hot *damn!* I always wanted tae fly a helicopter through time. That was awesome."

He was wearing breeches and a blue coat, with a high ruffled shirt collar, looking like a Founding Father. "Wasna it awesome, Mag Mòr?"

Magnus said, "Ye are a monster. Who are ye?"

The man's face fell. "Ye will call me Emperor Asgall, and ye dinna like it, Mag Mòr? Ye dinna think twas fun?"

"Nae, twas criminal and if I address ye at all, twill be as 'Arsegall'."

He chuckled. "Ye just had tae put on yer seatbelt and — but I see ye dinna hae a seatbelt. Oh well, tis fine, ye lived through it." He lifted the head of the pilot from the control panel. "This guy though, he dinna survive it. But twas an experiment, we learned something."

Magnus asked, "Where are we?"

"We are at one of my residences, ye are tae be my guests while I wait for yer ransom."

He ordered men to grab us and force us through the woods at dusk, the light was growing dim. We came to the lawn of a large colonial-style home.

I was walking behind Magnus. He was craning around, looking at everything. I was too, trying to figure out where we were. Any clue. Or else it would be near impossible to find us.

It was humid but cool, and felt like there was a river nearby.

The forest hadn't seemed like the south. It was sunset, and I could hear noisy bugs.

It didn't seem like the southeast. Something told me it was a Mid-Atlantic state, possibly the North.

Did it seem like Maine?

Unfortunately there were a lot of states I hadn't traveled to… I didn't really know. But I had seen houses like this in Virginia and Pennsylvania when Emma and I had been scanning Zillow looking to buy more safe houses.

Our feet thudded across the porch, and we were shoved through the front door to a foyer. The floors were wood, there was a fancy wooden stair that went up to the second floor. There was wallpaper. I looked for light switches, but there were just oil lamps on the wall. There was a grandfather clock in the entry…

A s we passed through the kitchen. I took a quick scan, there was no… I looked over my other shoulder: no refrigerator.

Definitely Colonial. Eighteenth century, probably. But where?

Magnus raced for the kitchen counter, but was grabbed and shoved, hard against the doorframe. Groaning with the jolt of pain.

I could see Magnus's back ahead of me stretched in his shirt. His arms were bound, he was surrounded by mercenaries: he looked tight and ready to fight. Angry. Deeply angry.

I was angry too. It was very hard to get the sound of my children's screams out of my mind.

The mercenaries pushed us out the back door and into a backyard, thick air and bugs buzzing. There were fireflies flashing over the grass. Then a hatch door was opened and Magnus and I were shoved down the steps into a cellar under the house.

It was dark, grungy, musty and damp, and frigidly cold.

Magnus hit the wall, stumbled, then righted himself.

A soldier stepped aside and Asgall sat down on the top step. It was difficult to make out his expression because he was lit from behind by the ambient light of the moon. We looked up as if we were down in a cave.

He lit a cigarette, dragged from it, exhaled smoke, then said, "Magnus, the reason I hae asked ye here today—"

Magnus grumbled. "Ye hae seized me, the rightful King of Scotland, against m'will."

"Och, ye hae done worse tae me. *I* was the rightful King of Scotland. Ye usurped m'throne with yer time traveling and stole m'queen and the son she was carrying. These are the acts of a usurper and a fiend. Did ye ken, Magnus, I had tae rebuild m'compound? And now I hae been lookin' for m'queen through time."

"Och, these are the reasonings of a lunatic. I was crowned king at Scone in—"

He drew in a long drag of cigarette and blew smoke out, making rings against the sky. "Daena be ridiculous, Magnus, it is all as I said it was. But now I hae set this all tae rights. Ye hae been overthrown. Edward has intervened and will be appointin' his own man tae the throne, probably John Balliol." He shrugged. "Whoever, the important thing is that Edward will be beholden tae me... he will do whatever I want—"

"How long hae ye been advisin' the English King?"

"He has been workin' for me for a verra long time." He grinned. "As will yer mother." He jabbed out his cigarette on the step.

Magnus said, "That is not possible. Lady Mairead would *never*."

"Well, not yet, mind ye, but she *will* work for me, once she finds ye hae been captured. Once asked...she will be highly persuadable, she just has tae learn what I am capable of. Case in point, I easily gained control of Scotland, England, the Colonies, and then the European continent. When I think on all that I own or rule over... even I am shocked by how easy twas." He jabbed out his cigarette on the steps above and with tobacco-stained fingers lit another.

"I rule *all* of it, Magnus." He drew in a long puff of the cigarette and exhaled smoke in puffs around his head. "Tis an empire."

Magnus groaned.

"What, ye daena like what I am tellin' ye?"

Magnus said, "Nae, I think tis stupid. I think ye need friends tae run these soliloquies past, so they can tell ye that ye sound like an idiot. A friend would say, 'Och nae, Arsegall, daena say such stupid things tae Magnus, ye are goin' tae give him even more reasons tae kill ye, just tae shut ye up—'"

He watched the burning end of his cigarette and spoke lazily, "Ye forget, Magnus, I am holdin' yer wife as well. Dost ye want me tae teach her a lesson for yer insolence?"

I shrank back behind Magnus.

Magnus said, "Ye daena hae a lot of listenin' comprehension, Arsegall. Ye see, twas not me sayin' it, twas yer friends that ought tae hae said it. I canna help it that ye dinna get very good advice. Perhaps ye daena hae any friends, maybe."

I said, softly. "Likely."

Asgall said, "What did ye say, bitch?"

Magnus's breathing was heavy. "Ye take—"

I said, "Only my friends can call me 'bitch'. You and I are barely acquainted."

He laughed, a menacing, overly loud laugh. "Ye are both in a great deal of trouble. I truly hope yer mother trades well for ye, and fast."

From behind Magnus's shoulder, I asked, "Curious… what are you asking for in trade?"

"Riaghalbane. That kingdom will complete m'collection." He drew in another long puff of the cigarette.

I asked, "Where are we?"

He stood and chuckled. "Och, ye wouldna think as highly of me if I were that dumb — right, bitch? Why would I tell ye that?" He jabbed the second cigarette out on the steps.

I said, "Because what does it matter? There's nothing we can do about it."

He humphed and stood on the top step, leveling his eyes on Magnus. "Emperor Asgall... say it."

"Say what?"

"*Say* 'Emperor Asgall.'"

"Umpire Arsegall is an arse of epic proportions."

"Ah yes, hopefully yer mother will trade for ye soon, every minute that she waits will become more uncomfortable for ye."

Magnus stiffened.

Asgall stepped fully out through the door and closed the hatch over us, blocking the last of the light with a finality that was terrifying.

CHAPTER 57 - KAITLYN

A CELLAR UNDER A BROTHEL IN STAUNTON, VIRGINIA - 1775

*T*he hatch was bolted above us and we were in total darkness.

I could hear Asgall's footsteps recede on the damp ground, then I heard his creaking steps above us as he crossed the wooden floor.

Then I realized, very far away, like on the second floor I could hear moaning, *what was...?*

Someone was having loud sex.

I said, "Someone is having sex? What is happening?"

Magnus's voice through the darkness near me. "Aye, tis a brothel. I want ye tae stay behind me."

I stepped closer and stood there, both of us facing the door until it became obvious that no one was coming for us. That was it, we were locked in a dark basement.

He asked, "Dost ye hae a knife on ye?"

"I did, for the first time I did, Magnus, but they removed it before they threw me onto the helicopter."

"Och nae, ye finally learned the lesson and yet were foiled. Well, we need tae find something tae cut the bindings from my wrists."

"Yes, definitely." With my hands in front of me I felt around at the height of my waist, but then finding nothing I started looking higher, being very cautious not to... I banged my knee hard. "Owie." I rubbed it.

Magnus's voice through the darkness, "Ye are well, Kaitlyn?"

It took me a beat to get my breath back, but then I said, "Yeah, yeah, fine. It was just a..." I felt a piece of vertical wood. "...a stud where I—" Something sliced the pad of my left middle finger. "Ow, shit, I sliced myself."

It was instantly damp, that was going to be...

Magnus asked, "Tis bad?"

"Let me see... or rather, I can't see, let me... hold on." I wrapped my hand in my skirt and held it tight. Then I put it in my mouth for a second. It was still bleeding. I put the finger back against my skirt. "It's not bleeding much, it's going to be okay, I think."

"I will kill him."

"But the good news, there's something sharp near here, bad news, it bites." I added, "Let me use the force... see if I can figure it out without getting cut again."

Magnus said, "The force like in Star Wars."

"I can see you are a good modern boy."

"Ye canna see anything, tis why ye are usin' the force."

I chuckled and used my foot to prod around. I was in a corner. I felt along the bottom of the walls, keeping my face well away, and established that about two feet up was where the sharp thing was situated.

I wadded up my skirts and carefully reached forward, making small swipes and tentative juts until I felt something out of place and homed in on it. I came in from the side and figured out it was hard and flat, the sharp place was pointing left. Then I figured out I could lower my bundled hand down the length of... it was a blade, a long blade, and then finally a handle.

I whispered, "There's a machete right here, it's a gardening implement, I think, stored between the studs. It's blade up

though, the handle is down, it's not going to be easy to get out."
I added, "Man, it is dark, wish my eyes would adjust."

"Aye. Maybe ye daena hae tae get it out, could I just rub the
bindings against the blade?"

"I don't think so, it's too… how much room do you have
between your wrists for a blade?"

"Barely any light between them."

"Yeah, we're not doing that, I'm going to get this knife out of
the wall. I'm going to be very slow and cautious, the kind of
slow and cautious that means no one gets hurt."

I crouched and moved slow like in tai-chi. "Slowly…
slooowwwwlllly…" I added, "Can you step back just a bit?"

He did, but asked, "How come, if ye are being cautious?"

"Because I changed my mind." I reached out and with the
fabric around my hand, grabbed where I assumed the handle
was. I lift-tossed it up — it dropped back.

"Trying again, one, two, three…" I lift-tossed it, knocked it
away from the wall, and jumped back. The machete flipped out
and clattered to the ground.

We both listened.

There was nothing but the sounds of someone going, *oh, oh,
oh, oh,* and a man going *grunt grunt.* "How long will that last?"

"Depends on how drunk he is." He put his foot out to feel
the blade, where it was, tapping back and forth and then he
reached down and with the machete in his hand said, "Here,
hold it out like this. Daena move it. I am going tae put m'wrists
against the blade."

I held it in both hands. I held it as still as I could.

He was close, his breathing shallow with exertion as he
worked on the bindings.

He asked, "Tis alright, ye hae it?"

I said, "Yeah, go for it, I got it." The end of the blade went
up and down against his force. I wished I could hold it more
securely, but I did my best. Finally there was a strong downward
push,

He said, "I am free."

"Oh thank God." He put his arm around my shoulders, feeling down my arm, and pulled the knife from my hand. "I will hide the blade, how is yer finger?"

I put it in my mouth again. "It's good, stopped bleeding."

"Good, now we are goin' tae sit down."

He shifted his feet around, checking the floor. "Sit behind me, I'm goin' tae face the door."

We lowered to the floor at the same time and then I hugged around his back. I kissed his shoulder and nestled my head against the back of it. "Do you think the kids are okay?"

"I think they are verra frightened, but Emma is there, and Hayley. They will take care of them for us, until we return."

I nodded my head against his shoulder. The tears were coming, welling up. "I am so sorry about Sean, so so sorry, my love." I held him tighter.

I felt him nod quietly. He lifted my hand and kissed my closest finger. "I ken."

We sat quietly, until he said, "I canna believe he is gone, he has been the most important man in m'life since I can remember. He was always m'older brother, the one who would look after me. He died tryin' tae look after me. He wanted tae build m'walls and keep m'son safe, och nae, his sons are goin' tae miss him. He was goin' tae be important. I was goin' tae make him a laird of his own castle, as soon as this was over."

I didn't know what to say, so I kissed his shoulder and held on.

He said, "I ken we are in dire straights, and I ought tae be fightin' our way free, but seein' m'brother slain in front of me has knocked me loose from m'moorings. I daena ken how tae do any of this."

I tightened my grip.

He said, "He was always the head of the castle. He had gained the job well before twas his. He was a better leader than the Earl. He was more skilled than Uncle Baldie. And after

Baldie passed, Sean assumed the position of head of the castle. The Earl's son dinna have a thing tae say on it. He left and went tae Edinburgh, because Sean was the only man the Campbells would follow."

"And Maggie loved him, he was a good man."

His hand stroked the back of mine. "Aye, she will be devastated."

We were quiet as sounds above us went from *ungh, ungh, ungh, ungh,* to a loud *uuuunnngggghhhhh.*

Magnus said, "Thank God, *that* is over."

We were quiet for a moment until I said, "It was distracting at least, now I'm thirsty."

"Aye, I hae been imprisoned before, tis the thirst and hunger that will break ye."

Tears welled up. "Is anyone looking for us, will they find us?"

"Aye, they will find us, once they are looking, and the good news is that they will be lookin' for us, because he plans tae trade us for something. He will tell Lady Mairead that he has the King and Queen of Riaghalbane and I expect she will find us within about three minutes. She might already ken where we are."

I nodded. "That makes me feel better."

He said, "And once they open the door at the top of the steps. I will fight us free."

"Don't die, my love."

"I winna." He joked, "I canna die, I hae too much revenge tae seek."

"Plus Jack needs you. He's barely met us — if something happens to us when he's one year old, he will never remember."

"He will remember us in his heart, but I ken what ye mean. It has not been enough, and goes back tae what I was saying, I will kill him for this. Asgall is maggot-food, he just haena realized it yet."

CHAPTER 58 - KAITLYN

A BROTHEL IN STAUNTON, VIRGINIA - 1775

I felt Magnus's back tense as footsteps crossed the floor above us. There was more light, streaming through a crack in the door. He lumbered to his feet, and moved to the blade. I scrambled up and stood behind him. "You got it?"

"Aye."

The bolt slid on the hatch and the doors swung open.

I looked up at the morning light, blinking — so thirsty.

Magnus tensed, ready to spring.

I had my hand on his hip. I knew the drill, as soon as he sprung into action, I would run. That was how I would help.

Asgall stepped down the steps, a gun drawn, pointing at Magnus. I hadn't really gotten a good look at him, he was wearing the white, high-collared shirt from yesterday, open at the neck, wrinkled and crumpled, and the cream colored breeches, and high leather boots. He was big and ugly, his beard wiry and sparse. He said, "Ye found the blade? Och ye are verra resourceful, seems a shame tae kill ye."

I said, "Why are you killing anyone? I thought you were ransoming us?"

He sneered, his gun leveled on Magnus. "I hae sent my demands, Magnus, yer bitch mother best not make me wait."

Magnus shrugged. "She does how she likes."

Asgall said, "As do I, Katie, come here."

I shook my head.

His brow went up. "Nae? Ye say nae tae me?"

Magnus said, "Daena go with him."

Asgall said, "Ye just proved yerself clever, Magsie, and now ye are ill-advisin' yer wife! Let us work it through — ye are guests in m'home. I am Emperor Asgall, I hae asked yer wife tae come with me. What makes ye think ye can refuse my request?"

Magnus was breathing heavily, and looked furious. I did *not* want to go with this guy up into his brothel, but it was the only way to survive this encounter. "Okay, I will." I put up my hands.

Magnus's eyes were locked on Asgall. "Nae, Kaitlyn, daena."

Asgall said, "Hands on yer head, Magsie."

Magnus put his hands on his head, "Och nae."

"Och nae is right, Magsie, but daena fret, if yer wife is forthcoming I will give ye some food and water. Twould be a good thing, daena ye think?"

I stepped around Magnus and went to the stairs.

He groaned behind me. "Kaitlyn, be careful."

"I will be." I climbed the stairs.

Asgall grabbed my arm, yanked me up the steps, and slammed the doors shut on my husband's face. He bent over the trap doors for a second to lock the bolt.

I thought, *jump on his back, strangle him, fight for the gun,* but he stood up and looked at me with a laugh.

"Ye arna strong enough."

"Likely, but there is a chance — I'm the mother-fucking matriarch and you've taken me away from my babies. I wouldn't turn your back on me again."

He shoved me in through the back door of the house and down the hall into a living room. The room was decorated with ornate wallpaper, carved wooden furniture, cherry wood stain, and upholstered seats. The end tables held oil lamps.

Everything fit olden times, except for an iPhone and a full

ashtray of cigarettes on the coffee table. He sat down on an upholstered, claw-footed chair, and patted his knee.

I shook my head. "No way."

"Aye, come sit here on m'knee." He gestured with the gun still in his hand.

"I don't want to."

He fired the gun at the wall. I clamped my hands over my ears and shrieked.

From under the floorboards I heard the muffled voice of Magnus yelling my name.

Asgall gestured at his lap.

I shook all over as I stepped forward and perched on his knee. The proximity made me gag.

He put the gun down on the table and picked up the phone. He held it out like he was posing for a selfie. "See how handsome I am?" He raised his chin, as if he were searching for his best side. His nose was misshapen, his face rounded, he was flabby instead of fit.

He hit record. "How are ye doin', Katie? Tell Lady Mairead."

I paused.

He grabbed a fistful of my hair and yanked my head back, hard.

I sobbed, "Not good."

"Lady Mairead shouldna take time with our negotiations, daena ye think? Time is of importance. Would ye like her tae go fast?"

He yanked my hair back even more. It hurt terribly. Tears rolled down my face. "Yes, please."

He twisted my hair even more as he leaned forward. "Grab that newspaper."

I pulled the newspaper to my chest, but couldn't look down on it. I was arched back, facing the ceiling, my eyes watering, clamped tight in pain.

He said, "Turn it over so she can see the date."

I turned it over. He said, "Fine, 'tis good enough."

Then he said, "Lady Mairead, ye see I winna take hesitation kindly, I hae yer son and yer daughter-in-law. They are at my mercy. Ye must sign the contract."

He put down the phone with a slam on the table.

I said, "Owie, owie, my scalp, it hurts."

He let go of my hair with a shove on the back of my head, knocking me forward. He grabbed the newspaper from my grip and tossed it on the table.

I got a quick glimpse — The Virginian, or something. That old drawing of the snake cut into parts, *that was revolutionary war, right — not civil war?* Then a flash, near the title: 1775… Virginia in 1775, that was helpful.

He drew his fingertips across my shirt, and fondled my breast through my dress. I shoved his hand away and tried to get up but he grasped my wrist, yanked me back down, and stuffed his hot sweaty panting mouth beside my ear. He started kissing me there. His other hand fondled my breast and I whimpered, *stop, please stop,* but it seemed to drive his excitement, so instead I stared right at his cheek. I stared at his swollen pock-marked pig-face, and didn't move, submit, or struggle, I just glared.

Finally he pulled his face away from my ear and looked at me. "What?"

I glared back.

"Och nae, I knew ye were a bitch." He shoved me hard off his knee.

I fell on the ground, hitting my back on the way down on the edge of a coffee table. "Ow."

"Get up. I'm bored of ye."

I scrambled up, even though the pain had knocked the air out of me. But then —the gun! I dove forward and grabbed it.

I held it up, my arms shaking and tried to steady it.

He laughed.

I squeezed the trigger, but nothing happened. It was empty. "It's not loaded?"

He got up fast, grabbed my wrists, and twisted hard, until

the gun dropped, then shoved me to the wall. I stumbled and fell. He yanked me up and shoved me again, banging my shoulder and head. I fell forward onto a knee.

"Ye are so clumsy, Katie, so unattractive." He yanked me up and shoved me against another wall, and another. "Such a clumsy bitch!" All the way down the hall he shoved me against the walls, until I ached all over from the knocks and bangs.

"Yer husband is goin' tae hate that ye dinna even bargain for a meal or a glass of water for him." He shoved me against another door jamb.

I collapsed down the wall, crumbling on the floor in a heap. "Please, can I have a drink for Magnus? Please, we're thirsty."

Another man walked down the stairs from the upper floors. "This the Queen Bitch?"

Asgall said, "Aye, if ye are finally finished with the girls upstairs ye can make yerself useful and return her tae the cellar."

The man was disgusting, he leered with wet lips and the stench of sex. "Want me tae teach her a lesson?"

"Later, put her in the cellar for now, I'm tired of lookin' at her."

CHAPTER 59 - KAITLYN

THE WILDERNESS OF VIRGINIA - 1775

*T*hat man shoved me against the exterior door and down the two steps to the cellar hatch. He was so gross and handsy, putting his hand on my breast as he forced me toward the dungeon. He smelled drunk and seemed unsteady.

He swayed as he crouched over the hatch to pull away the bolt and then there was a giant forceful heave from below. My husband threw the doors up with his back, knocking Drunk Guy off balance. Drunk Guy careened. Magnus meanwhile leapt through the doors and I shoved Drunk Guy, hard. While he stumbled and fell I grabbed his gun from his holster.

Magnus swung the machete and sliced off the dude's arm, I shrieked because blood was everywhere — above us, a man carrying a rifle slammed through the back door.

Magnus grabbed my arm and yanked me around the side of the building, tweaking my ankle, as the man shot at us.

I pressed to the house, breathing heavily, Magnus took the gun from my hand, put it in the back of his belt, and jerked his head across the side lawn toward the woods. We ran.

It wasn't far, we made it to the cover, but it was thick under-brush and tightly packed old trees. It was tough going as we fought our way through brambles and woods. Branches clawed at me as we ran. We scrambled over a boulder, and then our path was clear. We hit the ground and ran until we were so deep into the woods that we collapsed behind a boulder to breathe.

I thought my heart would explode. I was so out of breath. He put a finger to his lips and then breathed deep, and put his hand out palm down, lower, then lower, he breathed in again slower, looking me in the eye. We matched our breaths — in long, hold, out long. He whispered, "Better?"

I nodded and whispered, "I'm so thirsty."

He said, "There is a river next tae us, we are goin' tae hae tae calm ourselves before we approach."

"I'm going to drink so much water."

He squeezed my hand. "Ye good?"

I nodded.

He waved for me to follow.

We crept through the underbrush and came to the edge of the river. It was so delicious looking — wide, sparkling water, calm, like the Amelia river, with a blue heron wading between tall grasses at the edge. It looked timeless.

Magnus peered out from behind the tree for a long time, then he nodded. We crept forward, collapsed to our hands and knees, scooped water, and drank from our cupped palms.

I said, "Thank God we have water, I can do anything now."

He splashed water all over his face and head and whipped his hair back in a spray. Then he slicked it back, looking a lot less like a wild man. I washed my hands in the water taking care to make sure the cut I had gotten was clean.

He asked, "Did he hurt ye?"

I nodded.

"Did he do anything else tae ye?"

"He tried, but... he, he didn't. But ow..." I pushed my sleeve up, there was a bruise on my lower arm. I pulled my skirt up, there was a big gnarly bruise on my shin, and an even bigger one on my thigh.

He said, "Ye hae bruises on yer face as well."

He reached out and said, "There is one here on yer brow and another here on yer jaw."

I frowned, "I didn't realize, I was just trying to stay alive."

He nodded. Then he drank from his cupped hands again. "Dost ye think a fish might jump in my mouth if I will it?"

"Like a bear?" I shook my head. "I doubt it, we'll need to fish for our supper I think and—"

There was a shout and horses coming through the woods.

Magnus scrambled to his feet, grabbed my arm, and dragged me up. We raced into the woods, disappearing into the deep wooded growth, heading in the opposite direction.

We were slower on foot, but we snuck, until finally we came to a spot on the river that was shallow and fordable. We hid behind a tree while we took off our boots, then peeled off our socks. We held them in our hands. Magnus looked out, up and down the river, listening. Then he nodded.

I raced into the river and waded across. Magnus followed, then passed me, leading me into the woods. We headed up a hillside.

We ran until we couldn't run any more.

He pulled up under a stand of trees and hanging his head, breathing heavily, he tried to get on top of his breathing. "Och nae, they are makin' it hard tae escape."

We were on a rise. I could see the river sparkling not far below us. But through the trees we could see some of the valley. I asked, "Can you see the house?"

He pointed, "Tis there, by that river bend, dost ye see the gray of the roof?"

I nodded. "We ran a long way."

"Aye."

Then beyond the house we witnessed the swirling of a storm and above it big banking black clouds, rising into the sky.

I asked, "Coming or going?"

He watched for a moment, hands on his hips, trying to calm his breathing. "I think goin'."

"Damn, he had a live vessel in there, I can't believe I didn't grab it. That should have been the *first* thing I did."

He chuckled. "Och nae, ye are a terrible arse, listen tae ye — ye wish we had risked more afore we escaped? Ye wish ye had looted him on the way out? We barely survived, mo reul-iuil! It could hae been the end of us, and look at what we hae!" He pulled the gun from the back of his belt with a grin. "Ye did good."

"I did do good, didn't I?"

"Absolutely, ye had a knife on ye, but ye were disarmed. Ye went with him upstairs, took a pretty profound beatin', and then ye dinna run away like I hae told ye tae do around a million times, instead ye thought tae grab the gun.... Tis a terrible arsery thing tae do."

I leaned back on my arms, but then said, "Ow," and rubbed my wrists. "He twisted them." I frowned.

"Och nae, I am sorry he hurt ye, mo reul-iuil. But think how sweet our revenge will be." He took my arm and kissed me on the inside of my wrists on the pulse points.

"That feels much better."

"I ken, my kisses are magical." He chuckled.

I pretended to pout and put my arm up against his lips again. He kissed there. Then I said, "Highlander, I love you, I wish I could live on your kisses, but I am so hungry."

He checked the gun for bullets and said, "Tis why I am about tae find us some food."

"It's like the olden days."

"Aye, where are we, dost ye think?"

I grinned again. "I saw a newspaper! We're in Virginia, colonial times, the year is 1775." I stood up and looked around. "Looks pretty peaceful, but the colonies are at war with England…"

He joked, "I bet the colonial deer taste delicious."

I said, "Could you get us a deer? Just like that? Okay, then, after a venison feast we will talk about what to do next."

"Aye, right now I canna hear ye over m'stomach growling."

We stood up and went to hunt and forage for food.

"Where are we going to look?"

He joked, "Tis America, not Scotland, I thought ye were leadin'. Ye are the one from here."

I said, "Uh oh. I don't know anything about colonial America. I'm a Florida girl. I wonder if there's a drive-thru nearby." Then I groaned and held my stomach. "I'm too hungry to think—"

He put his hand out, stopping me mid-step. My heart caught, fearing we had been seen. I followed Magnus's eyes — he was looking at something in the foliage ahead of us. He raised the gun and aimed.

I stopped breathing. A long minute passed, then he fired.

Flocks of birds flapped up from the trees, tiny beasts scurried away through the brambles. Magnus rushed forward, yelling, "Follow me!"

A moment later he plucked up a dead squirrel, I rejoiced, but he kept running, carrying his kill, racing through the woods. We scrambled for about ten minutes east, up another hill. At long last we stopped at a good viewpoint.

We both doubled over, then collapsed onto our backs, our faces grimaced, to catch our breaths yet again.

"I don't think I've ever been this exhausted, or hungry."

"Aye." He lumbered up. "Stay there, I need tae make certain we werna followed." He walked away for a moment, while I stared at the sky thinking, *we are all alone in the world. Where are my babies? Are they worried without me?*

Finally, he returned. "Nae one is followin' us, and it daena seem like anyone heard the gunshots."

I asked, "If I um… help with the fire, will you deal with the um… dinner?"

He nodded. "Aye, ye are squeamish, I ken it."

I picked up branches for a fire.

Then he used the blade from the cellar to skin the squirrel while I built the fire using the flint he kept in his pocket all the time.

After he skinned it, he jammed a stick through it and put it over the fire with some sticks to hold it up. It took a bit of balancing and a couple of tries, but then it was up, the fire licking at its meat.

I licked my lips, nothing about it was *normally* tantalizing, but I was so very hungry. I stared at that little beast cooking the whole time as Magnus slowly turned it and we talked of nothing else except what it would taste like, how much we wanted spices, the want for salt, and that we missed Chef Zach.

Finally Magnus said, "Tis ready."

I put some leaves out on the flattest rock I could find and he placed the cooked squirrel on it. We both crouched beside the meal. He was in a hurry to pick some meat. "Ouch! Och nae, tis hot!" He shook his hand, but immediately tried again, pulling off a hunk and shoving it in his mouth. Chewing, he said, "The whole time I was goin' tae give ye the first piece but then I put it in m'own mouth, I couldna help it."

"It's okay, you've barely complained. I've complained so much I don't deserve first bite." I plucked off my own piece and chewed it. "Man, that is good, don't know if I've ever eaten squirrel before."

"Daena think Chef Zach considers it a proper meat."

"He would be wrong, it's the most delicious thing I ever tasted." I chewed. "But I was really hungry, I might be exaggerating." I swallowed. "Gamey." I took another hunk. "Want more."

We finished the squirrel and drank from the stream and then

sat side by side. I said, "What do you think the kids are doing? I miss them so much."

He said, "They are terribly worried on us, I hate that they witnessed us be taken away."

"Yeah, that was devastating. Archie was freaking out just a couple of days ago about you dying — he'll be inconsolable."

He nodded. "If only I could give him peace and prosperity, a throne with nae usurpers... I would, but I canna figure out how tae do it. I wasna prepared for Asgall tae gain so much power. I did nae suspect the English King was time traveling. I failed immensely."

"It's not your fault."

"I ken ye are tryin' tae set my mind at ease, Kaitlyn, but this is all m'fault. I dinna ken that the danger was comin', until I saw m'brother's life taken in front of me. What if something had happened tae Archibald? I put everyone in danger, and Sean lost his life because of it."

"He wanted to be there. Everyone was there because they wanted to be at the meeting. This is a lot to have on your shoulders. Please don't let it break you."

"Aye. I winna, mo reul-iuil." He ripped up a weed and pulled apart the leaves and tossed them in front of his feet. "There will be a wind at m'back. Asgall will rue what he has done."

I nodded. His jaw was set, he was angry and determined.

"What will we do?"

He chuckled dolefully. "First we are goin' tae need a miracle tae get out of this ancient forest."

I said, "Yep, a miracle would be nice. We are in a pickle."

He laughed.

"You never heard that before?"

"Nae, but aye, we are in a salty brine-filled barrel and we will need tae break out of it. Tis a good metaphor."

I asked, "What do you think Fraoch is doing right now?"

"He is raisin' an army, but..." He tossed a pebble in front of us. "He will need a vessel tae deliver the army tae Asgall's shore, an army is nae good if ye canna travel."

"It's true, we're stuck in a pickle, he's trapped in a dilemma."

"Aye, and we need tae get a message tae Lady Mairead tellin' her where we are. She is in a fog."

"How do we get a message to her?"

"I daena ken, so first we ought tae pray."

I nodded. "Yeah, we should." I clasped my hands and bowed my head.

He pressed his hands together and said, "Dear God in Heaven, please watch over our bairns in our absence. Guide them tae find courage while we are apart and solace in the arms of their friends and family. Father, please keep them from despair, and let them ken we are searching tae find our way home tae them. Give Jack, Isla, and Archibald comfort, and though I ken tis not usual, I ask that ye keep Haggis safe, so he may guard them well until m'return. And I ask of ye tae give our friends, Fraoch and Hayley, Zach and Emma, and their bairns, the strength and wisdom tae hold our family taegether until we reunite, please keep all our bairns safe. And please, Almighty Father, I ask also that ye welcome Sean intae yer arms," his voice broke, "tell him that I am sorry for it... in yer name we pray. Amen."

I said, "Amen," and put my arms around him and held him tight. "Want to talk about it?"

"Nae, not now." He took a deep long breath, then asked, "Which direction ought we go?"

"You're asking me because I am the native to these colonial shores?"

"Aye."

"Well, if we are in colonial America, then we need to walk east towards the ocean, that's where we will find the port towns, where we can, hopefully, get a message out."

"I agree." He stood up. "And though I am verra tired, we

ought tae walk for a time, we can sleep at nightfall." He teased, "Point the direction."

I stood and thought, "Umm.... I think..."

He laughed and started walking down the hill. "Follow me, mo reul-iuil, we must head east."

I laughed. "I knew that was the way, I just needed a minute."

"I ken."

We walked for a bit then emerged from the woods on a newly worn path, we walked a bit then he stopped in his tracks.. "Ye see it, Kaitlyn?" He pointed at three marks slashed on a tree trunk. "Tis a road."

"Good, I think."

"At the end of it will be a town."

"These are the miracles you were talking about."

"Aye."

CHAPTER 60 - BLAKELY

LIAM AND BLAKELY CAMPBELL BESIDE THE RIVER TAY - PRESENT DAY

I was sitting on a boulder on the bank of the river, sipping from a mug of coffee, and reading over the letter that Lady Mairead had dictated to me. She had commanded Liam to carry it in his pocket.

It made no sense.

I said, "It says here that we are bringing him a vessel—"

"I ken, I was there when ye wrote it."

"Who is him? And what does she mean by bringing it to him?"

"She told me tae dig, tis all I ken, dig the hole."

Liam was all hotness in front of me digging with a shovel around the base of a tree. "Your ass is very fine when you're shoveling, my love, this is a lovely view." He chuckled. "Ye are just randy because of the Scottish air, tis fresh and invigoratin'. Ye are thinkin' ye want tae hae yer way with me."

"That must be it, not at all the pull of your pants across your..." I stood up, walked over, and stuffed the letter in his pocket. I kissed him on the cheek. "I don't want to cross her."

"Plus twas a chance tae touch m'arse, I ken how ye are, Woodshee." He grinned. Then he stepped on the shovel and dug up a shovelful of dirt. "Ye canna proposition me out here, I am a man who has been turned upside down — we slept all day, and almost missed the sunlight, I hae been asked tae dig a hole by a time traveling Lady from the future who matches the description of a Lady from the past. I hae been given a mission, I must dig..." Another shovelful was dumped to the side. "But whatever we are looking for, it must not be here."

He stood looking up at the trees and then around at the base of them. "Maybe I picked the wrong one. This might be..." He walked six paces to another tree. "Aye, this is this one." He dug the shovel intae the dirt at the base.

I said, "So we're just believing her, she's a time traveler, but time travel doesn't exist..."

"Occam's razor, Woodshee, the simplest explanation must be true."

"How do you know *anything* about Occam's razor?"

He chuckled. "I spent a lot of time in locker rooms."

I rolled my eyes. "That is not an explanation. But whatever, how, pray tell, is time travel the simplest explanation? It's very *very* complicated for time travel to exist."

"Tis not. Ye are thinking tis because ye are still in the mindset that it daena exist. Twenty-four hours ago ye dinna believe time travel occurred. Ye were livin' in a simple time and yet, remember, Woodshee — we couldna come up with a single good reason why we found those letters stuffed in a Harry Potter book in an old library in an ancient castle. It dinna make sense. But then..." He dug the shovel into the dirt again. "*Then* we heard there was time travel. We dinna ken it before, but now we ken it exists, and now *all* the events make sense. That is why we hae been given this castle. That is why we hae a full bank account. That is why there is a Harry Potter book on our shelf that looks three hundred years old — because tis. Tis three hundred years old, Woodshee. And time travel explains why the men we met, James and Quentin, put a letter there for someone tae find. They put the letter from centuries ago, inside a book that is twenty-five years old, in a library that is hundreds of years old, inside a castle that was locked up and unused for at least fifty years. Did ye remember that part?"

I sipped coffee, "Yeah, I heard that, and you're right it doesn't make any sense. How could a twenty-five year old book be dusty on a shelf that has been locked up for fifty years? It's nonsensical."

"Aye, and it's been fifty years since the building was used, and that was just the main floor. It's likely that the library hasn't been used for a hundred years, easy." He leaned on the shovel and mopped his brow.

I fanned myself. "Unless one of the workers who was fixing it up this past year, getting it ready for us, maybe if... maybe one of them put it there..."

"How would the letter get there?"

"A prank, I don't know."

His brow went up. "A *prank*, Woodshee? I hae a bank account that daena look like a prank."

"I know, I know."

He went back to digging.

I said, "There's nothing there, right? I mean, if she was wrong about there being a box, maybe she was wrong about—"

His shovel hit something hard and metal.

I said, "Uh oh, what's that?"

"Somethin' proving the simplest explanation is real."

He used his hands to pull dirt away from the edges of a chest. And then went back to digging with more confidence. He uncovered the top and then shimmied the shovel edge between the chest and dirt and pried it up. He changed sides and worked from all directions until the box finally dislodged.

"'Tis the chest! She told me right where twas!"

I laughed because he had dug three holes before he found it.

"You got the way to open it?" I pulled out my notes from the conversation.

He crouched down. "I remember the code she told me."

"Good, because my mind was spinning, and my notes are a mess."

"Aye, I hae lots of practice because I daena trust the devices. I keep it all up here." He tapped the side of his head, leaving a little dirt smear there, still sexy though.

He worked on the lock for a moment and the top lifted, pneumatically.

He grinned with his eyebrows up and down. "I live in a king's castle and I just opened a king's chest..." He rubbed his hands together. "I hope there is a king's treasure." He gingerly lifted a piece of velvet off the top and peered inside. "Hmmm.."

"What is it?"

"I daena ken, tis..." He picked something up. It was metal and about the size and shape of a Red Bull can. He held it on his palm. "Tis odd, it hums, it feels alive."

"She said not to touch it or twist it."

"Tis in m'palm, I am no'doin' anything tae it."

I stood beside him looking down on it.

"So what is this supposed to be?"

"She called it the vessel. I suppose tis tae time travel with? We need tae go call her and tell her we found it."

"So we're just going to accept *all* of this as fact?"

"What else are we goin' tae do, Woodshee? No' believe the lady who is callin' us from the year 2391?"

I narrowed my eyes. "Did we get proof?"

He shrugged. "I thought I would take her on her word, seems a farcical tale tae tell."

"Would you also believe a Nigerian Prince needs you to drain your bank account?"

"Tis not what this is, this is the Lady Mairead fillin' *our* bank account."

"Good point — and so far none of it is illegal." I poked the vessel. "I don't think—"

There was the sound of tires on gravel coming from the front of the castle.

He listened.

We both turned toward the building.

We were on the river bank behind a thin strip of trees, with a view across golf-course-style grass to the side of the castle. We had an oblique view of the driveway. Four SUVs drove up and parked in a line.

He asked, "Who could that be?"

I said, "Our first visitors—"

The SUV doors opened and soldiers stepped out, they were armed. A few headed up the steps while others walked around the side of the building, as if they were surrounding it. It looked as if they were there to make arrests.

Liam said, "Who the hell is that—?"

But then he looked down in surprise as the vessel in his hand began to vibrate. I grabbed his arm. "What is it doing—?"

Wind whipped through the trees above us. I looked up at billowing black clouds. There was a searing pain that rose up my hand to my elbow and spread across my shoulder. I put up my other arm to block the wind, and felt such intense pain inside my body that I felt like I was going to be ripped apart. I began to scream.

CHAPTER 61 - BLAKELY

LIAM AND BLAKELY CAMPBELL - 1301

I came-to first by feeling very sick. I clapped my hand over my mouth, realizing I was draped across Liam's chest. I shoved myself over, weakly retched in the grass, then collapsed back on the ground.

He asked, his voice a mumble, "Woodshee, are ye alright?"

I nodded, but then I sobbed and said, "No, what was that — are we okay?"

A low voice startled me. "Who are ye? What are ye doin'?"

I jerked up my head.

There was a large brown horse that was stamping left and right, and beside it was a man, wearing a long hooded cloak. The man looked young, he seemed to be about eighteen years old, and from what I could tell with his face half hidden in the shadow of his hood, very handsome, like a model, his hair was dark. Along with the cloak, he was wearing a belted tunic, high leather boots, and carrying a big sword, the tip of it casually down in the dirt. He looked like he was the king of the Ren Faire, as if he were cosplaying, except not like it was a costume — he looked real.

Real dark and ancient.

Actually everything looked dark, smoky, like someone

needed to turn on the lights. But it was day — was I brain damaged? My breathing was too loud, my heartbeat hammered in my chest.

I ached everywhere.

Liam shoved himself up to sitting. "Who are ye, what hae ye done tae us?"

"I am Archibald. I dinna do anythin' tae ye. Ye just time-jumped intae m'lands, and I haena seen a time-jumper in a verra long time."

~

The End.

EPILOGUE I - ARCHIE

NEAR INNIS CHONNEL CASTLE ON LOCH AWE - 1301

The man asked, "What do ye mean? Where is this place?"

"Ye are in the past, the long ago past. From the looks of yer clothes ye are not used tae it." I looked at my watch, one of the last vestiges that remained of our former modern lives.

Ben returned from checking for others, he said, "Nae one else."

I asked the travelers, "Ye are alone? Were ye chased?"

The man said, "Aye, we are alone... I daena ken how, but I brought ye somethin'."

He struggled tae reach his pocket, pulled out a letter, and passed it tae me.

I unfolded it and read. Twas from Lady Mairead, tellin' me tae take the working vessel and set this whole problem tae rights. "How did ye get this?"

"A woman named Lady Mairead—"

"My grandmother. How was she?"

The woman said, "We talked to her by video, she seemed fine, I guess, worried. She dictated it to us, we — I'm Blakely, by the way, this is Liam — aren't sure what happened, but—"

"Where did ye get the vessel?"

Liam said, "She told us tae dig it up. I promise we werna stealin', she told us we would be delivering it, we had nae idea what that meant."

I looked at Ben, "We have a vessel."

"*Finally*, should I tell everyone tae get ready tae go?"

I chewed m'lip and passed him the letter. "Nae, we canna — read it, Lady Mairead says nae, she says everyone needs tae stay while I try tae solve it."

Ben looked it over and said, "Damn it… But ye ken, *Mom*. Maybe ye could get her tae the hospital."

I nodded. "I ken."

"Dad will be pissed, she needs medicine, she's goin' tae lose the other foot."

"Aye, but if I can solve this, then I can rescue us earlier… before the accident. Before Jack grows up without parents. Haggis is at death's door."

Ben nodded, "Yeah, years ago would be good… aye, I agree. But maybe ye need a second person, I could come, if I could get some medicine and bring it back, just in case, so she's nae in pain, ye ken, in case ye canna get us earlier—"

I said, "Emma would never forgive me, I canna risk yer—"

Uncle Fraoch and Uncle Zach rode up on horses.

Uncle Zach said, "I wondered if I ought to cover my tattoos for company, but these guys are modern — Wait! These guys are modern! There's a vessel?"

Uncle Fraoch said, "Och aye! Time travelers, their vessel works!" He swung down off his horse, drew his sword and pointed it at Liam and Blakely. "Friend or foe?"

Liam put his hands up, "Friend, I think."

Uncle Fraoch sneered. "Prove it— " Then he peered at him, "What year are ye from? Och — I dinna recognize ye! Tis Liam, Liam Campbell! Ye ken…?" He looked around at us all as he sheathed his sword. "Och, none of ye were there. We gave him Balloch castle, he's a direct descendant of Sean!"

I looked him up and down. "Ye do look a bit like how I remember Uncle Sean."

Liam said, "That's right — ye're Fraoch! Last time I saw ye, twas a few months ago, ye were in my pub. Ye hae changed, yer hair is gray, this might be the first proof we hae of time travel — inna it, Woodshee?"

Uncle Fraoch said, "Seems a verra verra long time ago. Twas almost ten years as the wheel rolls... and ye daena believe in time travel yet ye are in the fourteenth century? Och nae, this has been an exciting day for ye, Liam Campbell, how was Balloch treatin' ye?

Liam said, "We were there for one night."

While they talked, I plucked the vessel from the dirt and held it, it did feel like twas alive. I passed it tae Uncle Zach.

He said, "It's working! Hot damn!" He kissed it.

Uncle Fraoch said, "But ye ken, Archibald, they happened tae be friends, but they might hae been foes. Ye canna ride out alone, especially chasin' storms tae meet time travelers—"

Ben said, "He wasna alone, I was with him."

"Aye, but he is an exiled king! Ye ken we are at war with Longshanks, tis a brutal lawless time. Ye are supposed tae be livin' in secrecy, Archibald — what if the visitors had meant ye harm?"

"I am armed, and they were lyin' in the dirt. They couldna hurt me. I could hae stabbed them through afore they wakened if I wanted."

Liam groaned.

Uncle Fraoch said, "I am only sayin', ye are a king, ye ought tae take more caution."

I said, "If I am truly the king, I daena think I ought tae be cautious at all. I am nae certain why I ought tae be anythin' but fierce while I take back m'father's throne."

Uncle Fraoch said, "I ken, Archibald, I ken, but we ought tae wheesht, the forest overhears."

Uncle Zach said, "Let's focus on the issue at hand — when do we leave? Florida is calling our name, we need to get Em to a hospital."

I chewed my lip.

Uncle Fraoch said, "From the looks on their faces, daena get yer hopes up, Chef Zach."

Ben said, "Dad, think it through, we daena get tae leave—"

Uncle Zach said, "What the—? But Emma needs a hospital, and we've been here for years! No, I won't stand for it, fuck that, no." He sighed. "Fine, I get it, yeah... if we get rescued before Emma's accident, before we run out of our first aid kit—"

Ben said, "Before Jack grows up without parents."

"Aye, I know, I understand, but damn... this sucks, right, Frookie?"

"Och, ye went through all the emotions, and aye, it sucks verra bad, but ye ken we will save Madame Emma long months of pain, and besides that, ye daena want tae get rescued in yer current state. I ken ye daena hae a mirror, but ye've gone well wrong."

"Speak for yourself, Frookie-bear. I look lovely, everyone thinks so."

Jack, Isla, and Zoe rode up. Uncle Zach said, "Isn't that right, Zoe?"

"What, Dad?"

"That I look lovely."

Isla and Zoe laughed.

Ben said, "Ye ken Mom wants ye tae cut yer beard."

Uncle Zach's beard was so long he kept it draped over his shoulder. "That's because your mom doesn't know anything about high Scottish medieval fashion."

Jack dropped down from his horse and stood beside Ben. "What's it say?"

I said, "Lady Mairead, our grandmother, sent us a message. She wants me tae take this vessel and go get our Ma and Da."

Jack nodded his head. "Can ye?"

"Aye, I think I can, Jack, I will—"

Jack said, "Promise?" Then he howled, "Awhooh!" like a wolf. I said, "Aye," and howled like a wolf back at him, "Awoooh!" Ben, Isla, and Zoe joined us, "Awoooh!" our full pack howl. Liam and Blakely seemed dazed as they quietly watched our discussion.

I said, "I promise I will either get them back, or I will return. I promise, ye winna miss me, Jack, because nae matter *what* I will be back. But, all that aside, the letter said I must move fast. This vessel was dug up, then used, it might be fleeting. It could terminate at any time."

Ben said, "I still think ye might need me though, I am offerin' tae lend ye my sword, ye ought tae consider it."

I said, "Ye ken what I am sayin', Ben…" I glanced at Jack. "I need ye tae stay behind and watch over the family."

Ben nodded. "Aye, I ken."

"And I will be right back as soon as I can."

Uncle Fraoch grinned, baring the hole where his tooth had been, now just a screw sticking out of his gum as he had broken the fake tooth off five years earlier. "What about me? Why canna I go? I ken a lot more about the vessels. Ye daena remember even usin' them, ye are just a bairn in the scheme of it. Ye ought tae stay and let Uncle Frookie solve all of this."

I exhaled, considerin'. "Uncle Fraoch, I need ye tae stay here, watch over Jack. Ye ken, I need ye tae, we need continuity in *case*, plus Aunt Hayley would kill me." I turned my attention tae Ben. "Besides we hae Uncle Wallace's battle comin' up, and we're helpin' Uncle Cailean build our army, when I get back we are goin' tae ride intae battle, we want tae retake my throne."

Ben said, "Aye, I understand, I get it, but when ye come back could ye bring medicine for Mom—?"

Jack said, "Ye will come home, right, Archie, *promise?*"

"I promise. I will come home, I will bring medicine."

Uncle Fraoch said, "Ye are verra young tae go on a dangerous trip alone, how old are ye, barely eighteen?"

Ben said, "Uncle Frookie, he's practically middle-aged."

Uncle Zach nodded, "If we can get rescued before Emma's accident that would be... you know, really good — need anything, want food for the trip?"

I said, "Nae, I ought tae get movin'."

Uncle Fraoch climbed off his horse and came over. "Ye hae some coins?"

"Aye, in the bag." He poured some gold coins in my hand anyways.

Ben said, "And ye hae yer sword. Tis all ye need."

Uncle Fraoch said, "Och, lads, it has been a long time since ye've been in the modern world. I can think of many things Archibald might need—"

Uncle Zach said, "A phone, a credit card, a—"

Jack asked, "What's a credit card?"

Chef Zach pretended tae cry. "Tis a glorious card with which ye can buy all the food ye want."

I said, "I hae all I need, and as soon as these people... Liam and Blakely are ready, we will jump."

Liam groaned. "Again? Och nae."

Isla interrupted and looked at Blakely, "Did ye bring anythin' with ye from modern days? We are out o'*everything*."

Blakely said, "Oh, let me see." She dug in her pockets. "My phone, the... I have a chapstick and a pack of gum."

Isla's eyes went wide.

Blakely stood with a groan and approached the lassies. "I wish I had more."

Zoe said, "Tis alright, we can share." She opened the pack and counted. "Jack, ye want a piece of gum?"

He put out his hand. "What is it?"

Uncle Fraoch said, "Ye chew it. Twill taste like mint and sweet honey, dost ye hae anymore, Zoe?"

Zoe said, "There are only three pieces, Uncle Frookie, ye can hae mine."

Uncle Fraoch said, "Nae, ye hae it, lassie, twas verra sweet ye offered. I will chew on that, twill keep me comforted."

Jack chewed three times and swallowed. "Twas verra good!"

Isla frowned. "Ye are supposed tae chew the whole time and not swallow, Jacky!" She tore her piece in half and gave him the other. Zoe tore her piece in half too and gave it tae Jack. We were always lookin' out for him, as he was verra young when he lost our ma and da. And we remembered them and he dinna, so we tried tae make it up tae him.

Blakely said, "I wish I had more."

Liam said, "Aye."

I said, "We need tae jump, as soon as ye are able, I hae tae get ye back. What was the date when ye left, Liam? I need tae ken, as far as I can tell this is the only vessel in the world that is still workin'."

Blakely said, "I don't understand any of what is going on at all."

Uncle Fraoch asked me, "Ye ken how tae set it?"

"Aye, ye hae instructed me, for many long years ye instructed me."

Ben said, "We all ken how tae do it."

Uncle Fraoch said, "In m'defense it has been verra borin', daena forget or ye will get stuck somewhere."

Uncle Zach said, "Check twice, jump once. That's the rule. There are a shit ton of people you have to rescue and get back here to rescue us before Emma had her accident in June of 1300."

I said, "Before that, definitely, I will do everythin' in my power tae get back before that."

Uncle Fraoch said, "As long as we are listing our dates, ye could come before we ran out of batteries."

I nodded.

Jack said, "Daena forget tae come home, Archie."

I said, "Of course I winna forget, Jack, I promise, I am goin' tae solve this."

Uncle Fraoch said, "And go fast, ye need tae gather everyone before that vessel gets shut down too."

Blakely said, "That's a thing that can happen? Ugh."

Liam told me the date they left.

I worked on the setting, when he said, "Somethin' tae mention though, I daena ken if this is applicable — we were at Taymouth Castle and right before that vessel thing, did... ye ken, what that thing *does,* there were armed men surroundin' the castle..."

My brow drew down. "Truly? Och nae."

Uncle Fraoch said, "Well, ye canna go back there, ye hae tae go somewhere else."

I asked, "Can I take ye tae... Florida?"

Uncle Zach put his hands over his ears, "I can't listen, it'll break my heart."

Liam checked his wallet. "We don't have our passports, I didn't—"

"Dost ye hae any money? I need tae drop ye somewhere and ye will hae tae get back, or ye hae tae come with me, but ye would hae tae ride a horse, possibly get in a sword fight, are ye an accomplished horse rider and sword fighter?"

Liam said, "Nae, I am no'... Blakely, can we get back from Florida?"

Blakely nodded. "We'll rent a car, we can do it. I have my phone in my pocket, we can do what we need to do."

I said, "Good, thank ye for understandin'."

I finished workin' on the settings on the vessel.

I shewed it tae Uncle Fraoch.

He nodded. "Aye, tis right."

"Uncle Zach, ye want tae look it over too?" I handed it tae him.

He looked it over. "I am so damn proud, you're a time traveler."

Ben said, "He will be in a minute. He gets all the glory." He brought my horse tae the center of the clearing. "Daena eat anything good without me."

Liam said, "I daena understand anything about this situation, but I am makin' out that ye want me tae touch that machine again."

I said, "Yer other option is tae stay here, but I warn ye, I am not comin' back tae this time, I'm returnin' years earlier, ye will be stuck."

Ben said, "Being stuck is nae fun."

Blakely asked, "What happens if we are stuck?"

Uncle Zach said, "Well, the food sucks, there's no television, and an over-turned cart can injure you terribly and there's no hospital." He exhaled.

Blakely nodded, "I don't want to get stuck."

I said, "Ben, tell yer mom that I am going tae either get medicine and get her tae a hospital, or rescue her before the accident. Make sure she kens I'm nae desertin' her."

"I will."

Uncle Zach said, "She'll understand, Archibald, she's proud of you."

I nodded, my eyes mistin'. "And tell Aunt Hayley I love her. Tell her I am solvin' it."

Uncle Fraoch nodded. "I will make sure she kens."

I wanted tae say goodbye tae everyone, but I dinna want tae frighten Jack, so instead I held m'horse's reins and repeated, "We ought tae go," and straightened m'back and said, "Jack, tell Haggis I love him, and he is a cù math. Tell him tae hold on, daena die, he needs tae wait for me. Tell him I am goin' tae get Da."

Jack said, "I will."

Liam and Blakely stood with me, formin' a circle.

Ben and Jack and everyone else moved tae the trees around the clearing, Ben called out, "Kick some arse."

Jack said, "Wolf King it!"

"Aye, I will," I howled, "Aarh-oooooooooooh!"

Ben and Jack and Isla and Zoe and Uncle Zach and Uncle Fraoch all called out, "Arh-ooooooooh!"

I said tae Liam and Blakely, "Hook yer elbows, daena let go."

EPILOGUE II - ARCHIE

SOUTH END OF AMELIA ISLAND - PRESENT DAY

I lumbered up slowly and brushed off the sand. We were on a windswept beach at the south end of Amelia Island. *How many times had I landed here?*

I muttered. "Och nae, that was worse than I remembered," and glanced at the two people I had traveled with. They were beginning tae stir, but I dinna have a lot of time tae converse.

I glanced up and down the beach, twas familiar, bringin' back memories.

I shaded my eyes and looked down the dunes. *Was that our auld house down there?* It had been a while since we had lived there. I missed it, it pulled at m'heartstrings tae see it, hulking on the dunes. Closed up.

I focused on it, flashes of runnin' down the beach with Uncle Lochie and Ben, chasing birds, and tossin' a football. I had barely remembered it but now twas clear in m'mind.

Och, I missed this place — I wished I could go in, explore, see m'auld room, but I couldna tarry. I needed tae go... as long as the vessel was workin' I needed tae get movin'.

Yet I already missed m'family...

Would I cease tae exist?

Twas all uncertain and terrible, but I had tae move forward, everyone depended upon my success.

I plucked the vessel up from the sand… Who would I go get first? I was not entirely certain, *Uncle Lochie?*

I pulled the letter from my sporran, unfolded it in m'lap, and read it once more. It sounded as if Colonel Quentin and James were stuck at Balloch, but Uncle Lochie's message sounded as if he were in dire danger.

I hated havin' tae choose who tae rescue first. What if I were responsible for the death of someone in m'family because I made the wrong choice?

I wanted tae go directly tae the thirteenth century tae lend my sword tae m'father, tae rescue m'parents, but I was there when I was eight, I remembered it like it was yesterday: I was in the courtyard of Stirling, m'heart poundin' in m'wee chest, I had been verra frightened, there was an arm around me holding me back. I wanted tae run tae the helicopter — it was big and hulking and… so loud. M'Da was on his knees with his hands bound, his face bloodied. I was holdin' ontae my Ma's arm, but she was pulled way. I held on as tight as I could, but her arm was yanked free. She was shoved toward Da, they were both thrown intae the helicopter and flown away.

I had been responsible for Jack and Isla and Haggis ever since.

Och I had felt confused and inconsequential. I had wanted tae help m'Ma and Da, but there was nothing I could do. Twas devastating. I had been left with shame that I hadna done anything tae save them.

All I did was howl like a wolf as they left.

The act of a boy.

A howl of fear and anguish, but m'family had decided tae call me the Wolf King ever since. As if it were a badge of honor. Over the years I had grown tae embrace the name, but in the beginning it had filled me with shame. I was just a boy who had been stranded in the past.

Not a king, and definitely not a wolf.

Now I had a vessel and I could do somethin', but I had tae be calculatin' and wise, I couldna allow the fear and confusion of m'youth tae dictate m'path.

For a moment I wished I had brought Ben for the company. We had fought alongside each other in many battles, beginnin' when we were mere lads, runnin' messages between Uncle Wallace and Uncle Fraoch at the Battle of Falkirk — we had been a wolf pack for a long long time.

Since I was eight.

Ten long years — where were my parents?

I watched a seagull's flight as it soared above the waves.

Ben would hae loved tae hae seen this beach again. But I couldna risk his life.

I put the date and time into the vessel and stuffed the paper back in my sporran. I looked down on the vessel. *Did it look right?*

I finally said, *Aye.*

Liam shifted in the sand, waking up.

I whispered, "I am leavin', thank ye for bringin' the vessel."

I began tae walk away, leading my horse, Mario.

He called, "Where are ye goin'?"

"Tae Balloch Castle, the year 1683."

He said, "I hope tae meet ye again sometime!"

I turned and put my arms out, "Tis unlikely as I am merely a traveler on the wheel — I doubt I will get tae come back round this way again."

EPILOGUE III - BLAKELY

SOUTH END OF AMELIA ISLAND - PRESENT DAY

I raised my head. "What did he say?"

Liam shook his head. "I daena get it, I think he is goin' tae go back and rescue himself when he's younger, but where do ye think *he* will go?"

"I don't know... but he's really literally leaving us, right here in the..." I looked all around. "Sandy beach of what looks like paradise?"

Liam joked, "He's a monster. He took our horrible painful terrible machine that—"

The wind rose, whipping and spinning, black storm clouds roiling into the sky just north of us. The sand spray burned our skin.

Liam rolled over me, shielding me with his back, then there was a clap of thunder and an arc of lightning. "Get up, run!"

We scrambled across the sand to some low bushes and got behind one. He put his arms around me and held on. The storm lasted for about fifteen minutes and then as quickly as it came on it ended.

I asked, "Is he still there?"

Liam twisted to look. "Nae, the storm is part of it. Och nae, we hae glimpsed something that canna possibly be true. We were in medieval times."

"Did we ever get proof? Maybe it was all just a delusion."

He said, "The kids seemed modern, they knew modern things, but they had never had gum. They were living in medieval times, we were a witness tae it. We were in Scotland and now we're in Florida."

I groaned, sat up, and shook the sand from the back of my head. "Yeah, that's right, my mind just keeps trying to come up with *any* other explanation."

"There is nae other explanation, Woodshee, tis time travel, and we are caught up in the excitement of it."

I said, "Speaking of excitement, we need to figure out how to get home."

THE NEXT BOOK:

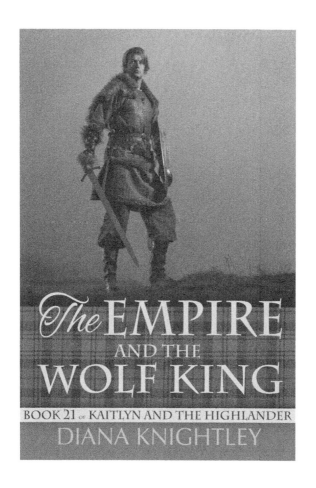

ACKNOWLEDGMENTS

Thank you so much Cynthia Tyler, for your bountiful notes and for reading through twice as you do, your edits, thoughts, historical advisements, your attention to detail and the appropriate word choice, and the eagle-eyed proofing. I appreciate your help so much.

~

Thank you to Kristen Schoenmann De Haan for your notes. And for finding things no one found, like Ash appearing in a scene that should have been Blakely. Editing is hard. I'm so grateful you're still helping me polish it up.

~

Thank you to Jessica Fox, for your notes, you are so good at finding things that all the rest of us miss, like realizing that they forgot to give Wallace his sword back and he was carrying one in the last scenes. At your urging, Magnus and Fraoch discussed it and returned Wallace's sword.

~

Thank you to *Jackie Malecki* and *Angelique Mahfood* (the admins) for beta-reading for me this go around. You were both so busy and going through so much, I am thrilled you took time to help.

And Angelique, thank you for your copious notebooks, keeping track of all of the details, I'm so grateful that you know who is related to whom and when they were born and when they were last seen and... etc. I couldn't keep it straight without you.

～

And thanks to David Sutton, for being willing to Beta read, even though time constraints and crazy circumstances made it impossible, Next time!

～

And more thanks to Jackie and Angelique for being admins of the big and growing FB group. 8.5K members! Your energy and positivity and humor and spirit, your calm demeanor when we need it, all the things you do and say and bring to the conversation fill me with gratitude.

You've blown me away with so many things. So many awesome things. Your enthusiasm is freaking amazing. Thank you.

～

Which brings me to a huge thank you to every single member of the FB group, Kaitlyn and the Highlander. If I could thank you individually I would, I do try. Thank you for every day, in every way, sharing your thoughts, joys, and loves with me. It's so amazing, thank you. You inspire me to try harder.

And for going beyond the ordinary and posting, commenting, contributing, and adding to discussions, thank you to all the top contributors!!!

Julia Burch, Cynthia Tyler, , Tonja Degroff, Sandra Barlow Powell, Nadeen Lough, Rena Sapko, Dawn Underferth, Tina Rox, Tina McCoy, Amy Brautigam, Marcia Coonie Christensen, Harley Moore, Lori Balise, Alana K Mahler, Kathleen Fullerton, JD Figueroa Diaz, Carol Stevens Owen, Cheryl Rushing, Maria Whitmer, Linda Anderson, Claire Stone, Jennifer Schwimley-Hensley, Julie Dath, Amy MacNeill, Sally MacIntosh, Joleen Ramirez, April Bochantin, Mitzy Roberts, Tomisa V Bates, Carol Wossidlo Leslie, Stacey Eddings, Toni Escudier Plonowski, Wanda Jo Burroughs-Taylor, Marie Smith, Retha Russell Martin, Roz Rice, Diane Emond, Helen Ramsey, Denise Carpentier Sillon, Kathy Janette Brown Murray, Ellen McManus, Jackie Briggs, Sonia Nuñez Estenoz, Lisa Zimmerman Moon, Lupe Skye, Linda Wildman, Diane McGroarty McGowan, Kalynne Connell, Nancy Josey Massengill, Lesli Muir Lytle, Shannon McNamara Sellstrom, Amanda Duke Branch, Susan Russell Valentine, Julia Waldman-Reeves, Darla Wallace Wiggins, Rebecca Bravo, Darlene Sciarra McCormack, Judy Megee Cravens, Anne Woolson, Jeannine Bennie Bishop, Pam Radford, Joann Splonskowski, Michelle Lynn Cochran, Lisa Lasell, Jessica Mitchell Guill, Margo Machnik, Barbara Baker, Tempe Garriott, Fran Doiron Mccarter, Carolyn Carter, Liz Leotsakos, Paula Flynn, Rhianna Cultrona Zisko, Jennifer DeWitt, Kathy Hansel, Beth Jones Walters, Jill Enterline McElroy, Carol Poate, Julie Lazaro, Sandra Mendez, Dorothy Chafin Hobbs, Natalie King, Jennifer Prince Reed, Kathy Ann Harper, Margot Schellhas, Cindy Straniero, Denise Riemer, Kim Shea, Susan Decker, Lori Carlson Jackson, Sharon Crowder, Amy McKenzie, Kristen Schoenmann De Haan, Samantha Killian Bowman, Azalee Salis, David Sutton, Monica Gronau Vazquez, and Haleigh Underwood

---

When I am writing and I get to a spot that needs research, or

there is a detail I can't remember, I go to Facebook, ask, and my loyal readers step up to help. You find answers to my questions, fill in my memory lapses, and come up with so many new and clever ideas... I am forever ever ever grateful.

~

I asked:
I need a good safe house/location for the gang in the year 2025, in America.
It would be good if it was easy to get to, not too far out of the way, needs to be stocked with what they need.
Thank you to **Holly Bowlby** for saying: Highlands, North Carolina.

(Side story: The week before I had been looking at Burt Reynolds's house in Highlands, NC after seeing it posted on Zillow Gone Wild!)

No one actually made it to the NC house though, but they did get to the Yulee, FL safe house, thank you, **Carol Stevens Owen** for that idea:

"What about Yulee, FL? They could get there rather quickly by car and while it's a small town, kinda rural, it's still got all the amenities for supplies if they need anything for an extended stay."

~

Then I asked:
I use books quite a lot for getting messages through time. And guess what? It's happening again.

I need a book that Lady Mairead has given to Lizbeth. Obviously it can be any book in time, but Lizbeth keeps it on her shelf, has read it, really likes it, and looks at it occasionally.

Thank you to **Sharon Aldridge Cantrell, Anna Spain, and Rachel Hepburn** for thinking of Harry Potter.

~

And I asked:

Asgall (Villain) has a preference for a place where he can smoke cigarettes and has some modern proclivities, but he does like the wild lawlessness of historical times.

He needs a lair. It can be flat out evil or a subtly lovely respite.

Where and when does he have his new hideout?

Thank you to **Carolyn Dawkins Ensminger** for this idea:

"1775 brothel in Philadelphia on Elfreth's Alley! All the women and alcohol he can want, easy access since there is no country yet and he gets to wear a tricorn and cool clothes."

I researched brothels in 1775 Philly, but ultimately wanted a wilderness area so I came up with Staunton, VA.

~

This was a quick question with like a million answers...

Quentin and James are making a list of things to take to the 13th century.

What supplies are they taking?

Beyond the basics, any new and novel ideas?

Anything funny that they take that is ridiculous?

So many great ideas, thank you everyone who weighed in, and thank you to **Rebecca Bravo** for mentioning Mac and Cheese.

~

and I asked:

I'm in a writing session and can't remember, when Lady Mairead showed up in Florida with the two friends and seemed confused about things, what book was that and who were the friends?

Also, she wants to go visit a past lover, are there any that we need to revisit? Besides Picasso, not sure if she wants to go visit him this go around...

Thank you for all the answers Lupe Skye, Kathy Hansel, Alison Caudle, Harley Moore, Maria Woltmann, Nancy Massengill, Alana K Mahler, Marie Smith, Kathleen Garrett, Jayne Allen, Amanda Richards, April Bochantin, Jan Werner, Tara Smith, Sarah Runyon, and Rena Sapko

~

And thank you to **Darlene McCormack** for the horse name, Finn. (I chose to turn it to Finny.)

~

Thank you to *Kevin Dowdee* for being there for me in the real world as I submerge into this world to write these stories of Magnus and Kaitlyn. I appreciate you so much.

Thank you to my kids, *Ean, Gwynnie, Fiona,* and *Isobel,* for listening to me go on and on about these characters, advising me whenever you can, and accepting them as real parts of our lives. I love you.

SOME THOUGHTS AND RESEARCH...

Characters:

Kaitlyn Maude Sheffield - Born December 5, 1993

Magnus Archibald Caelhin Campbell - born August 11, 1681

Archibald (Archie) Caelhin Campbell - Son of Magnus and Bella born August 12, 2382

Isla Peace Barbara Campbell - Daughter of Magnus and Kaitlyn, born October 4, 2020

Jack Duncan Campbell - Son of Magnus and Kaitlyn, born July 31, 1709

Lady Mairead (Campbell) Delapointe - Magnus's mother, born 1660

Hayley Sherman - Kaitlyn's best friend, now married to Fraoch MacDonald

Fraoch MacDonald - Married to Hayley. Born in 1714, meets Magnus in 1740, and pretends to be a MacLeod after his mother, Agnie MacLeod. His father is also Donnan, which makes him Magnus's brother.

Lochinvar - A son of Donnan, Half-brother to Magnus and Fraoch. Found living at Dunscaith Castle in 1589.

Ash - Lochinvar's new wife. Married on June 20, 1291

Quentin Peters - Magnus's security guard/colonel in his future army

Beaty Peters - Quentin's wife, born in the late 1680s

Noah Peters - Son of Quentin and Beaty, born June 1, 2024

Zach Greene- The chef, married to Emma

Emma Garcia - Household manager, married to Zach

Ben Greene - Son of Zach and Emma, born May 15, 2018

Zoe Greene - Daughter of Zach and Emma, born September 7, 2021

James Cook - Former boyfriend of Kaitlyn. Now friend and frequent traveler. He's a contractor, so it's handy to have him around.

Sophie - Wife of James Cook. She is the great-great-granddaughter of Lady Mairead, her mother is Rebecca.

Junior - Son of James and Sophie, born May 16, 2025

Sean Campbell - Magnus's older half-brother

Lizbeth Campbell - Magnus's older half-sister

Sean and Lizbeth are the children of Lady Mairead and her first husband, the Earl of Lowden. They live in the early 18th century, in Scotland, at Balloch Castle.

～

The horses:

Sunny once belonged to Magnus

Osna belongs to Kaitlyn

When Magnus and Kaitlyn were in the 16th century they rode Cynric and Hurley.

Hayley and Fraoch have the horses Gatorbelle and Thor

Lochinvar now has a horse named Cookie, he and Ash are now riding Finny.

Magnus now has Dràgon

Archie and Ben have a horse named Mario

～

The Kings of Riaghalbane from the Scottish Duke:
Normond I - 2167
Maximillian - 2196
Niall - 2221
Artair - 2249
Birk - 2276
Graeme - 2306
Donnan I - 2331
Donnan II - 2356
Magnus I - crowned August 11, 2382 the day before the birth of his son, Archibald Campbell, next in line for the throne.

(Because of Time Travel dates and names are subject to change...)

Some **Scottish and Gaelic words** that appear within the book series:
dreich - dull and miserable weather
mo reul-iuil - my North Star (nickname)
osna - a sigh
dinna ken - didn't know
tae - to
winna - won't or will not
daena - don't
tis - it is or there is. This is most often a contraction 'tis, but it looked messy and hard to read on the page so I removed the apostrophe. For Magnus it's not a contraction, it's a word.
och nae - Oh no.
ken, kent, kens - know, knew, knows
mucag - is Gaelic for piglet
m'bhean - my wife
m'bhean ghlan - means clean wife, Fraoch's nickname for Hayley.

baobhan sith - a female fae who appears as a beautiful woman. She seduces her victim before killing them.

cù - dog

Ruith - Run!

cù math - good dog

Locations:
> **Fernandina Beach** on Amelia Island, Florida, present day. Their beach house is on the south end of the island.

Magnus's homes in Scotland - **Balloch**. Built in 1552. In the early 1800s it was rebuilt as **Taymouth Castle**. It lays near Loch Tay near the River Tay

The kingdom of Magnus I, **Riaghalbane**, is in Scotland. Its name comes from *Riaghladh Albainn*, and like the name Breadalbane (from *Bràghad Albainn)* it was shortened as time went on. I decided it would now be **Riaghalbane**.

Magnus' castle, called, **Caisteal Morag,** is very near where Balloch Castle once stood, near Loch Tay.

The Palace Saloon. The oldest bar in Florida and the last American tavern to close during Prohibition. Once a favorite haunt of the Carnegies, the Rockefellers and other socialites, The Palace Saloon is still operating today.

Stirling Castle is in central Scotland and is one of the largest and most historically and architecturally important castles. It's the seat of Magnus's power in the 13th century.

Crieff is a Scottish market town in Perth and Kinross, famous for its history of cattle droving.

For a number of centuries Highlanders came south to Crieff to sell their black cattle, the town acting as a gathering point for the cattle sale held during the "October Tryst" each year, when the surrounding fields and hillsides would be black with some 30,000 cattle.

True people and events that happened:
Edward I, also known as **Edward Longshanks** and the **Hammer of the Scots**, was King of England from 1272 to 1307.

First interregnum (1290-1292)
The death of Margaret of Norway began a two-year interregnum in Scotland caused by a succession crisis.

(this is the time period when Magnus is king.)

Robert Roy MacGregor was a Jacobite Scottish outlaw, who later became a Scottish and Catholic folk hero. During this time period he operated an extralegal watch over the cattle herds of the gentry in return for protection money. James once went out for a long ride with him.

Sir William Wallace was a Scottish knight who became one of the main leaders during the First War of Scottish Independence.

He was appointed Guardian of Scotland and served until his defeat at the Battle of Falkirk in July 1298. In August 1305, Wallace was captured and handed over to King Edward I of England, who had him hanged, drawn and quartered for high treason and crimes against English civilians.

The **Earl of Breadalbane** (1636 - 1717) and his son John (1662 - 1752).

A Ship Against the Mewstone, at the Entrance to Plymouth Sound by JMW Turner:

I asked Grok.ai to make me an image of a Queen and King in 1291 and I'm not sure it's historically correct, but *shrug* liking the way they look!

The theme of the last book, *Long Live the King,* was finding the right time, beginning at the beginning, being first, dawn.

In this book, *Dawn,* almost everything happens, or begins to happen, in the morning, but the theme of this book is mostly about the other meaning of dawn: 'to begin to be perceived'. Everyone has a dawning realization how precarious their situation is.

As Magnus says to Chef Zach, "When ye put it like that, in the light of the day, we appear tae be on our back foot."

Also wolves...

THE SCOTTISH DUKE, THE RULES OF TIME TRAVEL, AND ME

The year is 1670 and a young Duke has ridden out to explore a mysterious gale. He finds, in the center of a clearing, a strange apparatus.

He reaches for it and—

In Florida, 2012, a young storm-chaser has gone to investigate a storm — lightning arcs, the winds howl, trees whip around her, but when the storm clears she sees it: a small weird piece of tech jutting out of the sand.

She reaches out and—

The portals — active in two different times, in two different places — vibrate, grab hold, and rip them both through time.

They have just learned the first rule: Don't touch an active portal.

THE KAITLYN AND THE HIGHLANDER SERIES

BOOKS IN THE CAMPBELL SONS SERIES...

Why would I, a successful woman, bring a date to a funeral like a psychopath?

Because Finch Mac, the deliciously hot, Scottish, bearded, tattooed, incredibly famous rock star, who was once the love of my life... will be there.

And it's to signal — that I have totally moved on.

But... at some point in the last six years I went from righteous fury to... something that might involve second chances and happy endings.

Because while Finch Mac is dealing with his son, a world tour, and a custody battle,

I've been learning about forgiveness and the kind of love that rises above the past.

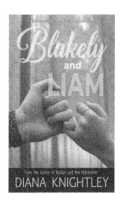

We were so lost until we found each other.

I left my husband because he's a great big cheater, but decided to go *alone* on our big, long hike in the-middle-of-nowhere anyway. Destroyed. Wrecked. I wandered into a pub and found... Liam Campbell, hot, Scottish, a former-rugby star, now turned owner of a small-town pub and hotel.

And he found me.

⤳

My dear old dad left me this failing pub, this run down motel and now m'days are spent worrying on money and how tae no'die of boredom in this wee town.

And then Blakely walked intae the pub, needing help.

The moment I lay eyes on her I knew she would be the love of m'life.

And that's where our story begins...

ABOUT ME, DIANA KNIGHTLEY

I write about heroes and tragedies and magical whisperings and always forever happily ever afters.

I love that scene where the two are desperate to be together but can't be because of war or apocalyptic-stuff or (scientifically sound!) time-jumping and he is begging the universe with a plea in his heart and she is distraught (yet still strong) and somehow — through kisses and steam and hope and heaps and piles of true love, they manage to come out on the other side.

My couples so far include Beckett and Luna, who battle their fear to search for each other during an apocalypse of rising waters.

Liam and Blakely, who find each other at the edge of a trail leading to big life changes.

Karrie and Finch Mac, who find forgiveness and a second chance at true love.

Nor and Livvy, who are beginning a grand adventure.

Hayley and Fraoch, Quentin and Beaty, Zach and Emma, and James and Sophie who have all taken their relationships from side stories in Kaitlyn and the Highlander to love stories in their own right.

And Magnus and Kaitlyn, who find themselves traveling through time to build a marriage and a family together.

I write under two pen names, this one here, Diana Knightley, and another one, H. D. Knightley, where I write books for Young Adults. (They are still romantic and fun and sometimes steamy though because love is grand at any age.)

DianaKnightley.com
Diana@dianaknightley.com
Substack: Diana Knightley's Stories

Made in the USA
Monee, IL
09 October 2024

67490364R00249